P9-DWD-727

CALGARY PUBLIC LIBRARY

DEC - - 2013

WEAPONIZED

WEAPONIZED

NICHOLAS MENNUTI
with DAVID GUGGENHEIM

MULHOLLAND BOOKS

Little, Brown and Company

New York Boston London

The characters and events in this book are fictitious. Any similarity to real persons, living or dead, is coincidental and not intended by the author.

Copyright © 2013 by Nicholas Mennuti with David Guggenheim

All rights reserved. In accordance with the U.S. Copyright Act of 1976, the scanning, uploading, and electronic sharing of any part of this book without the permission of the publisher constitute unlawful piracy and theft of the author's intellectual property. If you would like to use material from the book (other than for review purposes), prior written permission must be obtained by contacting the publisher at permissions@hbgusa.com. Thank you for your support of the author's rights.

Mulholland Books / Little, Brown and Company
Hachette Book Group
237 Park Avenue, New York, NY 10017
mulhollandbooks.com

First Edition: July 2013

Mulholland Books is an imprint of Little, Brown and Company, a division of Hachette Book Group, Inc. The Mulholland Books name and logo are trademarks of Hachette Book Group, Inc.

The publisher is not responsible for websites (or their content) that are not owned by the publisher.

The Hachette Speakers Bureau provides a wide range of authors for speaking events. To find out more, go to hachettespeakersbureau.com or call (866) 376-6591.

Library of Congress Cataloging-in-Publication Data
Mennuti, Nicholas, 1978-
    Weaponized / Nicholas Mennuti with David Guggenheim.—First edition.
        pages cm
    ISBN 978-0-316-19995-7
    1. Lookalikes--Fiction. I. Guggenheim, David. II. Title.
    PS3613.E492W43 2013
    813'.6--dc23   2013014382

10 9 8 7 6 5 4 3 2 1

RRD-C

Printed in the United States of America

For my father. My first and ideal reader.
—NM

To Dena, Penelope, and Leo. Everything is for you.
Everything is because of you.
—DG

[The speaker is Death.]

There was a merchant in Bagdad who sent his servant to market to buy provisions and in a little while the servant came back, white and trembling, and said, Master, just now when I was in the marketplace I was jostled by a woman in the crowd and when I turned I saw it was Death that jostled me. She looked at me and made a threatening gesture; now, lend me your horse, and I will ride away from this city and avoid my fate. I will go to Samarra and there Death will not find me.

The merchant lent him his horse, and the servant mounted it, and he dug his spurs in its flanks and as fast as the horse could gallop he went.

Then the merchant went down to the marketplace and he saw me standing in the crowd and he came to me and said, Why did you make a threatening gesture to my servant when you saw him this morning?

That was not a threatening gesture, I said, it was only a start of surprise. I was astonished to see him in Bagdad, for I had an appointment with him tonight in Samarra.

—*W. Somerset Maugham*

WEAPONIZED

1.

PHNOM PENH, CAMBODIA

Kyle West lies atop stiff sheets with his eyes half closed. It burns to keep them open, but shutting them is a paradoxical tease. He would kill for distraction, for the benevolent throb of a headache.

There's nothing worse than insomnia in a tropical climate.

He can't go much longer subsisting on stolen naps, he thinks. Falling asleep for five minutes on public transportation, chickens pecking his hands, children picking his pocket, and a background of hacking lungs.

His brain and body work overtime to fend off the inevitable systemic collapse.

His arms and legs vibrate, a plucked violin string beneath his skin replacing the beat of a pulse. He's hyperaware of the world around him, keyed in on an almost cellular level but unable to take in anything specific, the environment reduced to a passing blur in a rearview mirror.

He turns on his side and thinks, *Maybe not sleeping is a blessing. Maybe I'm looking at this all wrong.* Because when he does sleep, his dreams are ruthless, rooted in fact, absent of unconscious properties. There's no fever logic, no abstract questions answered, no deviant acts banned during waking hours fulfilled.

He tried to end the pain, picked up some natural remedies at the pharmacy. All they did was give him a dull drone of a headache and an erection lasting three and a half hours. He bought some capsules off the black market, purported pharmaceutical grade. Turned out to be expired Tamiflu.

He rolls onto his back and listens to the singed symphony of bug zappers.

The heat in the room is unbearable, a constant reminder. If you can't sleep, you can't forget your body, and forgetfulness is sleep's universal gift.

The walls around him are slathered in a white gloss. There's extensive water damage underneath. In response, the hotel management keeps adding more coats of paint. The wall is now several inches thick with subterfuge.

The only art is a print of Buddha in a chrome frame. The Bodhisattva sports almond eyes and an android smile. Behind him, the jungle explodes in plumes of purple and pink and green, its vines falling around his shoulders like fairy-tale hair.

The air-conditioning is a collapsed lung, helpless against the heat. The time before the rainy season. The time no one wants to be here. The daily room rate, normally twenty-two dollars, has dropped to sixteen while everyone waits for the storms to come and drown the city.

Even at sixteen dollars a night, the room is starting to strain Kyle's purse strings.

He exhales, puts his hand over his heart, hoping to slow it down.

This is how you measure the length of your exile, he thinks, *by the topography of your hotel rooms.*

He rises from the bed, runs his hand through his hair, and gets it caught in a knot. He hasn't cut it since he got here; hasn't shaved either. Which is fine. The expat populace isn't famed for their grooming. The West's prime export to Southeast Asia is tall blond surfer girls with unshaven armpits who do nude yoga on the beach while their scraggly boyfriends case the waves, looking for the perfect one to die in.

Kyle turns on the LCD television, flips the channel to CNN.

He was never a news junkie when he lived in the States, but now CNN has become a reminder of a world he misses terribly; Senate hearings trigger a warm rush of involuntary memory. Even though—as of late—those hearings have been focused on *him* and his former boss Christopher Chandler.

Kyle hears the rooster start up outside. Bastard lives on the balcony one floor below. One morning Kyle stood above him, ready to douse his head with ice water to cut short the dawn sonata, but after they locked eyes, Kyle decided it was best for them to peacefully coexist.

The rooster didn't look like he fucked around.

The tub is stopped up, filled with water that rose during the night. Kyle asked maintenance to take care of the drain, but they snaked the toilet instead. The hotel manager borders on Basil Fawlty when it comes to the operational side of things.

Kyle pours bottled water over his toothbrush, dumps the rest over his head. He should be immune to the tap water by now, but he sticks with the bottles. He still hasn't quite conquered the trauma of his first bout of sickness. The fever, the auditory hallucinations, the feeling there was a ball growing in the pit of your stomach and you had to keep throwing up until it burst.

Two days and ten pounds later, he had learned his lesson.

Don't drink the fucking water.

He goes back into the bedroom, brushes his teeth while watching the news-crawl at the bottom of the screen. National news, local headlines, human-interest stories, all interspersed with the postmodern cant of perpetual Tweeting. Viewers commenting on the news as it happens, present turned past in thirty seconds. His best friend, Neil, was right: Revolution is pointless today. The world moves too fast; we've fucked time. When the revolution finally figures out what it wants, it's already too late—the opposition has factored it into its own plan. The revolution becomes another cog. We're all working for the opposition now.

Back in the bathroom, Kyle spits out his toothpaste and avoids the mirror—a safety precaution. If you don't want to crack, shun surfaces, be a mystery to yourself.

He walks over to the desk and boots up his computer. While the laptop launches, he goes to the fridge, pulls out an Angkor beer, and holds the cold can against his forehead.

He taps his finger against the tab, trying to decide whether or not to pop it.

The pounding starts again in his chest. Hot fingers tight around his heart and squeezing. His heart *hurts.* Not metaphorically. It genuinely aches, like a leg muscle cramping with lactic acid after a hard mile.

His breaths are shallow. He can't take in air. His heart sends electric reminders down to his fingertips.

The air-conditioner starts to heave, a biometric groan suggesting imminent collapse.

He pops open the Angkor. It may not do much for his heart, but at least it's cold. He swallows, feels the alcohol start to build a barrier between his brain and body.

The panic goes gauzy, alcohol dulled but still there, bubbling.

These are the worst moments, the moments of clarity, the bone-deep time when Kyle knows, knows it and can't tell himself different:

I'm gonna die in this place and no one even knows my real name.

He stands before his laptop, signs onto the Internet, and activates his self-designed proxy server, hiding his IP address so he can't be tracked.

He scrolls around some music-downloading sites, finds a few tunes he likes, then opens up a real-time news stream and turns the volume up.

Christopher Chandler, his former boss, sits before a Senate subcommittee. He looks right in his element, like a lizard perched on a rock offering its throat to the sun. His suit is tailored to reveal only three-quarters of an inch of cuff. Chandler doesn't give anything away without a fight, not even fabric.

Chandler crosses his legs, blinding onlookers with a recent shoeshine, while a righteously indignant Democratic senator from Maine—utterly out of his depth—attempts to grill him about financial records no one seems to be able to recover.

Chandler's lawyer, Thomas Lozen, keeps putting his hand over the microphone and consulting with Chandler, who is preoccupied writing the first chapter of his memoirs on a yellow legal pad, finishing sentences with a fountain-pen flourish, not paying a bit of attention to the senator's questions.

Kyle knows something no one in that room except Chandler knows.

Chandler's been working on his memoirs for twenty years and has never gotten past the first chapter. He just keeps writing and rewriting, finding the joy in repetition, finding nothing but pure narcissistic renewal in waking up every day and sculpting the story of his own creation.

There are no references to his parents, to his childhood, nothing. It's as if Chandler were hatched fully formed, as if he hadn't required the traditional means of begetting.

He can exist as pure fact.

Besides, no one would ever let him publish his autobiography. He told Kyle once:

"Do you think it's an accident George H. W. Bush never wrote an autobiography? He's the only former president who hasn't. All we got were a series of letters he wrote during his time in office. That's it. Well, he and I have the same problem. But it doesn't take away the fun of writing it."

Kyle mutes the subcommittee, shrinks the window, moves on to a cluster of bookmarked news sites, and the panic starts again.

This morning, like too many mornings, he's headline news:

"Megalomaniac with Mommy and Daddy Issues."

"Tech Fascist Had Red Parents."

"Irony: Engineer Traded in Commie Parents for Chandler."

Kyle can't read the articles; even skimming causes the room to spin. He knows what they're about, knows where the information emanated from.

While working for Chandler, he started suffering from severe anxiety attacks, panic so intense he was sweating right through his skin; so intense he wanted to jump out a window to make it stop. Chandler sent Kyle to talk to the company's retained psychiatrist, and then, Daniel Ellsberg–style, someone from the inside leaked those files to the press.

He feels violated, vivisected for ratings, his personal tragedies reduced to casual breakfast-nook conversation.

Thank God his parents aren't around. Of course, if they'd been around, he never would have gone to work for Chandler in the first place.

2.

NEW YORK, NEW YORK

Neil O'Donnell sits at his desk and pours himself a Jack and ginger, raises his glass to a framed shot of Lech Walesa, and then goes a few inches to the right and stops at the one of Stalin. Neil's not a Communist, but he loves the way Stalin's photo kills conversation the minute someone walks into his apartment.

His desk is his mind made manifest. Envelopes opened but their contents never read. Magazine back issues featuring his most searing articles. A boneyard of half-smoked cigarettes. He can't concentrate long enough to finish a whole one.

He turns around and rests the drink on his treadmill, a relic of a valiant attempt at clean living, then gets up to fetch his computer from the bedroom.

Tangled in electric-blue sheets, bathed in the fluorescent glow of his fish tank—which is completely devoid of aquatic life and consists solely of cacti, coral, and sunken treasure—is his intern, Katie, a nineteen-year-old journalism student at the New School. Neil unplugs his laptop from the outlet on his side of the bed, and Katie stirs.

"When are you going to get some new fish?"

"Never," he says.

"Why?"

"The fish were a test."

"What kind of test?"

"Doesn't matter. I failed it." He runs his hand through her raven hair. "Go back to sleep."

Neil has a predilection for—actually, correct that, an addiction to—fucking his interns. He looks good for his age: thick, curly hair; skinny body in a uniform of ripped jeans and T-shirts preaching irony. But his fuckability bona fides come courtesy of being a bit of a rock-and-roll cyber-muckraker. And that's what makes the leftist undergrads look at him like some kind of sexual Ellis Island. You've got to fuck Neil O'Donnell when you're in New York if you want to be taken seriously at the next WTO protest.

Truth is, politically, Neil would label himself a Zen anarchist. In fact, he'd tell the Progressives after a few whiskeys that people had to worry about the health of the Left when its most prominent mouthpieces were an ex-rightist formerly married to a gay oil tycoon, and a socialist billionaire who'd sunk the British pound.

Neil started out as a freelance political journalist, contributing pieces to the likes of *Mother Jones,* the *New Republic, Rolling Stone,* and *Vanity Fair.* But he got sick of the lag time between his articles and the events of the real world, got sick of his big stories becoming sad commentary instead of *news.* He wanted his stories delivered moment to moment, fresh and uncut. So he became one of the first big-league bloggers, posting news in real time, making it a living, palpable thing. He had gotten his undergraduate degree at MIT, and no, he had to keep telling the interns, he didn't study with Chomsky. What he studied was international relations and computer science. So setting up the site and networking and server was no problem. And besides, he had all-around tech genius Kyle West, his college buddy, helping him out free of charge.

Neil bankrolled the site out of his own pocket and luckily it moved into the black before he went red—but, man, was it was close. Now he's got on-site advertisers; he's got *sponsorship,* as he puts it. He's got a whole army of freelancers who sit in their apartments all day waiting for something to happen so they can upload it instantly. He has his own media fiefdom, which he runs out of his two-bedroom in Greenwich Village while frequently naked and even more frequently drunk.

He lights a cigarette, watches the smoke coil around the bare bulb in his ceiling fixture, hears the steel-cello chirp of a connected call, and knows exactly who it is.

"How's my favorite exile?" Neil says when he sees Kyle's face in the corner of his screen. "Today the day you're gonna tell me where you are?"

Kyle's voice is low, suffused with fatigue. "Safer you don't know."

Neil puts out the cigarette. "I can't help you if I don't know."

"You *can't* help me. Not only can't you . . . you *shouldn't*." Kyle exhales hard. "See the news today?"

"Yeah." Neil nods. "Waited to hear from you. Wanted to give you some breathing room."

"Why the fuck didn't you tell me this was coming?"

"I didn't know."

"Bullshit," Kyle says. "You're the king of alternative media."

"When it comes to you, no one tells me shit. Look at my site . . . one of my freelancers posted the article. When it comes to you, man, I'm in the dark. They're afraid I might leak it back to you. I'm—you'll love the irony of this one—considered a security risk."

This has been a sore spot in Kyle and Neil's friendship for the past year. Ever since Kyle became permanent front-page news, Neil's been forced to sit on the sidelines, to farm the story out to freelancers. Too many people know about their shared history; know they were college roommates, know they remained best friends, know Kyle put up some capital to help Neil start his site.

And this kills Neil, *kills him,* because he'd love nothing more than to be out there eviscerating Chandler in print. Taking down guys like Chandler is the reason he got into the news business.

Kyle snaps his fingers, nothing rhythmic, a nervous tic. "What do you think?"

"Of what?"

"Of what to do. Can we do any damage control?"

"You're already damaged."

"Why are you talking to me like this?"

"Like what?"

"Like you don't care."

"'Cause I'm trying to hold back how much I do care. Because you're not the only one with insomnia... you're not the only one in exile."

"Why are you upset? I'm the one who just got creamed."

"I haven't seen my best friend in a year. I don't know where you are..."

Kyle tries to focus Neil. "My question was, what do I do now?"

"Same thing I told you on day one. You never should have gone to work for Chandler. Guy's most printable nickname is the Prince of Darkness." Neil picks up the half-smoked cigarette and relights it. "Remember the article I posted. The one about how on the eve of the Baghdad invasion Saddam sent out an urgent telegram. He was willing to make oil concessions, to let the UN in and inspect? He capitulated to all of our demands. And who does Saddam send this telegram to? Not Cheney... not W. ... not Rummy—he sent it to Chandler. He *knew* Chandler was the one with the power to stop the war. And you went and fucking worked for him."

"Where is this getting us?"

"Nowhere. This is me venting my frustration with you."

"I can't believe the legs this story has..."

"And you *really* shouldn't have run."

"What do you mean? I'm named in suits by Judicial Watch, Truth and Justice Watch, the ACLU... top of that, I was handed subpoenas from two different Senate subcommittees. I'm facing, at minimum, two years of jail time for contempt of Congress. I've been accused of helping to transform America into a fascist state. What did you want me to do? Sit on the couch and wait it out?"

"It made you look guilty, running."

"I should have stayed and fought?"

"If you didn't do anything."

"I *didn't*. That's why I ran."

"Right..."

"I've told you a thousand times, I did my *job*. That is all. I worked on weapons proliferation."

"Then come home, man. Come home. You *are* missed."

"I can't."

"You can. Cut a deal with the government."

"They're not offering."

"Make *them* an offer."

"Stop acting like this is some fucking choice I have."

"You need to make a deal with someone. It's your only option."

"It's not."

"Kyle... you worked in DC. You know this. Somewhere, someone wants to cut a deal."

"Chandler is the government."

"Then why is he on TV being grilled?"

"Public relations. Why do you think he agreed to show up? Does he look worried to you? This is a dog-and-pony show. They *asked him* to show up. He gave them his permission to do this to hide the really big issues."

"Make a deal."

Kyle exhales.

"I know that sound," Neil says. "Means you think, somehow, you give it another year, this shit's gonna blow over. Listen to me. Chandler put a live tap on every telecom circuit... and you've been accused of building the network to slice through everything his taps sucked up. You think this is blowing over? Even England, CCTV capital of the world, thought a live tap was nuts. They backed off. This makes Bush's FISA scandal look merely indecent. Reach out. Make a deal. Or don't reach out and make a deal. Just come home."

"Minute I get off the plane in the States, they'll throw the cuffs on me. I'm obstructing justice with my absence."

"And I'll be there for you, with a lawyer, and then I'll run an exclusive."

"No way, man... I'm not some martyr."

"Why'd you do it in the first place?"

"What?"

"Go work for Chandler. Why? You had to know how it was gonna go down; everyone around him has a habit of self-immolating."

"I thought I could make a difference... maybe."

"Right. Change-the-system-from-the-inside kinda thing, am I right?"

"Right."

"But at what cost?"

"Right," Kyle says.

Then the call goes dead.

3.

PHNOM PENH, CAMBODIA

Kyle signs off Skype, closes the window with Chandler's testimony, logs onto one of Neil's feeder publications, and is greeted by a color photograph of himself wearing a tuxedo that could charitably be called ostentatious. He remembers when the photo was snapped. Chandler was in the habit of holding seasonal banquets in his own honor. This particular fete celebrated his philanthropic endeavors, and Kyle was there to introduce several disadvantaged teenagers who would be summer interns at one of Chandler's sixteen companies.

Kyle looks at himself in the tux, clean-shaven, hair sculpted, genuine grin, and he shudders at what he must look like to most people these days. Above the picture, the headline shouts:

"From Revolutionary Son to Corporate Fascist: Kyle West in His Own Words."

Kyle sees all the trigger words below: born in Palestinian training camp...grew up in East Berlin under Stasi protection.

The feeling starts again. The heart squeeze, the arterial tightness, the cold sweat.

He slides open the balcony door and gets, instead of air, a gut punch of heat and haze.

The sky is pregnant with rain, ready to pop. The sun presses down like an anvil. Two bougainvillea plants rest on the balcony, one on either side, dying. Their plumed purple faces have turned pale.

A branch of heat lightning bisects a cloud.

April certainly is the cruelest month.

Kyle rests his hands on the metal railing and then withdraws them in shock. He can't believe the surface has soaked up so much heat this early in the morning.

He peers over the rail at the Mekong River. The lifeblood of the Khmer people. The water is a shade of rusted brass stained by silt carried in from Laos. Houseboats bob along, ramshackle materials, collage art as shelter. Gnarled doors, beach towels as curtains, rusted roofs, NGO-donated tarps, bullet-riddled plaster walls, torn screens, empty oil drums for furniture.

Several houseboats have been pushed together to form a floating village. The suburbs of the postapocalypse, a hellish atoll.

His skin starts to burn.

A naked child stands on a jagged metal plank jutting off the side of a houseboat and pisses into the river. His mother—a land-mine victim, Kyle assumes; she's missing her right arm and foot—pulls the laundry off a clothesline running between her boat and another. The father dumps their waste into a welcoming wave.

Fishermen are caught in the Mekong's version of morning grid-lock. Some have floated farther from the dock than others, and Kyle can make out only the shadows of their straw hats, dozens of Tom Sawyers steering splintered wooden boats. Fishing as a family business. Fathers steer, sons paddle, wives and daughters unfurl nets.

He feels the first buds of cold rise on his skin, signaling a deeper burn.

He puts on his sunglasses and tries to find a thought to hold on to, to ride out. His thoughts go in circles now. Extended exile opens the door to that habit. Actually, it opens the door to *two* habits: endless reflection and alcoholism. He tries to remember what his favorite philosopher in college—E. M. Cioran—said about exile; something about it beginning with exaltation and ending in tuberculosis and masturbation.

He raps his fingers against the railing, decides to head out to anywhere with people. It doesn't matter if he can't understand what's being said. He needs sound, needs to hear speech.

4.

Heat shimmers on tin roofs. Everything's gone aqueous, doubled. Kyle sprints out the back door of the hotel. He needs to keep moving, feels as if he's exploding out of his skin. Staying embodied is his main challenge these days. He wants to burst out, to become free of himself.

Across the street, there's a makeshift village of slum houses built side by side, no breathing room between. The shanties seem to wilt in the heat and lean on one another for support, a series of dislocated shoulders. Laundry stretches from window to window. A hunk of steel—probably the side of a building at one point—stands before the structures, the gateway to a cardboard kingdom.

But what dangles from the top of the steel stops him dead.

Ropes of human hair tied into perfect individual ponytails and drying in the sun like smoked meats. All the hair is the same length and color: dark brown and long enough to reach the small of a woman's back. It looks like the work of an executioner bored with lopping off heads and searching for a new thrill.

Kyle drifts, wonders where all the hair is going, then decides he doesn't want to know. There are some truths that don't enlighten, and he figures the ultimate destination of the hair is one of them.

He moves down the street, passes a shirtless teenager dragging an overflowing sack of iPhones and iPods, the weight too much for his growing bones to bear.

Kyle rounds the block, and a line of tuk-tuks compete for his attention.

"Where you go?" a driver calls, following him.

"Central Market."

"Get in."

"No, no . . . it's only ten minutes to walk."

"It's too hot. You die in five." The driver slows down. "Fifty cent. I take you anywhere."

"I'm . . ."

"People die in this heat. Especially American. You not made for this."

The driver has a salient point. Kyle gets into the tuk-tuk, a small motorcycle attached to a separate passenger carrier complete with a ramshackle roof.

"Wha's your name?"

"Jim," Kyle says. Every day he tries a new one.

"Sok," the driver says. "Today my birthday."

"Happy birthday."

"Every day my birthday. I born in the jungle. Khmer Rouge come and take everyone there. No one knew what day it was, what month, year, nothing. No calendar. I was born in no time." He laughs. "Have lots and lots of birthdays."

Kyle sinks into the back of the tuk-tuk.

Born in no time.

That's his existence in Phnom Penh boiled down. *No time.* He's lost twenty pounds of muscle since he touched down here, lost his resolve, his desire to get off the ground, his will to re-create rituals from home, those moments that personalize one's world.

But the most crushing loss has been losing his ability to write code.

Kyle's always felt that language, not the body, is the true prison house of the soul. When he lost coding, he lost his Edenic native tongue. Now he's forced to rely on the same words everyone has to work with.

Thus far, he's not impressed with the results.

He starts to drift, losing consciousness with his eyes open; like watching himself on television.

The traffic snaps him back to the present right about when Sok decides to pulls a double-lane cross and merge, using his horn as an exclamation point.

Driving in Southeast Asia is always dangerous, but Cambodia (and, in particular, Phnom Penh) is considered the crown jewel of potential catastrophe.

Two lanes of traffic on one side. Another two lanes running parallel. And no barrier to separate the flows. If people don't like one side, they simply swerve onto the other.

No signals, no warning; punk-rock driving, all attitude and swagger. Cars, motos, tuk-tuks, lone cyclists, hotel shuttle vans, freewheeling pedestrians, trucks hauling timber or waste all flow together in a motley mix, crisscrossing from one side to the other.

If one can be called an expert on such conditions, Sok deserves the title. His strategy seems to be driving straight up the middle and honking belligerently until someone lets him in.

They pass a tuk-tuk filled with tourists holding out their cell phones and recording the drive, living through the lens. They'll experience the trip when they get home. The ultimate authentication: sitting before your laptop with a glass of wine and watching yourself on vacation.

Sok swerves around a police truck with a water tank attached to the back. An officer stands at attention, holding a hose and power-washing fresh blood off the highway.

The tuk-tuk continues on, passing crumbling French architecture that survived the Khmer Rouge. Buildings like royalty in exile. Rococo palaces in disrepair, facades blasted. Ferroconcrete, glazed balconies, art deco, alien artifacts of former colonial status. The cracked jaw of a lost kingdom. And below these imposing structures, the Cambodians living like moles, so poor they hide under houses.

Sok drives on the wrong side of a city bus, then hammers on the horn as a bunch of Buddhist monks in flowing saffron robes cross the street, chanting.

Kyle taps Sok on the shoulder. "You can stop here. This is good."

5.

The Central Market is a prime tourist site; built in 1937, it's a massive art deco dome with four wings radiating from its center. The inside is a labyrinth of stands, merchants, and shops.

Kyle stands in the heart of it. The unreal city. Bruised-fruit sky dripping phosphorescence. Even abject poverty looks ethereal in its glow. The crowded outdoor stalls selling black-market electronics; the local dealers with Buddhist handicrafts and traditional Khmer instruments; the infants running around bottomless, reminding everyone that diapers are in short supply. All of it has the tint of gold left at the bottom of the sea.

No real pedestrian space. Bob-and-weave walking, like Sok moving through the traffic, and instead of horns, there's the squawk of loudspeakers, the pitch and pluck of Khmer music, the cacophony of commerce.

Kyle walks on. He scans faces, goes through his mental Rolodex, marks anyone who looks out of place. Distinct scents of stale urine, barbecue, fresh fish. Shadows with no source. "Want to drink blood?" someone asks. *God, I hope it's snake,* Kyle thinks, although you never know.

He passes a row of stands selling Chinese electronics; disposable cell phones; bootleg DVDs; computer software; wall outlets; pop-music CDs with no covers, just the artist's name and the album title written in mangled English.

Kyle points to a cell phone with prepaid minutes. He's out of minutes and doesn't like the feeling, even if he hasn't called anyone in weeks. The owner slides it off the rack and pulls a price out of thin air. Jacked up a few dollars for the color of Kyle's skin.

Although the globalized economy is starting to crack open the city, it's still free of occidental ornament. If all cities are whores, this is still Phnom Penh's first week working the corner. In 1975, she had been more than your common streetwalker, but Pol Pot and the Khmer Rouge took care of that.

Pol's was the pinnacle of the revolutionary ladder that started with the Soviets or, some would argue, with Robespierre. For all the zealots who wondered whether the great social revolution had failed on its prior attempts because it didn't go far enough, because of internal ossification, because the people lost their nerve and harbored secret bourgeois sympathies, Pol Pot provided the answer.

What would it look like if the revolution went all the way?

There would be no one left.

No one was loyal enough to survive. No one was worthy enough to live in paradise.

Extermination was the sole area in which Pol excelled. A failed technical student and a piss-poor electrician, capable of only a rudimentary understanding of Marxism—forget Hegel or Feuerbach—and an uninspired military leader who wasted thousands of troops in misguided offensives. Mao may have been the century's biggest butcher, but there are a billion people in China. We wouldn't talk of Pol Pot today if he hadn't killed off a quarter of all Cambodians. And Phnom Penh bore the brunt of it.

One of the first things Kyle noticed when he got here was the lack of middle-aged and elderly people. Pol and his Khmer Rouge had made sure of that: liquidate the cities, the intellectual classes, and then, as is de rigueur for all revolutions, liquidate yourselves. A country of orphans, average age of seventeen.

The UN wouldn't call what happened genocide because Pol Pot wasn't looking to exterminate a specific group of people.

He wanted to kill *everyone.*

The Cambodians put up monuments, counted the bones, and wanted to move on. You had to.

Kyle slows down, and the beggars and hustlers surround him. Some offer newspapers to rent so you can read while you eat, some a chance to squeeze off shotgun rounds at chickens, some visas for a hundred American dollars, some close-up views of skin diseases and the ravages of dengue fever, and some nothing but a glimpse of devastation.

He loses his bearings, loses track of the faces.

The girl is the victim of an acid attack, a frequent denouement to lovers' quarrels in this part of the world. Kyle's seen girls like her before, but this one has suffered horribly. Half her face has been scorched off—lips and one eye—and her arms and legs bear tremendous scars, tortured terrain. He figures she must have been wearing a sundress on the day of the attack. He tries to avoid looking at her mouth, a corrugated pinpoint, a scream that closed in around itself.

He swallows hard and drops a dollar in her hand.

He's a block from Armand's when he hears the shriek. Two cops have a monkey in a wire cage, and the fucker's going crazy. Banging around inside, trying to pry the bars apart. It takes both cops to hold the cage steady.

The monkey's a glue addict separated from his poison. He's one of a gang of fifteen most-wanted that the cops are trying to round up. Pictures of the criminal simians line the walls of restaurants, offices, and embassies.

They're considered public enemies.

The chief of police is on record as saying, "We treat them like people, like citizens. If they do crime, we will hunt them."

So how does a monkey end up sniffing glue and forming a habit? Street kids and criminals train them to pick pockets and snatch purses. One monkey scratches your leg or jumps on your back while the other snatches anything of value. On one such boost, a monkey scored a bottle of glue from a woman's handbag and then huffed it. He brought it back home, and everyone got a turn. Before you knew it, there was an epidemic.

The monkey keeps banging his head against the bars until he passes out.

6.

There's no door. Only a threadbare beaded curtain. If people want to come in, they're going to come in.

At least, that's how Armand sees it. It's his life's philosophy boiled down to a decorative flourish.

The mirror behind the bar is sweaty and streaked, and anything reflected in it looks like the cover of a 1970s glam-rock album: Vaselined lens, vaguely space age.

Kyle parts the beads, enters, approaches the bar, and leans on it with his elbow. He locks eyes with another Westerner, a woman wearing a muscle tee with a marijuana leaf on the front. The leaf curves around her breasts, and her tanned, toned shoulders finish off the fetching effect. Kyle can't stop staring, but it's not lust. He doesn't like seeing new faces in Armand's bar, especially new Western faces.

"Another round, Armand," she calls out.

"Coming, my love," he yells in return.

Armand's in the corner messing around with the television, playing with the picture. He finally gives up and broadsides the panel with his palm, causing it to miraculously come to life.

Kyle stares at the television tuned to CNN.

After several onsite suicides at a plant in the Chinese city of Taiyuan, the reporter says, management encircled the factory's exterior with inflatable mattresses. The restive workforce decided that was the final indignity and is rioting in response—smashing windows, starting fires, overturning management's luxury cars and dancing on the debris.

A journalist is able to get a few words with Li Bao, standing member of the CCP and former governor of Shanxi Province. Li is there to speak for the striking workers.

"You need to allow these people to unionize. No Communist country has ever allowed their workers to unionize. Why? Because it's supposed to be a workers' paradise. Well...paradise is burning," Li says into the camera, which quickly cuts back to the chaos, the real reason for being there.

"Turn the channel," the girl in the marijuana-leaf tee says. "If I wanted to watch CNN, I'd have stayed home."

Armand's body has moved past obesity and into the realm of existential claim. He wears a Hawaiian shirt, and entire petals are lost in the chasm between his chest and stomach. His shorts used to be jeans, and both of his exposed legs are as thick as someone's waist. There's a baby strapped to his chest, and its chubby legs kick nonstop, a machine working itself to death.

Armand pours the girl another drink. She goes off and sits alone.

"She got here two days ago," Armand says in a French accent muddled by years of overseas living. "Says her name is Violet." He laughs, a huge sound that obliterates every other noise in the room. "Bullshit, obviously. My bet...she stabbed her boyfriend and is on the run."

"Could be," Kyle says.

Phnom Penh lends itself to the mutability of identity. This is where you come to shed your current form, to mingle among other ghosts. It's the same as when you take a plane ride; you can lie to the person next to you for the entire trip.

Even Pol Pot changed his name, ten times.

"You see what happened to my fish," Armand says. "Electricity went out most of yesterday. Fucking power failures." Armand's fish tank—previously his pride and joy—is now a cemetery. His fish float atop brackish water, their gills clogged with drain scum. "The filter stopped working and they drowned in their own shit...I loved those fish."

"I know you did."

"This fucking city...it just takes and takes from you." Armand swats away his negativity. "It's always good to see you, Andrew."

Andrew was one of the first names Kyle toyed with upon arrival, and Armand seems to have taken to it. No sense in changing things now.

"Drink?" Armand says, and pulls an unmarked turquoise bottle from behind the bar.

"Yeah." Kyle squints. "The hell is that?"

"Do you trust me?"

"It looks like the stuff they use to clean combs at a barbershop."

Armand laughs, fills two shot glasses, and makes engine noises at the baby, who smiles.

Armand's a true child of Cambodia, raised in Phnom Penh until 1975, when most of the Westerners made a mad dash before Pol Pot's shock troops emerged from the jungle. Until Pol's revolution, Armand's dad owned and operated casinos. In a desperate attempt to balance the budget, Prince Sihanouk had granted licenses to gambling houses. He needed a way to signal to the West that he was trying to stanch the flow of Communism and didn't want his country to end up like Vietnam. The easiest way was to fly the flag for private enterprise. Financially, the casinos were a tremendous success, and both the prince and men like Armand's dad got fat off the proceeds. However, for the populace, they proved to be a disaster. People committed suicide after incurring insurmountable debts. Business activity bottomed out as everyone from factory owner to common laborer lost his life savings on a pillow of green felt.

Armand's dad still talked about the last days before Phnom Penh fell, talked about it like it was Rome under Caligula minus the midgets. One night, Armand's dad hosted a pool party. Everyone was embalmed in champagne and sniffing heroin from Laos. A Frenchwoman dove into the water and invited all the men in there with her. She traveled around the pool and fucked a stranger in every corner until they all met in the middle and had their way with her.

The other partygoers sipped gin and cheered them on.

Some Cambodians weren't upset when Pol Pot and his crew put an end to this strain of Western bacchanalia. Then they learned what was taking its place. Suddenly, orgies seemed almost quaint, a foreign lark.

Kyle and Armand do the shots, and it takes Kyle three tries to force it down. "Somehow, it tastes worse than it looks," he says, rubbing his teeth with his index finger, trying to scrub the taste away.

Armand notices Kyle's hand. "You're shaking."

"I...I haven't been sleeping well," Kyle says. "How do you sleep in this heat?"

"Air-conditioning," Armand says.

A Khmer song explodes from the jukebox. The singer's voice is absolute bubblegum—remnants of a style that went out in the West with Phil Spector's girl groups—and the stringed instruments sound like they're mourning. The contrast is the perfect sonic summation of Phnom Penh.

"Andrew...you have to sleep," Armand says. "Sleep is where we work out all our problems. It's elemental. Goes back to our origins. When it was hunting season and the men of the ancient tribes were up for days searching for prey, they would pay a shaman to dream for them."

Kyle points to the baby. "Maybe I could buy his brain for a night."

"Oh, no," Armand says. "He dreams for me."

"That explains a lot."

Armand lets out that huge laugh that devours all other sounds. "What I mean is, I've seen it before. Many people like you..."

"Americans."

"Westerners in general. But mostly Americans."

Kyle nods.

"They come here to get away from it all," Armand says. "You know, take some time. Lose the city hustle. Get some sun. Well, many...many of them take it too far. They forget they brought *their bodies* with them on vacation. They act as if touching down on another continent relieves them of all responsibility. Whatever you've been doing...don't do it anymore. Please."

"I appreciate your concern," Kyle says. "I do. It's the heat. Nothing more."

Armand points to the blue liquor. "Another?"

"Not even if Jesus was pouring."

Armand grins, pours himself a round. "Suit yourself." He tosses down the blue liquor with a full-body shudder and then wipes his lips with the back of his hand. "Your package is in my office."

"Right," Kyle says. "Thanks."

He nods, and as he walks toward Armand's office, he locks eyes again with Violet, who sits alone, sucking on a lime wedge.

7.

Armand's office has a stained sign on the door that says PRIVÉ. Three different locks dot the cherry wood, and none of them work. Armand says the illusion of security is all one needs. If someone's determined to break in, one lock—or three locks—isn't going to stop him. He says it's like the concept of the law: There is no law. There's only regulated punishment. Law exists solely to inform people of what they can—and will—be punished for, not to actually stop them from committing crimes. In fact, Armand would continue, the law is a vile institution, because it *goads* you into breaking it, just so it can punish you properly.

Kyle steps into the office, which is bare except for a metal desk holding spilled files and a potted plant. On the wall, there's a calendar from a local restaurant featuring girls in scanty bikinis lounging on muscle cars.

Kyle fishes his package out of the clutter on the desk and opens it. He gets all his packages shipped to Armand. His hotel isn't particularly skilled at or concerned about protecting the mail from marauding children.

He opens it up, and inside is a well-thumbed edition of Graham Greene's *Collected Short Stories*. Kyle wasn't much of a reader back in the States, but since arriving in Phnom Penh, he's been searching out the poets of exile—Durrell, Hemingway, Duras, Conrad, and, of course, Greene.

Kyle wonders if exile—either physical or mental—was what spurred all these authors to be so exceptionally prolific. Was each book a silent scream into the void with the hope a voice would answer and guide the author to a place to call home?

Kyle slides the book back into the packaging, tucks it under his arm, walks back into the bar, and sees Armand has his drink waiting for him with a napkin laid over the rim. Kyle nods in thanks, and Armand returns only a quick nod; he's occupied, talking to Violet. Armand would be the first to tell you that in the West, he'd have no shot fucking someone who looks like Violet, but—as he's fond of pointing out to Kyle—people do really *strange* shit when they're away from home.

Kyle grabs his drink, sits down at a table close to the door so he can get a hint of a breeze, takes a swallow, and cracks some ice with the back of his teeth. For a moment, his eyes do a slow close. Not because he's got any chance of sleeping; it's pure reflex.

His eyes are tired of being open.

Almost as soon as they close, they're brought back to bloodshot life.

The beads are swaying. Someone's crossed into the bar.

8.

Kyle registers the newcomer first as shadow, then as a cloud in the mirror behind the bar, then as shoulders, and finally as a man.

Definitely Western and, Kyle figures, judging from the color of his skin, new in town. His face and hands are freshly burned, crustacean pink and red, and look painful to the touch. The man doesn't yet have the obligatory tan. Even if you're not trying for one, you get it. It's part of the price of being here.

The guy is also *way* overdressed for Armand's.

His suit is exceptional, white linen offset by a perfectly folded pink handkerchief. The suit looks custom-made but not by a tailor in the West, not someone used to dealing with a bulky body and this man's height. The cut is a little too tight in the chest, and it's a little too short in the legs. With his pouty, pillowed lips and swept-back hair, this newcomer would have looked at home during French rule sipping gin at a bamboo table with a rotating fan overhead.

Kyle squints. *Another Westerner? Too many in one day.*

The man holds a Tumi briefcase in his left hand and casually loosens and tightens his grip on the handle.

He approaches the bar, takes in the tableau of Armand, Violet, and the kicking, squirming baby, and says: "Vodka. No ice."

Armand puts his hand atop Violet's, excuses himself, and approaches the stranger. "No ice?"

"What's the point? This heat's epic," the man says as Armand goes for the bottle.

Violet parts her lips but doesn't give him a smile, just a welcoming flick of the tongue. The man smiles at her. His teeth are magnificent alabaster squares ready to do his bidding.

"I'm Violet," she says, unconsciously rearranging her long legs for maximum effect.

The man nods, another flash of teeth.

Armand places the drink on the bar.

The man lights a cigarette, clenches it between his teeth, tilts his head slightly so the smoke stays out of his eyes, and drops a bill on the bar. "Keep the change."

As the man wanders away, both Violet and Armand look over to Kyle's table. Each wears the same expression, the same dazed stare Kyle suspects he's sporting as well.

Because this man, this stranger, looks uncomfortably like Kyle.

Similar height, give or take an inch or two. The same pronounced jaw. The same aquiline nose, dangerously close to becoming a beak but pulling back in time. The same eyes, green orbs with a coat of frost. The only big difference between them is their hair, both color and length. Kyle's is lighter, and his current look could be called unintentional bohemian; the new arrival has a close shave and a triple-digit haircut.

The man approaches Kyle's table, pulls out a seat, and settles in. "You look like you could use a friend."

Kyle shakes his head, subtle but forceful. "Not really."

"All right." The man throws up his hands, called out. "*I* could use one. And I nominate you for the job."

Kyle motions toward Violet with his head. "Looks like you already made one."

"That's not a friend. That's someone looking for death."

"Yours or hers?"

"I don't think it matters. She just wants to set up a meeting." The man crosses his legs, leans back in the chair. "I picked you be-cause... well, you're American. We search out our own kind, right?"

"That was the only requirement? You might want to think about shooting higher."

The man laughs. "Also, you don't look like you're here working for an NGO. I don't want to talk third-world politics, the evils of Western Imperialism, et cetera..."

"I see..."

The man raises his drink to his lips. Kyle sees a Patek Philippe watch, a chunk of gold for a bracelet, and what could be a wedding band. "Why are you here?" He takes a drag off the cigarette, then exhales, sending smoke through his nose like his adenoids are on fire.

"Vacation," Kyle says.

There's an uncomfortable subtext beneath the conversation, an almost hazy flirtation, as they both try to avoid bringing up the obvious. *You look like me.*

The man brings his briefcase onto the table and quickly enters a combination; the top pops open. Kyle jumps back, his instincts hardwired to react to any unexpected sounds that could presage violence.

The man laughs and removes a ham and cheese sandwich from inside the case. It's shrink-wrapped and looks so loaded with additives it could survive the apocalypse. The type of sandwich that's the staple of international airspace.

The man holds up the sandwich like someone surrendering or confessing. "I've been out of the developing world for too long. My insides have gone soft against parasites." He takes a bite of the sandwich, another drag off his cigarette. He's always doing something with his mouth. "So, vacation?"

"That's right."

"I'm on business. I think I've got my card around here somewhere." He starts searching through the various inner pockets of his linen suit. "I work in telecommunications. Southeast Asia is ripe for smartphones. Expendable income is up sixteen percent."

Kyle's interest is slightly piqued—is this a fellow tech guy, a brother in coding? "You an engineer?"

"Salesman. I work for a German telecom company. VodaFone. That's *Fone* with an *F,* then *o-n-e.*"

"But you're not German..."

"God, no." The man gives up the search for his card. "American. I pursued the Germans for a position. American telecom companies have lost their fire. All fat off their monopolies. While they rub their bloated bellies, the Chinese and Germans are buying up the contracts to build infrastructure throughout the developing world. The action isn't in the States anymore, and I adore the chase. I told the Germans, Look... turn me loose. I want to make all of you fucking *rich*."

Kyle looks over his shoulder, not used to staying in one place this long. "That's what it takes to make it in sales, I imagine."

"That and slightly jaundiced scruples. You have no idea who you have to deal with in order to get a contract signed in some of these places. Warlords who a few years back were eating young girls' hearts for power before riding off to slaughter. These same fucking lunatics now control the rights to half the infrastructure. And their idea of bargaining differs slightly from what they teach in MBA programs. But if we want to be competitive with the Chinese, we need to turn a blind eye to that, because the Chinese sure do." The man raises his glass. "They don't call them emerging markets for nothing."

"You like getting sent all over the world?"

"*Love it.* Massively. I love to sell." The man takes another bite of the sandwich, discreetly brushes some crumbs off his lower lip, and says: "Christ... manners. I'm Julian Robinson. My mother read the Forsyte Saga like the Bible. I'm the beneficiary of her Anglo lust."

Kyle sees a way around giving up a name. "Could be worse. She could have named you Trevor."

"Trevor's my younger brother." Robinson lights another cigarette. "So who are you?"

Kyle stares at the cigarette held between Robinson's thumb and index finger. "Andrew," he says. "I'm Andrew."

"Andrew," Robinson says. "And what do you do back in the States?"

"Tech support," Kyle says. "Databases. Networks, mostly."

"Deal with charts and graphs all day," Robinson says. "I don't know how you do it. Bores my tits off. The company sent me to an

Excel course to learn how to keep better expense reports. I left after an hour and told them, You want me to sell or fill in boxes?" He brings the cigarette to his lips. "Been at it long?"

Kyle tries to avoid specifics. "Freelance. I float from company to company."

"Like me," Robinson says.

"Except I don't sell anything."

"Sure you do. You sell yourself. You sell *confidence* in you. We all sell something. Been doing it long?" he asks again.

"Floating? Or tech support?"

"Either."

"Tech support . . . longer than I care to remember. Floating the past five years. Mostly New York."

"Well, it sounds great," Robinson says.

Kyle's relieved, assuming the conversation is over and he'll be rid of Robinson any moment now.

Robinson leans across the table. "For being complete bullshit."

"Sorry?" Kyle says, stunned, tensing up.

"It's okay, Kyle," Robinson says. "I know who you are."

Kyle starts to get out of his seat. Robinson holds Kyle down by his hand. "Hey. Hey. It's okay, Kyle. It's okay. I'm a friend. I'm here to help."

The reassuring words don't stop Kyle from trying to get loose. He looks to the bar, sees Armand giving Violet change for the jukebox.

"You're going to make a scene," Robinson says. "There's no need for it." He uses his free hand to raise the cigarette to his lips. "I'm a friend. I promise. Give me two minutes of your time. Two minutes."

Kyle doesn't sit back down.

"Two minutes," Robinson says. "All I ask. Christ. You've got me asking for permission to try and help you—"

Kyle cuts him off. "You have *one minute.*"

Violet gets off the stool, a leggy princess born from a mushroom, and glides over to the jukebox. She's taken off her shoes, revealing pink toenails and a ruby toe ring. She stops at the jukebox, selects some electro-pop, and starts dancing with herself.

Robinson shifts to keep both Kyle and Violet in view. "I couldn't believe my eyes. I just got here few days ago. I stop in here for a drink and you're at the bar talking to the big guy. Kyle West. In the flesh. At the end of the world."

"You've already lost twenty seconds. Better get to the point."

Robinson smiles. "The point is not what I want. The point is what I can give you." He leans in closer. "In exchange for your passport."

Kyle starts to get up again. "No. No thanks."

"Wait. What I'm offering benefits us *both*. I need to get into Africa to close a deal and . . . well, I had an unfortunate mishap the last time I was there."

"What kind of mishap?"

"Short version . . . due to a disagreement between myself, a finance minister, and a rebel warlord, there's a warrant out for me in Congo. I'm persona non grata. They claim I stole five million dollars worth of coltan."

"What's that?"

"Mineral they put in cell phones."

"Did you do it?"

"No," Robinson says. "I'd never jeopardize my position there. But I'm a convenient scapegoat for a corrupt rebel leader lining his pockets. There's no law there. There's no way for a businessman to protect himself. I *need* to get back there." He takes a drag off his cigarette. "I checked into it. There's no extradition agreement between the U.S. and the Africans for you. I can't get in there, but you . . . I mean, your passport can."

"So you want me to give you my papers?"

"And I give you mine."

"How long have you been following me?"

Robinson looks down at the table, decides to take another bite of his sandwich. "I haven't. I've been waiting."

"If you found me, someone else will too."

"I haven't noticed anyone else. And I've been careful to keep my distance."

Kyle circles back to the point at hand. "So I give you my papers . . . and I get exactly *what* in return?"

"Name Raymond Kuo mean anything to you?"

Kyle nods. "Yeah. Kuo heads the subcommittee looking into whether Chandler used federal dollars to set up his system. He's the guy who has me on contempt."

"Kuo is up to his neck in bribes with the CCP," Robinson says as he leans back in his chair to take in Violet's dance. "He's been passing them intel for years. Cyber stuff."

"The Chinese Communist Party?"

"I do a lot of work with the Chinese," Robinson says. "I'm good friends with a guy in the CCP. He owes me. Gave me very specific info on Kuo, because, well...Kuo is a pain in the ass to the telecom industry. My friend thought the info might come in handy for someone like me. Kuo controls a lot of regulation, throws a lot of weight around. Makes life difficult for corporations. Especially foreign ones trying to do business in the States. If I give you this info on Kuo, I guarantee you can go back to the States, no questions asked. If Kuo knows you've got it, this will all go away for you. No jail. No contempt. Nothing. Case dismissed. You can slide right back into your old life."

Violet extends her arms toward Robinson, beckoning him to come join her. He holds up an index finger, signaling he'll get to her soon. "A clean-document swap is always better than a forgery. Trust me. Always better to have real documents."

Kyle's trying to keep up with the specifics of Robinson's plan. "And what the hell do you have on this guy in the CCP, he's willing to hand you the info on Kuo?"

"The less you know about the CCP, the better. This guy's a friend. A good friend. All *you* need to know is your freedom rests in my office in England."

Kyle runs his hand through unruly hair, causing half of it fall over his face. "If this information exists on Kuo, someone like Chandler would have access to it. Why doesn't he have it? Why isn't he using it?"

Robinson replies in an eerie echo of Kyle's earlier sentiments. "Someone like Chandler doesn't need it. His testimony before the subcommittee is a show trial. The government looks inept. Chandler looks evil. Maybe they fine him a little bit and then kick the money back to him through a third source. Bottom line, ineptitude punishes evil and they keep using the program. They need to make it look like they're punishing the guilty while they keep using *your* program."

"I didn't invent *that* fucking thing."

"I never said you did. Believe me, we are totally simpatico on the topic of being fucked by the government. Our problem is the same. The rebel leader did the same thing to me that Chandler did to you. They used us. They took our trust and used us."

Kyle lets Robinson's words sink in, feels the beginnings of a slight camaraderie based on mutual misfortune, then cancels that emotion and reverts back to his normal state: paranoia. "Passing yourself off as me ... that's a hell of a risk."

"My deal in Africa is worth, minimum, eight figures ... *if* I can get there. It's essential I get there. I assume it's equally essential for you to get out of here."

Kyle's silent, then: "Why?"

"Why what?"

"Do you think it's essential for me to get out of here?"

Robinson's surprised. "I just assumed. I mean, you can't like *this* ... running. Sure, you've been lucky so far, gotten a grace period. But how long do you think you've really got? I give you my info on Kuo at least you've got a fighting chance. All you've got now is *chance* itself."

"This type of thing ... this trade ... it's really *done?*"

"It's becoming more and more common. Identity is the new currency of the world."

Kyle thinks, *Christ. Somehow, the death of hard cash has led to the rise of the self.* "You've been involved with it before?"

"No ... but I know people who have."

"Did it work?"

"Wouldn't be here if it didn't."

Kyle bites his lip. "I don't know ..." He can't look Robinson directly in the eye. "I need to think about it ..."

"I want us to help each other. I do. But I can't wait around either." Robinson rips off the corner of a napkin, scribbles down an address and phone number, and passes it to Kyle. "That's my hotel."

Kyle takes the paper, recognizes the address, and slides it back to Robinson. "I know it."

"Kyle...think about what I'm saying," Robinson says. "I mean, *really* think. We both need this. Equal risk, yes. But equal reward also, if it works out." Robinson stands, pushes his chair in. "Someone else needs a partner too." He glides over to the dancing Violet but turns back to Kyle one more time. "Hope to see you."

9.

Kyle sits inside a Buddhist temple surrounded by unarmed UN peacekeepers—a contradiction in terms, if you ask him.

The temple is an austere place of worship, not a tourist attraction. A towering pink Buddha rests atop a rusted altar surrounded by charcoal-penciled verses from the Dhammapada, gold bowls, and scented candles. A carpet before the statue is covered with dozens of the city's homeless, huddled together and drenched in sweat.

Kyle stares at the statue of Buddha and is reminded of the innate respect he's always had for Buddhism, a religion far closer to a philosophy in that it offers no sturdy solutions, only endless questions and quixotic steps that, even if completed, don't guarantee self-enlightenment. There's little to recommend it to those who find no comfort in *doubt* as the essence of spiritual catechism.

Kyle wants to call somebody, reach out for advice, talk to someone he trusts and ask:

Should I do this? Should I take Robinson's offer?

But he knows the answer: He shouldn't. You never feel the need to call someone for advice when you know you've got a solid plan. No one ever calls a friend and starts the conversation by saying:

I've got this terrific opportunity. I can't say enough positive things about this course of action. But I'd just like your opinion on it.

He looks at the homeless sprawled on the temple's carpet and thinks:

The only difference between them and me is that I haven't run out of people to sell myself to.

Kyle intones the name over and over: "Julian Robinson. Julian Robinson."

Robinson was right about one thing. All Kyle's been doing for the past year is enacting a sun-drenched rehearsal for death.

Kyle looks up at the Buddha, its face stripped of false worldly illusions, and thinks about what the West—his people—have done to Buddhism. They turned a religion based on nullifying the self and becoming an objective universal eye into an exploration of the self that can be combined with *exercise. Christ,* he thinks, *is there anything we can't commercialize?* But there is. There is one thing that cannot be totalized and absorbed into the system: Death.

Julian Robinson. Julian Robinson.

10.

Kyle sits before his computer sipping an Angkor beer and straining to keep his eyes open. He types a string of terms into a search engine, rubs his eyes, and gets up from the desk.

He walks into the bathroom, turns on the bare bulbs encircling the tiny square mirror, runs the water until it turns cold, cups his hands, fills them with water, and bathes his eyes.

The cold feels good against his swollen lids. He blinks back the water dripping down his lashes and then washes his eyes one more time.

He goes back into the bedroom, looks at the search results, and begins to read.

There are photos of Robinson at various telecom conferences. He's standing with government employees in charge of information regulation. Kyle clicks on more images. Pictures of Robinson with prominent European businessman, always either boarding a private plane or entering a bulletproof car.

Kyle opens up articles written by Robinson for trade journals, several of which are in German. Luckily, Kyle remembers enough German to be able to read them.

The first two deal with how Europe's overregulation is hindering sales and halting progress in the telecom industry. The last article is about the radical possibilities for political and personal emancipation in Asia and the Middle East as a result of technological innovation.

It's a cogent, well-argued piece. Kyle's impressed with Robinson's writing skill, even though Robinson seems to be wearing the garb of a technological utopian primarily to bolster sales.

Robinson appears to be legit, to be telling the truth about his identity.

Kyle closes down his computer, lies on the bed, and feels the potential for sleep. It's not that Robinson's offer has relaxed him. It's that for the first time in a year, he feels like he has an option. He can take it or not, but an actual option, a potentially viable way home, has been presented.

11.

Kyle turns on his back.

Awake for the past few hours, resting with his eyes closed, now he feels like reading. He stretches his arm to the nightstand, and his new book isn't there. He thinks back, realizes he left Armand's in such a hurry yesterday that he forgot it.

Shit.

He looks at the stack of books in the corner. He's read them all, several times; their spines are cracked and broken.

He doesn't like the idea of visiting the same location twice in two days, doesn't like setting up an obvious pattern, but if he waits for Armand to deliver his new book, he'll have that bloated scion of former colonialists drunk and singing outside his window at two in the morning, waving the book around like a white flag.

He throws his legs over the side of his bed, and his feet find his shoes in the dark.

12.

Kyle slides his sunglasses on and slips out the back door of the hotel. The sun's hardly pushed through the clouds, but it's boiling out. Even the banyan trees seem stunned, their branches straight, rigid with surprise, the leaves wilting, thirsty for water still a month away.

Kyle walks the block, sweating through his shirt after a few steps, keeps his eyes trained for a tuk-tuk. Today he won't argue with the driver. Today he'll happily accept a lift.

His mind wanders; images blur, dissolve into a stream of heightened blues and desiccated browns, the color scheme of his surrounding world, shanties and baked dirt.

Peripheral movement gets his attention, returns him to the present moment. The severe, elongated shadows of two men thrown against the slum steel give him pause.

This is what I get, taking the same route twice in two days.

He starts to pick up his pace. Could be nothing. All shadows are suspicious at first.

Calm down, he thinks. *Get in a tuk-tuk, get to the market, get to a crowded place.*

Then two bullets graze the side of his ear and lodge themselves in the wall a few feet ahead.

13.

He takes off in a sprint, looks back for a flash, and makes out two men dressed as tourists. Khaki shorts, garish polo shirts, baseball caps, and Bluetooth earpieces. The hallmarks of what Kyle calls mercenary casual.

The humidity enters his lungs and harpoons his heart, sending it into overdrive. He can't keep up this pace on an open street. He needs to get somewhere populated.

He takes another look back. The two men are dangerously close. The only thing weighing them down are ill-fitting ankle holsters mummified in tube socks.

Two thoughts cross Kyle's mind and battle for space. First: *He found me. Fucking Chandler finally found me.* Second: *I hope these two have scruples about shooting civilians because they're about to be swimming in them.*

Kyle knows where to lead the chase. He has one advantage over his pursuers: he knows the city, knows its nooks and crannies like a longtime resident.

He takes a hard right into a cardboard city and is greeted by a lake of sewer water over a foot deep. The smell rising from the fetid pond is noxious. There's a dozen naked children flopping around in the sludge, playing with a stripped mattress someone tossed in there.

Kyle stifles the urge to scream at the children, *Stop. You're all going to get fucking cholera.*

He rushes through the puddle, trying not to breathe in, hoping brief contact with the water doesn't eat away the skin on his ankles and heels.

He hears the two guys splashing through in pursuit, cursing the water, the smell, the fact they're wearing shorts.

He doesn't look back, keeps up his pace, side starting to hurt.

He cuts left and crosses into an open area, a space of slanted shanties sinking into the mud like the earth is trying to drag them back home.

The ground is a suction device. Kyle's shoes can barely trudge through, his soles dragged down into the grimy glue.

Then another obstacle thwarts his run.

People.

A seemingly endless stream, shuffling, too weak and too hot to move as fast as Kyle needs them to. They circle him and start begging once they see the color of his skin. Their hands outstretched, supplicating, the guttural cry of naked need:

"Please ... please, help us ..."

He wishes he had time for pity. Instead, he rockets himself into the deepest section of the crowd, shouting out "Sorry" when forced to toss people aside to clear a path.

He makes it through the huddled mass and careens into the center of town, which looks like a Greek polis after the Romans invaded. Groups of people stand around smoking cigarettes and gambling. Fires burn in trash cans so people can cook. Clotheslines everywhere, hundreds of them, towels and drying clothes acting as dividers between shanties.

Kyle runs through what seems like a solid mile of linens. As he inadvertently rips the poles from the earth, women rush up, start screaming and hitting him. He's ruined the only means of privacy and property demarcation these families have.

He hears the two tourists behind him:

"Move. Move!"

Residents scatter, knock up against them. Everyone's pissed. Too many white people fucking up their property for one day. Time to fight back.

One of the residents yells, *"Gun,"* and the chaos kicks up another notch.

The tourists curse aloud, can't get off a clean shot at Kyle in the middle of this.

Kyle's plan is working, but he needs to change things up. Open space has given him an advantage, but he can't run like this any longer. His knees are shaking and his breath rattles, the dirt and humidity causing his lungs to overflow with phlegm.

He dives into a squatter's shack and lands on his side in the middle of a makeshift classroom. An American NGO worker armed with only a dry-erase board and some secondhand copies of Babar books is trying to teach the slum children how to read. Fifty kids are crammed into this tiny, slanted space.

The teacher rushes over to Kyle, furious at his interruption. "What the hell do you think you're doing? This is a charity operation," she says, as if somehow *that* should provide insurance against an international felon diving into the middle of her reading lesson.

Kyle ignores her, fishes in his pocket, and pulls out a ten-dollar bill. Even the smallest kids know what it is. That's the beauty of money.

Kyle dangles the bill in the air and says:

"Follow me. Come on. Follow, follow!"

The kids rise from the floor in a screaming cluster and take off after him—the capitalist Pied Piper.

The NGO worker can't stop her class from stampeding. Her screamed entreaties of "Stay here, stay right here" fall on deaf ears.

Kyle leads the pack of children to the entrance of the shack and tells them to stay. He motions with his hands and keeps saying it.

"Stay. Stay. Don't move. Do not move."

He drops the ten-dollar bill into the mass of screaming kids, turns, and heads back inside.

14.

Kyle's khaki-clad pursuers come to a sudden stop when they hit the barricade of Lilliputian limbs. They try to push inside, past the kids fighting to be the one to get to hold the ten dollars.

Finally, one of the men loses his cool, decides to clear the doorway the old-fashioned way: violence. He fires two shots into the air. The bullets are a muffled burst, their sound absorbed into the vacuum of humidity.

But the kids get the general idea and scram back toward the classroom.

The two men get through the doorway, draw their guns, look left, right, aim at nothing, curse in unison, and then see Kyle at a rickety structure climbing a set of shaky homemade wooden steps that lead to an equally tossed-together upper level.

The men charge the staircase and ascend single file, taking two steps at a time. They're catching up to Kyle, who's just a few feet ahead, can barely keep going. He's not a trained mercenary. He's a cubicle dweller trying to catch his breath.

The staircase moans from the force of three pairs of feet stomping on its back and bones.

Kyle gets closer to the top. The men a few steps behind.

Their combined weight proves too much. The moan turns into a sustained wooden shriek. The stairs splinter at the seams, begin to buckle.

Kyle hits the second story and dives to the floor.

The other two aren't as fortunate. Before they have time to jump, the banister snaps, the steps cave in and devour their ankles, and then the entire improvised staircase follows suit, collapsing in on itself and crashing to the ground, burying the men and their tourist wear in a grave of diseased wood.

Kyle peers over from the safety of the second floor, sees his pursuers entombed, and, after the initial euphoria of survival passes, he realizes:

There's going to be more. No one ever sends just two people. I'm completely blown here.

Only one option left now.

15.

Robinson's hotel and Kyle's are a study in contrasts. In Robinson's hallway, there's no Cambodian John Cleese lurking around chain-smoking while picking up the charred corpses of errant mosquitoes that kamikazed into the bug light. No belch of rusted plumbing escapes from an open door. No crime-squad-ready stains on the carpets or walls.

This hallway, the passage to Robinson, is a testament to success. The day's financial newspapers and fresh flowers lie before doors. Dead room-service trays dot the ethereal white carpet. That the designers had the audacity to choose white carpeting for a hotel in Phnom Penh tells Kyle more about the guests who stay here than all the crystal dishes, fine caviar bowls, and hand-blown carafes.

He runs his fingers along the wall for material verification. *This is happening,* he thinks. *I am walking to Robinson's room.*

I am going to do this.

This is happening.

Kyle reaches Robinson's door, room 314, traces the knob with his fingers, closes his eyes, and finally knocks.

16.

Robinson opens on the third knock, chewing his omnipresent processed-ham sandwich and holding a cigarette. "Hey, stunner," he says to Kyle. "Come in."

Kyle hesitates.

"Come on," Robinson says. "I'm just fixing a drink."

"I don't know."

"About coming in? Or the drink?"

Kyle peers past the door into Robinson's suite: two rooms—sitting room and bedroom—separated by a plush carpeted rise in the floor.

Robinson goes to the freezer and opens it; Kyle sees it's stocked with two large bottles of whiskey, a bag of ice, and several cartons of cigarettes. "I visited the duty-free shop." He laughs, drags on the cigarette. "My mother was an inveterate coupon clipper. Even today, I can't resist a bargain." He drops some cubes in a glass. "Come in."

"We need to talk."

Robinson's voice drops. "Come in. Seriously."

Kyle knows Robinson's right. This isn't a hallway conversation.

"Lock it behind you," Robinson says; he pours two drinks, then descends into the bedroom. "What happened?"

"Two guys tried to kill me," Kyle says, locking the door behind him. "You said I was safe. *You said that.*"

Robinson hands Kyle a drink and raises his own glass to toast. "I never said you were *safe*. I said I didn't *notice* anyone following you. Someone like you is never going to be safe. You know that."

Kyle ignores the friendly gesture, takes a fast belt of whiskey. "You were smart enough to find me, but you didn't notice two guys out to kill me."

"I happened upon you. I wasn't looking. I told you that."

Robinson's right. He did say that. "Who do you think sent them?"

Robinson works an ice cube in his cheek. "No clue."

Kyle watches Robinson's teeth obliterate the ice. "Chandler?"

Robinson sits on the unmade bed, sliding the scalloped sheets over. "You're a popular guy. You probably can't keep track of all the people who want to kill you. Only thing I know is this: I'm not one of them. And that should carry some weight."

"I didn't do it. I didn't invent anything for Chandler."

"Then why'd you run?"

"I didn't do anything," Kyle says through clenched teeth, trying to contain his frustration. Robinson seems completely unmoved.

Kyle looks at the sheets, sees lipstick traces, wonders if Violet was here before him. "Is your exchange still an option?"

"Absolutely."

Kyle starts to worry a hole in the rug with his shoe. He's not quite so cavalier about his identity. "Good."

Robinson works his cigarette between thumb and forefinger. "I feel like you have some secrets you're not telling me. Secrets are different than sins. People get hurt over secrets. I need to know what I'm walking into."

"I don't have any secrets."

Robinson laughs. "Okay. Total bullshit, but okay." He takes a drink. "We'll try that one again later. You have your passport on you?"

"Back at my hotel."

"I'm going to need to see it," Robinson says.

"I figured."

Robinson rises from the bed. "Good. Let's go, then." He finishes off the drink, drops the cigarette in a can of Diet Coke, and looks

Kyle over from head to toe. "Kyle, if you are going to be me, you cannot—under any circumstances—continue to dress like *this*. You're, what? About a forty-two long?"

"Roughly."

"We'll get you fixed up proper. I've got some choice custom." Robinson pulls his car keys from between the bedsheets, jingles them at Kyle, and heads toward the door. "If you're gonna be me, might as well take advantage of some of the benefits."

Kyle opens up the wall safe; reaches to the back, past the dwindling stack of American bills; finds his passport; and then leaves it, reconsidering.

He's shaking, getting that trapped feeling. Everything's moving too fast. *Who is Robinson?* He tells himself he doesn't have to go back downstairs, doesn't have to get into Robinson's car and hand over his passport. Somewhere, there are still unexplored options.

He sits on the bed and thinks about the documents in his safe. They make him Kyle West in the eyes of the world. That's it. That's life in this century. It's not your parents, your job; it's not who loves you, not your political beliefs, not even your gender. All the things that once conferred identity are up for grabs. It's your papers that give you weight, that tell everyone who you are.

There's still time. He could stick his head out the window, call down to Robinson, and tell him it's off, that he'll figure something else out.

But he's a marked man. And he gets the feeling everyone he passes on the street knows it too. In this city, people look at a dead man with a sense of commiseration.

Stop debating. No matter who Robinson is, being him can't be any more trouble than being yourself right now.

He pulls the passport out of the safe and puts it in his shirt pocket, a psychic talisman against his chest.

17.

Kyle taps on the driver's-side window. The door is locked. Robinson's eyes are closed, and he's singing in dream murmurs to a Cambodian pop song on the radio.

Robinson stirs and his eyes snap open. He unlocks the passenger door, reaches into his suit pocket, pulls out a travel-size Tylenol bottle, and dry-swallows a fistful of them.

Kyle hands his passport over to Robinson for inspection. Robinson cracks open the navy-blue cover and smiles. "Perfect." He flips through, scrutinizes the immigration stamps.

"Look...how do we know this is going to work?"

"We don't," Robinson says.

"I've got plenty of risk right now. I don't need to invite any in."

"Fair enough."

"That's it?"

"You're right. We need to test it." Robinson hands the passport back to Kyle. "Time to shop."

Robinson pulls his car—windshield dotted with dirt and insect corpses—into the pharmacy's parking lot and squeezes it into a space between two tuk-tuks.

"Take mine," Robinson says, handing Kyle his passport. "Pick up what you need."

Kyle opens Robinson's passport, absently starts to flip the pages, putting off the moment of exchange.

"That means you give me yours too," Robinson says.

Kyle hesitates.

"If for some reason I was going to fuck you over, you think I'd do it here? In a parking lot full of people? I'm putting just as much trust in you."

Kyle nods. "All right. You're right." He hands Robinson his passport.

Kyle and Robinson burst through the automatic door.

One of the benefits of the continued French presence in Phnom Penh is that the pharmacies are unusually well stocked for the third world. There's a spiraling line at the counter, and in a mix of French, Khmer, and English, people plead for advice about stomach cramps, skin disease, and sunstroke.

"Meet up at the register," Robinson says and takes off down an aisle stocked with makeup and hair dye.

Kyle picks up a basket, looks at the aisles' signs.

If you keep moving, nothing can hurt you.

He studies Robinson's passport, then starts pulling items off the shelf with a shaky hand, dropping them in his basket.

Hair dye. Dark brown.

Electric razor. Regular razor plus blades. Shaving gel.

Blow-dryer and mousse. Robinson has thick, voluminous hair that will take some work for Kyle to achieve.

He checks Robinson's photo again to make sure he's not forgetting anything. He notices the stock boy looking at his trembling fingers and jams his hand into his pants pocket.

Don't stick out. Give no one a reason to remember you.

The standing water in the tub has risen several inches. Robinson sits on the lip, examining his purchases.

Kyle stands before the mirror with a pair of scissors, chopping his hair off in chunks and watching it collect around the drain. In the photo, Robinson's hair is semi-short on the sides and longer in the front. Kyle's is unruly all over.

"Mirror's yours," Kyle says to Robinson.

Then he walks over to the tub and slides on a pair of surgical gloves to work the hair dye in at his roots. He has to leave it in for the maximum time. His hair has lightened considerably because of constant exposure to the sun.

"I need the mirror back," Kyle says.

"Okay," Robinson says. Overheated, he takes off his shirt and wipes his chest and stomach down with it. "It's hot as hell in here."

"You decided to wear a suit."

"I refuse to have my fashion dictated by this country's climate." Robinson lights a cigarette, takes off his belt, undoes the top button of his slacks, and turns the shower knob as far as it goes toward the letter C. "I'm not coming out until you're done with the mirror."

Kyle goes to work on his beard, using the electric razor first and then shaving close to the skin with a Mach 3. There's less irritation underneath than he expected, but he applies aftershave to be sure he doesn't get a rash.

Even though he's turning himself into Robinson, he looks more like his old self than he has in months. He has to contend with the dual shock: the sight of his old face, and the new one he's making.

Avoid mirrors. Shun surfaces.

"We can switch," Kyle says, a little existentially queasy about rediscovering himself in a situation like this. "I need to wash out the dye."

The military checkpoint is about a hundred yards ahead of them. Kyle starts to fidget when he realizes what Robinson's plan entails. "This is your strategy?"

"You wanted to test it."

"Yeah, but..." Kyle motions to the checkpoint.

"We can't just go try to buy a six-pack—"

"What if it doesn't work?"

Robinson slows down. "Better to find out here than the airport. At least here we can make a getaway in a *car*. If it's going to fail, I want it to fail somewhere where I can either drive fast or pay someone off." He hands Kyle his passport. "Now give me yours."

Kyle pulls it from his shirt pocket.

Four men in uniform with automatic rifles strapped to their chests approach the Escalade. The leader raises his palm for the car to stop. They're all wearing the same regiment green, and they all have the same face and the same spent soldiers' eyes that light up only when they find fresh prey.

They aim their guns right at the Escalade.

"Yeah...so much better than the airport."

Robinson puts his hand on Kyle's knee. "In my experience, soldiers, like most third-world employees, are infinitely corruptible."

The soldiers come closer, fingers on triggers, and yell in unison:

"Why you here? Why you here?"

Robinson gets into character, rolls down the window. "What's the problem?"

"Road closed. Can't you see?"

"What wrong? Can't you see?"

"No go."

Robinson gestures toward the road behind them. "There's no sign."

"UN there—"

"De-mining—"

Robinson interrupts. "There's no sign. How am I supposed to know?"

"Mines—"

"Mines from Khmer Rouge—"

"Vietnam—"

"Very bad—"

"No go—"

"No—"

"Go."

The soldiers, their English almost exhausted, point their guns at Robinson and Kyle.

"Out."

"Get out."

"Out of car...both of you."

Robinson turns off the car and opens the door. "Okay." He motions to Kyle. "That means us."

Kyle gets out, the color already starting to drain from his face.

"Passports. Both of you."

Robinson hands them Kyle's without a care in the world while Kyle hands over Robinson's and grits his teeth. One of the soldiers inspects the passports. Kyle West. Julian Robinson. He looks up; down. Up; down. Up; down. The whole time with a movie slasher's empty stare.

The other soldiers search the car, looking in the glove compartment and under the seats, opening up the cooler and Robinson's duffel bag.

No such thing as the personal in a place like Phnom Penh.

"Open the back."

"Fine," Robinson says.

He goes to the rear and opens it. Two soldiers crawl inside while the third keeps the gun trained on Robinson's back. The two in the car talk in Khmer, throw things around, and then step out, satisfied.

They walk Robinson over to the side of the road, a gun pressed against his spine, and stand him next to Kyle.

"You."

Kyle points to his chest. "Me?"

"Robinson."

It takes a second to register. "Yes. Robinson."

"You are Robinson?"

"I am."

"You..."

"Yes." Kyle's heart drops to the soles of his feet.

"...have lost weight," the soldier finishes. "You look much less like child. No more round face."

The soldiers start back.

"Turn around and go. You done."

"You go..."

"Get on the highway."

Robinson and Kyle walk back to the car, settle in, return the seats to where they were before the search. Robinson starts the car, fiddles with the radio dial, and then offers Kyle his hand. "I'm Kyle. Kyle West. Nice to meet you."

Kyle lets a smile sneak out. "Julian Robinson."

They laugh together. Damned men in stereo.

"We need to celebrate," Robinson says, "our successful merger." He guns the engine.

"Where do you feel like going?"

"This is your town, isn't it? Surprise me. But while surprising me, make sure we go somewhere that shows some tits."

Kyle smiles. "Won't be a problem here."

"I think that soldier insinuated I look fat in my photo." He checks the rearview mirror for oncoming traffic. "Asshole."

"I don't think he insinuated it."

Robinson bursts out laughing. "No, he did not."

18.

Robinson has the tuk-tuk drop them off a block before the bar. The second that Robinson's tasseled shoe hits the ground, a studious-looking young man approaches him. "You speak the English?" He's college age and dressed like a Bible salesman, white shirt and short-sleeved blazer.

Kyle pays the driver and steps to the side to watch the exchange.

"Just want to practice," the young man says. "No one for me to practice with at school. No one want to learn English...they all lazy. I want to move to United States when I graduate. Great country."

Robinson pats him on the shoulder and tells him in flawless German that he doesn't speak English.

"Not possible," the student says.

Robinson and Kyle walk down the street. Phnom Penh at night, still hallucinatory with the lights off, like the love child of *Blade Runner* and Rudyard Kipling.

The outdoor market stalls are set for the dinner crowds; large spits spin meats round and round, like a carnivore's carnival ride. At a wooden butcher table, a grandmother carves up a side of beef that spurts blood in uneven intervals.

The banyan trees are thick, leafy inkblots against the moon.

Robinson and Kyle wait for a momentary break in traffic that doesn't come. They look at each other and decide to make a suicide run. They sprint, holding their hands up against the phalanx of vehicles and screaming "Shit" all the way across, and when they hit the other side, they're greeted by a local pissing in a sewer grate.

Across the Mekong, the Royal Palace drips with gold glitter, like a celestial chocolate box, and nearby, several floors of a new Western-style skyscraper are lit up as freshly indoctrinated capitalists work through the night.

A Catholic missionary stands outside the bar, hoping to find a few late-night converts before heading home. She offers Robinson a pamphlet and starts her spiel, but he waves away the booklet and takes her hand in his own. She seems shocked by the intimacy of his action. He puts ten American dollars in her palm and closes her fingers around the money as if they were precious petals.

"God bless," she says. "You are a wonderful man."

Robinson puts his arm around Kyle's shoulder and walks him toward the bar. The act of friendship, of bonding, would mean more if Robinson hadn't just shown the missionary the same unexpected familiarity. Kyle's beginning to learn that's Robinson's way; he's intimate with everyone.

19.

They walk into Bar 69.

The bar is fringed with blinking red and green party lights, an illuminative scheme somewhere between Christmas and the display window of an adult bookstore.

Atop the bar, girls in halter tops and miniskirts dance to a techno-tribal rhythm.

The girls are barefoot and trying to avoid stepping on the lights.

The crowd's a mix of expats, sketchy locals, journalists, and administrative staff from various embassies. Robinson and Kyle sit at the bar, and Robinson points to a group sitting at a back table. "North Koreans," he says.

Kyle squints to see them. "You sure? How can you tell?"

"They're partying like they might get sent back tomorrow. Hoarding all the good times, saving up, like squirrels in winter. Won't be like this when they get back home."

Kyle watches one of the bar girls put on a private show for Robinson. Her dance is a true ballet *mécanique,* drained of passion, just a fucking job she doesn't seem thrilled to have. But Robinson looks like he couldn't care less. He got a look up someone's skirt.

The bartender walks over to them.

"Vodka tonic naked. No ice," Robinson says.

"Scotch on the rocks," Kyle says.

Robinson finds his cigarettes and offers Kyle one.

"No, thanks... you gave that missionary a lot of money."

"It was ten bucks," Robinson says.

"That's a fucking fortune here."

"Been working up the balls to say that?"

"Are you a believer?" Kyle whispers in a tone usually reserved for something sexual.

"Not especially."

"Then, why?"

"The entire twentieth century was about finding alternatives to the Judeo-Christian narrative. And they all ended in unspeakable tragedy. Better to support the one that seems to do the least harm."

"The least harm?" Kyle looks at Robinson in shock. "I suppose... if you don't consider pedophilia to be particularly harmful."

"Half the people in this room are fucking pedophiles. Ever hear of the sex trade? You're in the armpit of it here."

"Yeah, but they're not wearing collars..."

"No, they just work for the government. Our government, their government. So pedophilia's okay as long as tax dollars are footing the bill?"

Kyle chooses to ignore the warped validity of Robinson's argument and presses on. "And don't even get me started on the pope—"

Robinson smiles. "I love the pope. If I'm going to be instructed not to masturbate, I want to be told in a German accent. It sounds more definitive..."

"The pope not allowing Catholics to wear condoms even though a huge number of people have AIDS and the countries don't have the resources to support the population explosion. All the massive growth is happening in the places least able to handle it, and most of them are Catholic. All the future resource wars, you can hang them on the Church's outmoded morality..."

"Kyle," Robinson says, "you're fucking *exhausting* me. These girls are nearly naked and smiling at you. I'm absolutely the least interesting thing here."

Kyle laughs. Robinson's got a valid point.

Their drinks arrive and they toast their new friendship forged in mutual risk. "I'm off to piss," Robinson says.

Kyle sips his drink, looks at the girl doing a robotic dance before him, a parody of eroticism.

The guy sitting next to Kyle speaks. "You like her?"

Kyle doesn't answer.

"She's my wife," his neighbor says. "Well...kinda my wife."

"Congratulations, then. Kinda."

"She's coming home with me. South Carolina. She wants to go to cosmetology school and do people's nails and hair and shit like that. It'll be great. Till I lose her."

"The loss of optimism usually comes later in the relationship—"

The guy ignores Kyle. "She's gonna get to the States and realize a big-shot American in Cambodia don't mean shit back home." He gets lost in the girl's dance, in the lace going up her legs. "Look at her...fucking beautiful...so fucking beautiful, it kills me. And she's gonna realize back home I don't mean shit." He brings the beer to his lips. "Here, I'm above average. Fuck...I'm fuckin' rich. Here, I mean. Home, I'm barely average. Below average, in fact. And she's gonna know the minute we get there. I'll lose her to a fuckin' banker in a month." He frowns at the imaginary banker. "Fuckin' cocksucker."

Robinson returns and puts his hand on Kyle's shoulder. "I've procured us a table."

20.

A new song with a heavy bass line starts up. Robinson does an indecent little dance with his head and neck, mimicking the girls atop the bar.

"What did you do before telecom?"

Robinson keeps the dance going, drags off his cigarette. "Have you been to the Killing Fields?"

"Yes."

"Astounding, isn't it. The Khmers have no money to build proper memorials, but maybe that's right, maybe that's the only way to show crimes against humanity. You go to Auschwitz and it's all so eerily preserved, it's like visiting a satanic art installation. The Killing Fields, though...just endless piles of skulls and a handwritten placard that says *Here, four hundred people died.* Maybe that's the only way, right? Just tell the truth. Here are the skulls of four hundred people who died for fucking nothing...What was your question?"

"What did you do before going into telecom?"

"Studied poli-sci and poetry at Yale. Then a year at Harvard Law. Then the rest of my life trying to unlearn all of it."

"So you're an anti-intellectual?"

"If you think Ivy League colleges create intellectuals..."

"No?"

Robinson smiles and shakes his head. "Where'd you go to college?"

"MIT."

"Meet any intellectuals?"

"Why only a year at Harvard Law?"

"I quickly realized law was the art of negotiation and compromise. Neither of which are skills of mine. Nor ones I wanted to develop."

"Then telecom?"

"Some false starts. Worked as a representative's aide for a while, but we fell out. He would say due to my ideological rigidity. I would say due to his utter lack of vision. Either way, I never put him down as a reference."

"You don't strike me as ideologically rigid."

"I was young."

"You *are* young." Kyle stares at his drink. "Do you think you have to lose your values to grow up?"

Robinson seems taken aback by the earnestness of the question. "No. It's just going to be really painful to be you."

"Guess so..."

"I mean, it's really gonna fucking hurt." Robinson drags on his cigarette. "See...business is fantastic because it has no memory. It's why I chose it. Good or bad, it remembers nothing. Henry Ford—great businessman, obviously—said history is basically bunk. And from a business standpoint, he's absolutely right. To be a truly successful businessman—not some nine-to-fiver who half-asses it to pay his mortgage but the *real* deal—you need to be a historical blank. You need to be a psychopath."

"Don't most psychopaths get caught?"

"Or rich."

"So I guess you haven't been affected by the global recession?"

"God, no. You have to remember—there's always someone *somewhere* making money."

"Where's the money now?"

"All in the East. Plus, war and disaster are great for telecom. And there's been no shortage of either the past few years. Hurricanes, earthquakes, tsunamis—nature's indigestion erupting all over the place. The War on Terror. Boom times. First city I ever got sent as a sales director was to Kabul after we invaded. The army was wired for networks, but there was no infrastructure there. So we built one. From the ground up in the moonscape. Then the telecoms started thinking, *Well, the stuff's all there now, shit... let's sell these people phones.* Fucking tremendous. Afghanistan—a country arguably still in the nineteenth century...if you're feeling generous, right? I talked to some soldiers there who were training the Afghan security forces. They had to explain to the fucking Afghans what a toilet was. But all those guys have cell phones now. Mostly because of me. Amazing."

"Is it also amazing how all these people who never had phones before figured out how to use them to set off IEDs and blow up our soldiers? You armed them all."

"The uses and misuses of technology are far above my pay grade. Tell you this—they may use my phones for IEDs, but know what else they use them for? Remittance payments. People who couldn't get money to their families back home can do it now. So, maybe, because of someone like me, one person might not take the money to become a suicide bomber because their sister or brother is able to get them money by pressing a key."

"That's just moral relativism," Kyle says, pissed.

"You say it like it's supposed to hurt me."

"It is."

"*You're* exiled here, need my passport, and you've got the fucking nerve to speak to me like Mr. Morality himself?"

"Eric." A girl appears next to Robinson. "Eric, it's Deanna." She's a stunning American, an inch shy of six feet with an untamed mane of blond hair she's pulled off her face.

Robinson squints. Kyle's stunned. He was so caught up in their conversation he missed this statuesque creature enter his line of sight.

"Deanna," she says again. "We met in Indonesia at the fair-trade protest."

"Deanna from Indonesia," Robinson says. "Love, I want to know you more than anything, but I'm afraid I don't."

"I work with COHRE. Housing rights."

"Pains me to say, but you've got the wrong guy." He offers her his hand. "I'm Julian."

"I could've sworn it was you. I usually have a photographic memory when it comes to faces."

"Sorry to break your streak," Robinson says. "What are you drinking?"

"Don't worry," Deanna says, "I'll let you two get back to your talk."

"Don't be silly," Robinson says. "Have a seat."

"No, I gotta go," Deanna says and walks off, clearly disappointed.

Robinson watches her ass in retreat, a perfect heart shape. "Fuck...I wish I was Eric. What a magnificent creature. God. Ever fuck a tall woman from behind?"

Kyle's taken aback. "No."

"Ahh...I mean, you look down and you just think, *Fuck...I've really been somewhere...accomplished something.* Dealing with the legs alone...like landing an airplane on water."

"I think she really liked Eric," Kyle says. "She seemed so sad."

"You should do something about that. No reason for someone like that to be sad."

"Nah," Kyle says. "I'm out of practice."

"And I am out of time." Robinson looks at his Patek. "I've got to make a conference call to work. Day's just starting there."

"I'll come back with you."

"Nonsense. You've got half your drink." He motions toward Deanna. "And new friends to make."

"She's not going to give me her number."

Robinson smiles. "No, she *isn't*...she's not going to at all."

Kyle laughs, stares into his glass. A little drunk and full of self-deprecation.

"I'd wish you luck tomorrow, but that'd mean I think something might go wrong," Robinson says.

"Same here."

Robinson dips into his pocket, removes his wallet, and hands Kyle his American Express card. "Don't forget this. You need it to get your ticket tomorrow."

"Right," Kyle says. "Thanks."

"Pleasure meeting you."

"You too."

"Really. I wish we had more time."

"Funny thing about meeting new people..." Kyle begins, then stops himself.

"What?"

"Nah... I'm drunk and you've gotta go."

"No. I want to hear."

Kyle may be drunk, but he's still touched. "Really?"

"I do."

"It's like this. When you're younger, you think, *There's so many interesting people I still have to meet, so many connections out there for me.* And then at some point, it just stops. You know everyone you're going to know. And you didn't even think you were that old yet."

"Worst thing about getting old, you forget about one word—*possibility*. And it changes your whole life."

"Yeah."

Robinson stands, pushes in his chair. "I'll see you on the other side." He puts his hand on Kyle's shoulder. "You take care."

21.

Kyle stands by his bed and contemplates Robinson's passport. Pages worn down from frequent flipping and the whole thing thick with official stamps.

Kyle thumbs through, charts Robinson's globe-hopping. Germany. Dozens of African countries. The UAE. Most of Asia, with a lot of time in China. Eastern Europe. Month in Croatia. A world traveler with the miles to prove it.

Kyle opens up the fridge, pops the tab on an Angkor beer, and drinks. The cold feels good against the lining of his mouth scorched by scotch.

He stares at his graphite-colored laptop sitting on the desk. No way he can take it with him. If anything should happen, the computer would only make things worse. But he pulls the flash drive out of the USB port and puts it in his pocket.

He imagines what Neil would say about Robinson's plan. Neil, his nagging moral compass, would tell him that he's making the wrong move, that he should go home and clear his name, that sacrificing someone like Kuo, no matter how corrupt, drags him down closer to Chandler's level.

Kyle would counter: *But what about all the risk involved on my end? How is this the easy play? I could be killed.*

Neil would answer: *Sure. There's great physical risk, but fucking over Kuo doesn't clear your name. It gets you even farther away from who you are.*

Swapping identities with someone so you can pick up info to blackmail Kuo isn't the way a victim would act. It's the way a guilty man or a man too weak to fight would act, and I would never want to see you as either one.

Yeah, Kyle would argue, *but getting the info on Kuo keeps me from being arrested and having to testify.*

Kyle can already hear Neil shutting him down with one of his favorite lines:

Some of the most honest people have had to do some time. Don't be afraid of the time; be afraid for your name.

Kyle brings the beer to his lips again. *Wash it all away. Just keep moving.*

22.

PHNOM PENH INTERNATIONAL AIRPORT

Phnom Penh International is the size of a shoebox. A small customer-service area and blue chairs bolted to the floor in front of the departure board. Its sole distinguishing features are a Dairy Queen, a few stands selling indigenous trinkets—mostly elephant statues, totems of eternal return—and a pizza place, overpriced, because it can be.

Outside, pilots unload UN rice and medicine from a fleet of small planes refueling for the flight home.

Kyle stands in line at the kiosks to print out his boarding pass. Pink shirt, pinstripe suit, red suspenders, puffed-up hair. He's more Robinson than himself now, and he can't keep his foot still. He's artificially awake, hopped up on adrenaline.

A kiosk opens up. He approaches it, takes out Robinson's AmEx, swipes it, and waits while the machine processes.

The computer freezes, then starts to hum like an overworked appliance. Kyle stands there, waiting for the system . . .

Waiting.

Waiting.

Long time.

Don't shake. Don't act suspicious. What would Robinson do? Probably have a cigarette and talk about his Anglophile mother.

The computer comes back to life.

And tells Kyle his card is denied and the system can't issue a boarding pass. It instructs him to speak to a service representative.

Fuck. Fuck. Fuck.

He hits the cancel button, swipes the card again, his foot keeping time with his anxiety.

Hum. Hum. Hum. Computer processes.

Waiting.

Same shit.

Still waiting.

Fucking frozen.

The computer refuses the card again. Instructs him to speak with a service representative.

He looks at the other machines; they're all occupied, and the lines are starting to wind around the rope. He can't get in another line; he'll lose too much time. He needs to make his plane.

Fucking hell cocksucking shit.

He's moved on to cluster cursing. Never an auspicious sign. He raises his hand to the side of the machine, ready to slap it. He tries to gain control of himself but loses it after one more quick glimpse at the blinking screen:

Card denied. Speak with a customer-service representative.

He doesn't want to speak with a customer-service representative. He wants his goddamn fucking ticket. The one he paid for with Robinson's fucking card.

That's what he wants.

He broadsides the machine with his palm. Not once. Not twice. Three times. Hits it so hard that it's shaking. Slapping the machine around like it's a gangster's moll momentarily pacifies his anger, but it also has an unforeseen side effect.

A uniformed security guard appears beside him and grimaces. "Problem, sir? Problem with machine?"

Kyle's hand is still in the air and he's contemplating a fourth slap. "Problem. No. No problem," he says. Act like nothing's wrong. Be Robinson. Smile in the face of adversity. But he can't. His hand is visibly shaking.

"Hit machine," the guard says. "Why you hitting machine?"

"Misunderstanding. Just a misunderstanding."

"What? Why you hit machine? Can't do. Can't hit."

"I was wrong. I'm going. I'm on my way out."

"Why? Why you hit?"

"I'm just leaving..."

The guard stares past Kyle at the face of the kiosk. "No leave. You need to see customer service. That all. Very simple. No hit. Customer service."

"No. Not necessary."

"To hit. Yes. Customer service. Follow me."

"No. Not necessary."

"Customer service. I take you."

"Oh, no, sir, I don't want to trouble—"

"Not trouble. This way."

"Sir..."

The guard gets on his walkie-talkie, speaks into the receiver in Khmer, then turns back to Kyle. "This way." He beckons for Kyle to follow. "This way. With me."

Kyle follows the guard's instructions. Too late to run. No way he can leave now without causing a scene, no way he won't be pursued, no way this won't be on camera, and no way it won't end up on the news once people figure out who he is.

No. No fucking way. He's got to see a customer-service rep.

The guard leads Kyle to the service area while smiling and beckoning with his hand. "Very close," he says.

Kyle trudges along, the unfamiliar sound of Robinson's Ferragamos echoing. He curses the noise and the way the shoes strangle circulation. How the hell does Robinson walk around the third world in these? Kyle's barely walked around the airport and already feels blisters blossoming.

The security guard plops Kyle down in a seat in front of a service rep, a Khmer girl blowing on a steaming cup of tea.

"Ticket trouble," the guard says to the girl as he walks off, "man have ticket trouble."

"I'm Mai. How may I help you?" she says to Kyle. She's young, barely drinking age, wearing a simple black dress and thick-rimmed glasses.

"The kiosk won't print my boarding pass," Kyle says, and sits on his hands so she can't see them shake.

"I'm sorry about that, sir."

"Will this take long?"

"Not at all."

"Good."

"I'm just going to need to see your passport and e-ticket."

Kyle dips into the jacket pocket, pulls out Robinson's passport, puts it on top of the e-ticket, and turns them over to Mai.

"Oh...and your credit card too."

"Fine," Kyle says, and hands her Robinson's black AmEx, then sits on his hands again.

Mai begins to type furiously. "Have you enjoyed your time in Phnom Penh?"

"Yes."

"What was your favorite thing to do?"

Kyle sucks on his left cheek, thinking, *Are we* seriously *going to do this shit, Mai?* "I think...I wasn't here very long. Just walked around the Central Market."

"My mother sews. She has a stand at Central Market."

Kyle tilts his head, trying to see what she's typing. "Great. Good. Good for her."

She opens up Robinson's passport, flips through the pages, punches a few more keys. "You look younger."

"What?"

"Than in this photo."

"Oh," Kyle says, shifting around on his hands. "I was tired when that was taken."

Mai giggles, showing her rabbit teeth, her pink tongue.

"Everything okay?" Kyle asks.

She punches a few more keys, drinks some tea, flinches at how hot it still is, and says, "Hmph. I can't...seem to override the system to print out your boarding pass."

Kyle's sweating like a man waiting for test results. *Christ,* he thinks, *I'm a total bomb as Robinson.*

Then Mai hands his passport back to him, leans over the desk, and says:

"You appear to be on a no-fly list, Mr. Robinson."

Within twenty seconds of Mai's verbal neutron bomb, three Asian men approach the desk dressed in corporate camouflage—sober suits and ties, the type of clothes designed and selected to be instantly forgotten.

One of them reveals himself to be the leader by removing his sunglasses and fixing his stare on Kyle. The other two look straight ahead, avoiding Kyle's eyes, as if he's committed a lurid crime.

"Mr. Robinson," the leader says. "Security. We're going to have to ask you to come with us. This is purely a formality." He tilts his head a bit. "I'm certain *you understand.*"

"I want to be put on a plane immediately," Kyle says. "I paid for my ticket. There is no reason for me to be on a no-fly list..."

"It's not us, Mr. Robinson. It's the computer." He motions subtly for Kyle to rise. "We want this straightened out as much as you do. If you'll just follow us."

"If you'd please just follow us," one of the other men says, still avoiding eye contact, echoing the leader.

"You're harassing me," Kyle continues. "I am an American citizen and I am being harassed—"

The leader interjects with a leer, "You would like us to call your embassy, then?"

Kyle's trying to conquer his overwhelming fear with indignation. "You are harassing an American citizen."

"We will happily call the embassy and they can come and—"

"I don't want my embassy," Kyle says, terrified they're going to choose that option. "I want to get on a fucking plane," he adds, his voice following a twelve-tone scale, starting low with general anxiety and ending in a soaring crescendo of panic.

"And you will, Mr. Robinson. Please follow us so we can straighten this out." The leader gives another head tilt, more threatening this time. "This isn't getting us anywhere."

"I don't belong on a no-fly list."

What would Robinson do? Well, apparently, he's done lots and lots of nasty shit or Kyle wouldn't be here.

Out of options, Kyle stands, defeated, and agrees to go with the three men.

The leader pulls a stray piece of lint off Kyle's shoulder. "What a wonderful suit." He flicks the piece of lint into Mai's garbage can. "Follow me," he says.

The leader and Kyle walk side by side out of the service area and into the airport proper. They pass a series of crowded boarding gates. Kyle looks at them longingly. All of these people on their way home to be greeted by loved ones the minute they pass through customs.

Kyle wishes he had told someone about this plan. But who? Neil's his only friend and would have told Kyle he'd finally lost his mind.

No two ways about it. He's stranded.

The leader leans into Kyle and whispers, "We appreciate you not making a *scene*. It would have been uncomfortable."

Kyle sees fewer people, notices he's being escorted to an increasingly remote section of the airport. "Where are we going?"

The leader doesn't answer, just turns back and urges the two following behind to pick up the pace.

Why didn't I run? he thinks. *Why did I follow that guard to the counter?*

The leader pushes open a service exit door and ushers Kyle through. The others follow. "Close that," the leader snaps at his underlings.

The hallway's empty except for a mop and a bucket filled with gray-green water. No windows, no air, no natural light; fluorescent lights flicker.

Kyle's through playing along with this routine. "We near it yet? The security office?"

"Sure," the leader says, smirking. "Right down this hall."

Kyle knows this is bullshit; this whole situation is total bullshit. "Who are you guys? Seriously." He feels the burn of the bleached floor in his nostrils. "Who are you? Tell me."

What he wants to do is scream out that he's not Robinson, that they've got the wrong guy. Problem is, he's not much better off being Kyle West.

Maybe it's best to just face the situation as Robinson.

Maybe somehow it'll work out and he'll get on the next plane.

Then it happens.

Bitter tang of chemical spray. Brutal. Sends Kyle's gag reflex into overdrive. And that's before it ends up in his eyes. He staggers, opens his mouth to scream, but the lingering chemical cloud is so strong, he chokes instead, a dry, hard hack.

A foot takes out Kyle's legs, hurling him down. "Eat the floor. Eat the fucking floor."

The foot stays put in the center of Kyle's back while someone ties his hands together with cord and pulls it tight in one fluid motion.

"Keep your head down...keep it down."

Kyle's pulled to his feet. He can barely see through the tears. The chemical taste on his tongue is like ingested insect spray.

He sees someone wave around a Taser.

"Keep your fucking eyes in front of you."

And then the hood goes over his head.

Claustrophobia kicks in. He can't breathe. Starts to panic.

A quick kiss from the Taser current sets his spine straight.

"Move. Move."

Someone steers Kyle by the waist and says:

"Nice to see you again, Robinson. Been too long."

Then kicks him in the small of the back.

23.

PHNOM PENH, CAMBODIA

Tom Fowler's bored as hell, so he's doing dumbbell work. Lateral raises, concentration curls, triceps kickbacks. For someone in his sixties, he cuts an imposing figure. Doorway-size shoulders. Neck bulging like a frog stretching to catch a fly. The thick veins on his forearm fence a memento from Vietnam, a massive tattoo of a dragon, multicolored wings spread, clutching a submachine gun. Another reminder of the war dangles close to his throat, a necklace of Buddhist charms given to him by a monk he rescued in Cambodia.

Now the Agency's sent him back here—the ashes of Southeast Asia.

His biceps starts to burn and he drops the weight on the office floor. He didn't shower this morning, and his sweat's mixed with the lavender of his girlfriend's soap.

Women.

Fowler's never forgotten what his first wife said as she slammed the bedroom door and never spoke to him again:

"When women are alone and bored, we play dress-up. We put on Mommy's makeup and try on her clothes. When men are bored, they play dress-up too. Only when they do it, they put on uniforms, go to someone else's country, and kill everyone."

Her name was Victoria Rose. That was it. No fucking nicknames for her. No Vicki, or Vic, or Rosie. Don't even think about it. Victoria Rose.

It's 1975. Fowler's just gotten back from Saigon. He's anxious; he's waiting for *something*. He meets Victoria Rose in a bar one night when he's wearing his civilian uniform, Levi's and a leather jacket, holstered gun close to his heart. At that moment, Fowler's seriously considering bank robbery as his next career move. Something that lets him carry a gun. But Victoria Rose gives him an outlet.

She's a peace activist, a graduate student in social work. But she fetishizes violence, specifically men of violence—men like Fowler. She likes to be close to it, to feel the weight of it lying on top of her. Like some of her hippie friends who called cops pigfuckers but secretly wanted that uniform, wanted to be on the other end of those handcuffs, the true unspoken Janus face of liberalism and power relations.

Because Fowler's a rare breed.

Most men came back from Vietnam with PTSD if they were lucky, if they were *real* lucky. Most of Fowler's buddies hit the booze, hit their wives, hit the heroin they had started fucking around with over there, or died horribly from cancer, courtesy of Agent Orange. But Fowler didn't come back with PTSD, didn't come back with the urge to drown all the memories in a sea of self-destruction.

Fowler wants another war. He gets Victoria Rose instead.

First day in Vietnam, September '69, Fowler goes on a raid. There's a firefight. He fends off the Communists and gets in a few close kills. Ted Shackley hears about the raid. And Shackley *is* the CIA in Laos; he pulls the strings. Locals call him the Blond Ghost.

And Shackley likes what Fowler did under enemy fire, under *pressure,* and recruits him into the Phoenix Project, a CIA-designed program of pacification that's all about punching up big kill numbers to show the suits in Washington that we're winning the war, that we're rounding up any South Vietnamese harboring Communist or anti-Western sympathies. Working for Shackley is like working on a satanic factory line. He's got to report quantifiable results back to the shareholders on the Hill.

And Fowler kills real good. He's employee of the month every month for several years straight.

When the war ends, in '75, Fowler goes home, and after settling down with Victoria Rose, he realizes he doesn't like the idea of being out of uniform. So he takes Shackley's advice and joins the Agency's training program, where Fowler learns there are two types of CIA. There's the intellectuals, the analysts, the guys who go to good climates under diplomatic cover and haunt embassy halls, blue bloods who pass notes to nuclear scientists at cocktail parties.

Then there's guys like Fowler. Guys who get sent to denied territory to root out subversion. Guys who work off the books, fly below the congressional radar.

After he graduates from the program, Fowler gets his next war, gets his marching orders to Angola.

And Victoria Rose calls him a fucking fascist while he's packing his bags to go.

But what she doesn't get is this: It's not that Fowler blindly follows orders. It's not that he doesn't question orders.

It's that he *likes* the orders.

He does four years in Angola and enhances his reputation for being one of the Agency's prime go-to guys for smash-and-grab ops. And just when he's turning the tide in Africa, he gets a call to take a night flight to Afghanistan.

Fowler's close to Bill Casey, Reagan's controversial CIA head. Casey picks Fowler up personally in Angola, waits with him on a hot tarmac, and says:

"This isn't 'Nam, Tommy. We're doing this one right. We're going over to win."

So Fowler's in Afghanistan, but he gets kicked out. Everyone around Fowler wonders the same thing—and with good reason: How in the fuck do you get *kicked out* of Afghanistan, Tom? I mean, *really*.

Here's how. He notices a certain disquieting trend in the makeup of his mujahideen. He notices that Egyptian intelligence is looking at the anti-Soviet jihad as the best news they've had in years. The bulk of Egyptian jihadists—the militant radicals who tried to whack Mubarak—are rotting in jail, and they're pissed. Pissed right the fuck off. 'Cause they're missing the big jihad, missing the chance to martyr themselves. Then the Egyptians get a bright idea: Let's let them out. Fuck it. Let these lunatics go out and die. Let them be someone else's problem.

Fowler's fucking problem.

So a wave of militant Islamists, the real deal, the sons of Sayyid Qutb, arrive and start radicalizing Fowler's troops. His freedom fighters weren't exactly secularists before, but after the Egyptians arrive, the troops start praying five times a day and stop listening to Fowler because they've been told he's an infidel.

So Fowler goes to the CIA director and gives him the frontline scoop: We've got to do something about these fucking Egyptians. I'm losing control of my troops. And Fowler's told to let it go, that they're all on the same side. And Fowler says, We're all on the same side right now, but wait. The director doesn't like Fowler's tone. And Fowler doesn't like this simple-minded anti-Communist who has never seen a day of frontline fire and doesn't know shit about radical Islam. And, well, words are exchanged, there's a hard shove against a filing cabinet, and Fowler's given his walking papers.

But thank God things are really heating up in Nicaragua, because there's no hard feelings, and Bill Casey puts Fowler on a plane that evening—to go train Contras.

And while Fowler's camped out in Nicaragua with wife number two, the unthinkable happens: The Soviet Union implodes. (Another historical game changer the CIA never saw coming, just like the Berlin Wall and Pakistan going nuclear and, hell, let's go there—9/11. Fowler always thought the Agency's analysts were using a crystal ball covered in cobwebs.)

So the Cold War is over and Fowler gets called back home and that's okay. He won't miss Nicaragua, and wife number two elects to stay behind, and he's okay with that too. Fowler doesn't go native wherever he's stationed. He knows the way the Agency works: the guy who's your best friend *today* may be the guy you have to kill tomorrow. He keeps to himself, keeps his attachments loose.

But Fowler's not someone who does well with peace.

When he gets back to DC, he's beached behind a desk, and he

panics. He's been running hostile ops for almost twenty-five years and now he's counting paper clips. Not a promising career trajectory. But thankfully—Fowler's particular luck—the Balkans start acting like the Balkans again after a fifty-year nap. Clinton's administration wants to help the Bosnian Muslims but doesn't want to commit troops; Bill still has severe Somalia agita. And the Republicans aren't big on humanitarian intervention yet. So Clinton turns to the Iranians and the Saudis to ship the guns and to guys like Fowler to show the Bosniaks how to use said weapons against the Serbs.

Plus the Agency needs boots on the ground, so they allow mosques throughout Europe and the Middle East to advertise this skirmish as "Afghanistan: The Sequel." And this time, the Agency starts to notice strange things about the imported freedom fighters. They're not only butchering Serbs—which no one minds, although the boiling-people-alive thing is a little *much*—but also starting to terrorize the moderate Muslim population, whom they consider just as bad as the Serbs for not following the "proper" path to Islam. And some of the CIA guys who knew Fowler in Afghanistan start coming up and saying: "Hey, Tommy, maybe you had a point back in '85. Maybe a bunch of godless Communists or Serbian socialists is less scary than the alternative."

No shit, Fowler thinks, but keeps his mouth shut. 'Cause Bosnia is the only war going right now, and he doesn't want to get sent home.

In '95, Milošević signs the Dayton Accord, and Fowler gets shipped back. He's sweating bullets because he knows Clinton and Gore are cutting the CIA to ribbons and subjecting it to open-market principles. So when he gets called into DCI John Deutch's office, he's sure he's getting handed a pink slip.

But he doesn't. He gets promoted, put in charge of a new Agency program.

Extraordinary rendition.

After the attempt on Mubarak's motorcade and the two bombings in Saudi Arabia targeting Americans, Clinton decided he needed to get serious about radical Islam. *Because the 1993 World Trade Center bombing wasn't a big enough tip-off?* Fowler thinks as he listens to the

DCI. But he keeps his mouth shut. Hardest lesson he's had to learn, but he's got it down pat.

"We need someone with your unique skill set for this," Deutch says.

Unique skill set, Fowler thinks. *Blow me.* No problem, though, because Fowler's back in business, sending eighty-something suspected jihadists to Egypt or Jordan for "questioning." And then the trouble starts.

Fowler's stationed in Milan—one of militant Islam's main arteries—and the Agency tells him to rendition a radical cleric named Abu Aziz. When he and his team jack Aziz, it's business as usual. The team waits for him to be out of public view, then a white van pulls up, someone shoots chemical spray in Aziz's eyes, and he's thrown into the back of the van. Hood and handcuffs follow. Then off to the airport, where Fowler's crew and Aziz are packed on a plane to Egypt.

The usual stirrings occur back in Milan.

A witness comes forward to say Aziz was forced into the back of a white van. Aziz's wife files a missing-person report, hires a lawyer and a private detective. In response, the Agency plants a trail suggesting Aziz might have taken a secret recruiting trip to Albania. It all dies down fast. Everything goes back to normal.

A year later, the Egyptians run out of reasons to hold on to Aziz. God knows they looked, but outside of being a loudmouth, he's strictly jihad lite. And the first thing Aziz does with his newfound freedom is call his wife. And he's got *shit* to say. He tells her the Americans kidnapped him and sent him to Egypt, where he was tortured nonstop for a year.

And here's where it gets messy for Fowler.

The Italians had been watching Aziz for years, and part of their operation involved tapping his phone. So the Italians hear Aziz bitching to his wife about his rendition at the hands of the Americans, and they go fucking ballistic. How dare the Americans come in and snatch their suspect before their operation bears fruit? Of course, Fowler would have told the Italians, you don't catch terrorists by *waiting* for them to do something.

The Italians take the Aziz tape to the state prosecutor, a man so fervent in his hatred of Bush and Iraq that he makes the Jacobins seem positively milquetoast about the Church and the monarchy. The prosecutor immediately opens up an investigation. And Fowler's been sloppy. He let his people use personal cell phones and stay in hotels under their real names. So unraveling the case of Aziz and determining the chain of events that led him to a basement in Egypt with electrodes hooked up to his nuts is no sweat.

The prosecutor goes public with his case and with the suspects' names, and he indicts them all for kidnapping, assault, and a whole smorgasbord of lesser charges. And the left-wing press on both continents is all over it, running exposés, signing book contracts. In fact, Kyle's buddy Neil wrote a book called *Torture Team,* all about Fowler's crew.

So in the middle of this shitstorm, the DCI travels to see Fowler in hiding.

"How the fuck did this happen, Tommy? How could you be so fucking sloppy?"

"I wasn't." Fowler's wearing a suit to look nice for his boss, but he never wears suits, and his shirt collar is strangling him. "The Italians told us not to worry. That everyone was in on it. They were acting like it was the old Gladio days. I'm not that fucking lame. If they hadn't said there was nothing to worry about, you think I would have taken such risks?"

"They want us to extradite you, want you to stand trial."

"Fuck them. The prosecutor's a Communist."

"And we all agree, Tommy. No one's gonna send you or any of your people back to Italy. This whole thing...pure politics."

Fowler nods.

"And the way the press is talking about you," the DCI says. "Treasonous."

"They're calling me a storm trooper. American Waffen-SS."

"Treasonous."

"Fuck them."

"And, Tommy, you know no one is going to let anything happen to you. You've been a soldier for us for thirty years. We take care of our own."

Now Fowler's nervous. He knows what "take care of our own" usually means.

"You're what now, Tommy, sixty-something?"

"Around that."

"You can retire with the Cadillac plan."

Fowler takes off his jacket, loosens his tie, rolls up his sleeves. "You want me to go out?"

"Not at all. But it's like when a bar closes: you don't have to stop drinking, but you can't keep doing it here."

"So where am I going?"

"Southeast Asia."

And Fowler perks up; tons of radical Islam there. "Indonesia?"

The DCI laughs. "Right...Indonesia." He laughs some more. "You get a respected cleric tortured for a year, and we're gonna send you to the most populous Muslim country on earth." He pulls a manila folder from his briefcase. "You're going to Cambodia." He stares at the tattoo on Fowler's forearm. "Your first field of action, right?"

"One of them."

"Two benefits, Tommy. One: It's a nonextradition country, so it'll shut the Italians up..."

"So I am a pariah to the administration."

"Of course you are. Right now. But no one stays one forever. Plus the other benefit..."

Fowler taps his foot. "Malaria? Done that one."

"The girl working under you is a right fucking tart." The DCI tosses the folder to Fowler. "Rebecca Harris. Her cover is that she's an ethnomusicologist. Know anything about Khmer music, Tommy?"

"It's all sad."

"Right, a lot of oral archives of atrocity."

"Isn't most music these days?"

The DCI laughs. "Rebecca was stationed in Ukraine. But she got too close to one of her agents and he burned her back. There were rumors of a relationship of a...sexual nature. She can thank the Clinton administration she's still got a job. We didn't have enough women or fags for their taste, so now it's impossible to fire either a woman or a fag." The DCI motions toward the folder, and Fowler takes out Rebecca's photo. "Nice, right?"

"Sure."

DCI points to the picture. "Doesn't do the tits justice."

Fowler gives him a fake smile.

"See, you're both exiles. Guy she bedded down with in Ukraine was a fifty-two-year-old professor—sorry, the guy she *allegedly* bedded down with." He makes a face of disgust. "I have to remember my corrective training." He recovers and smiles. "Maybe you two can be allegedly homesick together..."

Fowler bites his lower lip.

"They've already put your name on the door. It'll be your first executive placement: You're chief of station. And you ship out tomorrow morning."

So Fowler gets to Cambodia and meets Rebecca Harris and takes her out for drinks and she's giving Fowler the lay of the land when he bursts out with:

"I know this place."

"Yeah, but a lot's changed since you were here."

He raises his drink to his lips. "They got a few high-rises...a few hotels...they threw some paint on a cemetery. The Vietnamese still run this place. Nothing's gonna change until they don't."

"Still harboring some old prejudices."

"It's funny how your generation thinks *facts* that don't fit into their view of the world are just old prejudices."

"Right."

"How'd you end up here, anyway?"

Rebecca smiles. "Like you don't know."

"Why don't *you* tell me?"

"I was burned by my agent. Everyone thinks I let my guard down because we were having an affair."

Fowler says this one slowly, because his chances of an office romance hinge on her answer. "They shouldn't think that?"

"No. 'Cause I told them no. It's just...neither agency, theirs or ours, can imagine a woman not being blown away by the chance to mercy-fuck a sad crony Communist teaching agriculture."

"So you didn't do it?"

"And he burned me because I wouldn't."

"Why didn't you fight harder?"

"I did. They put me here. That was considered...generous."

"Why didn't you just quit? Fuck 'em."

"Because I am a goddamned good agent, and wherever they put me, I'm going to try to do good."

"You gonna ask how I ended up here?"

"Already know."

"Right," Fowler says. "Everyone knows. And?"

"What do *I* think?" Fowler nods, and she goes on. "I think what most people like me think: you're a menace to civil liberties and our standing in the West."

"Civil liberties don't matter if you're dead."

"What if I'd rather be dead than live in that world?"

"You mean that?"

"I do."

Fowler *really* likes this girl; shame his chances of a torrid affair seem null and void at this point. "So you think I'm shit?"

"Not at all. I think the policies you enforce are shit. I don't know *you* from anything."

"That's fair."

"Still like me?"

Fowler smiles. "Whaddya mean?"

"Come on, Fowler. You're an Agency guy...you were hoping these drinks would just be the start of the evening. I have a reputation."

Fowler sucks on his right cheek when he's embarrassed. "Yeah. I like you."

"Good. Then let's get out of here."

"Sorry?"

"I wasn't interested in fucking *the professor,* Fowler."

And Fowler's not a kiss-and-tell guy, but the girl is worth getting burned for. They're not exclusive, they both play around, but there's real warmth between them—the first time Fowler's ever felt that. She's the smartest agent he's ever worked with. She's insinuated herself into the Khmer community in a way he can't.

They see that tattoo on his forearm and they know he's one of their ghosts come home.

24.

Rebecca bursts into Fowler's office without knocking. "I got something," she says, holding up a printout of an e-mail.

"No knock?"

"Please, Fowler." She sits down in front of his desk. "When your door is closed, you're doing one of two things. Lifting weights or sleeping." She smiles, indulging him but never coddling.

Fowler sits behind his desk, lights a cigarette.

"I thought you stopped," Rebecca says with a slight shake of her head.

"You can smoke in elevators and hospitals here. This is my last chance to smoke with total impunity. I mean . . . the kids here smoke." And Fowler's about to start in on how half the diseases and ailments in the first world are because of people's luxury and boredom, as opposed to the *actual* epidemics in the third world, but he decides to keep quiet, because he can see Rebecca can't wait to talk. "What have you got?"

"Strange things going down at the airport."

"Usually are."

"Even stranger today."

"Locals' turf," he says. "We're here by the good graces of people who don't like us to stick our noses in over there."

"Right, but it's not sticking our noses in," she says. "See . . . we have due cause. There was a guy on a no-fly list."

Fowler perks up. "Say more."

"And by order of Langley, we have to—"

"I know all that. Say more. No-fly guy..."

"Yeah. Name is Julian Robinson. He'd been grounded."

"Know why?"

"Not yet."

"Did we ground him?"

Rebecca shakes her head. "Not us. No. Not the Agency. Someone did, though."

"Name like that. Julian Robinson. Two to one, it's money laundering. He doesn't pass my Muhammad test. Guys named Julian Robinson aren't gonna show up with a bomb in their underwear or shoes. Get a guy named Julian, and he's been laundering diverted UN money for a third-world despot."

"You're a caveman."

"Start asking around back home. But it's not strange yet. Just a no-fly guy."

"'Cause you never let me finish anything. He's *gone.*"

"Gone? Didn't security detain him?"

"Robinson goes to speak to someone about his ticket. Customer-service rep. She tells him he's no-flyed. Then three guys come and pick him up. Girl assumes they're security, so she thinks nothing. Then a minute later, *actual* airport security shows up, responding to the initial alarm set off by the boarding-pass kiosk. And no one can find Robinson anywhere. He's gone, and no one knows who these guys are who took him."

That's all Fowler needs to hear. He stands up, slides a blazer over his heavily worked-out shoulders. "First thing we need to figure out, did Robinson get carted away by friend or foe? 'Cause it obviously wasn't airport personnel."

"Right," Rebecca says.

"I'll call you from the airport." Fowler looks for his car keys. "Start checking around, see what Robinson was grounded for in the first place."

25.

Kyle wakes.

A series of hard slaps across the face, then a variation in tone, a few gentler ones, and then a final belt across the cheek.

Someone rips off the hood, and Kyle immediately wishes he had left it on.

His interrogator shakes out his hand; that last crack left him with some bodily feedback, a hand vibrating with violence.

The strobe lights are throbbing, suffocating. Kyle can't find an image to hold on to. Everything blends into an amorphous pulse that churns his stomach.

He's in a warehouse. That much he's sure of.

In between the strobe flutters, he tries to make out his surroundings. The windows are blacked out, boarded shut. Rain damage has pulped the walls. Industrial ooze drips; smells like sulfur, moves like grape jelly. Exposed wires everywhere, coiled insect antennae.

"Robinson!" a voice shouts. Chinese, but not a heavy accent; the voice's owner has spent years abroad. "Robinson, give me your eyes." Fingers snap. It's the guy from the airport, the leader of the crew that kidnapped him. "Give me your eyes right here."

But Kyle can't do that.

He feels like he's just been born and is learning the world. His hands and feet are bound, and he's seated on a metal chair that's been bolted to the floor. The strobes' rate picks up, an epileptic's heartbeat.

He cranes his neck, sees rats scamper across a bare mattress that's a mass of electrical wires hooked up to an enormous battery. The apparatus hugs you close and gives you a charge.

Kyle sniffs the air. Scorched skin and fear-sweat.

Flicker. Flicker.

Kyle sees several belts and pairs of shoes by the mattress. People who came in and never came out. He can feel the pain haunting this place.

"Robinson...listen to me. Look at me."

Kyle whispers, "I'm not Robinson. I'm not."

"Who are you?"

"Kyle West."

"That what you're calling yourself *now.* 'Bout time. You always were too attached to being Robinson."

A new voice. "Wasn't healthy."

"Why are you in Cambodia?"

A different voice. "Who is your target?"

Kyle can't stop turning his head. "What? What?"

"Who is your target?"

"I don't..."

"Why are you in Cambodia?"

"Who is your target?"

Kyle tries to answer but keeps stumbling, slurring out sentence slivers. "You're the same guys from the airport...the guys who...I'm Kyle West."

Another guy kneels down before Kyle. "Robinson." His voice is different, still Chinese, but he sounds like a mellifluous date rapist with an Ivy League degree. "Sorry, I mean Kyle. Know what...I can't get used to that one. You're Robinson to me."

Kyle's about to mumble *I'm not Robinson* but changes his mind.

"Say something?"

Kyle shakes his head no, focuses. There're three guys in here. Three he can make out.

"We both know what we're capable of doing to you. But, see, we don't have time to be so gentle. We don't have months to rebuild you. Don't have time for sensory deprivation and hydrotherapy and electric behavior modification and hypnosis." Date Rapist smiles, and his teeth are white bricks against the strobes. "We don't have time to break you and make you love us at the same time. Your specialty."

"Please," Kyle says. "Please. I'm not him. I'm not. I swear. I'm Kyle West. I'm Kyle West."

"Then why do you have Robinson's passport? Why do you have his credit cards? Why are you wearing his clothes?"

Kyle looks for a break. "I can explain... I can... Just give me..."

"I know you. I know who you are. I know your face."

"Robinson. You're among people who know you," another guy says.

The third guy laughs. "So just tell us who your fucking target is."

Kyle asks, "What target? Who? Listen, I'm Kyle West..."

"Why won't you just let us make this *quick?*"

"Quick... make what quick?"

"Tell us what you're doing here, and you won't feel a thing."

The other voice. "Tell us who hired you."

And then the third. "Who hired you?"

Kyle stumbles. "I don't know... I don't..."

"Yeah, you do."

"I don't... I don't know..."

"Why are you making this harder?"

"I'm not, I swear. I can't tell you anything. I don't know anything you want."

"Can't or won't?"

"I want to," Kyle pleads. "I do. I want to talk to you."

"Then do it. Let go."

"But I don't know anything. I swear it. I swear," Kyle sputters, starting to tear up. "I swear."

"All right." Date Rapist rises to his feet. "This has to move forward."

26.

One of the guys kills the strobes. Kyle tries to readjust his vision; tears sluice down his face.

Someone comes over and rests a laptop on Kyle's thighs.

Date Rapist talks again. "See, Robinson, I know something no one else does. You told it to me once. Years back. Right before you did this exact *thing* to someone else. I'd been sent there to learn from you." Those white teeth again. "I know that whatever we do to you, you won't care. The more pain we give you, the more spite you'll feel . . . the more you'll make *us* suffer. The more you'll hold out. 'Cause in your case, you live for anger. And if we show you any mercy, you'll hate us for it. And we don't have time to play that game."

And Kyle thinks, *Thank Christ for small favors. They're not going to torture me.*

"So we had a special friend follow Lara from the airport. This is a friend you know. You know his work well."

"Lara . . ."

"Yeah," Date Rapist goes on. "And you're going to watch while he tears her apart. You're going to watch her suffer. And, more to the point, *you'll* suffer. Because I know the thing that scares you most. I know her body is your body, because you love her. And I'm going to make you watch him destroy it."

"I'll tell you. I will," Kyle pleads. He doesn't want to watch this. "Please . . . let me help you."

"Too late," Date Rapist says. "She's gonna have to hurt a little, 'cause you made me wait." He punches Kyle hard in the mouth. "You shouldn't have made me wait." He powers up the laptop. "We told our special friend to make sure he's got the camera aimed right at her face."

Date Rapist goes to a secure site, passes through four stages of encryption. The screen fills up with the interior of a hotel room.

The bedroom.

Date Rapist turns to Kyle. "Can you see?"

"Please . . . whatever you're doing, don't. Don't," Kyle pleads.

"Can you see?"

Kyle nods. He can see.

Date Rapist uses the cursor to scroll around the room.

The lamp is shattered, green glass against the white carpet. There's a torn pair of black lace panties balled up beside the bed.

He keeps scrolling, and there's a pool of blood and a broken champagne bottle.

One of the kidnappers says: "Looks like our friend couldn't wait to get started. Problem with a man who loves his work."

The other one laughs. "Think he fucked her up, boss."

Date Rapist doesn't talk, just keeps scrolling.

He leaves the bedroom, makes his way to the bathroom. The shower's running.

There's more fresh blood en route.

Kyle's nauseous, swallows back fear. "No. Turn it off. Please, turn it off."

Date Rapist doesn't look at Kyle, just says, "Should've talked sooner."

"Please, turn it off. . . . Turn *it off.*"

The camera's getting closer to the shower. More blood, and a woman's blouse in tatters. Date Rapist is getting pissed off. Seems like his friend got too enthusiastic too early.

He zooms in on the shower, and his face starts to turn ashen.

He scrolls around faster and faster. Something's not right.

The shower curtain is open. Bloody handprints are smeared all over the sink and medicine cabinet.

The shower stall is in full view.

And before Kyle can figure out what's going on, Date Rapist rises in a rage, yanks his phone out of his pocket, and finger-pounds the keypad.

"What happened?" someone says.

Date Rapist fumes. "Shut the fuck up."

Kyle looks down to the screen. It's not a woman in the shower, not anyone who could conceivably be named Lara.

It's a man.

He's Chinese and bearded and muscle-bound, and his throat has been sliced so deeply that his head is attached to his neck by only a wing and a prayer and a bit of cracked bone and cartilage.

Date Rapist throws his phone against the wall. "Fucking bitch."

The two guys run over. "What the fuck? What happened?"

Date Rapist storms over and kicks Kyle in the head, then turns to his boys and says: "Fucking cunt killed him. Tore his throat out."

Both of the guys say in unison, "*She* killed him?"

Kyle reels, spits blood and part of a tooth, and throws up a little in shock.

Date Rapist barks to one of the two, "You. Get him ready to move. This place is blown. You"—he points to the other one—"get on the phone and call for backup. Who knows what our friend told her before she killed him."

The hood goes over Kyle's head again. He listens to someone scream muffled orders into a cell phone.

Darkness. Complete as the day before Creation.

Kyle squirms in his seat.

Seconds later, he feels the moisture of lips against his ear and then hears the words "Don't worry, baby. It's me." A woman's voice, deep; the accent sounds Russian, but from the outer provinces, nowhere near Moscow. Kyle can't help hoping he lives long enough to see what kind of body contains a voice like that.

Then the bullets start, a saturnalia of shells.

Kyle hears his kidnappers suffer, hears them slam into the wall, fall directly to the floor. Someone heaves like he's breaking open inside. Guttural gagging, murmurs without the strength to become a scream, limbs fluttering against linoleum. Kyle feels fluid collecting around his feet.

His savior scampers to the other side of the warehouse. She flips on the lights.

He swivels his head. Back and forth. Back and forth. He can pick up sense impressions, can feel movement.

He hears his savior's footsteps get closer and closer, and then he recoils, feels the cold of a blade against his skin, tries to bounce away on the bolted chair.

"Stay still, baby," she says.

Kyle's words are muffled. "What are you doing? What are you—"

She saws away at the cords on his hands and feet, frees him.

"We gotta go," she says, taking his hand, and they rocket down several flights of steps.

27.

She throws Kyle into the passenger seat of a two-door rental pock-marked with rust, a wounded warrior's chassis. There's nothing she can do to this car that it hasn't been through already.

She starts the car, waits until the engine's epic sputter turns into a sustained surge, then slams down on the gas.

She gropes around the dash, then reaches under the seat, grabs a pack of cigarettes and a lighter, hands them to Kyle. "Light one for me," she says, and then laughs, realizing she left the hood on him. "I'm sorry, baby," she says. "Things happened so fast."

She takes off Kyle's hood, grabs the nape of his neck and pulls him close, her nails gripping his jaw, and plants a long, ravenous kiss on his mouth—all the while steering with one hand. Right as she's slipping Kyle her tongue, she breaks away and throws him off, smack into the door handle.

Kyle winces.

"Who the fuck are you?" she yells.

Kyle's frozen by nerves and the passion of her kiss. No one has ever kissed him like *that* before.

She pulls a gun from her waistband and points it at Kyle. "Answer me. Who are you?"

He throws his hands up, shrinks into the corner. "Don't kill me. Christ. Don't kill me."

"Who are you?"

"Kyle. My name's Kyle."

"Kyle... Kyle what?"

Kyle's blinded by how fast the car's moving; his stomach's doing laps. She's blazing past throngs of Buddhists off to pray; past tourists snapping photos of temples and markets; past hands pounding on the car windows, hawking DVDs, fruit, and water; past lines of men and women turning the highway into a sidewalk; past banyan trees baking in the sun.

She waves the gun. "Kyle what?"

"You killed those guys. You killed all of them."

"Want to be next? Talk."

"Fuck... don't kill me. Don't."

"Where's Robinson? Why do those guys think you're Robinson?"

"I don't know. I don't know where he is."

She's screams at him as she floors the gas. "How do you know Robinson? How the fuck do you know him?"

"I don't know him. I met him. But I don't know him."

"How'd you meet?"

Kyle's reeling, can't keep up with her questions. "What?"

"Tell me where he is."

"I don't know. I swear it. I don't know where he is."

"Who do you work for?"

"No one. I don't work for anyone."

"Bullshit. Everyone works for someone."

"I don't. I don't."

She tightens her finger on the trigger. "Who do you work for?"

Kyle screams back at her, "*No one.* I don't know anything. I swear. Listen to me."

She looks in the rearview. There's an SUV with tinted windows trailing them, and closing the gap. She's got the gas floored. The car's doing ninety and leaving behind an ocean of oil and brake fluid. The speed is cannibalizing the carburetor; the transmission whistles like air through a bullet hole; the body of the car is shaking.

They don't have much time before the SUV catches up.

"Goddamn, Robinson," she says. "Why'd you have to send me to a place with no roads or sidewalks?"

Kyle's beached in the corner, rubbing his wrists, which are raw and swollen from the cord. His eyes are empty; he's staring off. "I don't know anything," he whispers to the girl he figures has to be Lara. "I don't." He's marooned inside himself.

She checks the rearview again. The car on their ass doesn't have a license plate. Not a good sign.

Kyle stares at the ornate tattoos on Lara's upper arm and shoulder. Can't figure out what language they're in, thinks it could be Slavic.

In a slightly softer voice, but while pressing the gun right against his forehead, Lara asks: "One last time . . . who the fuck *are* you?"

"Kyle West." He nods in affirmation, almost to reassure himself. "I'm Kyle West."

She presses the gun harder, leaving a mark. "That's your name. Not *who* you are."

Two bullets obliterate the back window before Kyle gets a chance to respond.

28.

Kyle throws himself against the door in shock, thinking the bullets came from Lara's gun. He's sure he's shot, searches his body for blood and wounds.

More bullets fly through the car's exposed back; they lodge in the upholstery and frame, shredding leather and throwing tufts of fabric.

Lara loses control of the car. Smoke overflows from the engine in a furious froth, obscuring her vision. She slams on the brakes, then pumps them, but the car keeps spinning until it ends up in a dead stop facing the wrong way—which is to say, directly at the SUV.

Lara tosses her hair off her forehead, breathes in, and picks up her gun from the floor.

On impulse, Kyle decides to seize the chance to flee. Throws open the passenger door and takes off running across the road.

Lara sticks her head out the window. "Where the fuck are you going?"

But he doesn't look back, doesn't answer. He's running to freedom or, at the very least, away from the crazy bitch who pointed a gun at his head.

Lara slams the car into reverse and floors it while unloading a fresh clip in the direction of the SUV.

Kyle crosses the road, streaks through dirt clumps and gravel that are surrounded on all sides by slum housing in a state of semicollapse. He's running hard, sucking in air, holding his sides since he's still in pain from his earlier beating. The shoes, Robinson's Ferragamos, are tearing up his soles and ankles.

Just keep moving. Do not stop to think.

Kyle looks back and sees the doors of the SUV open. Two Chinese guys wearing wired-up earpieces surge out in pursuit. One of them yells: "Robinson. Stop. Get in the car!"

Kyle picks up his pace, his chest and throat burning, then makes a right into the slum suburb and immediately regrets it. This place makes the shanties of Phnom Penh look like something out of a brochure begging for a wide vista shot.

He strips off the Ferragamos so he can move faster. Not a great idea, considering he's about to step in raw sewage.

He hops over a lake of indigo goo, something septic, and rips through an endless succession of clotheslines, strung up to both dry rags and separate makeshift housing.

No one he encounters pays much attention to this heavy-breathing American. They all seem to have other things on their minds—probably how happy they are he's not a government-sponsored bulldozer razing their homes, gobbling up the land, and displacing them even farther from the city.

He cuts into a corridor separating residences, pushes aside some naked children, and is about to fuck up a game of dice some locals are playing when bullets explode a few inches from his head. In response, the gamblers pick up their dice, avoid eye contact, and disappear into the shanty labyrinth.

"*Robinson,*" one of his pursuers yells. "Robinson. We need to talk to you."

Kyle keeps running, sees a clearing ahead, sees a street. He thinks he can make it.

The bullets are tearing up dirt in clumps around his feet.

"Stop," one of his pursuers says. "Goddamn it. Stay put."

Kyle does the exact opposite, makes a lung-shredding dash straight into the open road without looking—and is nearly crushed by Lara's car, which is smoking like a nineteenth-century steam engine.

"*Get in the fucking car,*" she yells to Kyle.

He turns back and sees the two guys screaming into their headsets, their guns fixed on him, a few hundred feet behind.

Kyle closes his eyes, prays for insight in the dark.

These people are going to kill me, he thinks. *This woman might kill me.*

"Get in here now," she says.

Okay. Play the odds.

He rips open the car door and jumps inside.

Lara floors it, and the radiator responds by belching fluid across the windshield.

29.

PHNOM PENH INTERNATIONAL AIRPORT

Fowler stands amid the crowds in the bustling airport. Just as he'd feared, he spent the past half hour on the phone with the police demanding a translator be sent over.

"Why wasn't one here in the first place?" Fowler asks.

Fowler's got the chief of police on the other end of the line, a man who's trying to placate him but who has a long memory of colonialism that he can't quite keep out of his voice. "Mr. Fowler, sir, the manager of the airport speaks English. Mr. Suong, I believe."

Fowler paces around a boarding gate. "Yeah, well. Apparently, Mr. Suong has left for the afternoon."

"*Our* translator will be back in the office at seven thirty tomorrow morning."

"I'll have shot someone by then."

"I understand your frustration."

"You seem to speak English pretty well."

"Thank you, sir. Not much choice in the matter."

"How about *you* come down here? Help me out."

"Looking into missing persons isn't what I do, Mr. Fowler."

"It's a crime, right?"

"Yes, sir."

"You're police, right?"

"Yes, sir."

"What *do* you do, then?"

"Major crimes, sir. I report directly to Hun Sen's chief of security. Our translator will happily accompany you to the airport at seven thirty tomorrow morning."

"I suppose it wouldn't do any good to remind you who I am."

"I could say the same to you, Mr. Fowler. People like you come and go, but I live here. Good day."

Fowler strolls over to the customer-service area and sits in front of Mai's desk, holding her police report.

"Speak English?"

Mai giggles. "Some."

Fowler offers her his hand. "I'm Tom Fowler."

"Mai."

"You're the one who helped Mr. Robinson when he had difficulty getting his ticket?"

Mai's face is a blank.

"Trouble. Mr. Robinson had *trouble* with ticket."

She nods. "Yes. I did help."

"Good. And how would you describe Mr. Robinson?"

Mai shrugs.

"Was he nervous? Angry? Guilty?" Fowler has a face to go with each emotion.

"Oh—angry. Very angry."

"Okay. So you tried to help him with his ticket, and then security showed up? Is that right?"

"Yes. I tried to help."

"How long was Mr. Robinson with you before security arrived?"

"Long?"

"Minutes. How many minutes did you speak with Robinson for?"

"Very few. Very few. One, two, maybe."

"Did you know the security guards? Recognize them?"

"No. But change often. High rate of turnover."

Fowler smiles. "Good. That's good." Mai's well versed in human resources–speak. Nice to know American corporate euphemisms for termination transcend native tongues.

"Okay." Fowler taps the top of her computer. "I'm going to need

Robinson's credit card info, Social, ticket number, all of it. Can you do that?"

"Yes."

"Good. You have security cameras here?"

"Excuse?"

Fowler makes the motion for a camera lens near his eye. Mai nods her head enthusiastically.

"Can you take me there? Help me find Robinson on the tape?"

"I'll try," she says.

Fowler gives her a warm grin. "All I can ask." He gets up, takes in the layout of the airport. "What direction did security escort Mr. Robinson?"

Mai looks around the airport and points.

"Okay." Fowler follows her finger. "And where is the security office?"

Mai points in the opposite direction.

Fowler gets part of the answer he was looking for. "That doesn't look right, does it?" he says, more to himself than Mai, who shrugs.

30.

Fowler watches the tech guys scroll through footage while Mai stands at his side, keeping a lookout for Robinson on the screen.

Fowler and Mai are drinking tea; Mai because she wanted tea, Fowler because he couldn't get her to understand that he wanted coffee.

Mai taps one of the techs on the shoulder. "That's him."

And there's a man standing at the kiosk struggling to understand why it won't print out his ticket and then assaulting the inanimate device.

Fowler squints. "Scroll forward. See if you can get me a frontal facial."

The camera follows the man from behind as he heel-toes it toward Mai's desk escorted by the security guard. Then he sits down, and his face comes into full view.

"Freeze there. Can you isolate that?"

Tech guys shake their heads in confusion. What?

Fowler looks to Mai. "I need a picture of him. Can you tell them that?"

She does, and they nod in response.

"Keep going on the archive," Fowler says. "I want to see if I can get a look at the security guards."

Fowler motions to the tech guys to move the tape ahead, and he watches as the three security guards approach the man, then lead him through the boarding area and completely out of the range of the cameras.

Fowler knows one thing:

These guys have done this before. They've been trained to get out of the camera's radius immediately. Even freeze-framing the images provides nothing but shadows and smears of gray suits.

Fowler moves away from the terminal, nods in thanks, turns to Mai. "Tell them I need a PDF of Robinson's picture e-mailed to these two phone numbers." He tears apart his cigarette pack, writes the numbers on the cardboard, and hands it to her. "Do you know what I want?"

Mai nods, and Fowler hopes she gets it. She's impeccably polite, but her eyes call to mind the famous saying "There's no *there* there."

Fowler steps back into the airport proper, sits in the departures lounge, and calls Rebecca.

"Hey there," he says. "You get the Robinson card info I sent?"

"Got it."

"You're gonna get a PDF of his face in a few. Run it through our system. See if it hits anyone we're watching."

"Fowler, I know how to do this."

"I'm sorry." And he is. He still hasn't adjusted to having someone smarter than him under his command.

"Anything at the airport?"

"Locals had already taken prints when I got here," he says. "Fuck knows what they picked up or smudged away. They aren't delicate when it comes to forensics."

She breathes deep in agreement. "I have some potentially good news. You know the airport manager you asked me to locate, Mr. Suong? I found him. Can you take down an address?"

Fowler gets ready to use the other half of his cigarette pack. "Yeah.... Go."

"Fowler, don't leave me working pics and card info while you run around. I can do more."

"I'll call you after I talk to Suong. Just see what you can do with the credit cards."

31.

Lara's driving as fast as the bruised chassis of the car allows. She's dropped the speed down to sixty, and the steam has subsided.

"I need you to pull over," Kyle says, losing the last vestiges of control over his nerves.

"Right."

"Pull over."

"No," she says, weaving between hotel shuttle vans and honking indiscriminately.

"I am not kidding." he says. *"Pull over."*

"We need to make tracks from here."

Kyle pounds his fist against the dash. "I've almost been killed *twice* today. I need to try and process this..."

"No stopping."

"I don't care. I do not care. I need you to pull over to the side of the road now." He raises his voice. "I am freaking the fuck out. No joke."

"If I stop the car, it's not starting again. Just scream. Let it all out."

Kyle turns to her, incredulous. "You're serious?"

"Scream or don't. But you've got to collect yourself. I want answers, and you're useless to me like this."

Lara clicks her tongue against the roof of her mouth, a trick she uses to focus her thoughts. Then Kyle emits a primal scream straight from the center of his stomach; his innards vibrate from the effort.

Lara's so shocked by the primal sound that she jumps, cracks her head against the roof of the car. "Fuck you," she says, more annoyed than angry. "You were supposed to scream...what was *that* sound?"

"Sorry," Kyle says. "Sorry."

Lara shakes her head.

"I think I feel better," Kyle says, shocked her suggested course of action worked.

"Your lip is still bleeding."

Kyle flips the visor to the mirrored side and gets a look at his face. "Holy shit," he says. "Holy shit." He holds his finger to his pulsing lip and winces. "This is not good."

"It looks worse because it's fresh. It'll be better once the blood dries."

He turns his battered face to her. "You think so?"

"We're gonna get you cleaned up. You can't be seen in public like this."

"Okay." Kyle turns back and stares into the mirror, touching his lip even though it stings.

"Stop playing with your face," she says. "You'll make it worse."

Kyle puts his hands in his lap. "Where are we going?"

Lara ignores him. "I ask questions now. First one: How did you get Robinson's passport? Second: Who the fuck are you?"

"I'm Kyle West. I met...I met Robinson two days ago. I was at a bar in Phnom Penh. He came in...introduced himself...we talked. He knew who I was."

"So what."

"I'm not traveling under my real name."

"Why not?"

Kyle exhales. "It's a long story."

"Shorten it."

"I can't go back to the United States. Well, to be exact, I can't go to the United States or to any country that has an extradition treaty with it. And Robinson knew that."

"So he just sat down with you and talked. That's it."

"That's it."

"Well, you achieved something few people do."

Kyle cranes his neck, a bodily question mark.

"You met Robinson and survived," she says.

Kyle nods. "Yeah. You could look at it that way."

"What way do you look at it?"

"That he fucked me over. That he promised to help me..."

Lara laughs. Kyle's taken aback.

"God," she says. "You must have really wanted to believe him."

"He said he could help me if we traded passports. He said he had information for me in England. I use his passport to go to England and get the information...and he uses mine."

"Why did he want your passport?"

"He said he needed to go to Africa...he had a deal going down there."

"What sort of deal?"

"Something telecom related. I don't know....I barely met him. I couldn't have spent more than six hours with the guy, total."

"More than most."

"Right." Kyle looks in the mirror again, raises his hand to touch his lip, then reconsiders but keeps staring at it. "Thank you for saving me."

"You're welcome," she says with an undisguised sneer. "Lot of good it did me." She swerves around a cluster of tuk-tuks. "Look. The people who kidnapped you are the same people who came to kill me. They're not going to stop. As long as they think you're Robinson, they will not *stop*. Follow me?"

Kyle nods. "I think."

"So we need to find Robinson right *now*. You met him in a bar. Did you two go anywhere else?"

"Yeah. His hotel."

"You remember it?"

"Yeah. Absolutely."

"Then that's where we're going."

"What if he checked out already?"

"Maybe he didn't. And if he's gone, then you convince them you're him. We need to get into his room."

113

"Wait. Wait," Kyle says. "Now *I've* got a question. What are you to Robinson?"

No answer; she just presses the gas.

"I mean . . . you know who I am. Who are *you?*"

"Your only chance of staying alive," she says. "That's all you need to know."

"That's not an answer."

"No. But it's what you're getting."

"Look," he says, "I'm holding Robinson's passport. If anything goes down at the hotel, it's over for me. I think it's better for me to keep moving."

"Fine. Then get out. Go back to being Robinson on your own." She motions toward Kyle's face. "Seems to be working out well for you. I'm going to the hotel."

She's got a salient argument, he thinks; any hope he has of staying alive involves her. "All right."

"Plus," she says, "if he's there, maybe we can get your passport back."

32.

Mr. Suong, errant airport-manager extraordinaire, is spending the afternoon attending to matters of personal pulchritude.

When Fowler finds him, Suong's sitting in a high-backed salon chair letting Kaffir lime juice soak into his luxurious black locks. An organic oatmeal face mask has been spread across his visage to cleanse his pores of toxins, and an impossibly green cucumber slice resides over each eye.

New Age music heavy on the sitar and chirping birds plays over the speakers. Suong sips on mineral water garnished with a lime slice.

Fowler sits in the chair beside Suong, taps his shoulder, and rolls a cigarette between his fingers. "Mr. Suong," he says. "Tom Fowler. CIA. Wanted to ask you some questions about an occurrence at your airport this morning."

"I recommend talking to security," Suong says. "I've been here all day. I have an engagement this evening at Hun Sen's. We're celebrating the sale of over one hundred thousand hectares of arable land to Kuwait. And the Kuwaitis... well, for a people whose official religion forbids images, they're quite judgmental about appearance."

Suong expects the mention of Hun Sen's name to force Fowler to retreat; however, Fowler's realized anyone who runs a business of value or consequence in Cambodia is on Hun Sen's guest list. If Fowler didn't talk to Hun Sen's associates, he'd have no one to talk to. "Sure. Sure. Understood," Fowler says. "Thing is, your security people seem to be a little hazy about the details of recent events in *your* airport."

"Such as?"

"This morning, a man on a no-fly list, Julian Robinson, attempted to board a plane. He went to customer service for help and was apprehended by security. Problem is, these men weren't your security detail. They aren't security personnel, period. They were professionals."

"I hire professionals..."

"What I mean is, they escorted Robinson out of the camera's range in close to thirty seconds. And they never allowed their own faces to be captured in a frontal. That takes tactical planning and prior knowledge of the airport."

Suong purses his lips. "And you know this because?"

Fowler can't exactly come clean on this. "I just do."

"And my men aren't capable of this?"

"Your men showed up two minutes later looking for Robinson, only to find he'd already been escorted out. No one's seen or heard from Robinson since."

"And?"

"It would appear he was either kidnapped by hostiles or helped to escape."

"Why would someone on a no-fly list attempt to board a commercial airliner?"

"That's why I'm talking to you. My feeling...maybe it was a signal for his friends to come pick him up."

"I will perform a thorough investigation tomorrow. No stone will be left unturned."

"If I could just—"

"It is so hard to find good help, Mr. Fowler. The fruits of Pol Pot's revolution included leaving us with a devastated intellectual class." Suong's mask has started to harden around his wrinkles and frown lines, cleansing deeper. "I take this quite seriously, Mr. Fowler."

Women in floral smocks scamper around the salon, checking on customers. One of them examines Suong's face mask, adds a little more to it, whispers something in Khmer, and Suong smiles. "I'm making progress," he relates to Fowler. "I have extremely oily skin. Comes from an excess of hormones. A blessing and a curse, I assure you." Suong spares no expense on his upkeep. He is his *own* greatest love affair.

Fowler gets around to lighting the cigarette. "See, here's the thing. Southeast Asia has pockets of heavy terrorist activity. I've placed some of these guys on no-fly lists myself in the past few months, and fuck if I know how, but they keep getting *other* places."

"Catastrophic. Corruption holds our country back."

"And I know guys like you, not necessarily sympathetic to the terrorists' goals but—let's face it—a little *dirty*, might let them on a plane for a little do-re-mi. Well, I'll give you some credit, Mr. Suong—a lot of do-re-mi."

"I would never aid or abet known terrorists."

"I'm not saying anything. But do you remember Abu Bakar Bashir?"

"Who?"

"Bashir blew up a nightclub in Indonesia a while back."

"Means nothing…"

"I ordered him no-flyed, and he gained entrance through your airport. We nailed him in Bali anyway, but…"

"I had nothing to do with that."

"And I didn't say you did. Your day off, obviously."

"Mr. Fowler, I feel this is a line of questioning best engaged in at your office, not in a place of business and *indigenous culture*." Suong says this last part with an upturned lip and sneer.

"All I want to know is…is it possible anyone on your staff could be involved in aiding Robinson's escape or in handing him over to forces outside this country? I've checked the criminal records and pay stubs of your security. It's not beyond the realm of possibility."

Suong tries to remove the cucumbers from his eyes for dramatic effect, but one of the beauticians stops him and wags a disapproving finger. "Are you talking about rendition?" Suong says to Fowler in feigned horror. "Are you asking if my staff aids in renditions?"

"I don't know yet."

"I have no idea of this man's..."

"Robinson."

"Of this Robinson's whereabouts. His name means nothing to me."

"I can look at this in one of two ways. One, you're a garden-variety greedy bastard...which is to say, you're like every single one of us walking the earth. And you're paid a retainer by certain people not to ask questions about what goes on in your airport. Or, two, you were in on it. You know who Robinson's friends are, know who helped him escape, and I'm going to have you charged with conspiracy for running a ratline for people on no-flys. They get tagged by the computer, and you help them leave before someone comes to pick them up." Fowler leans in close to the rail of Suong's chair and puts his thick hand over Suong's slender, nearly hairless forearm. "I'm CIA, Mr. Suong. I don't even have to charge you with anything. I can have you disappeared, send you someplace for questioning where no one'll ever find you. So tell me: Are you just dirty, or are you a friend of Robinson's? If you tell me the truth, nothing will happen to you."

"Nothing will happen to *me* regardless." And without missing a beat, Suong turns his cucumber eyes toward Fowler and says, "I'm an entrepreneur. I don't know Robinson. He is not my friend. But my airport is always open for business for friendly countries. And people know that. I think you have your answer now." Suong touches his hair, then inhales the lingering scent of lime juice.

Fowler knows now it wasn't an inside job. These people took it upon themselves to grab Robinson, with Suong's implicit blessing. Which leaves Fowler with an even larger question, one Mr. Suong can't answer.

Who the hell is Robinson?

And why is he worth either helping or grabbing?

33.

The Caltex gas station is about fifteen minutes outside of Phnom Penh. Its bathroom is a wooden outhouse with a rubber hose in the corner. There's no floor, just a layer of hard dirt that cracks under Kyle's new canvas shoes purchased inside the gift shop. The hose coughs gray water that smells both mineral and toxic. Kyle keeps his eyes and mouth shut while he runs the sporadic stream over his head.

In addition to the shoes, Kyle picked up a small pocket mirror with a yellow kitten embossed in the corner. He holds it up to take stock. His face is puffy around the eyes and lips. He looks even *more* like Robinson now that his face has a little heaviness to it and his lower lip is a swollen heart. He runs a wet finger over his gums and teeth to wipe away the dried blood. He looks one more time in the mirror. *At least I have the pain to remind me that it's still my body and not just Robinson's rental.*

He steps outside into a sea of motos and rusted 1970s gas-guzzlers.

The fuel station is a row of blue drums with a siphon attached to the side of each one. He slides on a pair of sunglasses and looks up to the sky. He's never seen one like it. Lizard-skin surface. Butter sun. Clouds shiny and plump and with such curly tails, they remind him of fattened pigs ready for slaughter. And it all combines to make him obsess over one fact.

I'm going to die here.

I'm never leaving this place.

All the subterfuge, all the residence changes, all the deliberate artifice—all of it was a prelude, a rehearsal for his meeting with Robinson.

Kyle's been knocking on death's door for a year. Eventually, someone was going to answer. And it turned out to be Robinson, wearing his exceptional suit, offering drinks and casual conversation.

Time to knock on Robinson's door one last time.

Kyle walks over to Lara, who is filling up the gas tank while smoking a cigarette. "This look any better?"

"Good enough," she says. "Just keep the sunglasses on. I'm checking the oil before we go. Get in the car and wait."

Kyle nods. Lara's conversation is distinctly lacking in ornament.

34.

Robinson's hotel appears to be part of a French plan to reconquer all its former colonies by way of affordable luxury. The hotel is a familiar chain, but instead of the faceless slab of franchise glass and concrete that the chain's hotels hide behind in most Western cities, here, the building is all rococo and bamboo, decked out with the gossamer lanterns the French favored before they were kicked out after the Battle of Dien Bien Phu. Colonial kitsch for tourists, a theme park for ersatz glory.

Kyle and Lara walk into the lobby, and it's packed with men and women in suits. A business convention just ended in the hotel's conference center, and the French manager—slick-bald, the chandelier's bulbs causing the beads of sweat on his forehead to twinkle—is walking around shaking hands and making sure everyone found the service agreeable.

Kyle stares at the businessman bouillabaisse. Goddamn, practically every country on the map is represented here. It makes him think of one of Neil's drunken stream-of-consciousness rants about business in the twenty-first century:

"These people are the reason you need regulation...because they don't have *countries* anymore. Any company worth its salt is multinational, and the responsibilities of its management are to the shareholders, not to the citizens. The individual laws of countries are things to be squeezed around, not obeyed. There's no loyalty. These fuckers will tank a country's economy if it keeps the board happy and their pockets lined. And a government can't stop them . . . fuck, they can just buy a new one. Our 'elected' leaders serve at their pleasure. Like everyone else."

Lara drags Kyle by the elbow over to the check-in counter.

There's no line. They walk right up to the clerk, who says with a huge smile: "Hi. How may I help you?"

"Hello," Kyle says, starting to sweat noticeably and having trouble getting his mouth and brain to sync. "My name is Julian Robinson and I'm a guest at this hotel . . ."

Lara gives Kyle a quick jolt to the ribs, reminding him not to be so formal; he's supposed to be a guy who forgot his room key.

The clerk runs her tongue over her teeth, checking for any mishaps with her freshly applied cinnamon lipstick. "Are you here for one of the conventions?"

"Actually, I was out enjoying your lovely city with my friend"—Kyle motions with his head toward Lara—"when I realized . . . I seem to have misplaced my room key."

"Oh, dear . . ."

Kyle's face falls. "Is that a problem?"

"Not at all. Your name and room number again?"

"Robinson. Julian Robinson. Room three fourteen."

"Okay. I need to see your passport, sir."

"Certainly." Kyle hands her Robinson's passport.

The clerk scrunches up her face as she inspects the picture and the man before her with a swelling lip and sunglasses.

Lara picks up on it and says: "Mr. Robinson is having an allergic reaction to some fish we ate for dinner. It's why his face is . . . *swelling*."

The clerk looks at Kyle. "Too bad, Mr. Robinson."

Kyle's heart sinks. *This is what happens when you choose the worst possible option.* He hears a ticking in the back of his head.

"About the fish," the clerk says. "Happens to so many people when they visit." She reaches under the counter, then hands Kyle a plastic key card with a magnetized stripe. "My name is Carola, and I'm here all night to help you."

"Thank you," Kyle says. "You've been most..."

Lara gives him a none-too-subtle shove toward the bank of elevators.

They stand outside room 314. The embossed number on the door frame floods Kyle with trepidation. Thus far, nothing positive has come from his time in that room, and he doubts a second trip is going to reverse the trend.

Kyle's about to run the key card over the contact strip when Lara stops him. She checks how many bullets she has in the chamber of her Walther PPK and then nods.

Kyle raises the key. Stops.

Lara turns, eyeballs the hall, then turns back to him. "What is it?"

Kyle points to the pulsing green light. "It's not locked."

Lara's stunned, pushes on the door. It gives, no resistance.

Kyle doesn't like this *at all*. Robinson doesn't strike him as the kind of guy who spends quality time in an unlocked room.

Lara runs her finger along the wall looking for the light switch.

"Robinson," she says.

Kyle stands behind her. "Maybe he already left town?"

The curtains are drawn.

"Then why would they give us his room key? He didn't check out. He's still here." Her finger finds the light switch. "Robinson...I'm gonna turn on the light."

She lets a few seconds pass, opens the door a little farther, and then they notice the smell.

Like warm semiconductors. And cordite.

"Robinson," she says. "I'm turning on the light."

But neither one of them really wants to.

One more time.

"Robinson," she says.

And this time she turns on the light.

35.

This man didn't want to die.

The nightstand is overturned; the lampshade is askew; the mirror looks to Kyle like it's trying to avert its glass glaze.

Lara lingers as Kyle approaches the wall, puts his hand to it.

The blood is still warm.

A few feet away, a Chinese man dressed similarly to Kyle's kidnappers lies in a pool of blood. The stain flares out from under his outstretched arms and keeps growing. He's been shot several times. Forehead. Side of the face. Chest. An intimate kill. Someone got within a lover's distance when he did the deed.

The exit wounds of the facial shots took his jaw and ear with them.

Kyle moves closer, trying to steer around the blood, but there's no way to do it. For some reason, he finds it more appropriate to crawl over. You can't tower over someone who's suffered this kind of abuse. You owe him a primal level of respect. You have to go down on hands and knees.

Even though Kyle knows it's futile, he lowers his ear to the man's chest. Shocking silence. Not even a distant drum.

"What are you doing?" Lara says. "There's no point."

Kyle ignores her, sits next to the body, and takes the man's hand in his own. Obviously it's too late, but Kyle wants the man to know that someone held him, that someone knew there was no reason, no matter who he was, for him to die alone, far from home, in such a horrible way.

Kyle also does it because he knows it could easily *have been him* sprawled out and shot up on Robinson's floor, and he hopes that some similarly kind stranger would have shown his corpse the same mercy.

Then the wave of nausea hits, not the kind that can be ignored. Kyle rises, pushes Lara out of the way, and races to the bathroom, leaving bloody footprints in his wake.

He falls to the floor, knees hugging the bowl, and everything comes up in a trail of acid from the base of his stomach. When there's nothing left to throw up, he rests against the cold outer door of the shower stall, closes his eyes, and sucks in air.

Panic breaths. Opening his mouth to swallow all the air in the world. He'd scream if he could find enough air to start.

And when he opens his eyes, he realizes he's been sitting in a puddle of blood. He shifts; his clothes sound like a sopping sponge.

He struggles to focus, spent from vomiting.

He lines up his planes of vision and sees another dead body—this one also Chinese and likely the victim of the same bullet enthusiast responsible for the body in the other room. More of this man's insides are sliding down the wall than remain in the cracked container of his body.

Kyle shakes his head, starts to laugh. It had to be two bodies. It had to. Somehow, one wouldn't have sufficed. He yells out:

"Lara . . . you better get in here."

Fowler whips his car into the hotel's underground parking garage while talking on his cell to Rebecca. "I just pulled in."

"You got my e-mail, then?"

"Yeah."

"The credit trace popped up immediately. He used the card there last night," she says. "But I haven't been able to tie anything using the Social or passport number."

"Keep going." Fowler scans the parking lot, row after row of rental cars. "I want you to take that picture of Robinson and go to all the expat places you can think of. You know the scene better than I do. See if anyone knows him." Fowler pulls up to a valet and says, "Lot's packed. You guys giving something away in there?"

"Meetings are finishing up," the valet says. "People should be leaving soon."

Fowler starts doing laps around the tiered lot. "I'll call back," he tells Rebecca.

Kyle steps out of the bathroom, still in a daze.

Lara's stripped down to a black tank top and jeans. He's transfixed by her exposed shoulder blades. They jut out of her back like the mourning stumps of mythic wings.

She notices Kyle's sleeve drenched in blood. "Go put on one of Robinson's suits. You can't go back downstairs like that."

Kyle checks the sleeve. "Yeah. That's a good—"

"Fast. We don't want to be here."

There's a darkness, a terrible depth to Lara's beauty, something that moves beyond the boundaries of traditional aesthetics and into the realm of transcendence. Her beauty inspires fear. It physically scares Kyle to be in proximity to it.

"Faster," she says, clicking her tongue like a clock.

"Hey," Kyle says, sorting through the suits and wire hangers, "would it kill you to be the slightest bit polite? I'm not asking for nice—okay, I know we're not even in the vicinity of nice. But could you at least not bark at me?"

"Do something right," she says.

He pulls a charcoal suit from the closet and strips down.

He goes to the wastebasket to toss his soiled shirt inside and stops short when he sees his own passport lying on the corner of the desk. He opens it, flips through the pages—nothing's changed. "Why did he leave this behind?" he says to Lara, holding up his passport.

Lara walks over, inspects the pages. "I have no . . ."

Then Kyle looks at the bed. Amid the tumult of twisted sheets are the clothes he lent Robinson to add more realism to the plan.

He points at the bed. "That's . . . that's really bad too." There's no other way to interpret these signs. "We...we walked right into a crime scene. That he wanted to pin on me." He's been set up; *framed* is not nearly an active enough verb to describe this type of *absolute fucking*. Passport plus clothes plus two dead bodies equals even more trouble than he's in back home. "He set me up for these two. He set me up."

Lara pockets Kyle's passport. "Look," she says, indicating the bed, "I'll take care of this. Go change."

Fowler makes his way across the grounds, past the domed gazebos overflowing with indigenous shrubbery, past the floodlit pool packed with convention guests, several of whom sip champagne in the emerald-tiled Jacuzzi. "I'll call you if I find anything," he says to Rebecca as he whirls through the revolving glass door into the lobby.

He approaches the check-in desk, hands one of the two uniformed women his ID, rests his elbows on the counter, and says, "I'd like to know when one of your guests checked out."

The check-in girl stares at Fowler's ID, not comprehending.

"I'm CIA."

"Oh." She looks again. "I see."

Fowler does his best impression of a smile. "Yeah. They got us everywhere."

"What was the guest's name?"

"Robinson. Julian Robinson."

A clerk nearby perks up. "Mr. Robinson."

Fowler slides over to her. "You know him?"

"Mr. Robinson didn't check out. He's in his room. Is he expecting you?"

"No."

The clerk frowns. "Well, I have to call him. It's hotel policy. I must announce you."

Fowler takes his ID from the first clerk and hands it to the second. "No, you don't." The clerk scrutinizes it. "It's real," he says, and grabs it back.

She nods and says, "I have to get the manager, Monsieur Fresson, to let you in. There are rules here. This is not some boarding house," she adds with the propriety of someone who grew up in one. "We...I must call the manager. We are the representatives of a major multinational chain, and there are rules..."

She's still going when Fowler makes a break for the elevators. "Tell the manager to meet me up there!" he shouts.

Fowler loses his momentum at the bank of elevator doors. They're making local stops. Sclerotic slowness. He curses under his breath, pulls out a cigarette.

He checks his two guns, one holstered on the shoulder, one on the ankle, easy access. He changes his mind about the cigarette, puts it behind his ear, and waits on the fucking elevators congested by convention-goers.

The door of one pops open, revealing a tableau of executives in bathing suits. Fowler watches the parade of middle-aged spread given form by forgiving elastic waistbands and padded cups.

Fowler can't get over the number of them. They just keep coming. How many bloated plutocrats can this gilded box hold?

He pushes his way in, not bothering to wait for everyone to get out.

Kyle buckles his belt, slides the suit jacket on. "I'm ready." The pounding glare of salmon and green city lights filters in through the curtains.

Lara doesn't respond. She's stripped the bed bare and is now relieving the dead men of their identification

Kyle crosses the room and stands before her, trying to figure out the best way to engage her in actual conversation. "I want to thank you for everything you've done. Really. Thank you."

Nothing. She pockets the dead men's documents.

He doesn't let her silence deter him. "But I'm going to ask you to drop me off at the American embassy. I have...I have to try to explain this."

"How are you gonna do that? Show them Robinson's passport?"

"No. I've got mine back."

"No. *I've got yours.*"

"Wait a minute..."

"You go there as Robinson, you're responsible for killing two people..."

"I'm going as me. I have to try and get someone to believe me."

"And if you show them *your* passport, what happens? You said yourself you're in trouble back home. They'll bounce you back to the States. So you can go as Robinson or yourself. And you'll end up in jail either way. Least, that's how I see it."

"I want my passport back."

Fowler's sprinting down the corridor, taking in the room numbers through his peripheral vision. He dodges around a room-service tray covered in dishes—discreet lobster claw jutting out from under a china cover—necking couples dressed to the nines, and more convention guests sporting swimwear, starched hotel towels wrapped around their sagging shoulders.

Fowler sprints to room 314 and pulls his gun out of his shoulder holster right as a maid emerges from a side stairwell. She's in full uniform, cuffs and frills, vacuum cleaner in tow, and when she sees Fowler, gun at his side, she yells:

"*Gun. Gun.*"

Lara rushes to the door, peers through the peephole to check the source of the chaos. The maid is still standing in the hallway screaming, "*Gun.*"

A man's trying to shut her up, but it's not working, because he's waving the cause of her stress around.

Kyle storms over to the door.

For the first time since he met Lara, he's more pissed off than nervous, and he tries to throw her out of his way. "You can give me all the logic you want, but I'm going to the embassy. I'm telling them everything. I may be wanted, but I still have some rights. And I want my passport."

She throws him to the floor, draws the gun on him. "I can't let you do that."

"I swear I won't mention you. I never met you . . ."

"That's not—"

"You will not be brought into this."

"That's not it." She aims the gun at his head. "*You* are Robinson now."

"I am . . . what . . ."

"You are, because I say you are."

"I can't be Robinson. I can't . . ."

"Better learn to be," she says, not moving the gun an inch.

Fowler stands before room 314, braces his leg against the frame, puts his ear to the vault door, and tightens his finger on the trigger. "*Robinson,*" he yells. "This is the CIA. Open the door or I blow it off."

Kyle can't pry his tongue from the roof of his mouth; it's cemented there. His throat is parched from fear.

"Don't you even think of giving yourself up," Lara whispers.

Kyle quickly weighs his options. He can explain to the CIA agent about to bust down the door who he is, how he ended up with the passport of someone on a no-fly list, and—if that weren't enough of a hurdle—what he's doing at the scene of a *double homicide*. If, through some cosmic alignment of events, the CIA guy somehow buys his explanation for these dead bodies, he'll still get shipped home, sent to jail, and let out only occasionally to testify against Chandler.

Or he can go with Lara.

She motions to the balcony with her gun.

Fowler bites his lip, ready to fire, his face flushed with adrenaline. He blasts two rounds into the door and blows it off its hinges.

Kyle and Lara stand on the steel balcony, the city's nocturnal neon flashing through a scrim of fog. She reaches back and shuts the curtain, sealing them off, then peers over the ledge.

"We can drop to the floor below," she says. "There's a balcony."

* * *

Fowler shoulders inside, kicks the wrecked door to the ground, extends his gun, and hits the lights in one fluid motion.

He scans the room.

And the only thing moving is a sheet over a body, stirring to the rhythm of the air conditioner.

Lara puts one leg over the balcony railing, straddles the structure, then swings over the other leg and stands atop the steel rail. She bends her knees and drops onto the balcony one floor below.

She holds up her arms for Kyle, waving him along, trying to simultaneously encourage him and hurry him up.

"Just let go," she says. "Follow me."

Fowler walks over to the sheet covering the body and pulls it away.

"Fuck," he says as he looks at what's left of the victim. Times have changed. Back when he was growing up, if you wore a suit like that, the chances of your ending up in a hotel room with your head blown off were pretty slim.

Fowler turns around, sees the balcony door wide open with the curtain drawn. He rushes to it, throws it open, and peers ahead.

Kyle comes face to face with him for a flash, a flicker. Now that he's lost the opportunity to join Lara on the balcony below, he's got to do something drastic. Without internal debate, Kyle launches himself off the balcony before the man has time to even line up a shot.

However, he does have enough time to yell out "Robinson" as Kyle plummets to the pool below and tries to stifle a scream.

Kyle drops like a stone, knees against his chest and announces his presence to the other swimmers with a lounge-clearing splash. German tourists scatter, scram to the shallow end; everyone screams.

Kyle stays under, producing bubbles, until he's sure no one's going to try to shoot at him from the balcony.

* * *

Fowler stares over the balcony, watches as the guy surfaces and makes a mad dash across the parking lot, upsetting a few topiary displays on the way.

Fowler couldn't fire even if he wanted to. He's too far away to get a clean shot, and the risk of collateral damage is too high.

Fowler steps back into the room, pissed off, shaking his head in disappointment.

Then, to top off Fowler's personal farce, Monsieur Fresson—the bulb-headed hotel manager—arrives, takes one look at the blown-off door, curses in French, shakes his finger at Fowler, looks down, sees the body on the floor, passes out, and lands in a puddle of blood.

Fowler closes his eyes for a moment, really *understands* why the French don't bother having an army anymore, and then holsters his gun.

He pulls out his cell phone, ignoring Fresson's coma, and calls Rebecca. "What's up?" she says. Fowler offers a guttural exhale she's on intimate terms with. "Okay," she says. "What do you need?"

"Get in touch with our Indonesian office. Tell them I need Lawrence Grant. He's the best forensics guy in the Southeast. Try and keep the locals far away from here long as you can. I need some time with Larry before they come and contaminate the scene."

"Can we do that? Not inform the locals?"

"I'm doing it."

"What did you find there?"

"Something that needs Grant. And something not phone-friendly." He pauses, considers pacing, then realizes he can't avoid all the blood. "I need you here."

Rebecca can barely contain her excitement. "Really?"

"Yeah," Fowler says, already feeling guilty. "I really do."

Purposely leaving out why he needs her:

To keep Fresson occupied while he and Grant get the place scrubbed down.

36.

Kyle sits on a cement bench in the neon night waiting for Lara to emerge from inside a local market.

The severe heat, unleavened by the appearance of moon and stars, has partially dried his clothes soaked from the unexpected dive. He's still breathless, and gradually coming to realize it's going to be his permanent state until he finds Robinson. He's going to have to learn to live with his heart hammering and the feel of a spear in his side.

Right now though, he needs to focus on slowing his brain down long enough so something coherent can burst through the neuronal bedlam.

He begins with a dialectic that's served him well in the past. General Freudian castigation. He knows this situation is almost entirely his own fault, as much as he'd *love* to lay it all at Robinson's feet. It all goes back to his own overwhelming need for safety, and his inability to move past seeking it in the sanctuary of someone older or braver.

First, it was his father who turned out to be a fraud, although the most loving fraud Kyle could have asked for. All fathers are mostly faking it, and at least Kyle's dad got the *father* part right. He just happened to be on shakier terrain with the whole identity and truth thing.

Then it was Chandler who, in his modern-art mausoleum of an office, offered to become Kyle's new father, who promised to make it all go away, to make Kyle his rich and spoiled little boy. Kyle would be relieved of the burden of self. He could code all day. It would only cost him his freedom.

Next, Robinson sprang onto the scene with promises of deliverance, promises Kyle could avoid further pain if he followed instructions, continued to embrace entropy, went back to sleep, and let the adults clean up his mess.

That's how you end up like this, Kyle thinks. *You keep waiting for someone to come along and save you, to absolve you of responsibility. You do that dance long enough, and the inevitable happens: You get older; you get desperate; you get less picky about your path to absolution; and someone like Robinson starts to look like divine grace instead of a dime-store Satan.*

But this clarity, the result of a year of nothing but time to think, hasn't gotten Kyle any closer to the root of his current problem.

He needs to find Robinson, needs to find out why he seems intent on destroying the meager remains of Kyle's life.

And now his potential savior has come down to this:

Lara.

The one who jammed a gun against his forehead.

Yeah. Things have gotten to that point. And if Robinson was rough trade in a good suit, now Kyle's got to work with the woman who already boasts a body count of three and could charitably be called a wild card.

So he's got to double down on the killing machine, a woman who also happens to be—in one of those ironies peculiar to a God who also made asses the perfect height for kicking—the best kisser he's ever encountered.

Lara emerges from the market and snaps her fingers to prompt Kyle. "I can't believe you jumped in the fucking pool," she says, shaking her head. "Get in the car, Jacques Cousteau."

37.

Upon entering Robinson's hotel room, Lawrence Grant, one of Fowler's CIA brethren and a forensics specialist, utters: "Fuck."

Fowler's watched Grant work before. He's a guy so inured to carnage that his face remains a funereal tabula rasa even when confronted by the horror of a dead body left locked up in a hot room for so long that it exploded. To inspire Lawrence Grant to mumble "Fuck," someone has to leave behind a hot fucking mess.

Grant is silent as he combs the scene for potentially usable evidence, then he turns to Fowler and says: "Should have told me to wear my boots."

And he's not kidding. Not all the blood and guts have finished drying, and Grant's loafers are starting to look like part of the crime scene.

"I'm gonna check the closet," Fowler says.

Grant doesn't look back, continues to read the room, searching for the story. "Another one in the bathroom, right?"

"Yup," Fowler says.

Grant kneels beside the first Chinese man, puts down a briefcase. "I'll start with him."

"You need me out of the room?"

"No." Grant tosses Fowler a pack of surgical gloves. "Just don't touch anything."

"I know the drill." Fowler's walking toward the closet when Grant whistles and says, "Fowler. No smoking in here."

Fowler's about to respond when he looks back and sees Grant rooting around in what's left of the man's jaw, placing portions of broken bone and loose skin on the floor, while trying to extract part of a shell casing from what's left of the cheek.

Fowler's lunch rises to midchest and bubbles. He's aware of the deep contradiction. He has no problem maiming people when they're *alive,* but he hates to see bodies desecrated. It sickens him. For some unknown reason, he has far more respect and sensitivity for a body once it ceases to matter to its former occupant.

Fowler opens the door to the walk-in closet, puts a penlight between his teeth, and moves all the empty wire hangers to the end of the rail. He goes through the pockets of the clothing Robinson left behind, a pair of slacks, a purple-striped oxford shirt, a black blazer. They're all empty, nothing but lint.

Fowler peers up and feels around the top shelf. Nothing. No luggage.

Next, he drops to the floor and runs the penlight beam along the carpet. He crawls the length of the closet, reaches the wall, and feels something digging into his knee. He turns around, backs into the corner, and examines the object.

It's a poker chip. Bright red.

Fowler flips the chip and reads the number inscribed on the back. This chip is worth ten thousand American dollars. Not ten thousand riels. Ten grand is big money here. He holds it by the rim, brings it up to the penlight, trying to touch the surface gingerly to preserve any markings.

"I got something," he says to Grant.

"Come out here and get a bag," Grant yells back. "I'm busy."

Fowler leaves the closet, sees Grant is now working on the victim's back, and averts his eyes from the spinal spelunking.

"Bags are on the bed," Grant says.

Fowler pulls one out of a plastic dispenser, drops the chip inside, and seals it. "How long until you need the bathroom?"

Grant's cracking vertebrae in the victim's spine so he can root around deeper for an errant slug. "You got time." He's visibly sweating from the effort of pushing and pulling the man's body apart. "Can you turn up the air in here?" he says to Fowler while removing a serrated spreader and hacksaw from the briefcase, catching Fowler's stunned reflection in the silver teeth.

Fowler adjusts the air, drops the temperature to sixty-five. He hears Grant crack the victim's spine in several spots and doesn't want to turn around.

Christ, Fowler thinks, *the human body is a lot of effort. It takes a lot of sweat and tears to love it and an equal amount to destroy it.*

Fowler hits the lights in the bathroom, steps inside.

He steps over the seepage from the body in the corner, does a quick search around the sink, then looks inside the medicine cabinet, where he finds nothing except an unopened box of pills for nausea.

Fowler rounds the space between the sink and toilet, stops, lifts the toilet lid, and sees vomit inside. "Larry," Fowler yells, "I got some puke in here."

"And?"

"Do you need that?"

"I'm set."

Fowler flushes the vomit, then removes his shoes and steps inside the shower. He checks the walls for stray hairs, subtle prints, forgotten fluids. Doesn't see anything. Then he notices the drain. A small pool of water has collected around the stopper. He kneels down, pops the plug off with a small penknife, sticks his gloved hand inside, and exhumes a clump of hair.

It's long and wispy with split ends from too much blow-drying and the chemical treatment that turned it hot pink. Fowler holds it by its black roots and rises from the tub.

The hair still smells a little like avocado shampoo.

There was definitely a woman here with Robinson in the past few hours.

38.

Lara punches a code into the sunken keypad next to a drab gray door. A green access light pulses, and she walks inside.

The apartment's never been lived in; all the furniture and appliances are wrapped in clear plastic. An indistinct but conspicuous chemical smell suffuses the air, but Lara puts an end to it by lighting a cigarette.

"Come in," she says.

Kyle remains in the doorway, frozen. This is like entering Robinson's hotel room all over again. He's got the same eerie presentiment his life is about to change irrevocably and that somehow he unconsciously invited it to happen.

Kyle takes a few tentative steps inside.

"I said come in."

Her face, Kyle thinks. *Her body.* She's a literal *lustmord* in casual clothes. She and Robinson belong together. They both harbor some personal power that can't be articulated but could lure you willingly into just about *anything.* A power completely alien to Kyle, who's used to a world of charts and boxes, facts and figures.

"Whose place is this?" Kyle asks.

"A friend."

"That a good idea?"

"You got something better?"

"Isn't it dangerous to go to a friend of yours right now? All things considered."

"He's a friend of *mine*. Not Robinson's. He's just a businessman."

"That's what Robinson told me *he* was. Seems like everyone's a businessman these days."

"This guy's a salesman."

"Another booming field."

"I *fuck* him. Okay, I fuck him for old times' sake. He doesn't know Robinson. He doesn't know what I do He's the first person I met when I came to Europe. He thinks I study fashion. He brokers apartment complexes all over the Middle East and Southeast Asia."

"Oh," Kyle says with a hint of disapproval.

"Oh? The fuck is that?"

"I thought you and Robinson..."

"What?"

"Were a...thing."

"You don't know anything about me and Robinson."

"I don't know anything about you, period."

No response.

Kyle looks around the apartment, trying to find some speck of human warmth. "Can I have a glass of water?"

"You want me to get it for you?"

"No. It's just...this isn't my place."

"Not mine either," she says. "Sink is over here."

Kyle opens up several cabinets looking for glasses, but they're all bare except for floral shelf paper. He turns on the tap, sticks his lips to the faucet, and drinks until his tongue doesn't feel like it has a sock wrapped around it.

Lara leans against the counter, pitches the cigarette into the sink—where it dies with a soft sizzle—and folds her arms.

"At the hotel," Kyle says, "you said you needed me to be Robinson."

"There are people I need to talk to," she says. "People I can't talk to without Robinson. I don't have him. But I have *you*. You can open a lot of doors for me."

"I barely knew him."

"How well does anyone know anyone?" She locks eyes with him. "You need to find Robinson to get yourself out of this. I need to find him too."

"Look. There are other options. We have similar problems. I'm sure we can come up with something."

She looks at him like he's an insect she's *allowing* to fly around the room. "You and I have very different problems. We just have the same solution."

"You don't think very much of me, do you?"

"Why should I?"

Kyle knocks his knuckle against his front teeth. "I don't know."

"Are you always so... direct with your questions?"

"No," he says. "Seems like only around you or Robinson." And it's true. There's something about the sphinxlike quality of these two that makes him want to confess his deepest sins.

"Well, if I may be as direct as you," she says, "you're not the only one who Robinson's fucked over recently. And you're going to help me undo that."

39.

Lara's never been comfortable alone in a room. Being alone in *life,* that's a different story, but being alone in a room horrifies her. She doesn't want to remember how many men and women she's spent a night with, weeks with, months with, just to avoid the terror of the empty room. She's currently fighting the syndrome by watching television, listening to synth-pop through ear buds, chain-smoking, and painting her toenails.

She figures her phobia probably stems from her childhood growing up in Russia in that grim, functional brutalism called public housing. Several families crammed into two or three rooms at the State's largesse. She never had a room of her own, was unprepared for the privacy and spaciousness of the West.

Robinson used to tell her that never having had her own room made her far more adapted to the world than someone who had grown up like he did. "Because this is a world both atomized and Balkanized," he'd say. "This world...our world...is about feeling alone and isolated and primed to explode no matter how many different sets of eyes are watching you. The room is never empty. Only you."

She takes an aggressive drag on her cigarette. The filter is stained red from her lipstick.

Kyle emerges from the bathroom, sits on a chair, and sinks into the cushions.

Lara turns down the TV. "So this is what you need to know. No one meets Robinson," she says to him. "To the public, I am Robinson."

"So you're like his representative?"

"Not *like*. I *am*. I take meetings for him. I name a price. And if that price is right, Robinson decides whether he wants the job." She takes a long drag off a cigarette. Kyle listens to the paper burn. "Six weeks ago, Robinson disappeared. I don't know if he decided to go or if someone took him. But I haven't seen him since. And since he's been gone, he's fucked four jobs for me I had him booked for. So I've got to come up with the fronted cash or produce Robinson...or I'm dead. I can't come up with the fronted cash, because he's got it. So I've got to come up with *him*."

"Lara," Kyle says, "what does Robinson do?"

"Whatever you want him to."

"Such as?"

"When I met him, he had just been in the Balkans. That war was his first gig. He was working on shoring up the mines in Kosovo for the occupation forces. Coal mines. He was working with the Germans, the U.S., and the KLA. He never told me who ran him. But it didn't really matter...no one actually runs Robinson. He was also operating an escape line for Bosnian Muslims and a ratline for Serbs wanted for war crimes, making some pocket money for himself."

"Isn't that a contradiction?"

"That's what war is. Armed contradiction."

Kyle rubs his eyes. There's far too much moral ambiguity going on for him. "What types of jobs did you book him for?"

"Robinson studied to be a lawyer." She laughs. "He's capable of anything."

"Who runs him now?"

"No one. No one runs him. He's private."

"Are the Chinese his clients?"

"Not through me. I've tried to steer him away from the Chinese. They're *cheap*. *Notoriously* cheap. They don't want to pay for someone like Robinson. They'd rather blackmail or guilt-trip some first- or second-generation Chinese living in California or DC into spying for them. Chinese are the worst employers in the world."

"Okay, but..."

"Mainly he works with multinationals or the governments that control multinationals. That way he can use business as his cover. He *was* a businessman, so it comes natural for him. Then when Robinson finishes his assignment, he resigns and moves onto the next industry."

"He told me worked for a German telecom. VodaFone, I think."

"Right. He did. That's an old one. He used an old cover when he met you." She furrows her forehead. "Those guys who took you were Chinese... just like our friends in the hotel room. What did they say to you?"

"They kept asking me why I was in Cambodia and who my target was."

"The target..."

Kyle nods.

"It's not a deal of mine," Lara says. "I never made a deal for Robinson with the Chinese."

"Well, someone did. And, more important, I think that CIA guy got a good look at me before I jumped."

"Yeah. Your midnight dive. How good of a look do you think he got?"

"Good enough."

40.

Fowler sits behind his desk typing with two fingers aided by some occasional thumb music to the space bar. His inefficient typing method isn't helped by his desperate need for a stronger prescription for his glasses. It's gotten to the point where he sees better with them perched at the end of his nose, making him resemble some fin-de-siècle Austrian prince ruling his empire in a room of polished brass and painted ladies. He needs bifocals, but refuses. That's Fowler's hidden secret—even in his sixties, he's hopelessly vain. Warriors don't wear bifocals.

He reads over what he's written thus far and shakes his head, still pissed.

Rebecca walks in without knocking—as is her wont—stands before Fowler's desk, and says absolutely nothing, just fixes him with a subzero stare.

Fowler decides to break the ice. "Know what my least favorite sentence in the world is?"

Her gaze doesn't relent.

He continues, "'Suspect eluded capture because he dove from a balcony into a pool packed with German tourists, thus impairing my ability to fire a shot without risking significant collateral damage.'"

"Fuck you," she says. "How do you like that for a sentence?"

"Outside of the fact it's not a sentence"—he stretches his arms over his head—"it's not thrilling. But it does benefit from the absence of German tourists."

"You told me you *needed* me at the scene. You wanted me to babysit a comatose Frenchman while you and Grant did all the work."

"Which we couldn't have done if you hadn't kept him occupied."

"He slept the whole time."

"He took things pretty hard, what do you want me to say?"

She doesn't reply but obviously wants Fowler to say *something*.

"Look," he says, "Grant and I needed time. You're the only one I could trust with Fresson. What I did wasn't exactly following the rules the U.S. agreed on to get a station here. I needed Fresson occupied and not talking to the cops." Fowler sees this line of reasoning is getting him nowhere. "No one said this job was sexy all the time."

She gives up, sits down. "You are so not getting laid tonight."

"Withholding sex. Seems extreme to me..."

"I am extreme."

"I probably won't be in the mood anyway. I have to go see someone both you and I consider distasteful. And you won't be upset I'm going alone on this errand."

Rebecca leans in, her curiosity piqued, forgetting how pissed she is. "Who?"

"Pang."

"Passport Pang?"

Fowler nods.

"Sex-club, gambling-den, drug-running Pang..."

"His résumé is diverse," Fowler says. "To paraphrase Whitman, Pang contains multitudes."

"When did you start reading Whitman?"

"I was bored at your place one night. You were asleep. It was on your night table."

"Did you like it?"

"No."

She laughs a little. "How would Pang get himself wrapped up with Robinson?"

"Don't know. But"—Fowler pulls the evidence bag with the casino chip out of his shirt pocket—"I found this in the back of Robinson's closet. He must have left it behind when he bolted." He tosses it to Rebecca, who studies it under the flickering office fluorescents. "It's worth ten grand American," Fowler says. "Pang's got the only game in the town that lets people play for stakes that high and has the dollars to back it up. No one else wants that kind of risk." He motions to another evidence bag on the side of the desk. "I found that too."

"Hair?"

"A woman showered in that hotel room not long before everyone got dead."

"One of Pang's girls?"

"We'll find out." Fowler leans back in the chair, then starts typing. "Let me wrap this up. Sooner I shoot this off to Langley, sooner they can tell me what they've got about Robinson."

"You want to release photos of Robinson to the media?"

"The airport photos?" Fowler says, then answers himself before Rebecca gets a chance, "No. I sent them around to the locals and CIA in the area. But I don't want to get the media involved yet. Robinson is on a no-fly, so his travel options are extremely limited. If he wants to fly, he's gonna have to come up with a new ID, and that'll take time. Even here. As a client, he carries a lot of risk, so he can't just go to some forger. He's going to need good papers. That's time he doesn't have." Fowler leans in over the desk. "We've got him somewhat boxed in due to circumstance, but if we get the media involved, he's gonna panic, and we may lose him altogether. There must be something here he *wants*. I mean, he escaped from the airport and went back to his hotel. Regardless of whether those guys at the airport were friends or foes...he got away and still went back. That's either dumb or desperate. And if he was smart enough to get himself out of the airport situation, he's got a damn good reason to be here. I don't want to give him any additional excuse to try and run. We hold off on the media."

41.

Lara and Kyle located some glasses and are drinking vodka with ice. Kyle raises the glass to his lips, listens to the cubes crack, and then sips.

"I can't believe Robinson got himself mixed up with the Chinese," Lara says. "It's not something he would do."

"The Chinese certainly think he has."

"The guys who took you... what did they seem like?"

"Like they wanted to kill me."

"Right," Lara says, rolling her eyes. "What else? What were they wearing? Did you get a good look at any of them?"

"Suits. They were in suits. That's all I remember. They wanted to know who the target was. That's all they kept asking. 'Who is your target? And why are you in Cambodia?'"

"Target? What target?"

"You tell me."

"I don't know."

"Well... sure sounds like part of Robinson's skill set is murder."

"Someone like you or me gets murdered. You *assassinate* the people who Robinson goes after."

"So that *is* part of his skill set?"

"Part of it. His least favorite. He finds it anticlimactic. All that buildup for one good shot. He likes blackmail, interrogation... the things that last. The ones that make people remember him. If he's going to assassinate someone either the Chinese gave him a sweet deal or they have something big hanging over him."

"Christ," Kyle says.

"He's in a lot of danger either way," Lara says. "The Chinese. Did they seem like government or hired thugs?"

Kyle takes another slug of vodka. It hits him hard. "There's a difference?"

"Why can't you remember more?" She rises from the bed.

"Hey. You met one of them in your hotel room. You didn't question him either."

"Don't compare us."

"It was dark." Kyle runs through the litany: "I got Tasered, beaten. And then you killed everyone."

"Fuck."

"Sit down," Kyle says. "You're making me woozy."

"You have to help me find him," she says. "You're the one who threw me off my path."

"Threw you off your path? You found me, remember."

"And lost valuable time doing it."

"How am I supposed to help you find him?"

"I don't know. Just do something. Make yourself useful, for fuck's sake."

"I thought I was supposed to *be Robinson*. That's *my job*."

"Yes. But first we have to find a reason for you to be him."

"How am I supposed . . ."

"I don't know. *Think . . .*" She can't hold back her frustration. "We don't have much time. This place will be blown soon too. The CIA saw you; the Chinese are onto both of us . . ."

"Just sit down, okay?" Kyle says. "The room's spinning. I can't think and watch you at the same time."

She sits down but bounces her leg.

Kyle places the glass of vodka on the carpet, leans back in the chair, and closes his eyes.

"Are you fucking sleeping?"

Kyle keeps his eyes closed. "I'm trying to think."

Lara lights a cigarette and says through the exhale, "It sure looks like sleeping."

You used to be good at this, Kyle thinks. *This used to be your job. You used to be able to find anything. No one wants to be found. No one. This is just one man. One man who has to be somewhere on the grid.*

Kyle's always been preternaturally gifted at seeing the world as a network, as a series of interconnected nodes able to function without a center. Those talents made him a hot commodity during the tech boom of the 1990s, but to achieve real fame and glory, he needed al-Qaeda to come along.

So how did bin Laden inadvertently turn Kyle into a celebrity in the—granted, extremely small—world of networking engineers?

After 9/11, Kyle, like everyone else, was moved, shocked, and furious. However, he channeled those feelings and did something constructive with his rage. He used the concepts and algorithms of game theory, applied them to the exploding field of social-network analysis, and created a graph that in six easy connections linked all nineteen hijackers together.

He posted his thought experiment on his website and allowed the world—well, other network engineers—to take in his handiwork, the product of nothing but open-source data available to everyone on the Internet.

DARPA, the Department of Defense's research wing, had also been playing around with ways to link the nineteen hijackers. They had a twenty-foot-long chart and had been able to tie only twelve of the men together. The project had ballooned to such proportions that internal memoranda referred to it as the Big-Ass Graph, or BAG, program.

Kyle's six steps versus DARPA's ever-expanding org chart.

Harnessing someone like him could open up surveillance possibilities no one had ever considered. Actually, Christopher Chandler *had* considered them after checking out Kyle's website.

A week after he uploaded his results, Kyle received a call from the director of National Intelligence asking him to fly out to DC and brief his staff and certain private contractors about his methods.

Kyle spoke to a packed room about *information,* about how he was able to connect the hijackers with such ease. The information was already out there in plain sight. The knowledge base already existed.

He was able to do it so fast because it was already too late.

He compared it to when average people on the street are able to spot a trend. They're able to spot it because the moment has wound down, played itself out. The fad has reached maximum market saturation. Same thing with information. When you can make out the clear contours of a connection, you've already lost your chance.

He said the challenge facing national security was learning to think in nodes and networks. The agencies had to be hunters, not gatherers. They had to write algorithms that searched out valuable information from the outset, as opposed to the current institutional standard: suck up everything in sight and then write code to sift through it later. If you don't have an underlying information base, you end up with everything and nothing.

After Kyle finished talking, everyone in the room offered him a job, but only one invitation intrigued him. Chandler's. Of course, the man himself wasn't present. He sent his emissary, his omnipresent lawyer Thomas Lozen, to deliver a meeting request.

You got to the power behind the throne in Washington because you tied nineteen hijackers together faster than DARPA, Kyle thinks. *All you need to do now is turn that skill set to finding one man—admittedly, one who doesn't want to be found.*

What can he use? What was it Chandler always said when Kyle couldn't crack a problem? What was Chandler's mantra?

"Follow the money."

42.

L ara," Kyle says.

She perks up.

"If you were Robinson's public face, if people paid you, you must have access to his bank accounts."

"Yeah. But he changed his passwords. I can't get in anymore. I've had every hacker I know try to cut through. And they were Russians. They practically invented Internet scams."

"Show me where he keeps his accounts. If you show me, I think I can look around. If we find out where he's spending his money, we can track him."

"You're saying you can crack his new passwords?"

"I'm not saying I can or can't until I see it."

Lara gets up, walks over to the wall, unplugs her laptop, and hands it to Kyle. "Have at it."

After watching Kyle attempt to break through the encryption for a while, Lara declares she is officially bored off her tits and is taking a nap. She tells Kyle to wake her when he has some news.

Kyle asks if she's an easy person to rouse.

"Do I look easy?"

An hour and a half later, Kyle's biggest concern isn't how to wake up Lara without incurring bodily harm. No.

Not his biggest concern right now at all—*not by a long shot.*

Kyle was able to crack Robinson's account, find a recent transfer in excess of five million dollars to a dummy account, and then ferret out the actual identity of the mystery recipient behind a barrage of false cyber-identities.

And he really wishes he hadn't found his man.

For starters, Interpol has issued a red notice for this gentleman, which means cooperating countries are to arrest him on sight. Additionally, a chunk of his assets have been ordered frozen by Executive Order 13348—and the authorities plan to freeze said assets *once they can find them.* He's also been convicted in absentia by a court in the Central African Republic for document forging, and been asked to testify before The Hague for purported business dealings with several Serbian war criminals. If you Google this man's name, articles with headlines like "The World's Most Dangerous Gangster" and "From Red Mafiya to Royalty" flash before your eyes.

And then there's the coup de grace:

This gentleman was kicked out of Russia. Putin and his men considered his continued presence a risk to state power due his fathomless finances and personal army.

His name is Andrei Protosevitch.

And as Kyle's about to scream in abject terror, Lara does it for him. Kyle rushes over, holds her down. "Quiet, quiet. It's me."

She's thrashing around under the sheet, shrieking in her sleep.

He puts his hand on her forehead. "Quiet. Quiet, Lara. It's me." She starts to wake up, to recognize the room.

Kyle moves his hand away. "You okay?"

"Nightmare," she says. "Fuck...I was in such a deep sleep."

Kyle sits at the edge of the bed facing away giving her privacy until she comes down from the dream.

"It's the same one I've had for years." She reaches over for her cigarettes.

Kyle turns around, looks at her. "What's your dream?"

"Why?"

"You said it was recurring." Kyle laughs. "When I had a nightmare, my dad always told me to tell him about it. He said if you tell someone, you're not alone anymore. Dream can't get you then because you broke the bond between the two of you."

"You're serious?"

"Yeah."

"That's stupid."

"Humor me," Kyle says.

She lights her cigarette, takes a drag. "I'm waiting tables at this banquet on the top of a skyscraper. It's so tall that it's touching the clouds. The guests are all rich, almost royalty. I keep getting them more wine. I wheel out a roasted pig for dinner. They're all loud and fat and drunk and getting worse. And they never stop laughing. Even if no one's saying anything, they're all laughing. I bring around pieces of the pig for everyone, put them down on the table, and then... one of the guests puts a huge knife through another guest's palm. And they're both laughing. The stuck one pulls out the knife, laughs at the blood. He takes the same knife and puts it through the other one's chest, and that guy's heart comes out the other end. The one who lost his heart, he puts his hand through the hole and starts laughing harder." She crushes the cigarette, sick of smoking it. "And everyone follows suit. Just tearing each other apart with knives and hands. And I realize, These people can't die. They can't. And they do this often."

Kyle nods. "I'd wake up screaming."

"There's more. So, when they're not looking, I split. I run one level up to the roof. And I'm so close to the sky and the moon and all the stars. I hold my hand out and touch it, I touch the sky, and it's ice-cold. The sky is freezing. Then I start to cry uncontrollably. I can't take it that I've touched the sky and it's cold." She lies back down, stays silent for a while, and then starts to laugh. "I think... I think I actually feel a lot better."

"Told you," he says, going back to the chair. "You okay to talk?"

"Yeah," she says. "I'm okay."

"Well... this isn't much of an improvement over your dream. I got into Robinson's account. He just made an enormous transaction. And it all went to one person."

"Who?"

"It's bad ... really bad."

"Just tell me who."

"Andrei Protosevitch."

"Oh, Andrei," Lara says.

" 'Oh, Andrei,' " Kyle repeats. "Fuck yes, *Andrei.* I've been reading about him for the past hour. His press makes Satan look effete and ... balanced."

"He's all right, you know, once you get to know him."

"I don't want to get to know him. He's a fucking killer."

"So's Robinson ..."

"I know that now ..."

"Well, who the fuck did you expect someone like Robinson to be friends with? Lara points to the laptop. "We need to find out what Robinson paid him all that money for."

"I can't figure that out through the accounts. I only know the amount that was transferred."

"That's what we have to find out."

"How?"

"We ask Protosevitch."

Kyle's totally lost. "How? You going to call him or something?"

"No." Lara laughs. "No. You can't talk about something like this with Andrei over a phone."

"Then ..."

"We're going to ask him in person." She smiles. "You're on. *Robinson.*"

"No. No. No way," Kyle says. "No fucking way. The guy was thrown out of Russia. Putin threw him out of the country. *Putin.*" He's getting even more flustered. "And you want to just go there and *ask him* what Robinson paid him all this money for?"

"First off, he got kicked out of Russia because he had more money than the state and refused to give Putin his cut. He's a businessman ..."

"He's wanted by The Hague ..."

"I disregard all international courts of law ..."

· "*I don't.*"

"We're going to see him. Andrei's going to tell us what we want to know because *Robinson* is coming to see him. And *everyone* talks to Robinson."

"Impossible," Kyle says.

"Protosevitch and Robinson haven't seen each other in years. Ten years, at least. I see Andrei on Robinson's behalf. I mean, if I didn't *know* Robinson, I would buy that you're him."

"I cannot take a meeting with *Andrei Protosevitch*."

"Like you said, we have to follow the money."

Kyle breathes in. "We're going to get caught. And then he's going to kill us."

"You're probably gonna get killed regardless. And so am I," she says without any obvious opinion on the subject. "It's just a question of who does it. It's a shit state of affairs for the two of us right now. We need to stick together."

"But . . ."

"I'll get in touch with Protosevitch. Set up the meet."

Kyle sinks into the chair, can't get over his assignment. Needless to say, he's stressed. He closes his eyes and sees patterns of molecular upheaval, floating galaxies of anxiety, red streaks of cosmic pulsations portending his headache to come.

He raises his hand to his face, lets his forehead fall into its forgiving cup, and then looks down and sees his shirt cuff dotted with tiny drops of blood.

He's shocked; his thoughts scramble. Then he raises his hand to his nose. Dollops of blood streak his knuckles. He's really bleeding hard.

Shit. Not again, he thinks. This always happens.

He gets up, sprints to the bathroom, and Lara doesn't even raise her head.

43.

Kyle sits on the toilet, drops his head back, and pinches his nose tight with a wad of tissues. Since he was a kid, whenever his stress level shot up, it all came out through his nose.

He knows he can't be Robinson. He fucking *can't*. He met the man socially, had drinks with him in a hotel room. He didn't absorb a personality, and he certainly didn't meet the man Lara's been describing.

A professional black operative. A man able to make a call and get a friendly meeting with Andrei Protosevitch. *Protosevitch.* The guy has seventeen billion dollars the public knows about. Kyle doesn't even want to consider what you have to do to get that kind of money, although it seems like he'll have a pretty good idea in a few hours.

His nose is really bleeding; he feels faint. He tosses the soaked batch of tissues into the trash and grabs a new one.

Lara knocks on the door.

Kyle sniffles, says he's fine.

Lara opens it anyway. "What's wrong?"

"Bloody nose."

Lara looks at the pile of Kleenex in the garbage. "Christ. . . . You're gushing."

"I'm aware."

"Will you be okay?"

"Yeah."

"Are you sick?"

"No...I get these when..." He hangs his head.

"What?"

"When I'm nervous."

"Can I do anything?"

"Could you talk to me for a second? I know it sounds stupid but...can we just talk like two people? Not about Robinson or Protosevitch. Just talk to me. The way people do."

She kneels down next to him. "What do you want to talk about?"

"I don't know. Where are you from?"

"Volgograd. Used to be Stalingrad. Do you know it?"

He looks over. She's still in her lace underwear, having stripped down for her nap, and her bra barely contains her breasts. "No." That's the cruel part of desire—it always seems to present itself when you're at your lowest moments.

"You're not missing much. I got the fuck out when I was eighteen."

"Where'd you go?"

"Germany. Berlin. Friend of mine heard they were looking for au pairs there and signed up. I did too. Ended up being bullshit...got sent to work in a nightclub instead."

Kyle tosses the bunch of tissues and gets another. "So you were...trafficked?"

"Yeah. That's right."

"I'm sorry. Really sorry."

She lowers her head a little.

"Can I ask something?"

Lara nods.

"How'd you get hooked up with Robinson?"

"His best friend, guy named Radek, owned the club I worked at. Robinson came in all the time. I knew him a little. Robinson told Radek he needed a courier, someone to be his face. He asked Radek if he could have me."

"But Robinson is your...boyfriend, right?"

"In time, he was that too."

Kyle stares at the blood under his fingernails.

She looks up at him. "How's the bleeding?"

"A little better."

She keeps talking. "My name isn't really Lara. Robinson named me that. His favorite book is *Doctor Zhivago*. He said I reminded him of the girl in it."

"I read it in college," Kyle says. "You reminded him of a metaphor for the schism in a nation's soul?"

She smiles. "I guess I did."

"Do you still want me to call you Lara?"

"Yeah. I do."

Kyle pulls the tissues away from his nose. He's better.

Lara rises. "I'm gonna make the call to—"

"Don't say it," Kyle says. "I think I finally got things under control."

She nods, stands by the door. "Try to get some rest. You've got a big day tomorrow."

44.

The banana-yellow awning over the brick building reads, simply, *Lounge,* in Khmer. Fowler bangs on the red door—which vibrates from the pounding bass on the other side—and waits for four thick dead bolts and a chain to be undone.

The doorman stands before him cradling a collie puppy barking like a machine gun on helium. "Shhh, Songha," the doorman says as he puts the dog down. A cherubic snowball with a brown patch around its eye.

Fowler peers inside and sees the doorman's chair, a steel bar stool with arachnid legs. A Škorpion submachine gun rests where the man's ass was thirty seconds ago.

"Here to see Pang."

Party lights throw pinwheels of primary colors across the doorman. Reds and blues, emergency lights whirling to the beat. "He expecting you?"

Songha lies down at Fowler's feet and starts to chew on his shoelaces.

"No," Fowler says.

"Everyone gets announced." The doorman picks up the house phone. "Who are you?"

Fowler hands over his ID. The humidity is unbearable; you end up drenched standing still. He feels the salt sting of sweat streaming into his eyes.

The doorman dials a number, scrutinizes Fowler's ID. "CIA. Haven't seen you boys around here for a while."

"We've been busy."

"Whole War on Terror thing?"

Fowler smiles. "Yeah."

The doorman cradles the phone between his chin and shoulder, waiting for a voice. "Thought Obama ended that."

"The *Times* ended it. Obama still seems to be all in."

Someone finally picks up on the other end. The doorman utters a quick Khmer sentence, then listens. "You can go back," he says to Fowler. "But you gotta leave your gun with me."

"Not gonna happen."

The doorman uses his massive shoulder to block the entrance. "Then you don't go back."

Songha perks up, sensing impending violence.

Fowler bites his lower lip. "Does Pang really pay you enough to fuck with someone like me?"

The doorman doesn't take much time considering. "He's in the back office."

45.

On a raised stage alive with blinking lights, a young local girl in a Stetson and a jean skirt karaokes. She works the microphone in her hands, oblivious to the sexual overtones. Behind her, on a flat-screen television, the lyrics bounce and stream, which is helpful for the audience, because she's massacring the song.

Rapid lyrics don't translate to the torpor of the Khmer tongue without casualties.

In the lounge area, a gaggle of young girls entertains the local press corps—middle-aged men with pitted salamander faces. They lean back on leather couches while the girls straddle their chests or sit in their laps.

One of the girls puts a reporter's hand over her hint of breast, takes a hit of smoked heroin, and blows a thick cloud into his mouth.

Two others have gone down to their panties for a reporter who sits there looking as if he can't be bothered to glance at the pair scissoring each other on a sofa.

Fowler looks over at the two girls. One has pink streaks in her hair. The other one has red. *Yeah,* he thinks. *I've come to the right place.* Find clues in a reprobate foreigner's hotel room, and they'll likely lead you to Pang.

In a room cordoned off by a muscular gargoyle of a guard, Fowler sees a soccer game playing on a flat-screen, sees a blackboard listing the teams, sees men holding fistfuls of bills before a roulette wheel, sees the elderly feeding coins into slot machines and drinking down complimentary beer.

The gargoyle telegraphs a message: *Move it the fuck along.*

The reason Pang took it upon himself to "entertain" the press corps had everything to do with that room. A few months ago, one of Prime Minister Hun Sen's men went into an underground gambling den and lost close to eight hundred grand in one evening, and the press broke the story. In a country where the bulk of the population lives on less than a dollar a day, it caused a furor. If a government minister could afford to drop that kind of money, then surely those corruption charges must be true.

In response, Hun Sen ordered his officials to shut down the dens and told citizens it was their solemn duty to tip off the government if they knew of any establishments his people had missed. He even set up an anonymous hotline.

Pang decided the easiest course was to get the press corps laid and throw them a few hundred American a month. They were the reason the dens got busted in the first place. So Pang fed them girls and drugs, and they in turn fed Pang's disinformation to the people and—more important—Hun Sen's ministers, and in record time, Pang was back up and running.

Gambling is an essential and tragic piece of the Khmer DNA. Fowler's seen men bet on the amount of rainfall during a monsoon. When the storm passed, the guys would get a ruler, climb up to the roof, and crown the winner.

Fowler reaches the end of the corridor, bangs on the door to Pang's office.

46.

Pang answers after undoing four or five dead bolts and a chain and punching in a code. He's on the phone, working the filter of a cigarette between his teeth like a nervous test-taker with a pencil while shouting orders in Khmer.

He beckons for Fowler to enter.

Fowler takes a seat, listens to Pang conducting heated business—although most conversations in Khmer sound heated to Fowler, since he understands about 20 percent of the content, at best. He taps his foot on the floor and lights a cigarette.

Pang finishes his call, tosses the prepaid cell into the garbage, where it joins a graveyard of junked phones. "I'm so sorry for making you wait."

"It's okay," Fowler says. "I've got time."

Pang dusts clumps of cigarette ash from his seat cushion before he sits down. "Oh no. You're an American who has time. You've been here too long, haven't you?" Pang laughs at his own joke. His English is functionally perfect; he speaks it with as much of a French accent as a Khmer one. "You'll have to excuse me...this is most embarrassing...but I can't seem to remember you."

"We met a while ago," Fowler says.

"Under what circumstances?"

The singer outside switches from Lady Gaga to Wall of Voodoo's new-wave classic "Mexican Radio."

"It's terrible, isn't it?" Pang shakes his head before Fowler can answer. "She practices every day and never gets any better. It's a sin, an absolute sin, what she does to music."

Fowler nods and smiles. "It is...certainly awful."

"But she's my niece...what can I do? If I don't let her sing, God knows what she'll do with her mouth."

"Not a lot of good options for girls her age around here."

"Not at all."

Fowler takes a drag off his cigarette. "Passports. That's how we know each other."

Pang remembers, then tries to laugh it off. "Such an unfortunate incident. Really. Not the best foot for the two of us to start on. And your name again?"

"Fowler. And the unfortunate incident, *Pang,* was that I had to let you go. You were guilty as hell. I found a whole box of stolen passports in here."

"That's not my line of business anymore, if it ever was," Pang says, coy. "So if that's why you're here, we have nothing to talk about."

"It's not why I'm here." Fowler reaches into his pocket, places the ten-thousand-dollar chip on Pang's desk. "It's one of yours."

Pang picks it up, holds it to the light. "There are dozens of casinos in this city. Maybe more."

"None of them let people play for stakes like that. *You* do. Because you're the only one who can guarantee that kind of payout if someone wins. Because you got your little nonexistent passport-and-prostitution business."

"Is that all?"

"I got more."

"Continue."

The way he says *continue* makes Fowler realize Pang's most irritating quality: every word he utters sounds like an act of martyrdom he's enduring on your behalf. "This guy," Fowler says, and hands over the photo. "He was here recently. I found your chip in his hotel room. You see him? Remember him?"

Pang glances at the picture. "Doesn't look familiar. But I do most of my work back here. I don't often mingle with the customers."

"Even when they're dropping ten grand a hand?"

"I have people for that."

"You've also got a pink-haired dancer. I know you do. I saw her when I came in."

"I very well could," Pang says.

"You very well do."

"Look, Mr. Fowler. I don't hire the girls. I don't mingle with the customers. I run this club. I do all my work from back here. I'm not the ... concierge," he says, with evident distaste.

"I found some of what I'm pretty sure is her hair in the shower." Fowler points to the photo. "In that man's shower."

"And what did this man do?"

"Escaped from the airport, killed two men that I know of, eluded me at a hotel."

"Oh, dear." Pang leans back in his chair. "But, you see, I don't know him. I've never seen him. He escaped from you?"

Fowler grits his teeth. "He did."

"Obviously this is personal, then."

"Do you know him or not?"

"I told you no. But what I can do is let you talk to the girl with pink hair." He laughs. "Really. I don't even know her name." He picks up the phone, dials, waits for someone to pick up, and then speaks in Khmer to whoever's on the other end.

"She'll be here in a moment," Pang says.

47.

About thirty seconds later, instead of a supple private dancer with hot highlights, two of Pang's personal bodyguards come into the office, and tip Fowler's chair over before he has a chance to react.

While Fowler's splayed on the floor, one bodyguard puts a boot on his throat. The other puts similar footwear across Fowler's knees. They've got him trapped.

Fowler cranes his neck to the side, sees Pang bolt out the emergency exit, which sets off the fire alarm.

What Pang's guards don't know—and, really, how could they?—is that Fowler hasn't had a chance to inflict violence on anyone in a while, and instead of getting rusty, he's been hoarding his worst impulses.

Fowler sizes up the situation, readies his attack. The first thing Pang's guys have going against them is they're bulky and squat. Too may steroids and not enough natural height. Fowler can use gravity and their mass against them. Plus, like most rank amateurs, they thought securing Fowler's legs was the crucial thing, not realizing someone with his kind of training is equally fluent with his arms.

Fowler reaches up to the one with a shoe on his throat, grabs his nuts in the palm of his hand, twists, squeezes, and drags him down to the floor by the soft sack.

That guy is downed, disabled, and rolling around the carpet screaming in falsetto.

Fowler takes care of his partner in five seconds with a few well-placed chops to the windpipe and neck that rob him of consciousness. His eyes roll back and he lands on Pang's desk.

Fowler takes half a second to catch his breath, fight the burning in his lungs, and he can't help but laugh as he thinks:

Yeah. I think that chip definitely was Pang's.

Fowler unholsters his gun, barrels through the emergency exit.

48.

Fowler rushes into the street—lozenges of city light streaming over him—and spots Pang jumping into the back of a tuk-tuk.

Fowler points his gun at him. "Pang. Stop. I'm the goddamned CIA. Don't do this."

Instead of the desired—from Fowler's perspective—effect of freezing Pang in his tracks and forcing him to walk over with his hands up, Pang turns around and squeezes off two shots at Fowler.

Fowler ducks, and even though both shots miss, the margin isn't exactly comfortable.

Pedestrians and tourists scream, scramble from the bullets, block Fowler's field of vision. He loses Pang in the shuffle.

Fowler sprints over to the tuk-tuk, gun drawn. Pang isn't in the backseat anymore.

Fowler turns the gun on the tuk-tuk driver and yells, "Where the fuck did he go?"

The driver points across the street, to a hotel that burned down a few weeks back. The building's scorched spine has been converted into a squatter's shack, like any city property, charred or not, left unoccupied for more than twenty-four hours.

The exterior is gone—you can see into the rooms, and they're packed with families existing in lurid semidarkness.

Fowler cuts across traffic, holding up his hand, making his gun apparent, and bolts through the gaping tunnel that used to be a door.

Pang hauls through the lobby, a crumbling crematorium of scorched furniture, unsettled floorboards, and stray pages of financial documents and guest logs that fly through the asbestos air.

Fowler fires a warning shot at Pang. "Stop!" he yells, coughing. The air is noxious. He can hardly breathe.

Pang is running too fast to turn around and shoot at Fowler.

Fowler picks up the pace, gags.

Fowler's right on Pang's ass but can't overtake him; the bastard's too fast and lean. Fowler pivots, lunges forward, grabs Pang by the shoulders, and tries to drag him down.

But Pang's built up too much momentum to stop, even with Fowler hitching a ride on his shoulders. He ends up dragging Fowler for a few feet before crashing into what remains of a wall. Given their combined weight, they go right through it and end up back on the street, covered in plaster and ash.

They're on their backs, coughing, wheezing, trying to recover from a high-speed chase between two unrepentant chain-smokers past middle age.

Fowler rolls over, plants his knees around Pang's torso, shakes the plaster from his hair, then hauls off and punches Pang in the face.

Pang responds with a piglet squeal, shocked and annoyed. "That wasn't necessary," he says, wheezing.

"Yes, it was," Fowler says. "You're an asshole."

Fowler rises to his feet, pulls out a pair of flexi-cuffs. "Send in your fucking boys to work me over." He kicks Pang in the ribs, hauls him to his feet, and cuffs his wrists. "I know you know Hun Sen, but you still don't get to shoot at me." He marches Pang in front of him back toward the club. "Now I get to meet this girl with pink hair you don't know."

49.

Kyle stands before the bedroom mirror, knotting a silk tie and studying his face. The swelling has gone down, but his lips and cheeks don't sync up with the rest of his features, like the work of a carpenter stuck with an uneven level.

Lara steps out of the bathroom toweling her hair, which when wet becomes a basket of black ringlets. She hands Kyle two thumb-size bottles of Absolut left over from her plane ride. "Found them in my luggage. Liquid courage."

Kyle stares at them in his palm. "Thanks."

She walks over to the bed, opens her suitcase, and takes out a small safe. "Robinson never brings his jewels with him on business. He always has me carry them." She puts a key in the lock. "They're yours for today."

She puts a pinkie ring the size of a doorknob on his finger, hands him a diamond-encrusted watch that twinkles like icicles in the sun, then wraps the same watch around her own wrist. "For our anniversary."

Kyle looks at the watch up close, astounded by the wealth. "Christ . . . where do you get something like this?"

"You don't." She laughs. "It's custom. Everything Robinson owns is custom. The suit you have on. Linen. Hand-sewn for him in Milan. He never wants anything that isn't made specifically for *him*." Lara notices Kyle hasn't cracked open either of the bottles. "Drink up."

Kyle downs the first shot, grits his teeth. "Can I ask you something?"

Lara adjusts the towel tighter over her breasts. "Go 'head."

"What you *did* to the guys who kidnapped me . . . they never stood a chance. From what I could hear, they barely had time to draw on you. And you didn't miss. How did you do that?"

"My brother was ten years older than me. He was a soldier, won medals for his shooting. Best sniper in the army. He was sure Russia would be invaded by the Muslim caucuses one day and he might not be there to protect us. I was the most athletic one in the family, so he taught me how to shoot." She points to the tattoo that wraps around her shoulder and trails toward her neck. "That's for him. We lost him in Chechnya."

"I'm sorry."

"I don't think he planned on coming back. That was his last stand. He was making one last kamikaze effort to save the empire personally. For that alone, he was the most honest man in Russia. It wasn't about terrorism or Islam to him. He was too pure. It was a total property grab."

"Robinson know your brother taught you to do that?"

"Sure, but that wasn't his main interest in me. Robinson's capable of all that on his own." Her eyes zero in on him. "And since we're asking questions, I got one for you."

"Okay," Kyle says, not sure where this is going.

"I Googled you last night," she says. "And got about ten million hits. You've been holding out on me. Holy shit right, you got *some* passport issues. You worked for Christopher Chandler. They called you Chandler's brain."

Kyle nods. "Not at all . . ."

"Come on. You're famous. I know all about you. I've read about it for months. I didn't recognize you."

"Why would you? I'm not *me* anymore. I'm supposed to be Julian Robinson."

"Right," she says. "So you're a genius or something. That's what everyone says, right?"

Kyle can't help but smile. "If I'm a genius, why am I in this situation?"

"I'll give you that." She laughs. "But you really do what they say?"

"No."

Lara's eyes search him. "So why'd you run?"

"A lot of people who I didn't want to talk to really wanted to talk to me."

"So those people think you did it."

"That's right."

"Like that guy Kuo. The Senate guy. He's on TV all the time talking about you and Chandler. He really doesn't like you."

"Right. Which is how Robinson got me into this. He told me he had info on Kuo."

"It might not have been a lie. I'm sure he does. He has info on everyone."

Kyle takes another drink of vodka. "Not much help to me now."

"Okay, but still, holy *shit*. You're a total celebrity," Lara says. "You're way more wanted than Robinson. Think about it, right? That's kind of crazy."

"It's something."

"All the tech guys I know in Europe and Russia . . . you're like their god. When the newspapers printed what you did for Chandler . . . I mean, wow. But you didn't do it, so what does it matter? Now I've got no story for them."

Kyle avoids her eyes.

"What's Chandler like?" she asks.

Kyle shrugs. "As a person?"

"You go around the world, everyone's got a theory about him. Go to the Middle East and they think he was the real U.S. president for eight years."

Before Kyle can answer, Lara's cell phone rings. She checks the number, picks up, and answers in Russian. The call is quick, thirty seconds at most, no pleasantries.

"Andrei is expecting us in an hour," she says.

Kyle tries to hide his panic, but it comes out in his hands, his feet, and his right eye, blinking back fear.

"How's your nose?"

Kyle breathes in. "Okay. Tell me straight. Andrei doesn't buy this, neither one of us is walking out of there. Right?"

"That's right."

"And if things go wrong, there's no way you can shoot us out of this one?"

"Nope," she says. "So you gotta do good and get us what we need."

Kyle feels the pressure building in the center of his forehead and trying to run an express line to his nose. He takes another shot of vodka.

You are Robinson.

You are the kind of man who can walk into a room and collapse it to your will.

50.

Pang is one pissed-off translator. He holds a pack of frozen vegetables—broccoli, to be exact—against his steadily swelling cheek and lips. Occasionally, he removes the frozen food from his face and shoots Fowler a withering look complete with some lip-smacking to reinforce his already evident displeasure.

Fowler sits across the desk from Pang. He's not in a much better mood than Pang, but at least he's getting to talk to the two girls—Pink Hair and her partner in crime Red Hair—and they remember Robinson. The girls speak simultaneously in overlapping sentences—like a Cambodian Robert Altman movie—and then Pang translates the Khmer for Fowler.

Fowler can't help but be distracted by their appearance. Pink Hair wears a silvery, spangled bikini that resembles Christmas tinsel and is held together with a few gold rings. Red Hair wears a structurally similar two-piece but in gold and with one breast that refuses to stay housed. Every time she bends over to scratch a series of mosquito bites on her ankle, Fowler gets a glimpse of her pierced nipple.

Fowler's never interrogated a woman who is basically naked, much less two of them. When he first arrived in Southeast Asia years ago, as a kid, he was under the impression that the people—especially the women—were liberated and laid-back when it came to their bodies and nudity. Flesh was another fact of life; sex was just something you did. It didn't come wrapped up with oppressive feelings of sin and guilt, like back home.

When he came back to Cambodia a few years ago, past his sexual prime, he realized the nudity here was something far sadder and insidious than he'd thought. Some of these girls working at Pang's have been part of the sex trade since they were eleven or twelve, some even before they got their first periods. Walking around half naked is habit for them. It's what they do at work. It's not comfort in their own bodies; it's forgetting they own their bodies. Point of fact, there's nothing particularly embodied about Pink Hair and Red Hair at all—they are ghosts to themselves.

"Mr. Robinson," Pang says, "apparently was quite memorable. He came into the club, had a few drinks, and then started a gambling binge. He played for hours, winning and losing huge sums. Tens of thousands. Betting however the mood struck him. He wasn't there to win. He said to the girls ... hold on ..."

Pang consults with them.

"He said when he gambled, he played against God. Not the dealer or other players. He said some people say God doesn't play dice, but his God *does*. He said on that night, he had gotten the better of God, but it didn't always go that way. The girls liked that. Liked his attitude." Pang raises an eyebrow. "They liked *him* very much."

Fowler's taken aback. "How do they know so much about him?"

"Mr. Robinson spoke Khmer," Pang says. "Spoke it quite well."

Christ, Fowler thinks. *Who the hell is this guy?* "When did Robinson start talking to the girls?"

Pang asks. "He didn't. The girls came up to him because he was winning huge sums. The three of them hit it off. Robinson would let the girls play hands for him while he disappeared and made phone calls. He let the girls keep the money they won playing for him. After he had enough of gambling, he asked the girls to come back to his hotel. Both of them. They accepted."

Fowler crosses his legs, leans in. "Didn't he cash in his chips?"

Pang consults with his girls again. "No," he says to Fowler. "He

175

just wanted to play. He didn't care about the money. He just liked the game."

Fowler watches Pink Hair. She's so thin that her tattoos move with her bones, so thin you can watch her breath start in her lower abdomen and make its way to her mouth.

"Where was the hotel?"

The girls give Fowler the address and room number, and it's the same place he found Robinson. He bites his lip to avoid a smile, knows he's getting closer. "What happened at his hotel?"

The girls talk for a while as Pang nods, letting them go on. "Robinson wanted to be dominated and to watch the girls. He wanted to be tied up. He wanted to be whipped... hit. He wanted to be made love to with a tightening belt around his neck. He liked to watch the two girls, put them in exact positions. He was very *exact*." Pang shoots Fowler an evil eye. They are never going to get along. "The three of them stayed up all night and most of the next day, coking and fucking. They said he was inhuman. He never got off himself, and seemed to have no interest in it. He just wanted to keep going."

Fowler pulls out a pen. Writes down two notes on a pad. *Control freak. Likes to stage-manage.*

"Mr. Robinson told them how much he loved it in Southeast Asia. Said he felt at home here," Pang says.

Fowler takes more notes. "Did he mention to them where he was from?"

Pang asks; the girls answer. "No. They think he was either an American who spent a long time abroad or a European who worked in America. There was something about the way he talked... they couldn't place it."

Fowler puts down the pen. "Were the girls scared of him?"

"No. They liked him," Pang says. "They said he wasn't like most tourists or politicians here. He was actually having fun. He was interested in pleasure. They hope he comes back soon."

Fowler smiles, nods to the girls, and uses the only Khmer he knows. Thank you so much, he tells them. You have been most helpful.

51.

The two girls leave the room in a cloud of body glitter and the smell of stale champagne.

Fowler watches them go, then turns to Pang. "All right. On your feet. You're coming to jail."

"You're arresting me?"

Fowler nods several times in quick succession. "You bet."

"Mr. Fowler. Why must we keep doing this? You know I won't be in jail for more than ten minutes before someone lets me out."

"One: I don't think so. You shot at a CIA agent. Even Hun Sen might agree you need to do a little time for that. And two: If they do let you out in ten minutes, I'll just follow you day and night until you do something else I can pick you up for. Even if you only stay in jail for ten minutes, it'll sure make me feel better. Besides, I'm really not that busy. I've got time to make your life hell."

Pang seems entirely shocked. "Did I really upset you this much, Mr. Fowler?"

"You *shot at me,* Pang."

"But I fully intended to miss."

Fowler motions him up with his hand. "Come on. Let's go."

"Really?"

"What part of 'I'm incredibly pissed off at you' don't you fucking get?"

"I see," Pang says. "I see."

"Glad we agree. Now up."

Pang stands. "Mr. Fowler, I could be of considerably more help to you."

"Not interested."

"Don't be coy. Of course you are."

Fowler knows this game, knows he has to play it carefully. Pang's played it longer and better. Fowler knows from experience *this* is the moment all interrogations work toward, the moment when you and your prey have to take a leap of faith together and believe in each other.

It's like falling in love with attached electrodes.

"If I tell you what I know, then we forget this whole situation."

"Depends on how good it is," Fowler says.

"It's very good," Pang says.

"I'll be the judge of that."

"You must promise if I talk, you won't arrest me."

"You shot at me."

"Mr. Fowler. Do you think I would have shot at you if I didn't have a backup plan in case it didn't work? I'm no fool. I don't go around shooting at the CIA. I'd have preferred not to talk to you, but if I had to, I knew I could get you to forget a few friendly shots."

Checkmate, Fowler thinks. "All right," Fowler says. "I'll bite. God knows I'll probably get another crack at you soon enough."

"You say you are hunting Robinson," Pang says. "However, the man in the picture you showed me... that man is not Robinson."

Fowler sits down. "Okay..."

Pang sits down too. Things are cordial again. "I lied to you. I did meet Robinson when he came in here."

Fowler pulls out a cigarette, doesn't bother hiding his sarcasm behind a plume of smoke, "Shocking, Pang. Shocking."

Pang ignores him. "However, I have also met the man in that picture, and they are two completely different people."

"Pang, if you are fucking with me, I swear..."

"The man in your picture is not the man who was in my casino two days ago. The man *you're* calling Robinson I met six months ago. He said his name was Andrew. I assume it's an alias, but Andrew is what he called himself when he came in here."

"What'd you meet Andrew about?"

"Documents. He wanted documents."

"And..."

"I told him I didn't deal in them."

"Okay," Fowler says. "But you referred him somewhere, right?"

"No. Andrew said I'd been recommended highly—"

"He mention who recommended you?"

"No," Pang says. "Can I finish?"

Fowler holds up his hands, a half-assed apology. "Go 'head."

"He said I'd been recommended highly and he'd wait to see if I could come up with something."

"And you didn't come up with something?"

"No."

"Did Andrew leave you a way to contact him in case you *were* able to come up with something?"

"He doesn't use phones," Pang says. "He left me an address where I could get a message to him."

"Okay," Fowler says. "And you're gonna give that to me, right?"

"Of course." Pang starts to scroll through his BlackBerry.

"Is that normal procedure? People not leaving numbers?"

"Yes," Pang says. "People change numbers here daily. Nothing about the address option struck me as odd."

"What was your impression of Andrew?"

Pang keeps working through his endless list of contacts. "Friendly enough. He definitely didn't want to hang around and talk. Had no interest in the girls, unlike our other friend."

"And the other Robinson, the one who came into your casino, how much time you spend with him?"

"Very little. He was on a streak. I came out to offer him drinks on the house."

"What was he like?"

"Lovely. A man very comfortable with his desires," Pang says. "You know how it is, Mr. Fowler. If someone's up, you keep him around as long as it takes to get the money back. No house wants to part with that amount in cash." Pang pulls out a sheet of monogrammed paper and scribbles down an address. "You'll find a way to reach Andrew there."

Fowler pockets the address. "I'm coming back if he's not there."

"Yes." Pang sighs. "I'm aware you are."

52.

Lara's car passes through a cloud of colored incense marking a Buddhist holiday. Wipers wash away the purple fog. They've been driving toward Preah Vihear, on the Thai-Cambodian border.

Kyle sits with his head tilted, near catatonic, trying to keep his brain from pouring out his nose.

Lara lights a cigarette, whispers, "You've got to hold it together."

"I am."

"You haven't spoken since we left."

"Neither have you," Kyle points out.

She doesn't respond.

Kyle sits up, drums his fingers against the dashboard.

"Take the wheel for a sec," Lara says to Kyle.

Lara gets involved in a series of text messages, gets frustrated, starts muttering.

"The Chinese are all over my associates," she says, pointing to her phone. "Guy named Dean just got in touch. He's a business friend of Robinson's. Said he was followed all day and then interrogated by a branch of the Chinese secret service." She drags on the cigarette. "Last night I asked a girlfriend to check on my place."

"Where's home?"

"Berlin. Someone wrecked it from top to bottom."

She hands Kyle her iPhone. He looks at the photos of what's left of her apartment. Someone cleared off the photos and pictures and took a sledgehammer to the walls. All the furniture has been sliced open and the stuffing dumped out. Food and papers lie haphazardly on the floor.

"They took my computer too," she says.

"Sorry." He hands her the phone. "Sorry that happened."

"Honestly," she says, "I always kind of hated the place. Robinson bought it for me. It's his taste. Not mine. When he gets me a gift, it's never anything I want or like. He thinks he knows better."

She stops short to let a dozen cows pass. They stare at her with empty moon eyes. Kyle looks to the side of the road, spots a python that's just eaten. The face is smug, satiated. Kyle watches the slow pilgrim's progress of dinner through the swollen scales.

Lara honks the horn, throws up her hands. The cows don't care; the snake snaps its head, its digestion disturbed.

She goes around the cows, and they drive through unvarnished rural poverty. Starving wild dogs living under shacks and terrorizing the inhabitants. A family sleeping in a hammock, limbs peeking through the netting, a treasure dredged from the sea. Busted barbed fencing, a thatched roof on fire from the drought, an unbroken field of baked dirt and banyan trees.

Then the radio dies without warning. No stations. No static. No signal.

"Where'd it go?" Kyle asks. He pulls out his BlackBerry. Frozen. Someone's jamming the area's frequency. He puts his head back and closes his eyes. "Fantastic."

Lara slows down.

There are two armored Maybach 62s blocking the road, all four corners of each car guarded by men with guns.

Kyle sits up and takes notice. "Shit," he mutters. "Shit. Is this normal?"

"What's normal these days, Kyle?"

One of the guards walks to the middle of the road and holds his hand up for Lara to stop. He's flanked by two comrades, both of whom slide H & Ks off their shoulders and aim directly at the car. They all sport the same outfit, triplets of the security-rental generation. Flesh-tone wireless earpieces. White shirts, no ties, buttons undone enough to show off seriously worked-out chests. Their matching black suits are standard issue straight out of Medellín—bulletproof.

Lara rolls the car to a stop. "Looks like we're on."

53.

They step out of the car and immediately the guards yell:
   "Hands. See your hands."
   As Kyle watches the three guards approach he wonders, Why do these private-security guys always seem to come in threes? Is it so if you shoot one, the other two still have someone to talk to?
   "Against the car," says one guard in an English accent. He's middle aged. Bullet-bald. Day or two of beard. Kyle figures he's probably former SAS fresh from pacification work near a pipeline. He knows the type; these are the guys who guard Chandler.
   English steps to the side, keeping his H & K trained on them, and sends his two associates over to search Lara and Kyle. They strip her of her Walther, run a wand and then a bug sweeper. One of the guards—fucker's got a neck thick as someone's thigh—decides to spend a little extra time searching Lara's legs and torso.
   Until English puts an end to it with a hand slice and a disapproving head shake.
   "Move," English says to Lara and Kyle, and he leads them to one of the Maybachs.
   "What about my car?" Lara says.
   "We'll take care of it." English says.
   "Need my keys?"
   "Not necessary."
   Lara brings a cigarette to her lips.

"No smoking in the Maybach," English says.

Lara and Kyle step into the car's opulent cocoon. The windows aren't blacked out; they're silk curtained. There's a flat-screen television in the corner. News is splayed across the screen—stock graphs like a sick man's EKG, insolvency fears, Chinese bitching about T-bonds.

The steel divide separating front and back opens. A guard turns around and tosses two black woolen masks sans eyeholes to Kyle and Lara. "Put them on," he says, and watches them do it.

As Kyle slides on the mask, he thinks, *Christ, I really hope this works out better than the last time I had to wear something over my head.*

54.

Hands pull Kyle and Lara out of the backseat.

"You can take them off," someone says.

They comply, wait for their eyes to adjust to the light.

They're encircled by eight guards—somewhere, these guys managed to pick up a few more. English steps to the front, dangles Lara's Walther by the trigger ring as if it were a pair of scissors. "We'll leave this in your glove compartment."

She nods.

"Now walk," English says, and points ahead to a private airstrip, smack in the middle of rural farmland.

Resting there is a personalized Airbus A380 superjumbo—one of only three such jets under private ownership—with the word *Comanche* written on the side in swirling pink letters, like the opening credits of a 1980s teen movie.

Kyle stops in his tracks. A few hundred feet away, the scourge of post-Communist Russia is waiting to see Robinson. And it's not like Kyle wants this to happen, but his legs freeze.

"We can't stop here," she says.

"I know. I'm just... I'm..." He whispers, "I'm *fucking freaking*."

"Hold it together," Lara says, and takes his hand for an instant. "I'm right here."

English shouts through cupped hands, "Shake it, boys and girls. No stopping."

Kyle stares at the body of the jet. The fucking thing is equipped with missile jammers. *Don't bleed. Don't bleed.*

Yes. This is worse, far worse, than you imagined, but you signed on for this. The minute you ran from home, you signed on for this. The minute you decided it was easier to take Robinson's passport than it was to face down your problems at home, you signed on for this. Protosevitch may very well be your road to Calvary. Your only hope of freedom runs right through this jet. If you have any interest in getting your life back from Robinson, you better pull this off.

Protosevitch stands at the top of the stairs, waiting for his guests.

He spots Lara and Kyle and starts to wave with his whole arm. A welcoming gesture—except he's got a .500 Magnum crammed down the front of his tailored slacks. He extracts the gun and fires twice into the air, which is so choked by humidity, that the shots sound like holding a shell to your ear. "That's how happy I am to see you. Hurry up inside," he yells, and opens his arms wide.

Lara starts up the red-carpeted steps, then turns back to Kyle. "See. He's happy to see us."

55.

Protosevitch greets them at the top of the steps. "Come in. Come in," he says, putting the Magnum back in his pants and ushering them into the gutted cabin of the jet, built to seat close to a thousand and converted into his own airborne condominium. "I can't wait to show you around," he says like an eager realtor.

He opens a gold door, something out of Bluebeard's legend, and leads them into the belly of the plane.

Inside, two of Protosevitch's adolescent sons are playing video games on a 3-D television. They're both dressed like proper Etonian schoolboys, in black shorts and blazers featuring the school crest, and they have similarly turned-out friends cheering them on while they play a first-person racing game.

Protosevitch ruffles everyone's hair to schoolyard shrieks, then kisses his sons' heads. "Don't stand so close to the screen, babies," he says to them. They all answer in unison, "Okay." The mélange of accents is striking: Russian, English, and French.

"I don't want to brag, but my kids are so popular in school. It's amazing they're mine. I didn't speak till I was five. My mother thought I was retarded." Protosevitch lights a cigarette. "I just didn't want to talk to her."

He flings open another gold door, this one leading to his gym. Housed inside is the newest Nautilus equipment; sleek cardio machines riveted to the floor and topped off with TVs; racks of glimmering free weights. His two teenage daughters are working with a personal trainer who's encouraging them to go lower to the floor with their squats. Dance music pours from a speaker, and the trainer claps along to it, reminding the girls it's bikini season and the tabloids are going to be all over the beaches.

In the corner rests a gleaming marble Jacuzzi. Protosevitch's wife lounges in it, totally nude, fake breasts floating atop the bubbles. She sips a margarita and licks the salt from her cartoon lips. Protosevitch's oldest daughter, noticeably pregnant and also noticeably *older* than his wife, is getting her shoulders rubbed by her baby daddy, a young man who clenches a cigarette between his teeth.

Protosevitch walks up and slaps him across the face. "Don't you fucking smoke near her." He drags on his own cigarette. "That's my grandchild in there. Breathing in all your shit. You fucking peasant."

Baby Daddy answers in a Cockney accent, "Sorry, Dad."

Protosevitch walks back to Kyle and Lara. "You like the place so far?"

"It's amazing," Lara says.

"Amazing," Kyle chimes in. Amazing, he thinks, how much it reminds him of the berserk splendor of Chandler's office, with its omnipresent marble, smoked glass, modern art, and wall after wall of framed awards and achievements. Amazing how the only difference between the absurdity of American and Russian splendor boils down to this: Americans use their wealth to celebrate themselves, while Russians use their wealth to celebrate *wealth*. This makes sense, given that one country is rooted in individualism and the other abolished private property for seventy years.

They walk down a long hallway, the space on planes where the air hostesses would hang out and bitch about customers. Protosevitch begins, "The terrorists can't get you...well, it's harder for them to get you if you have your own plane. There's five private airports to every public one. Terrorism is a middle- to upper-middle-class problem. It's why politicians run on it. 'Cause those are the people who vote, the people who fly commercial and could get blown up. If you're poor, you never take a plane, you never go anywhere, so you're safe...well, unless we're talking poor in Africa, then you're just fucked. I mean, I got so many people trying to kill me, I don't need to add Muslims to the mix."

Another gold door and into the kitchen. Protosevitch's personal chef, complete with chef's toque, rushes over, and the two men kiss. The chef leads Protosevitch to a bubbling pot, pulls off the lid, and dips in a spoon. "Taste," he says.

The kitchen is brand-new, practically untouched. Copper pots hang over a center island, and the metal shines under gentle chandelier light.

Protosevitch hugs the chef. "Your food is the only thing that gives me my home back." Then he pulls the Magnum from his pants, puts it in the microwave. "So the children don't get it."

A four-year-old wearing a tiara sprints through the kitchen and says, "Hi, Daddy! Bye, Daddy!" while the babysitter chases after her.

One more gold door and they enter Protosevitch's private office. Armed guards sit on the bloodred-leather couches, smoking cigarettes and playing cards. There's an aquarium built into the opposite wall in which iridescent fish float. Protosevitch turns off the television, and the gray face of the screen reflects the tank; glowing fish flicker across like shadow puppets.

"We're going to need some alone time," Protosevitch says to his guards.

"We'll be right outside watching everything on camera."

Protosevitch waves them off; he's had enough. "I love them, I need them, but I don't *want* them. Know what I mean, Julian?" He crushes his cigarette in a standing swan-shaped ashtray. "I started off poor and I was in danger all the time. I'm not poor anymore"—he motions around the room—"but I'm still in danger all the time. Tell me how that's fair."

There's a gap in the conversation. Lara realizes she needs to fill it. Kyle's trying to acclimate, not quite ready to assume his role.

"You look amazing, Andrei," she says. "So tan."

"We moved to the French Riviera. I love it there. It'd be the most perfect place in the world *if it weren't for the fucking French.* I tell you,

Lara, I tell you, the French don't deserve France. Most beautiful coun- try in the world, and its citizens treat it like shit. These ungrateful bastards act like Hitler won, like there's not a damn thing to be proud of in being French. Go to a café and listen...unbelievable. Where is their pride?"

"So you left England, then?"

"I still have my flat in Chelsea and the Fyning Hill estate. My wife is obsessed with England. She grew up under Yeltsin reading Victorian novels and Tolstoy. Russia hasn't had a proper aristocracy since the revolution, and since that crew is gone, it's okay for girls to want to be princesses again. To dream of horses and gowns and balls. The English countryside is the only place left that offers that sense of royal *tradition*. Fucking Bolsheviks destroyed it. Russians who grew up under Yeltsin, see, they have no tradition anymore. You know this. It's why my wife needs to live in a Jane Austen book." He scowls. "It's why Russia is dying, why Europe is dying. There's no tradition anymore. Who wants to bring children into a world where noth- ing means anything, where two and two make three? No tradition, *no fucking.* It's why in Russia they have to offer people cars and mi- crowaves to fuck. I love Russia. I'm still proud. It's why I can't stop *fucking.* I just fuck and fuck, even more since I got *invited"*—he spits the word out—"to leave my home. All my kids speak English and want to work in public relations and television. Fuck it all." He looks to Kyle. "Hey, handsome. Where's my hug?" He opens his arms. "Where is it?"

Kyle walks over with trepidation—the same death march you'd take to meet a girlfriend's father who is twice your size—and holds Protosevitch. His torso is a pack of muscles; motherfucker is a bear, wingspan like his jet's, the perfect melding of machine and owner. He puts his hands on Kyle's shoulders. "You look good. Lost weight like I told you to."

Kyle pats his belly. "You thought I was fat?" He's almost offended on behalf of Robinson.

"No. What did I say to you? Remember?"

Kyle mimics thinking, gives up.

"What I said was, you're too young to gain weight like that."

Protosevitch motions for them to sit. He walks over to his desk, pulls a paper bag out of the top drawer, and points to Kyle. "Little surprise for you." He sits down on the couch opposite them, legs spread wide apart. The way the man walks and sits—pure, unfettered cock. He holds the paper bag up. "Remember last time we saw each other?"

Kyle winces. He's been waiting for a question he can't answer; he just didn't expect it so soon. "God... I can't." He leans his head back. *Don't bleed. Don't bleed.* "It must have been... God..."

"I don't either. It's been that fucking long. Must be at least ten years." Protosevitch tosses the bag over to him. "A gift from Marseilles," he says. "Last time we met, you couldn't get enough of it. I remember it was your favorite in the world. And you would know."

Kyle opens the bag, looks inside; everything's bubble-wrapped. "Should I open it?"

"Yes, you should."

He tears through the packaging. A dozen fat vials of uncut cocaine. Protosevitch smiles. "You're shocked, right?"

Kyle nods, says, "Mmmm..." Having trouble finding a complete word to sum it all up.

"Didn't think I remembered?" Protosevitch nods. "I always pay attention to what my friends love."

Kyle smiles, tries to keep his reaction under wraps, and passes the bag to Lara. "Thank you, Andrei. You're too good to me."

"You're among people who love you," Protosevitch says.

Lara opens the bag and her eyes go huge, a puppy whacked with a paper.

Protosevitch cracks up, leans over, and slaps Kyle's knee. "And since you're here in the *flesh,* we can do it up together. Like old times. You first. You're the guest of honor."

"No, really... you go first."

"Nonsense." Protosevitch laughs.

Lara puts her hand on Kyle's leg. "Andrei wants you to go first."

"But I want him to go first... and then you."

"But *he* doesn't want that," Lara says.

Protosevitch laughs, looks to Kyle. "You take a sharing class? Last time I was with you, you'd break the arm of anyone who touched your stuff. You were all nose on that trip."

"Was he?" Lara laughs.

"All nose. Nothing the fuck but it."

Lara laughs, grabs Kyle's knee, too hard for it to be meant as affection. "I'll bet he was. Show me."

Kyle sucks on his lower lip. *You fucking bitch.* "So . . . I'm up." He opens a vial slowly, 'cause he's never done coke before. He's never done anything harder than pot, commonly considered a gateway drug, but not if your sole pot experience consisted of smoking up, watching *The Fifth Element,* nearly shitting your pants from paranoia, and hiding under your best friend Neil's bed.

So Kyle's abstained from drugs for seventeen years, and he's getting reintroduced with uncut French cocaine, kind of like a thirty-five-year-old virgin who decides to get it all over with in a gangbang.

Kyle sprinkles a trail of coke on the table and pulls out a credit card from Robinson's wallet.

"The fuck are you doing?" Protosevitch asks.

"I was going to cut it," he says, thinking back to every time he's seen a movie character do coke.

"Its uncut, baby. You just need a straw and away you go." Protosevitch looks down at the table. "Give yourself a real line." Kyle keeps sprinkling more and more. Protosevitch smiles. "Now, *that's* a real Robinson line. Whenever I'm among friends, I pour out a nice line like *that* and I call it my Robinson line. And everyone who knows you laughs."

Lara hands him a dollar bill rolled into a straw. Kyle grabs it, pissed off, and says like a petulant teenager, "Thanks." He plunges his head down and snorts the line.

It hits him in the heart, one hard shot, then branches out in clusters of pounding nodes. Pure electricity pulses through his veins. The center of his body radiates heat, throws off sparks.

And that's the first thirty seconds.

Instinctively, he grabs the table for support, afraid he's going to die.

Then he stabilizes, throws his head back, rubs his eyes, and feels the coke drip down the back of his throat like granulated snot, like sleeping on your back with a cold. He coughs. "Holy shit," he says.

"One hundred percent pure," Protosevitch says. "You're not gonna neglect the other nostril, are you? It's gonna get jealous."

Kyle lays out another line, looks at Lara and Protosevitch, and inhales it.

And before Kyle's even aware, he's out of his seat like it's on fire, walking around, shaking out his hands, doing a kind of coke-fueled chicken dance. "Andrei...Andrei, that is the real shit, friend." He raises his voice. "That is just the *real shit,* right *fucking* there."

Protosevitch and Lara crack up, although Lara's laugh has an undertone of nerves. "Getting loud."

Protosevitch swats that away. "No worries. The room is soundproof."

That snaps Kyle back to his senses. A soundproof room. That sounds like a reason to worry.

Lara sprinkles a line for herself, ponders it.

Protosevitch walks to a small fridge in the corner of his office, takes out a jug, sets down three glasses, and pours a shot in each one. "Robinson, I made this myself."

Kyle notes the glass jug. "What is it...is it moonshine?" He's talking fast and he can't feel his teeth, but he's in an incredible mood. "Is it moonshine? That's moonshine, isn't it?"

"No, baby." Protosevitch hands a glass to Kyle and then to Lara. "Red-pepper-infused vodka."

"Oh God," Kyle says.

Lara's rubbing her face. "Holy shit," she says. "I can't feel it...*my face is gone.*"

Protosevitch drops a line for himself, an enormous trail, like directions on a treasure map. "A Robinson line," he says, and his head plunges. He finishes up, resurfaces, and pours another line, even bigger. "That one's not a Robinson line. Know what it is? Take a guess."

Kyle shakes his head and can't stop, like a fish flopping on land. Lara says, "No idea."

"It's an *Andrei* line," he says, then cracks up and snorts the line. He picks up the glass of vodka and raises it. "To us. Back in business." He tosses the shot down fast, like it's water.

Kyle raises it to his lips. Lara leans over and says under her breath, "Do it fast. All at once."

He does, and as it blazes a trail down his throat, he springs to his feet again, screams, and then, to stop screaming, he switches to yelling, *"Andrei."* He pumps his fist in the air. *"You know how to party, my motherfucker."* And he keeps on yelling. *"Oh my God..."*

Protosevitch is doubled over on the couch. "That's the man I love. There he is. Just like Marseilles. This is just like Marseilles."

Lara pulls Kyle down to the couch.

Protosevitch leans back, lights a cigarette, then tosses his pack to Kyle. "You forget yours?"

Kyle takes out one of the cigarettes. Why not? He's already tried uncut coke. He's never smoked before, so he thinks back to Neil, whom he affectionately calls the human ashtray, and tries to summon his essence. Kyle pops the cigarette in his mouth, lights it up, takes a long drag, and stifles the urge to simultaneously cough and vomit.

Protosevitch leans forward, cigarette in his mouth. "I was flattered when you wanted my help on this one. I hadn't heard from you in a while. I thought you wrote me off too."

Kyle drags on the cigarette, head swirling, drunk, stoned, semistupefied, but—and he hesitates to admit it—kind of enjoying the hell out of it. "Why?"

"Well. I'm damaged goods. Too hot for most."

Kyle nods. "We all are."

Protosevitch laughs, and Kyle makes out at least three gold teeth. "But you didn't get kicked out of your country, *mon ami*."

Kyle can't help but smile. "I wouldn't be so sure of that."

"They'll never get rid of you. Baby, you are America. Only America could give the world Marilyn Monroe." He sprinkles another line. "Because she was America. She bedded down with everyone but was furious when anyone called her a slut. That's you. That's all Americans." He sucks up the line. "That's why Islam hates you more than anyone else. It's not just the foreign policy... it's the promiscuity... the fact you dangle your sexy little pussy in the holy land, sell it to the highest bidder." Protosevitch leans back, trying to make himself coke comfortable. "You're just like Russia before we went down."

"No," Lara says. "I remember when it happened to us. The States are a democracy. It won't end the same."

Kyle interjects, speaking from a coke-fueled site of knowledge and passion, "You really think democracy will protect you from the state?"

Protosevitch raises his glass. "And this is from a man who knows. A man who has been *undermining* democracy for the better part of his life."

Kyle sinks into himself. He's high, he's muddled, but Protosevitch struck a nerve. Undermining democracy. Christ, how much of Robinson does Kyle really have lurking inside? Was there a reason, outside of his looks, that Robinson chose him? Maybe he sensed some karmic kinship, something Kyle's been hiding from himself all these years—a certain leniency concerning the foundations of freedom.

Protosevitch leans in closer and puts his huge hand on Kyle's knee. Touching a normal human body is like palming a basketball to this fucking guy. "It does mean something to me that you came out of the cold to visit me. Even people without your... profile don't take the risk these days."

"Don't worry about it."

"No." Protosevitch is adamant. "It means something. It means we are friends. And it pleases me that you are here in person to collect the fruits of having me as a friend." He gets up, walks over to his desk, and selects a key from an overflowing ring. "I really outdid myself on this one, Julian. I was so sad at the thought of handing this over to one of your minions and not seeing the look on your face when you opened it."

Kyle says under his breath, "The hell is he doing?" while Protosevitch opens the triple-locked bottom cabinet of his slate desk.

Lara's response is a shoulder shrug. Kyle mimics her shrug, exasperated, and mutters: "That's all you got?"

She shushes him, whispers, "Let's see where it goes."

Protosevitch drops back down on the couch, whistling, and places two medium-size flat-panel cases on the table. "These can take a beating. I know you're gonna be working in tight quarters." He raps atop the cases with a boulder-size knuckle. "Ethafoam interiors. Static control. Retractable handle. Even had them sprayed and powdered with chemical-agent-resistant coating."

"Thank you," Kyle says, hoping that's the right tone.

Protosevitch can barely contain himself. "Open them up."

Kyle's positive there's a fucking bomb in there, swears he hears it ticking. He knows it's irrational, knows he's still jacked up on coke and paranoid. He knows all these things, but he's still convinced it's a fucking bomb.

He closes his eyes, pops the release latch, and hears the top opens with a whisper-click.

The smell is the first thing that strikes him. The case is brand-new, freshly oiled.

His eyes flutter open. He breathes in through his nose. It's not a bomb. Not at all.

Although what's inside isn't what he'd call a major situational improvement.

It's individual silver sections of the *biggest fucking rifle* Kyle has ever seen.

"I picked it out myself," Andrei says. "I knew you'd be working tight, so I had an engineer break it down into two small cases instead of one big one. That way you won't get weighed down. Isn't it beautiful? I mean, it is, right? Right?"

Lara pushes Kyle out of the way. She doesn't to want to minimize his importance in the conversation, but she is lusting after this piece of hardware. She runs her hand over the collapsed stock and the suppressor. "This is British."

"Right you are, my love," Protosevitch says.

She puts the pieces inside their slots. "What's the range?"

"Up to fifteen hundred meters." Protosevitch turns to Robinson. "That'll get the job done, right?"

Kyle has no clue. However, he's hard-pressed to imagine a job that a gun like this couldn't get done. "I'm certain."

Lara runs her hand over the pieces, listing off the attributes in a mesmerized state. "Bolt-action...iron sights...twenty-five-by-fifty-six scope...adjustable bipod...it's all here."

Protosevitch leans back into the couch, his bulk swallowed by throw pillows. "Did I make you happy?"

Kyle has no words, can only nod, but he does so *enthusiastically.* He feels like that's how one should respond to such a gift. Very enthusiastically.

Lara holds and balances the pieces in her hands. "It's lighter than it looks."

"Has to be," Protosevitch says. "Guys have gotta be able to lug that around the desert all day."

As Lara lusts and Protosevitch beams over his successful acquisition, Kyle's stress decamps from his nose and sets up separate condominiums of pain all across his face. His jaw throbs; his eyes blink and tear. He can hear the blood beating in his ears.

Holy shit, his whole face screams. *This is happening. A displaced Russian oligarch just gifted you a goddamn hand cannon.*

Protosevitch leans into the two of them. He's unable to stay in one position or, for that matter, one mood for more than thirty seconds. He seems to exist to destabilize. "For the thing tomorrow," he says, "you need something else?" He nods toward the case. "You're gonna want to be carrying something smaller than that."

Kyle knows he needs to calm down, to get deep into character, because this is the opening he's been waiting for. He has to make Protosevitch feel comfortable, feel like he's having the kind of conversation he and Robinson have presumably had before. He tries to get the words out, but they stick on his tongue and roll out in a lexical blur.

Luckily, Lara intercedes. "Smaller than that, yes. But still heavy, right?"

Protosevitch smiles, nods toward Kyle. "Like you always say: A body is something to be wounded. They think that way. So must we. You go heavy."

Kyle dives in, finds his voice. "What's the head count tomorrow? How many you figure?"

"The courier." Protosevitch raises his fingers. "Figure he's going heavy. Then figure in his backup. No one travels alone with intel like this. It's too valuable."

Kyle wants to ask how valuable but knows better.

Lara interjects. "Numbers?"

"Not sure. Just him and backup," Protosevitch says. "I wasn't able to get backup numbers on such short notice. I'm sorry. I could only get profile and price."

"No. No. It's fine. Time is something we don't have." Kyle breathes in, takes a big risk. "Same location as you said?"

"Yeah. Siem Reap," Protosevitch says. "Courier's plane touches down, then he hops the boat to the harbor. You'll find him once he lands. You got lucky on this one, Julie. It's tough to shake someone down in an airport. Harbor's gonna be much easier."

"Time?"

"Same. Ten thirty. Morning," Protosevitch says.

Lara cuts in. "Do we know if his backup is going to be local or Chinese?"

"It's gonna be Chinese," Protosevitch says. "No hired muscle from here is gonna make this guy feel safe enough. He'll want his home crew." Protosevitch leans back on the couch, lights a cigarette. "Now we gotta talk figures. The gun was bought and paid for. We're good on that. But for this shit, now, I've gotta ask for cash. Whether or not you pull this off, you're gonna be so hot afterward, I can't be seen taking a transfer from you. I'm already on everyone's watch list. It's gotta be cash. Especially if you're successful."

Kyle nods. "You'll get it."

"I know I will," Protosevitch says, with his first real hint of intimidation.

Kyle shares a look with Lara that radiates clarity of purpose.

Time to get the hell out of here and over to Siem Reap posthaste so they can crash Robinson's deal.

Protosevitch looks pensive. "Julian..."

Kyle meets his gaze. "Yeah."

"You that bored with living or something?"

"As in?"

"This job. You fuck it up, they kill you. You do it right, someone's gonna kill you for knowing. It can't just be the money."

"You're gonna talk to me about doing things for money?"

Protosevitch is almost insulted. "I never did anything for money. You know that."

"Then why?"

"I never told you?"

Kyle shakes his head. "No."

"I did it because...because no one stopped me."

Kyle's taken aback. Protosevitch sounds exactly like Chandler. The raging, near psychotic accumulation of power for no other reason than to see how much you can get away with taking.

Lara laughs. "Come on...getting rich has always been the secondary thing for you two. You're both lucky enough to make money off the things you'd do for free."

There's total silence, until Protosevitch cracks up and points at her. "She's right, you know. She knows us better than we know ourselves." He laughs even louder. "She knows you too well, Julie. You're gonna have to kill her one of these days."

56.

A woman wearing striped pajamas leads Fowler up the twisting steps of the guesthouse. Most women in Cambodia wear these *pajamas,* and Fowler—even after spending the better part of a war here—still has no idea why. He also doesn't understand the local women who go into the ocean fully clothed. It's not custom. It's not exaggerated modesty either. Not in a city where every third storefront offers a Bacchanalian catalog of bar-dancing and illicit carnality.

She opens up the room and silently leaves Fowler to his business. The floor-unit air conditioner has been switched off, and the room suffers for it. Fowler starts sweating before he even commences his search. He takes off his jacket, rolls up his sleeves, and abandons all thoughts of lighting a cigarette. There's not enough space in the air for smoke.

He approaches the bed, rips off the covers, runs his hand under the sheets, then tosses the mattress onto its side. Nothing. He sinks to the floor, takes a look under the bed, bare except for a few Diet Coke cans among dust bunnies.

The nightstand is next. A Bible, some allergy medicine, green-tinted antacids in a plastic wrapper, and an extension cord.

Fowler's trying to concentrate, to keep calm, but it's hard, because this is his favorite part of the job. He built his career on being a soldier, but snooping, being a voyeur with a badge, that's his passion. There's nothing more thrilling than rifling through someone's shit. And the best, the absolute apex, is when the site of your search is a woman's apartment. But not for the reasons you'd think.

Women are so much *better* at hiding their secrets. They really make you work to find them.

No time for fantasy. Fowler's got Andrew to focus on.

He moves into the bathroom, hits the lights. *Now, this is more noteworthy,* he thinks. The drain is clogged with thick clumps of brown hair. The sink's surface and basin has a sandpaper feel, courtesy of beard growth floating in shaving cream.

Fowler turns, checks out the shower. The tub and drain are sticky with hair-dye residue. And the garbage can overflows with stained rubber gloves, tubes of dye, a comb choked with hair, and several worn razor blades.

Fowler digs into his pocket, pulls out his phone, and takes pictures of the scene. *Someone left here in a hurry.*

Back in the bedroom, he runs his fingers along the wall, feeling for anything out of the ordinary. He stops at the picture of Buddha, studies it, gives the surrounding wall a couple of sturdy knocks, and then removes the Bodhisattva, revealing a small built-in safe.

There's a combination lock on it, nothing serious, just a twist-and-pull kind of deal. But Fowler doesn't have the time to crack it manually. He takes the butt of his gun, pounds the dial until it breaks, and then opens the safe.

Inside, there's a few stacks of American bills in small denominations, and that's it. Fowler's disappointed. The adrenaline juice of discovery fading in record time.

He takes another look around.

Sitting on the desk is a laptop. Fowler approaches it. *Fucking strange,* he thinks. This room he's in—Andrew's room—this guy clearly thought he was coming back at some point. You don't leave your laptop and cash behind if you're pulling a permanent disappearing act.

Fowler hits the power key on the laptop, and the screen comes to life. But before any information displays, the computer asks for a password.

Thing is locked.

Fowler's not a Luddite, but he's certainly not a hacker. He unplugs the laptop from the wall outlet and takes it with him.

57.

owler walks into the cafeteria at the Royal University of Phnom Penh and makes his way around the lunch line, past the stacks of trays and students calling out orders to cooks sweating through paper hats.

Fowler cuts between dining tables that resemble plastic spiders, a large circle with six sprouting connected legs.

He keeps walking until he finds an eighteen-year-old sitting by himself and reading a textbook on C++. The kid is named Ricki, and it looks like he hasn't started shaving yet.

The first time Fowler met Ricki—whom he calls Rick—he told the kid he looked like a school shooter: camouflage shorts, hoodie, shaved head, and weight-lifting gloves. Fowler liked him—the kid had a certain tropical Dickensian flair—and he threw Rick a few bucks to buy some decent clothes. Even though Fowler was there to arrest him.

Fowler pulls out a chair, gets comfortable, crosses his legs.

Ricki freezes. "The hell you doing here, Fowler?"

"It's okay. I'm not on official business."

Ricki, like many industrious kids in the third world without money or parents, found solace on the Internet. Unfortunately, his hobbies included setting up sharing sites for music, movies, and porn. This wasn't Fowler's problem—those small sins fell into ICE's wheelhouse—but Ricki decided not to stop there.

Fowler *did* have to get involved when Ricki started an online casino site and the government ordered it shut down because their kickback money was drying up. Ricki had cornered the market on their turf. When Fowler broke down Ricki's door, he found a sixteen-year-old kid worth two million dollars.

Hun Sen's government was more than happy, jubilant even, to settle with Ricki and not press charges. All Ricki had to do was forfeit every cent of his ill-gotten gains directly to the treasury. After that, Ricki "retired," and Fowler made a few calls to get him enrolled in the university.

Fowler folds his arms on the table and tries to sound like a concerned parent. "Studying hard, I hope."

"I knew all this shit when I was twelve," Rick answers. "Got a cigarette?"

"Why you reading it, then?"

"Book is filled with mistakes. I'm writing them all down. Send it back to the publisher. Tell them they're fucking idiots. Ripping off the school."

Fowler slides him a cigarette. "I need your expertise on something."

Ricki lights the butt. "What?"

Fowler puts the laptop on the table. "I need you to open this thing up for me."

"First thing you do is press power."

Fowler smiles. "You're such a prick. Now, listen. I didn't exactly come into this"—he motions to the laptop—"in a clean manner. So I can't have our guys look at it. This is strictly a you-and-me kind of thing."

"Better you came to me. Your guys couldn't open it anyway."

"They caught you."

"Nope. I read the records. You guys got tipped off. You never would have found me otherwise."

Fowler tries to sound paternal again. "Everyone gets caught."

"No, they don't." Ricki opens up the laptop, presses the power button, and faces the password encryption.

"Can you get through that?"

"Don't know yet." Ricki tries a quick work-around he uses for unsophisticated encryption. The computer immediately freezes, then shuts down. "Yeah. This could take some time."

"How long?"

"Depends on how good it is."

"How good is it?"

"Well, thing is, this fucker looks homemade to me. He took the shell of a PC and cleaned out everything from the ground floor."

"Meaning what?"

"Meaning you're not dealing with someone looking to illegally download porn. I've got to look under the hood, see what makes her tick." He runs his hand along the side of the laptop as if it were the small of a woman's back. "She'll talk to me eventually."

Fowler laughs. "Ever do that to a girl?"

"Sure," Ricki says. "Your mom, last night."

"Ouch. Defaming dear Mrs. Fowler like that. It's almost like you know her." Fowler reaches across and takes Rick's sandwich off the tray.

Ricki looks down at his empty plate. "Help yourself, by the way."

Fowler chews. "I can't leave this thing with you. It's evidence. You got someplace we can work on it?"

"Yeah. My place."

"Let's hit it."

"I drive," Ricki says. "I hate it when you drive."

"Why?"

Ricki rises, slings his backpack over his shoulder. "Because I don't think you care if you live or die. And as your passenger, it concerns me."

58.

Kyle's in the shower trying to scrub off the sticky sheen of Protosevitch-induced perspiration. He rests his arms against the jade-tiled wall and lets the water run over his hair and shoulders.

Lara opens the shower curtain partially and pokes her head in. "I want to get out of here soon. How much longer do you need?"

"Not much. Where are we going?"

"I want to get to a hotel closer to the ferry. I need time to scope out the site and not have to deal with traffic."

"How are we gonna pay for a room? I can't use Robinson's cards or my own. The Chinese are probably watching your accounts."

"There's this amazing invention called cash. You give it to people here, and they don't care where it came from."

"Yeah." Kyle laughs. "That was stupid."

She runs her fingers along the scalloped edge of the curtain. "You said the CIA guy saw your face in Robinson's hotel room..."

"Right."

"Did he say his name?"

"Maybe. I don't know. I mean...you were there. It happened so fast."

"See, that bothers me. He's CIA. Why has there been no media coverage? Why has no one released any photos of you? There were two dead bodies, and you were in the room. Someone's keeping this a black-ops thing. That means I don't want to stay in the same place."

Kyle respects her logic. "I understand. We'll go."

Lara closes the curtain but stays in the bathroom. "You did a good job today."

"Was that a compliment?"

"Don't get carried away. I said *good.*"

He laughs, shuts his eyes, and works shampoo into his hair with his fingertips.

Lara pulls open the shower curtain and steps inside. She's naked and has her hair back in a ponytail. "Is this a problem?"

He can't eke out more than a nod and a "No."

She moves closer. "Get the shampoo out of your hair before it goes into your eyes."

He turns around, rinses off quickly while she finds some room under the nozzle and washes her face.

After he finishes, Lara holds him by the back of the neck, pulls him in close, and kisses him until they both have to stop because they're out of breath.

Kyle backs up, spinning.

"Know how I knew you weren't Robinson, even before I saw your face?"

"How?" Kyle says, still recovering, beads of water running down his face, dropping off his chin.

"You kissed me like you needed it. Like it was the most important thing in the world. Robinson's never done that. Ever." She runs her hands up and down his chest and stomach. "Do you do everything like that?"

"What about Robinson?"

"He lets me do whatever I want. He's more interested in hearing about me fucking other guys. The stories turn him on more than fucking." She kisses his earlobe, works her tongue down his neck. "You don't need to worry about him."

"Do you want to do it in here?"

Lara looks up. "That was the plan."

Kyle can respond only with "Wow."

She laughs. "Thankfully, your body is quicker than your brain."

She moves in close again. The water cascades over their kiss.

Kyle stares at her face. "Your eyes are two different colors."

"Yeah." She laughs. "My body can't seem to make up its mind about things."

She switches positions with him, leans against the wall, and wraps her right leg around his waist. He moves in response, buries himself against her body, holds her breasts in his hands. She runs her leg across his back, rubs herself all over him, back and forth. It feels like velvet. She teases him with the prospect of getting inside—back and forth—but not letting it happen yet.

Kyle leans his head against her neck.

Lara smiles. "Still okay with this?"

59.

Ricki works at his shitty plastic dorm-room desk surrounded by the tools of his trade. He uses a multiblade precision screwdriver to poke around inside the laptop's hard drive while his own computer simultaneously streams through data.

The stereo blasts Scandinavian death metal. Fowler's slouched in a junked chair—probably rescued from the street—that has zero traction and beer stains on the armrests. He's zoning out, teetering on sleep, and shocked he doesn't entirely dislike this music. He can't put his finger on it, but he suspects it's the primal screams. They sound like someone begging not to be born.

Ricki pokes around the circuits, a confounded scientist confronted with a new species.

Fowler's pocket starts to vibrate; he looks at his cell, and it's Grant calling from Indonesia.

Fowler walks over to Ricki's stereo and turns down the volume.

"What's the matter, Fowler?" Ricki says. "Can't take a little music while you work?"

"I gotta take a call," Fowler says.

"Cool." Ricki points at him with the screwdriver. "Gimme a cigarette."

Fowler answers the line, hands Ricki a smoke. "You should quit."

"Why?"

"'Cause I'm broke." Fowler speaks into the phone. "Hey, Larry."

"I got some preliminaries back from the samples."

"Okay." Fowler frantically searches Ricki's junked-tech graveyard for a pen. Ricki, frustrated as hell, finally slaps Fowler's hand and gives him what he's looking for. "Okay. Go 'head."

"Fingerprints came back nada. Those two weren't in our system. I've sent copies to a few select people I know at Interpol, but until I hear back, consider that a dead end. Sent out dental, nothing so far. But let's be honest . . . wasn't much left on that front, so it's gonna take some time. Here's the part you'll be interested in. The two guys—Chinese, obviously. But I had some of the clothing samples analyzed. Everything those two had on down to their drawers was custom-made from African cotton. The clothes were local. They weren't whacked with all the synthetics you get on the open market. And our two were tanner than you'd expect Chinese to be. It's why I thought they might be local at first. These guys hadn't spent much time home. So why would Chinese muscle be spending most of their time in Africa?"

Fowler knows this one. "Guarding Chinese third-world interests. Oil and farmland. You think they were military?"

"Can't tell. There were no tats or markings to indicate military. My guess is they were private security."

"Thanks, Larry. This is good."

"I'll call you if I hear anything about the fingerprints."

Fowler hangs up.

Ricki's been bursting to speak the entire time Fowler's been on the phone. "Fowler, I don't know where you got this, but this has got to be the sweetest fucking thing I've ever seen. You have no clue. It's like Fort Knox, man. This should be fucking studied. Then hung in a museum."

Fowler leans over Ricki's shoulder and examines the insides of the laptop. "Chinese hired muscle. Supercomputers. The hell is going on in my city?"

"Sounds good to me. This city needs some excitement."

Fowler begins to massage Ricki's shoulders with his grizzly-like grip. "You know, Rick," he says. "Well . . . you know how much I like you, right?"

Ricki is withering under Fowler's hands.

"I consider you a friend," Fowler says. "And a friend is someone you can trust."

Ricki bunches up his shoulders, tries to make like a turtle in defense. "Christ, Fowler...you don't want me to blow you or something, do you?"

"Rick." Fowler continues kneading the poor kid's shoulders and neck like a sadistic baker. "I'm going to have to leave you for a while with a valuable piece of illegally obtained evidence. That's a level of trust I don't place in anyone."

"Christ, you *are* gonna make me blow you."

"After you find what I need to know, you are going to reassemble this thing and give it back to me directly. And I don't want you to consider keeping any souvenirs for yourself, either for your own study or to sell to any of your little friends."

"Okay," Ricki says. "Okay. Just stop. Stop."

Fowler tightens his hands. "Promise me, Rick."

"I promise. I promise. I do."

"Not one single fucking thing."

"Just like it was. I won't keep anything."

Fowler ruffles Ricki's hair. "I'm glad we understand each other. I really am."

60.

Upon entering the hotel room, Lara immediately closes all the curtains, blotting out the semiotic seizure of neon from the street.

The room could charitably be called functional. However, if one was feeling uncharitable, then blighted with bugs and stains and having a rank smell emanating from the walls—a scent generally associated with advanced decay—would also apply.

Lara slams the door, checks the locks—none of which work—and shakes her head. She moves the sad carcass of a floral lounge chair over, tries to jam it under the doorknob, but it doesn't fit. "That's not promising." She moves the chair back and continues her security check in the bathroom.

Kyle watches her, lost in her lithe movements. Even her most casual motions have a feral fluidity that's hypnotic. He feels the fear rise and push against the wall of his stomach. It's terrifying to be this close to your object of desire, especially when said object can actually kill you.

"Let's get a drink," she says. "I'll kill myself if I have to do more than sleep here."

All the black lights not presently in college dorm rooms next to Led Zeppelin posters have ended up in this bar. The place is bathed in carnival tones of blue, orange, and green. The bottled alcohol looks like something a witch would give you for potency problems. The polka dots on the cocktail napkins are surreal children's vitamins.

Kyle's gin-based drink glows green. He takes a sip and notes a distressing fact about black lights: They don't reflect anything. They don't throw off any shadows. They siphon off all the objects around them and give nothing back. It's a vampiric form of lighting. Cancels out all chance of duality.

"What is this place?"

"All the expats hang here. That's why I chose it. Westerners don't stick out."

"It looks like the inside of a clown's stomach," Kyle says. "Tell me something. What exactly is our plan for tomorrow?"

"Robinson is going to show up to get his intel at ten thirty. And we're going to meet him there."

"You're sure he knows."

"The way Andrei talked to us about it, Robinson knows. He'll be there."

"What if he doesn't show?"

"Then he'll send someone. He'll send his own courier to meet the guy. We just need to watch for the Chinese holding the intel. He's the key. We find that guy, we find Robinson."

"Then what?"

"If Robinson shows, problem solved. If not, we grab whoever Robinson sends in his place and force him to take us to Robinson."

"We don't know what the guy holding the intel looks like. He's going to be an Asian guy just hanging out by the harbor. That's not an odd sight in Cambodia."

"You did a great job today. But don't get ahead of yourself. I'll make this work. This isn't the part you're supposed to be good at."

"Okay," Kyle says.

"Really?"

"What choice do I have?"

"Now tell me something," Lara says. "How'd you get into tech stuff?"

"You want to hear about Chandler again. It's okay. Everyone

does. He's our generation's Howard Hughes and I was behind the curtain."

"I don't care about Chandler. I want to know about you. How'd you get into tech?"

"You really want to know about me?"

"We're sitting in a bar together, relaxing, drinking. Isn't that what people do? Talk about their careers and stuff?"

Kyle nods. "Yeah. They do." It's been so long that he's forgotten. His only friend and drinking buddy for the past year has been Armand, and their whole relationship is predicated on the fact neither of them ever asks the other anything directly personal.

"I got into tech because of my mother," Kyle says. "She was a revolutionary. A *social revolutionary,* to use her exact words."

Lara laughs. "Your mom was a Commie?"

Kyle nods, laughs, sips his drink.

"You're like half of Russia," she says. "A tech geek with an anarchist in the family."

"When I was a kid, she saw this news special on home computers. It really blew her away. She was all excited, said technology was going to be the path to the new revolution. She made my dad buy me a computer the next day. I've been programming and writing code ever since."

"What's your mom doing now?"

"Everyone's gone. I got sent to live with my grandparents when I was fifteen."

"So your parents were social revolutionaries and you ended up working for Chandler. How does that happen?"

"It's...it's like, when you can't rebel against your parents, when they're more out there than you, the only thing you can do is embrace sanity. You...you become a square. Become a corporate drone. You become me and go to work for Chandler."

"Why'd you get sent to live with your grandparents?"

"It's a long story."

"It's a long night in general."

"I'm gonna need more gin."

"Not a problem."

He finishes off the drink. Lara flags down a waitress, her black hair gone arctic blue under the light, and orders another round.

Kyle begins. "In the late sixties, my mom was going to Columbia. Total hotbed of radical student activity. SDS, all those guys. Her sophomore year, she was an exchange student in West Germany. Met my dad there. He was German. Mom had always been a radical...her folks were Communists. She was one of the original red-diaper babies."

Lara's riveted, moves her hand to pick up her drink but forgets about it halfway through the motion.

"Mom got involved with the second generation of the Red Army Faction while she was in Berlin. It was a natural step for her. My dad fell in with the RAF too, but that was because he was trying to fall in with my mom. The whole goal of second-generation RAF was to get the first generation of fighters sprung from prison. So my mom and dad's cell teamed up with another cell from Palestine and kidnapped an ex-Nazi industrialist. They released videos. Said they were going to hold him hostage until their comrades were let out of prison. The state wouldn't give in, called their bluff. So thirty-something days later, the RAF killed the industrialist. Dumped his body in a field. My parents were murderers now. No going back."

Lara nods, not in response but in commiseration. Kyle's life feels achingly familiar. Failed revolution, family on the run, death and the state.

"So my folks ran to Palestine," he continues. "I was born there. We moved around a lot, lived in a bunch of revolution-friendly countries. Mozambique, Syria, Iraq. Then, out of the blue, two Stasi agents show up in Baghdad looking for my mom and dad. They *invited* us to come live in East Germany. Mom and Dad were considered model fighters for the Communist cause, and the German worker state would be happy to protect them. So I ended up living in East Berlin."

"Damn," Lara says. "You grew up crazier than me."

"It's all subjective."

"Keep going."

"Things were quiet for a long time. My folks got state jobs and housing. Mom was a teacher. Dad worked in a lab. Then the Wall came down, and the security services crumbled with it. The Stasi was liquidated. There went our protection. All the Stasi records were turned over to the reunified Germany. My folks were still wanted for murder in the West. The records gave everyone away. All the terrorists the state was protecting."

The waitress drops off their drinks. Kyle takes a long sip.

"My folks never made it to trial," he says. "They...they killed themselves. Utopia had finally been dismantled." He keeps his emotions in check. "That's the hardest thing, I guess...I mean, for me. The thing I've never been able to work past. I hoped I'd have been reason enough for them to stay around. I mean, even if the dream was dead, at least they still had me. But I suppose I wasn't."

"I'm sure that's not what they were thinking," Lara says. "I'm sure they *weren't* thinking."

"Twenty years later, every fucking morning I still wake up and think, *I'm an orphan.* Even on a day like today."

Lara smiles. "It's kind of ironic, if you think about it. I mean, you and your parents. They spend their whole lives rebelling against the state. You go and work for the state. I mean, Chandler is basically the state. And you both end up running. The state always gets you. Whether you rebel against it or serve it, it fucks you in the end."

Kyle returns her smile. "Fair point."

"Or maybe you just got so used to running, you were looking for a way to keep going. Working for Chandler certainly fits that bill. You're just like me and Robinson. We've lived everywhere and still have no home."

"I thought Robinson went where the money took him."

"I don't think it's ever been about the money for him."

"What, then?"

"He's terrified of quiet. I don't think at any point in his life things were...*calm.* He doesn't talk about his family, ever. Which means it must have been terrible. People who can't shut up about their families aren't nearly as fucked up as people who never say a word." She laughs. "He can never be still. Ever. He only seems alive when someone wants to kill him. Love certainly never did that for him."

"What did it for him, then?"

"Planning. He loves to plan. I always tell him he should have been a director. He loves to set stages. Before he'll even engage you, he has to make sure the lighting in the room is right, has to check his hair."

Kyle thinks back to his brief time with Robinson, and what Lara's saying adds up. When he visited Robinson's hotel room, everything down to the ice cubes seemed selected for maximum effect.

"Before I meet anyone for him," she says, "he has to bathe me, pick out my clothes, fix my hair for hours. But there's not any affection in it. We're all his props. He blocks us how he sees fit. You know that as well as I do."

"But *you* love him, right? You're together."

"That's right."

"It doesn't make any sense. You told me...you said he abandoned you. Hung you out to dry with a bunch of contracts. Left you with a price on your head. But you...you're still...you're still out here loving him and *looking for him.*"

"Robinson and I are a matched set. Don't get in the way of that."

"Why don't you walk away?"

"I can't. Look...subtracting my feelings for Robinson, I owe a hell of a lot of money because of him."

"Then get someone else to do the jobs."

"People pay for Robinson, they want Robinson."

"Take away the money, then. Just take that off the table for one question. Why else are you looking for him?"

"Kyle," she says sadly, "don't start getting ideas about what you don't understand."

"Then make me understand. Because it doesn't seem to me like he loves you. Nothing you told me makes me think that."

"What? You and me are gonna walk off into the sunset together when this is over?" She takes a drink. "God. I fuck you once in the shower, and your brain gets shot to shit. You think you can take Robinson's place? Be my partner? Think."

Although she's absolutely right, Kyle's still hurt.

"When you talk about me and Robinson," she says, "you're not talking about sex and love and commitment. You're talking about something bigger than that. You're talking about identity."

"I don't understand."

She smiles. "Then you're lucky."

Kyle looks around the bar, at the clusters of expats partying under the psychedelic lights, at servicemen and -women—mostly American and Israeli—blowing off steam, dropping drugs on their tongues, and dancing.

"It doesn't mean *we* can't have fun," Lara says. "You had fun before, didn't you?"

"Of course."

"Then stop asking questions you don't want answers to and let's do something more constructive."

She leans over the table and kisses him. Their talk is over.

61.

Fowler walks into his office and is greeted by Rebecca, who's sitting behind his desk, working on his computer, wearing his glasses perched on the bridge of her pert nose.

"Make yourself at home."

She motions to his glasses. "How do you see out of these things?"

"Not all that well."

"I cleaned off all the smudges. How did you read?"

"I pretty much didn't."

"I've got a few things for you to not read." She hands him a sheet of paper.

Fowler squints like a mole trying to decide where to burrow.

"I'll summarize," she says. "It's from Langley. Telling us Robinson isn't worth our man-hours and to let the locals handle it. What do we do about it?"

"It reopens a long-standing question I've had about our employers: Are they criminal, or just criminally inept?"

"That's not an answer."

"I don't recall receiving that letter. Do you?"

"Fowler..."

"They already tossed us here. What fresh hell are they going to invent to dump us in if we keep going on Robinson?"

"There're always new hells."

"So I retire and you go work in the private sector. What's next?"

"You consider the matter settled?"

Fowler nods. "To my satisfaction. But you don't have to take my path."

"I would have happily jumped off, but then I found this." She motions him to join her behind the desk.

Fowler stands behind her. She tilts the monitor so they can both see the screen. It's the Web site for a German telecommunications firm called VodaFone.

Rebecca's blown up a particular employee's curriculum vitae, and, in true European fashion, the candidate has included a recent head shot on the first page. This particular résumé quirk is considered an illegal discriminatory practice in the United States; however, fortress Europe is clearly willing to cede the higher moral ground so it can hold on to the inalienable right not to hire old or fat people.

Rebecca zooms in on the head shot, shrinks the surrounding text, and blows up the photo. "Does he look familiar to you?"

Fowler squints again.

Rebecca shrinks the photo and blows up the text. The top of the résumé clearly reads:

JULIAN ROBINSON

Below the name is an address and a telephone number.

"How did you find this?"

"A couple thousand name and image searches, plus Google translate," Rebecca says. "Mostly innate brilliance."

"Very good."

"I want a better compliment, Fowler."

He puts his hand on her shoulder. "You've outdone yourself. Seriously."

"I know."

"Pull up everything you can about VodaFone. And go through the rest of Robinson's résumé. Check out all those other companies he listed. See if they're all legit, like VodaFone. See if any of them have had charges filed against them recently. I want to know how anyone employed by VodaFone could end up on a no-fly list."

"What happened at Pang's?"

"Besides him shooting at me?"

"We'll get back to that one."

Fowler's surprised. "You don't seem concerned."

"Clearly he didn't hit you."

Fowler can't argue with that. "Couple of things. The most important being, he told me the guy in that photo we've been showing around isn't Robinson. Apparently, he's a local guy calling himself Andrew. Another American. Guy went to Pang looking for documents a few months back." He points to the computer screen. "About two days ago, *that* guy, Robinson, came into Pang's club and had a huge streak. I get an address from Pang for this Andrew. I go check out his place. It's cleared out—except in the bathroom, I find this." He pulls out his phone, starts flipping through pictures of the bathroom's tub and sink. "This Andrew was clearly making some cosmetic changes. I've got someone helping me try to identify him."

Rebecca screws up her face. "Who?"

"No one. Just someone I use for help every once in a while."

"Who?"

"What are you, a fucking owl?"

"Who?"

"Rick."

"Rick . . . Internet-casino Rick?"

"Yup."

"Ever since we busted him, he's been e-mailing me inappropriate pictures."

"He's lacked strong male guidance in life."

"I thought you had taken him under your wing—oh, never mind," she says, realizing her error.

Fowler abruptly changes the subject. "I feel like our best play at this point is to call that number"—he points to Robinson's CV—"and see what happens. See who answers and if he can tell us anything."

62.

Lara stands before the closed curtain, naked, smoking a cigarette. The neon lights bleed through the fine fabric and flash over her torso in Khmer cuneiform. The standing air conditioner has flooded and is pushing out dust instead of cold air. The room is hot enough to arrest thought, but she still can't slow down her mind.

Kyle, however, is fucked out, half drunk, also naked, and asleep on top of the sheet.

Lara ashes the cigarette, listens to the Dionysian sounds from the crowd outside, and reflexively leaps when her cell phone rings. She looks at the number, doesn't recognize it, and darts into the bathroom so as not to wake Kyle.

"Hello," she says, closing the door behind her. "Who's calling, please?"

"I'm looking for Julian Robinson."

"I'm sorry," Lara says, sounding like a practiced gatekeeper. "Julian's not available right now. Can I help?"

"Who is this?"

"I'm Julian's personal assistant."

"I'd like to schedule a time to talk with Julian."

"His schedule is pretty filled up for the next few days." She takes a look in the mirror, sees the dark half-moons under her eyes. "Are you calling regarding a preexisting account or to set up a new one?"

"New account."

"Understood. And how did you hear about us?"

"Excuse me?"

"Personal recommendation? Professional recommendation? We like to keep track of these things."

"Online. I found you online."

"Okay," Lara says, pacing around the small room and already running out of space. "And your name, please."

"My name is Tom Fowler."

"And this number that came up on my cell, is this the best number for Julian or myself to reach you?"

"It is."

"Would you like to leave an e-mail address as an additional option?"

"No. The phone is fine."

"Spell the last name, please."

"Fowler. *Fowl* with a *w* and then an *e-r*."

"Okay, Mr. Fowler. I'll pass this message along to Julian. He's traveling, so it may take a day or two for him to respond."

"That's fine. I'll wait for him."

Lara hangs up the phone, sits down on the toilet lid.

63.

SIEM REAP, CAMBODIA

K yle and Lara sit inside a rental car waiting for the ferry to dock. A local man, obviously high, does a narcoleptic-downer dance, defying gravity by standing and falling at the same time.

A hot purple–crimson sky—like someone got stabbed behind the clouds and is bleeding through—douses the cityscape, composed of claptrap architecture and the steel spines and sternums of high-rises.

Lara opens her Walther, dumps the ammunition into her lap, and works the firing pin and safety to ensure maximum fluidity at a crucial moment.

Kyle knocks his knuckle against his front teeth. He's in a jumpy, confessional mood. "Last night, you asked me...you asked how someone like me ends up working for Chandler. I told you I didn't know, but I do."

She finishes with the Walther, satisfied, and moves on to a smaller handgun.

"He said he understood what it was like to be a genius, to be special and not have the same perspective as everyone else."

Lara's not looking at him, but she's listening intently while working the gun.

"He said it makes you lonely. Incredibly lonely. That being smart pretty much guarantees you a lonely life. I felt like he really understood. Later on, I figured out Chandler's never been lonely. Not once in his life. He was just smarter than me and knew what I needed to hear."

Lara's finishes with the second gun, rolls down the window, and cups her hand to light a cigarette.

"You know, everyone's got these grand theories about how the world works. The scheming, the politics, the espionage, the back rooms. And it's all bullshit. I know that now. It's just window-dressing." He bangs against his front teeth again. "The only rule is survival. Base survival. And the root of survival is money. No matter how big you get, that's all you think about. Someone wants what you have, and you need to keep it. Some people wear suits while trying to keep it, and others don't. And that's the only fucking difference there is."

The strangled avian sound of the speedboat's horn warns other crafts as it approaches the dock.

Lara nods. "Time to go."

64.

Kyle and Lara climb the concrete steps, move to the middle of the dock, and swerve around a growing throng waiting to either board the speedboat for the next ride or meet friends and family getting off.

The Mekong River surrounds them, water and waste speckled by the morning sun, like a corroded jewel box the color of snakeskin.

The guttural growl of the boat's motor gets closer. Kyle sees the craft, sees topless tourists dangling over the bow or tanning on the deck, sees the captain—sporting a royal-blue hat with a gold crest—flashing the lights to get the fishermen to move out of his way.

Kyle and Lara scan the crowd for anyone resembling Robinson, trying to pick out faces in the constant stream.

Kyle turns to Lara. "Should we get closer?"

"Not yet. He's not going to show until he has to."

"What if he changed his looks?"

"I'll know him anywhere," Lara says.

The speedboat docks and the passengers disappear from the craft's two levels. Some of them don't feel like dealing with the rush and hop the rusted railings.

Tourists step onto the dock and continually take digital pictures, marking the end of their journey, wrapping up the narrative of their day trip.

Kyle starts to move, to inch closer to the crowd.

Lara puts her hand on his arm. "Stay still. Calm down. We don't do anything yet."

The crowd begins to thin, most of the people heading toward the parking lot. The cluster of new tourists makes its disorderly way onto the craft while the captain admonishes everyone:

"Slow down. Slow. Plenty of room. Let the other people off."

Kyle's able to see past the pocket of tourists to a Chinese man wearing jeans and a white windbreaker open to midchest, no shirt underneath. He's making himself visible but not *noticeable,* lingering by the dock near a fleet of fishing boats.

"That's got to be the courier," Kyle says.

"Wait," Lara says. "Wait for Robinson. He'll be here."

Kyle locks his eyes on the courier, who slides on a pair of wraparound sunglasses and turns his back from the breeze off the water to light a cigarette. Kyle looks at Lara. She's not focused on the courier; she's waiting on Robinson, and it's going to be tougher than either of them expected. There are more Westerners here, more tourists, than they anticipated. Robinson's not going to stick out as much as they'd hoped.

The courier drags off his cigarette, pulls a cell phone from the windbreaker's pocket, and makes a call. The entire time he talks, he swivels his head left and right.

"Lara," Kyle says. "The guy's on the phone. He's jumpy."

"You're jumpy," she says.

"Robinson's not going to show," Kyle says. "And this guy's gonna bolt."

"Shhh... I'm handling it."

"That's got to be his man," Kyle says. "It has to be."

Lara pulls Kyle closer to the speedboat; the crowd has mostly boarded, and she can see the area around the courier better from this new angle.

The courier ends his call, pitches his cigarette into the Mekong. It floats among the discarded oil drums bobbing in the water.

The crowd finishes boarding, and the captain sounds the bell; just a few strays remain.

Lara and Kyle watch the courier, and he watches them from behind his sunglasses.

A pause. No one moves.

Lara looks over the landscape. She whispers to Kyle in disbelief, "Robinson's not coming. He's not..."

The speedboat pushes off from the dock; the captain sounds the horn to signal he's backing up.

The courier checks his phone, punches a few keys, and begins to slowly stroll away.

Kyle's adrenaline spikes. He actually feels heat in his veins, something boiling beneath his skin, forcing movement, bypassing his brain. *Don't think,* his body says. *It won't help you here.* But he can't stop himself.

I'm sick of running as myself. I'm even sicker of running as Robinson. I'm ending this here. I don't care what it costs.

"Fuck it," he says to Lara. "I'm going to get him."

65.

Kyle sprints over to the courier, who has lit another cigarette and is making his way to the parking lot.

"Wait. Wait."

The courier turns back, slides the shades lower on his nose, and stops.

Kyle reaches him and can tell from the guy's facial expression that he feels exceptionally put out by this whole process.

"I'm Robinson," Kyle says. "I'm Robinson. I had to be sure it was you."

The courier doesn't respond, just looks him up and down, like Kyle's a disappointing blind date. "Money."

Just keep him here, Kyle thinks. *Just fucking keep him here. You don't have to be definitive. Just say whatever it takes to keep him from leaving.* "The money gets transferred into your account after I have my product. It will be there once I'm satisfied."

"Unacceptable," the courier says. "The deal is for cash."

"You're right. You are absolutely right."

"I know," says the expressionless courier, chewing on his lower lip.

"It's in the car," Kyle says. "I'm parked right over there." He points to Lara's car. "Take a walk with me and we'll finish this."

"I'll wait here. Bring it to me."

"I'm parked right there." Kyle points again for emphasis. "Just come with me."

"I'll wait."

"I'm not carrying that kind of money out in the open."

"Good-bye," the courier says.

"Wait...you're going—"

The courier walks toward the parking lot.

"Wait, man. Just wait," Kyle says. "I want to finish this up. Just walk with me."

The courier keeps moving. "It is finished."

Kyle speeds up, crosses in front of the courier. "Come on. Just work with me."

No answer, just movement.

Kyle puts his hand to the courier's chest to stop him.

"Remove your hand," the courier says. "It will be met with a response."

"The money's in the car. Just come with me."

Before the courier can say no again, Lara's there; she flips him around by the shoulder to face her.

"Give it to me," she says.

"I told your associate the deal is done," the courier says. "Protocol has been violated." He fixes his sunglasses-shielded eyes on her. "Move."

"Fuck this," Lara says, and shoots him in the kneecap.

Kyle jumps back, shocked by the swiftness and rawness of Lara's violence.

The courier is on the ground, gritting his teeth, spitting, cursing. Lara kneels, pats down his windbreaker and pants. "Where is it?"

He stays silent, spits at Lara's feet, and then turns his head.

Lara puts her hand over the courier's mouth, takes the butt of the Walther, and bangs it against the exposed, protruding bone of his leg.

Kyle turns away. The courier screams through Lara's fingers. *"In my jacket. In my jacket."*

Lara fishes inside, grabs a flash drive, rises to her feet, and takes Kyle's arm. They look like a happy couple casually walking away as Lara shoots the courier in the head without needing to look back.

Before the cordite echo has dissolved in the Mekong wind, suppressed gunfire erupts from the parking lot, the bullets narrowly missing Kyle and Lara. The shots are rigorously controlled and carefully selected but deafening and numerous nonetheless.

Lara shoves Kyle down, throws herself across him, and returns fire as she shields him. Kyle can't put together the psychic disconnect in Lara. He just watched her kill someone, and now he's watching her risk her life to save him.

"Well," Lara says, "there's his backup."

The few remaining tourists scream and search for cover. Fishermen and dockworkers hide behind their wooden boats.

Lara looks up and sees where the shots are emanating from.

The courier's backup guys are nestled between cars in the parking lot, and they're firing directly down onto the dock.

Kyle lifts up his head to talk.

"Keep your fucking head down and follow me," she yells as more gunfire erupts, and she moves them behind several plastic orange benches left for tourists who are waiting for speedboats.

While reloading her clip, Lara hands Kyle her car keys. "Go get the car. I'm going to hold them off here. I can't win, but I can hold them back while you run." She hands Kyle the loaded Walther, then pulls the second gun from her ankle holster. "Can you shoot this?"

"Never tried."

"The Walther is a good gun. Just aim and pull." A chain of shots rips up the orange bench, cracking the plastic seats. *"Go,"* she yells to Kyle. "Bring the car around and get me."

While Kyle makes a stealth run to the parking lot, Lara provides flanking fire, unleashing a dozen shots and killing one of the backup guys in the process.

Kyle sees the end result of the shot. The guy she tagged sprawls against a car hood, blood seeping from his head, and then lolls to the ground.

Lara keeps firing to flush them out, to keep their attention off Kyle.

Kyle gets to the car, throws open the driver's-side door, and steadies his hands. The two remaining gunmen take turns answering Lara's shots—one shoots while the other hides behind a car, and then they switch. The gunfire sounds like pocket change shot from a cannon and embedding in steel.

Kyle starts the car, pumps the gas. He's got to accelerate fast.

He straightens the side mirror and sees Lara. Her face is a serene blank, almost placid. *She seems calmest when everyone's trying to kill her. She's caught Robinson's disease.*

He guns the engine.

Lara hears it and, in response, lets off a sustained series of shots to distract the backup, taking out a second guy with a bullet to the temple that sends part of his brain out his ear in a gelatinous geyser.

The final gunman lashes out in retaliation and, mostly, fear, unloading a full clip into the bench Lara's been using as a sanctuary.

The cheap plastic shield suffers so many hits that it goes airborne, does a lazy spin, and lands, leaving Lara exposed.

Luckily, within a matter of seconds, Kyle takes out a railing, slaloms the steps, and grinds to a semi-stop in front of Lara, allowing her to jump into the passenger side.

"Slide over," she says. "I'm driving."

While the car screeches across the lot, the remaining gunman makes a last-ditch effort to take them out.

But they're moving so fast, his bullets miss the car and lodge in two parking meters, which erupt in a cascade of glimmering change. The stoned guy they saw earlier—still slouching but not asleep—makes a dash for the money while trying to avoid bullets.

Lara reverses straight across the lot. "Take the wheel," she says to Kyle, then, keeping her foot slammed on the gas, she fires the Walther.

Kyle steers, and she strips off her blazer, then ratchets up a gear, takes the wheel back, and drives them directly onto the highway.

66.

They're no more than a few feet into traffic before the cops arrive and start chasing them. Apparently, even in Cambodia, you can't kill people and riddle a dock with bullets without someone calling the police.

Kyle has to laugh. The notion of a car chase on one of Cambodia's highways is absurd. There's more than enough potential automotive apocalypse to go around without the addition of high-speed flight.

Lara weaves, speeding through endless motos and tuk-tuks transporting tourists and locals who stop and stare or hurl profanity or pull out their phones to preserve Lara's wild ride for posterity.

"Okay," she says to Kyle. "Here's our problem."

Kyle's relieved she's boiled this unholy clusterfuck down to a single issue.

"They're behind us. Which means I can only drive ahead. I can't defend. We need to be behind them. We need to not be the ones being chased."

"How?"

"I go in reverse."

Kyle shakes his head. She can't be serious.

"I'm serious," she says. "Get in the back. Take the gun. And be my eyes. Once I start, we're gonna lose the mirrors and then some. Shoot at whatever you have to so I can get behind those cars." She tosses him the Walther.

The cops pull alongside Lara in a cratered Oldsmobile, and the driver motions for her to pull over, using his gun for emphasis and punctuation.

Lara responds by giving her car more gas.

Kyle crawls into the back, peers through the window, and takes in the state of the chase. Honestly, there's so much chaos, *not including the cops,* it's hard for him to tell what their biggest concern is.

"Tell me what you see," Lara says.

"Three cop cars," Kyle says. "One's behind us. The second to your right. And the third flanking the second. And according to your plan, we need to get behind all of them?"

"That's right."

"Okay," Kyle says, breathing in.

"Make me space. And if they don't move, you shoot."

"There's a shitload of normal people. Riding bikes...motorcycles... tuk-tuks. I'm supposed to fucking shoot at them?"

"I'm not asking you to kill them. I want you to *move them.* I'm going."

"Wait, wait..."

Kyle rolls down the window, sticks his head out. "Okay. *Go,*" he yells to Lara, and then grandly gesticulates to the drivers and pedestrians to get out of the way.

"Move. Move!"

He's screaming over the shriek of tires.

Everyone on the highway stares at him in confusion.

Lara puts the car in reverse, swerves and mashes her way between two lanes of traffic, and starts traveling in the extremely limited available space, making room as she tears off other cars' mirrors, bumpers, door handles, paint, and pretty much anything in her way.

Sparks fly, tires smoke. They lose both side mirrors, plus a door handle.

Kyle has to fight his instinct to close his eyes as drivers and pedestrians scream and career into one another.

For a while, Lara's plan works.

Until they end up stuck between two cars stopped in traffic. One of which happens to be the cops'.

Fuck.

Not enough room to squeeze past or between them. Lara's sure as hell trying, but she's boxed in.

The cop smiles at his good fortune, points a gun right at Kyle, and motions for him to get out of the car.

"We're stuck. And this cop is gonna shoot me," Kyle shouts to Lara.

Lara grinds in reverse but she can't get out from between the two cars. Reek of ruined rubber. Black smoke from bald tires.

Drivers have evacuated their smoking, wrecked cars and are surveying the damage, shaking their heads in commiseration with one another. Some of them pull out cell phones, presumably to call in more police.

Everyone's honking. Total standstill.

Lara drums the wheel with her fingers.

Kyle yells, "Whatta we do? Whatta we do?"

Lara tries to move the car forward but just kisses side doors and throws off metal sparks.

The cop pulls back on his safety and motions that Kyle should get out of the car or he's going to use the gun.

"Lara," he yells. "This fucking guy's going to shoot me."

"Start shooting when I tell you," Lara says. "We gotta go forward again."

She guns the engine, builds up energy, then throttles the stick and throws the car into drive. "Shoot."

The pent-up force rockets them out from between the two cars, leaving behind most of their car's bumper.

But they're free.

All of Kyle's shots missed the people in the cop car, but he managed to disable the vehicle by obliterating the windshield and punching several holes through the grille.

Also, Kyle's learned an intriguing new fact about himself: Apparently, when he shoots, he screams at the top of his lungs.

"Christ, will you stop screaming," Lara says. "It's over. Okay? It's over." She grinds the gears between second and third, hurtling between lanes of traffic. "We lost them." She checks the shattered shards of the side mirror. "We did." There's no one coming, and she's left enough vehicular carnage behind that no one's getting through.

All true.

Lara did manage to elude the cops; however, other adversaries have been biding their time, and they now decide to make their presence known. A Dodge Caravan that's been driving in front of Lara brakes suddenly and then reverses into her.

Then, from behind, a Toyota rams them.

They're sandwiched. The chassis of Lara's car is screaming as if somehow the metal has become conscious, and aware of the abuse being heaped upon it.

A shadow behind the Dodge's tinted windows kicks out the frame and shows himself, gun-first. He's Chinese. He unloads a few dozen shots from an AK-47 into the front of Lara and Kyle's car.

Kyle screams. Then screams some more.

Bullets tear up the hood, shred the steel, and lodge in the frame. The windshield spiderwebs at several impact points, and air seeps inside through the fissures.

Lara looks front, then back, appraising things. "I can't go up against the Dodge. But I can take the Toyota."

"What?"

Her hand grips the clutch. "I'm gonna take him. We weigh more."

"*What?*"

"We've got to try to lose one of them."

Lara jerks the car into second, gets room to build momentum by pulling right up to the bumper of the Dodge, and then, in one wrist snap, she reverses into the front of the Toyota.

The trunk, the left rear tire, and the remains of their bumper are gone.

But the Toyota gets the worst of it.

The Toyota's driver loses control, and, since he isn't wearing a seat belt, he's hurled through his own windshield, a spraying, speeding projectile whose impromptu flight climaxes with him landing in the middle of the road, causing several cars to wreck as their drivers swerve to avoid the man's corpse.

The Dodge returns to finish the job. The Chinese gunman emerges from the back window again and unloads a partial clip into what remains of the hood of Lara's car.

The hood can't withstand the assault. First it pops up, blinding Lara, and then, under the continued fire, it flies off, spins, and crashes somewhere in the center of traffic.

The gunman opens fire again, and this time he hits the fuel line of Lara's car.

And now they're fucked. The exterior has caught fire.

The fire wraps the car in a quilt of flames, spreads inside, engulfs the dash, and—Kyle's legs catch fire.

"Oh my God. Oh my God. Fuck."

He starts shaking them out.

Lara keeps one hand on the wheel, stretches into the backseat, grabs her blazer, and throws it atop Kyle's legs. "Pat them down," she says. "Pat them down." He does. Smoke rises through the fabric.

"We gotta bail," Kyle screams. "Right now."

Lara doesn't answer. She switches to first gear, keeps accelerating, faster and faster; errant pieces of the car fly off into traffic.

She screams out to Kyle:

"Jump!"

He wraps the blazer around his hand, throws open the flaming door, and lands in the middle of the highway. And he is now certain, *fucking certain,* that jumping out of a moving vehicle is the most painful thing he will ever experience.

But Lara's plan worked.

The Dodge didn't have enough time to swerve from the path of her vehicular Molotov cocktail and is engulfed in flames.

Lara walks the highway, dazed, screaming out Kyle's name.

Kyle raises his hand. "I'm here."

She stops short, catches her breath, and stares at her handiwork. Sections of the Dodge are melting off, collecting in puddles of liquefied metal and steel; the sun streams across the surface, leaving a rainbow.

She reaches Kyle, leans in close, extends her hand. "Come on."

He rises and balances against her until he can stand on his own. "Is the flash drive still intact?"

She checks her pocket, pulls out the flash drive—it's still in one piece. "Can you move?"

Kyle nods. "Yeah."

"Good. We're gonna walk up a little farther and get a new car."

Kyle, who is becoming quite conversant in Lara-speak, under-stands that this means she's going to force someone out of a car—probably at gunpoint—and take off in it after rendering the for-mer occupant unconscious.

67.

PHNOM PENH, CAMBODIA

Most men Fowler's age have a houseful of memories; some even have to rent storage space for all the memories they can't fit in the current house.

Fowler doesn't have that problem. Over a lifetime, he's adopted the living patterns and conditions of the guerrillas he used to train and hunt.

He rents a one-story stucco sandcastle close to the water. The inside is functional, shorn of any aesthetic frill. He has no photos, no cherished childhood items, no secret stash of love letters, nothing personal. This is the way he prefers it. Dostoevsky once said that hell was perhaps nothing more than a room with a chair. To Fowler, that sounds like home, and he lives accordingly.

Fowler's standing by the sink finishing yesterday's coffee when his cell phone rings. "Talk to me, Rick."

"I'm going to be famous." The kid is gushing. "I mean, really fucking famous. Like the hacker hall of fame. They're going to have a dinner every year in my honor."

"The point."

"Do you have any idea whose computer you jacked?"

"I didn't jack it."

"You straight jacked it. And you know whose it is?"

"Obviously not."

"Kyle motherfucking West. Kyle West. Fowler, I just hacked Kyle West's computer. Do you know what this means?"

"Not a clue."

"You don't know who Kyle West is?"

"Maybe...vaguely."

"You're a fucking idiot."

"Better men than you, Rick, have called me worse."

"Kyle West created Christopher Chandler's computer network. He's been missing and presumed dead for a year. He's considered by many, me included, to be the Heisenberg, the von Braun of the network age. He created something we can't even process yet. Don't you watch the fucking news, Fowler?"

"Not since I was starring in it most nights."

"Fowler, no matter what you got up to in Milan, you are small-fucking-fry. I haven't even begun to crack this thing yet. All I could do was get into the finder box. And that took me hours. It would take weeks to strip the rest of this. And even if I had the time, I don't think I could. You don't understand what this guy can do to a computer."

"Kyle West," Fowler says, almost interrogative.

"You have to let me keep this for a while. You have to. Just for reasons of pride."

"You cannot tell *anyone* about this."

"No one...but do you have any idea what I've done?"

"I do. And that's why I'm saying tell no one. No one."

"How can you ask me to hack Kyle West and then keep it a secret?"

"Rick, you tell a soul, a single fucking soul, I will drop you in a cell until you shrivel."

"That's just mean, Fowler."

"I am mean."

Ricki's a kid at Christmas. "Can I keep working on it? Please. Can I keep going?"

Fowler waves it off. "Fine. You get a few more hours. But I'm coming for that thing soon."

Kyle West, Fowler thinks. *Kyle West. I know the name, a vague recollection.* He wants to call Rebecca and ask, but he knows even her infinite patience might be tested if she finds out he doesn't know someone Rick compared to Heisenberg, a person Fowler also doesn't know but who, since the name sounds German, probably did something terrifying to the very fabric of reality itself.

Fowler sits down on his couch, lights a cigarette, and boots up his computer. It's Rebecca's old model; she gave it to him when she upgraded. He signs on to Google Video, enters *Kyle West,* and ends up getting more hits than the last time he visited a porn site and typed in *kinky brunette.*

He settles on a CNN news stream from a few days back and takes another drag while the episode loads.

The stream covers Christopher Chandler returning after a long weekend to continue giving testimony before a Senate judiciary committee.

There's ominous drone music followed by the standard stock shots of Chandler, the images the news always deploys when trying to make him look sinister: Chandler getting out of a limo with sunglasses on, his bevy of bodyguards hiding his face; Chandler sitting at a round table with Rumsfeld and Condoleezza Rice, caught midsentence; Chandler standing behind a podium at a corporate function; Chandler sipping coffee with the president of Azerbaijan; Chandler walking through a hotel lobby in the UAE with the sheikh of Abu Dhabi holding his hand.

For the rest of the running time, the stream's focus switches to Kyle West, and pictures of him fly across the screen.

Fowler pauses the stream, stares at the photos. *Darken the hair, take off a few pounds, and I'll be damned,* he thinks. *This is the guy I chased down in Robinson's hotel room.*

A reporter is shown standing in front of Kyle's postmodern loft in Maryland; next, he's at Chandler's office being turned away by security.

In a voice-over, the reporter summarizes the history for those unfamiliar with Kyle's disappearance. The unofficial story is that an ethically affronted employee of Chandler's passed incriminating documents to the newspapers that outlined all the salacious details of

Chandler's live tap and listed Kyle's breakthroughs in filtering that had made it all possible. Those documents offered undeniable proof to the American people that all the conspiracy theorists and civil-liberties tub-thumpers were right: they were all being spied on.

The flashback portion wraps up with the reporter back in front of Kyle's loft, saying:

"Two days before his disappearance, Mr. West was subpoenaed to appear before a Senate judiciary committee headed by Raymond Kuo to respond to allegations stemming from the leaked documents. The committee was to determine two things: whether the documents were authentic and, if they were, whether any federal funds had been allocated to the project."

The stream then cuts to the reporter sitting across from Senator Arthur Diamond, Democrat from Illinois, who's built like a greyhound but who barks like a Rottweiler. When questioned about Kyle's disappearance, Diamond has this to say:

"We would love nothing more than to speak with Mr. West. Without him, Mr. Chandler is in a position of superior deniability. We have documentation of his alleged crimes, but no one to back any of them up. We have leaked documents, but no whistle-blower. Right now, it's a case of the report-says-this and Chandler-says-that. Mr. West is the architect of the system...without his testimony, this is another in a long line of PR disasters for Mr. Chandler, but nothing, judging by his long history, that he'll be unable to recover from."

"Where do you think Mr. West is?" asks the reporter.

"Unfortunately, at this point, we have no choice but to imagine the worst."

The video ends with that line, then cuts to credits, backed by the recurring ominous drone score.

Fowler picks up his cell, speed-dials Rebecca. "Hey. Where are you?"

"Home."

"We're not after Julian Robinson," Fowler says. "We're after Kyle West. He's the guy in the airport photo. He's the guy I saw in the hotel. Pang wasn't lying to me...I can't believe I just said that."

"Why the hell would someone like Kyle West have Robinson's passport?"

"West was looking for clean documents. He was desperate. My guess...he and Robinson look alike; West kills Robinson for his passport. West's bathroom had hair dye, shaving gel, razors. He was changing his appearance. He was making himself look like Robinson."

"And, what—West shows up at the airport and finds out the guy he killed was on a no-fly list? And speaking of which, I still haven't been able to figure out who put Robinson on a no-fly or why. This guy is a ghost. He's just a résumé floating in cyberspace."

"West took this guy's identity."

"We are talking about the same Kyle West, correct?"

"Yeah," Fowler says. "The guy tied in with Chandler."

"Fowler, that guy doesn't strike me as a killer."

"Who does? It's never the ones you expect."

"Kyle West is a network nerd. Come on...he didn't kill Robinson for his passport."

"I'm not as sure as you are."

"Maybe someone sold the passport to him. Maybe he didn't know what he bought. He tries to make himself over so it works..."

Fowler's getting frustrated. She's making sense, too much sense for his taste right now. He wants forward motion, not evidence deconstruction. "The motive isn't the point; the point is that Kyle West has Robinson's passport. And I saw West with two dead bodies in a hotel room. And he got away. That's the point. How he got the passport is not important. He *has* it. And he is running around as Robinson."

"What do you need me to do?"

"I want total media saturation. Either West is a murderer or, going with your theory, he's in completely over his head. Bottom line, I need to find him and talk to him before anyone else does. Blanket the media with his photos. Say he's wanted for questioning regarding the disappearance of Julian Robinson and in connection with two other missing persons. Then post a reward for information. Bounty goes up if he's captured because of that information. Leave the amount undisclosed. Just level a reward on him."

"What about Langley? They're gonna be furious."

"They told me not to go after Robinson. I'm not. I'm going after Kyle West, who happens to have Robinson's passport."

"That sounds pretty evasive."

"It is. It's extremely flimsy and *evasive,* but I need to smoke out West, force him into the open. Put money on his head, and someone will cough him up. I can't imagine he's got anyone all that loyal to him. You don't go on the run for a year if you do."

Fowler hangs up, and he's crushing out his cigarette when two bullets shatter his living room window and lodge themselves in the couch, sending clots of stuffing soaring.

68.

Fowler dives to the floor, stunned but alert; a few years of peaceful living haven't undone a lifetime of training. He turns back, sees the gunman kicking out the remnants of the living room window and entering, legs-first.

Fowler does a quick once-over of the room's contents—TV, coffee table, couch, stray coffee mugs, ashtrays, newspapers, laptop computer. Nothing that can be converted into an improvised weapon.

He's got to get out of this room.

His knives and guns are in the bedroom on the other side of the house. He's not sure he can make it there before this guy sees him.

The gunman eyes the room, his finger on the trigger, while a second of set of legs starts the same journey through the shattered window. He's got a partner.

No more looking for DIY weapons and planning in here, Fowler thinks. This is the time to fucking move.

He takes off out of the living room and rounds the bend into the hall. Slugs follow him, splintering the walls, embedding themselves with a bruised thunk.

Sprinting along the hall, Fowler breaks down the situation. *There's two of them, heavily armed. If I lead them into the bedroom, the field of battle is against me. Even though my guns are in there, there's too much open space, and they might be faster than me. They certainly appear to be younger. No,* he continues. *My best hope is to trap them in close quarters and take down at least one of them. I need to even the odds.*

With that settled, he makes a bee line to the bathroom, locks the door, and ducks into the tub, which is situated at an angle to the door so if they start shooting through it, none of the slugs will hit him in his porcelain fortress.

He sticks close to the back of the tub, listening for footfalls and forming the rudiments of a plan.

He undoes the first few shower rings, frees the plastic curtain, and rips it off, leaving only the rod. Then he slides the rod out of the wall, holds it in his hand, and waits.

The footsteps stop outside the door. They don't bother with the lock, just blow it right off and storm in.

Fowler's fast as hell, and before the first gunman has a chance to fully enter the room, he takes the shower curtain rod and drives it into the gunman's jugular vein.

The gunman belches up a pearled rope of blood and spit. His gurgle sounds eerily electronic because Fowler also pierced his voice box. He flails around, but he's blinded by blood. Fowler drives him into the corner with his shoulder, drops him over the toilet, and forces the rod deeper into the gunman's neck until it finally kills him.

The second gunman is stunned by Fowler's sustained attack, and while Fowler has that advantage, he rips the rod out of the partner's neck and then cracks the new guy across the cheek with it, breaking part of his face, right below the eye.

The second gunman stumbles, and Fowler cracks him across the cheek again, forcing him out of the bathroom and into the hallway.

Fowler wrestles the guy to the ground, straddles his chest, tosses the rod, picks up the fallen firearm, and places it directly against the guy's shattered cheekbone, which is rising like a ridged rock under the skin.

"Who sent you?" Fowler yells.

The gunman is trying to regain his composure; his cheekbone is pressing against the skin, and he needs to scream out before he can talk.

Fowler lets him scream and then continues. "Who sent you?"

"Robinson," he says. "Robinson sent me."

Fowler can barely process this. "Why?"

"Because . . . because you made a phone call."

"You work for him, for Robinson?"

"Sometimes," he says. "When he asks me."

"I'm CIA," Fowler says. "You can't just come into my home and kill me."

"*Robinson can.* The people he works for . . . they tell your people what to do. You're CIA. So what? You live in Robinson's world."

Fowler takes a moment to breathe but stays on the gunman's chest. He lowers his head, trying to find some air.

69.

SIEM REAP, CAMBODIA

Lara goes into the hotel room first, gun extended, expecting anything. Once she decides it's clear, she motions for Kyle to come in.

She doesn't put the gun down, just walks straight over to the fridge, removes a bottle of vodka, and takes a long swig of it.

Kyle crashes down on the couch, head pounding.

Lara walks over, hands the bottle to him. "Get to work," she says, and tosses him the flash drive. "And do it fast. You don't cause the wreck we just did and stay in town. We gotta move."

"How long you think before they tie it to us?"

"They've probably started. Surveillance cameras in traffic. They'll talk to people on the docks, get our descriptions, have sketches up and blurry CCTV in an hour or two. After two or three hours, we won't be able to leave this city. It'll be on lockdown for us."

Kyle holds up the flash drive. "I don't know what's on this...how long it's gonna take—"

"Get as much as you can." Lara starts to leave the room to let him work. "I want to know what we're looking at before we have to move."

"You okay?" Kyle says.

"Fine. I'm fine."

"You look like you're gonna pass out."

"I'm fine."

"No, you're not. Show me."

She exhales, walks to him, and opens her blouse; her breasts and sternum are covered in bruises from the impact of the steering wheel against her torso.

"Shit. Lara..."

"It's okay. It's okay," she says, more to herself than to Kyle.

"We've got to get you to a doctor."

"Where? The two of us can't just pop into the ER."

Kyle has to concede that point.

"Start working," she says.

Kyle pulls Lara's laptop close, inserts the flash, and waits for it to load. The computer installs the information from the flash drive, shows the file on the desktop. Kyle scrolls over to it and is given a list of programs the computer is trying to use to open the file.

None of them work.

The first thing that pops up on the screen is a password prompt. Kyle doesn't want to waste his time on this, because he's pretty sure there's something bigger behind it. *"Lara,"* he yells. "In the suit jacket I was wearing yesterday is my flash drive; can you bring it here?"

Lara comes back from the bathroom, hands him the flash, and watches him work.

Kyle ejects the courier's flash, inserts his own, selects a file called Brute-Forcing, and sets it to work against the password protection.

"What's brute-forcing?"

"Password cruncher. Runs through a million dictionary words in a second," Kyle says. "If that fails, it starts in with numbers, lowercase characters, uppercase, special symbols, all possible combinations. It'll probably crack the password in five minutes or so."

"It's hacking stuff?"

"Yeah."

"And you can do this, right?"

"This I can. Yeah. We'll see what comes after the password. Tell you this much, though—this file is stolen. Even if Robinson made a deal, it's hot. Because this kind of password protection is meant to

keep people out. And I guarantee you whoever owns this flash drive is going to want it back."

The brute-forcing works and plows through to the password. However, in response to the password, the screen splits into a square cut down the middle, and both boxes overflow with code, vomiting out information faster than the eye can follow.

"And there's your encryption," Kyle says. "Waiting behind the password."

Lara stares at the screen. "Holy fuck. Can you break that?"

"I think I can."

"You think? You gotta tell me the truth. If not, we need to get out of here and find someone who can."

"I think I can," Kyle says again. He watches the encryption engulf the screen. "It's really good, though."

"Whatever is in that code can help us find Robinson. And I'm asking you directly: Can you do this or can't you?"

"Probably."

"How can I be sure? I *need* to be sure."

"Lara, if anyone can get through this, it's me."

She's getting frenzied. "Give me a straight fucking answer. I need an answer *now*. No more *if* this or *if* that."

"I can."

"How do you know..."

Kyle's anger rises too. He doesn't like to have his technical prowess challenged. He's the best and he knows it. It's a point of pride.

"Because I built Chandler's fucking system," he says. "I did it, okay? I did it. I'm guilty of what everyone says I am. I built the fucking thing. Those leaked plans—they're mine. I did it. It's why I ran. It's why I don't sleep. It's the guilt. I let the fucking genie out of the bottle and no one's going to put it back. Chandler had a live tap and I taught him how to weaponize it. Same as your brother weaponized you. Same as someone weaponized Robinson. We're all guilty."

Lara begins to laugh, a soft chuckle she can't suppress that ends up spreading across her whole face.

Kyle can't believe he told her the truth because she pricked his sensitive spot by questioning exactly how good he is. "You're laughing?"

"I'm sorry," she says. "It's just—" She catches her breath. "It's just, I actually feel a lot more comfortable around you now. You're crooked. You're as crooked as me. People with a moral disconnect can never *really* trust each other. But now we can. Now I trust you."

"I'm not a crook," he barks back. "I'm *compromised.*"

"God," she says. "You're such an American. Even when you admit you're dirty, you still have to tart it up. You can't just be commonly dirty like the rest of us."

"Okay." He gives in. "Okay. You're right. I'm dirty." He says it again, with a palpable sense of relief: "I'm dirty." He lowers his head, almost weighed down by the enormity of his sin. Even after confessing it, it's still oppressive. "You're the only one I've ever told."

"No one else?"

"Not even my closest friends."

She gives him a conspiratorial smile. "I'm honored."

"I'd rather run than tell anyone."

Lara looks down at the screen, still multiplying with encrypted expressions. "So your program for Chandler can cut through this?"

"Yeah." Kyle nods. "Its specialty is adapting to any blocking algorithm that you throw at it. The program maps out the curves in algorithms and begins to learn from its mistakes. Then I can design a reverse algorithm to undo it. Of course, I usually have about a hundred interconnected computers helping me with it."

"So no piece of communication is safe from your work."

"Not unless it's encrypted by someone better than me."

Lara scrunches her face. "Kyle, that's...Christ. No wonder you didn't tell anyone."

"I've seen you shoot people—kill people—and you're gonna take that tone?"

"Yeah, but I just shot a few scumbags...you changed the world. Why'd you want to do that? What was wrong with the world?"

Kyle's defenses are down. "It excited me. Chandler told me about the live tap, how his people had gotten that down. He knew the work I'd done in algorithms and filtering. He asked me if I had any ideas. I did. I wanted to know if they would work. I couldn't resist trying them out."

"Guess they did," she says. "And *that's* why you did it?"

"That's *everything*. It's like the guys who built the bomb, right? It's something you don't think you can *actually* do. It's just . . . technically sweet. And then, when it starts working—shit. You realize it can't be undone. Once you break the social contract, which is already hanging by a pretty thin thread, you can never go back. You have to start running. Like me. You do the things I did, you can't go home."

"So it was just curiosity?"

"And ego. I can say that now."

"Well, you could go home, technically."

"Right, but I don't want to go to jail."

"Are you sorry?"

"Yeah. I'm sorry," he says. "But some days . . . it's fucked up."

"What?"

"Some days, I'm still a little impressed with myself."

"No. You're sorry or you're not."

"Is it really that simple?"

"You know who you sound like?" Lara smiles.

Kyle knows exactly who she's thinking of. "I'm not like *him*."

"Robinson uses his job to justify everything he does. So do you, right? If Chandler hadn't asked you to do it, you would've found someone else to ask you. Just to see if you could."

"I'm not like Robinson."

This is hard for her. "You keep living the way you are . . . not admitting what you did, surviving on your own guilt and spite. You'll end up like him."

"I'm not like him."

"How far away from being him do you think you are right now? Take a look at us."

Kyle stares at the coding, then opens up the Internet, starts to prepare.

"I forgive you," Lara says, knowing she needs Kyle to focus on the task at hand. "You're still my friend."

Kyle smiles. "You forgive me?"

"Yeah. I do."

Kyle nods. "Thank you. I mean it."

"See how easy that was? You say what you did, and someone forgives you."

"Yeah. Now I just need to say it to the whole world."

70.

PHNOM PENH, CAMBODIA

Fowler has dragged his would-be assassin into the kitchen, propped him up against the fridge, and flexi-cuffed his hands and feet together. He dumps a pitcher of ice water over his head to restore him to consciousness since the guy passed out from the pain in his busted cheek.

"Fuck," the gunman says when the water hits. "Fuck you, man."

Fowler kneels down next to him. "Who is Robinson? And why are you here?"

"You don't want to know that shit. You know...you'll never be safe again."

Fowler grabs the gunman by the chin. "You tried to kill me in my home. I don't feel very safe."

"This is a different kind of not safe."

"I haven't been safe since I was eighteen. Try again."

"Come on, man...they'll kill me."

Fowler has no remorse. "So will I. You pick: me or them."

"I don't...I don't..."

"Yes, you do."

"Can I have some water?"

"I just gave you some."

The gunman's in genuine pain. "To drink, you fuck."

"Start talking," Fowler says. "Work up a thirst. Then you get water."

"Fuck you," the gunman says, which is what Fowler wanted to hear. He knows these hard cases. You're not going to get them to talk for any reason other than spite. "Fine. Fucking fine," the gunman says. "I'll tell you. I'll tell you everything. 'Cause now I want you to die from knowing."

Fowler's plan worked. Anger tends to loosen the tongue.

"You know what the Flock is?"

"Yeah," Fowler says. "World War Two. Guys who thought Wild Bill's OSS were a bunch of blue bloods on vacation in Europe. The Flock wanted to really get their hands dirty."

"Right. But what made them special?"

Fowler shrugs.

"See, that's the whole thing, man. You don't know what you're dealing with."

"Then tell me."

"The Flock's operatives hid inside corporations," the gunman says. "They posed as executives in American Express, Philips, Sullivan and Cromwell. They used their corporate identities as a mask... way for them to be global without being suspicious. The operations were paid for and funneled through the corporations. After the end of the war, they kept it going, handling the stuff the OSS wouldn't touch. Then the head of the Flock got too chummy with McCarthy. He also got too chummy with Jack Daniel's and had a meltdown."

"It happens." Fowler thinks back to Bill Casey dying of brain cancer. But Fowler thinks maybe what killed Bill was keeping all those secrets—or finding out how many secrets had been kept from him.

"The Flock was dissolved and folded into Dulles's CIA. Then came the Bay of Pigs; Kennedy tossed Dulles, and that was that. No more Flock. New management at the CIA." The gunman licks his dry lips with his coated tongue. "Can I have *my fucking water* now?"

Fowler walks to the sink, runs the water until it gets cold. "Keep going."

"Then the Church Committee—"

"I know it." Fowler had been traipsing around a jungle while Congress was ripping the fingernails out of the CIA, one by one.

"Church Committee stripped it of the ability to conduct overseas ops without congressional oversight and approval. Considering very little of what the Agency had done since it started would get congressional approval, the people left in it scrambled for a work-around."

Fowler kneels again, hands the gunman his water, and waits while he drinks it all down. "Can I have some more?"

"Yeah," Fowler says. Time to reward his subject; he's cooperating.

"So they clean house in what's left of CIA, bring Bush the First back from his post in China, and install him as the head. Bush knows how to run slush through corporate books. He was the only man who couldn't find oil in Texas, but he still sold his companies at profit. You do the math. CIA guys like Shackley..."

Fowler nods. He knew Shackley from Vietnam. Shackley gave him his career.

"Edwin Wilson. All the Vietnam guys. CIA was back in business. Behaving on paper, but fully slush-funded. Then the fucking unthinkable, right? Carter gets elected on the platform of taming the CIA. He's going after the rogue elephant. Carter gets in, installs Stansfield Turner as head. Turner denies Shackley and his crew. They bail. So Shackley, Bush, and the boys privatize the CIA. They restart the Flock to get around Church and Turner. All the seed money for Latin America, for the start of Afghanistan, for Iran-Contra—all of it was Flock money."

"Right," Fowler says, remembering the lunar landscape of Afghanistan.

"Problem is, the Flock had to scramble to get front-organization cover. Corporations couldn't be trusted the way they could in World War Two when everyone was on America's side. Shit was different now. Vietnam tore this country apart and not everyone wanted to be part of the Flock's resurrection and lend them cover. So...so these fucking guys *built corporations* from the ground up. And they installed business emperors, not intelligence guys, to run them. Guys who knew how to make money. More CEOs than you want to know about were and are trained by the Flock. Why do you think the government had to bail out some of these companies you never heard of in 2008?

Why was it so important? Because they're doing the government's dirty work and couldn't go under. Why do you think no one went to jail for that mess? They're our people. And that's me, man. That's me, and that was Robinson."

"Robinson *was?* Until when?"

"He still freelances for them. He was never a corporate guy. He...doesn't like bureaucracy. They were grooming him to be one of the emperors."

"So he would hop to all these different Flock corporations, depending on the location of his job," Fowler says. "That about right?"

"Yeah. That's right."

"Who is he working for now? Which company?"

"I don't know. I got a call from his girlfriend after you called her. That's all."

"So VodaFone is one of the Flock's corporations?"

"Right."

"They built a legitimate corporation in Germany for European action, and they made Robinson a sales exec on paper to create the legend?" Fowler pauses, putting it together. "And I called the wrong number," Fowler says. "They backgrounded me and sent in the kill order."

The gunman nods. "More water." He touches his cheek, recoils in pain. "God—you fucked my face."

Fowler's still stunned. "These people sent in an order to kill me. My own people."

"They're not your people, Fowler. They're no one's people." The gunman can't stop touching the bone in this cheek, even though it hurts like hell. "Listen, we gotta get outta here. I was supposed to call after the job was finished. Either kill me or keep talking, but we can't stay here. In a few minutes, there's gonna be a second team coming."

71.

SIEM REAP, CAMBODIA

Kyle's sitting on the bed, typing furiously on Lara's laptop. The artist before his canvas, contemplating color and space.

Lara's pacing around the room. "I'm bored," she says. "You did *this* for a living?"

"Not this exactly."

She plops down on a chair. "Explain it to me."

"You remember in 2005, the domestic-eavesdropping scandal in the U.S.? Bush administration, civil liberties, all that?"

"Yeah."

Kyle punches a few keys, thinks, raps his knuckle against his front tooth, then deletes and retypes. "They put the attorney general under the hot lights."

"I remember."

"Well, after that—to cover their asses, because they were never actually going to toss the eavesdropping program—Congress immunized the telecoms. Congress may have hated Bush for it, but the program worked too well to destroy. You immunize the telecoms, it means that eavesdropping can go on unabated, legally. But see, the problem wasn't uppity telecom employees. All the leaks were coming out of NSA. NSA was the one who told the public, not Sprint and Verizon. So eavesdropping was privatized, outsourced to my boss."

"Chandler. So Chandler took over for NSA?"

"He didn't just take over. He'd been waiting years to try something and this gave him the cover to do it. A live tap. The British tried to implement it at one point. It's a system that sucks up *everything* around the clock. All communication. Worldwide. Twenty-four-seven."

"What about something like Echelon? I see it all the time in movies."

"So twentieth-century," Kyle says. "Echelon works only if countries are cooperating. Countries, nations—all outmoded terms now. We're talking about corporations. Corporations taking the place of nation-states. Corporations paid to watch you, because they're better at it than the government. Someone like Chandler, although not a figure like Cameron or Obama, is actually far more important to the daily functioning of the world. You kill the president, and the world weeps. You kill Chandler, and the world *stops*."

Lara nods.

"The live tap picks up all e-mails, texts, calls," Kyle continues. "But the Brits abandoned it because it was useless without a way to filter all the information. They'd be sucking up the equivalent of the Library of Congress every single day, and no one could stream through it all."

Lara points to her laptop. "What's it doing now?"

"Trying to learn the algorithm while breaking it."

"How close were you and Chandler?"

"He was the most impressive person I've ever met."

"Is that why you ran?"

"To keep Chandler out of trouble? Nah. No. I wish I could say that. I ran because I was scared—"

"Because you did it."

"Right. And I'm not a good liar. If I got called before a subcommittee, I'd tell them the truth."

"So why'd you take Robinson's passport if you didn't want to go home?"

"Someone found me here. Probably someone who was following Robinson and lucked onto me. Then I had no choice. I had to take Robinson's deal."

"Chandler found you?"

"Probably."

"You two were friends, right? Why would he want to kill you?"

"This situation goes beyond personal feelings. The project is too big. And as much as he cares for me—and I think he does, or at least did—it's better for him to have me dead. You can't know as much as I do and live. Also, he doesn't really need me anymore. He's got my system. I'm not all that necessary to him now."

Lara watches the screen moving. "Christ. How fast is that going?"

Kyle laughs. "This is just a fraction of what my program can do. I would need a room of Cray computers to show you what it can cut through at optimal speed. But since we're only trying to decrypt one small file"—he gives Lara's laptop a teasing slap—"this'll have to do."

"You really love this, don't you?"

"Oh yeah. When I don't have this—you are what you do, right?"

"I hope not," Lara says. "So how exactly did the shit hit the fan for you?"

"Someone internal leaked my program's coding and schematics to the press and everyone went . . . fucking crazy. Said we were living under a fascist dictatorship."

"Why would someone leak your stuff?"

"Couple of reasons. To fuck Chandler. Or just general moral rage. Chandler seemed to think the latter."

"Don't they have a point?"

"The government's been listening to all of us for years. Chandler's just better at it. The administration was completely scandalized. Civil liberties were supposed to improve under Obama. It was supposed to be hope and change. And we were doing thirty, forty percent more domestic wiretaps under his administration. Why not? Telecoms were immunized."

"Shit."

"I got served with lawsuits by every civil-liberties organization imaginable. Every day I got a new one. But my lawyer told me not to worry about those. The only problem was Congress. The program's a violation of constitutional law if Chandler took any tax money to develop it. I got subpoenaed. I panicked...I ran. And now, even if it's proven that Chandler didn't take any federal money, I'm still in contempt of Congress by my absence and have a minimum two-year sentence if I step on American soil."

"Wow," Lara says.

"Yeah." Kyle punches a few keys. "I'm *fucked.*"

"How much longer do you think this will take?"

"I don't know."

"I'm gonna watch TV for a while. See if we made the news."

"I'll let you know when I've got something."

Kyle stares at the screen. His program is filtering so fast, he actually has to turn away from it. The speed is more than his eyes can take. He opens up the browser and runs a system report. He doesn't want the computer to crash before it has a chance to finish processing.

"Kyle," Lara yells. "Kyle, get in here."

72.

Kyle rushes in. "What?" he asks, worried something's happened to her. "What?"

She points to the television, and he sees his image staring back.

"Oh shit," he says, and kneels before the television as if he's decided to start praying to his own pixelated self. He turns up the volume, listens to the anchor:

"Mr. West, already in trouble with the law, is now wanted for questioning regarding the disappearance of Julian Robinson. There has also been a reward issued—"

Kyle mutes the television. He smiles, almost finding a holy fool's sort of detachment within all this danger. "I'm never going to be able to get a corporate job again. They're gonna make me teach."

Lara smiles.

"I guess this answers your question about the CIA and the media. Apparently, they were biding their time. What do we do?"

Lara points to the bedroom. "I'd say work faster. We had maybe three hours before this place was locked down, but we don't anymore. Can you work in the car?"

"No," Kyle says. "The signals are too sporadic. It'd keep cutting in and out. I've got to do it here."

"Okay," Lara says. "See what you can do. Worse comes to worst, we'll hold them off in here."

"Great," Kyle says, trying to work up a little enthusiasm for guaranteed joint suicide.

73.

PHNOM PENH, CAMBODIA

Fowler's banging on Rebecca's door with one hand while keeping his other arm tight around his assassin's waist.

Rebecca, expecting Fowler alone, answers the door in a bra and jeans, a towel wrapped around her freshly washed hair. "Fowler. What the..."

Fowler pushes the assassin past her and into the apartment. "Sweetie," he says, "meet the asshole who tried to kill me."

Rebecca finds an old T-shirt on the couch and throws it on. "This guy tried to kill you?" she says while pulling it over her head.

Fowler's absolutely thrilled he nailed this guy. Years of dormant violence awakened and satisfied. He can't keep it out of his voice. "Yeah. Can you believe it?"

Even someone as inured to Fowler's antics as Rebecca is stunned. "Why the fuck did you bring him here? To show me or something? Like a dog with a dead bird?"

"No. I'm going to keep him here."

Rebecca is ready to explode. "You want me to babysit your assassin?"

Fowler tosses the gunman onto the couch, checks the flexi-cuffs around his wrists, then wraps a cord around his feet and slides the knot under the couch's leg. "Not in those words..."

"How would you put it, then?"

"I can't throw him in jail here. He's not good enough to kill me, but he can break out of the locals' cells without much fuss. I certainly can't call DC and tell them I got him, because I'm not supposed to be working Robinson."

"I thought we were chasing Kyle West."

The gunman is trying to make himself comfortable on Rebecca's couch, not paying any attention to the domestic squabble.

"Listen." Fowler slows down, needing her to stay with him. "You were right, okay? You were right. Kyle West somehow got himself mixed up with Robinson. He's in way over his head. He's running around with Robinson's passport while the real Robinson is out there doing God knows what. I'm not gonna find Robinson. But if I can get to Kyle West, I can use him to smoke out Robinson. One way or another, I need to find Robinson . . . because he wants me dead."

Rebecca points to the couch. "That's Robinson's assassin, then?"

"Yes. He works for Robinson."

"You're not leaving him here."

Fowler's cell phone goes off. "Hold on." He motions toward the couch. "Just watch him." He answers the phone. "Ferris. It's me."

"Tommy, baby, how's your dick?" Ferris says by way of greeting.

The crude argot has a story behind it. It's not simply a shared dialect of arrested masculine development. Ferris is CIA in the Siem Reap area, and both he and Fowler are Vietnam vets. Back in Vietnam, the state of one's cock was a valuable piece of information. In Laos, there were thousands of men at their sexual peaks always on the hunt for relaxation—no need to draw the inevitable sex and death connections—and there weren't nearly enough willing women for all of them. Inevitably, they were all, to put it bluntly, dipping into the same pool. So if a man had a certain undeniable fiery sensation in his cock, he knew one of those women had to take a few weeks off, or, if he could swing it, he'd get the girl a hush-hush shot by a willing medic from his unit.

After the war, the question continued as a greeting between veterans, and, ironically, in the world Fowler and Ferris run in, the inquiry still means basically the same thing.

"Slightly chafing," Fowler offers.

"Got some interesting news for you."

"Go 'head."

Fowler watches Rebecca try to decide whether to talk to the assassin.

"I've got a fairly significant stack of injured folks over here. We had a shootout and a chase through traffic. I've got downed locals and some critically injured Chinese."

"Christ," Fowler says.

"Yeah, and the witness reports and surveillance video ties back to you. It was your airport guy who was responsible for it. Plus, it looks like he picked up a girl along the way."

"Lock the city down."

"Oh, we did that an hour ago. We're on lockdown here, and so are all cities north and south. Those two aren't going anywhere."

"Good. I had his photo put all over TV with a reward. Between that and the lockdown, this guy's not getting out."

"I saw that. Nice touch on the undisclosed amount."

"I don't like paying," he says. "Thanks for the call. I'm on my way."

"How fast can you get here?"

"Try my best. Can you hold tight?"

"Course, baby. You just keep this shit pussy-tight, though. Don't go spreading it around."

Another piece of Laos lingo Ferris has never been able to part with.

All wars birth their own languages. Vietnam was the first one to incorporate everything from surf-brand Sufism to ghetto slang to institutionalized blue-blood racism. It was the first postmodern war, obliterating high and low culture, guerrilla, psychotropic. The same way Gulf War part 1 would be the bridge from Vietnam's postmodernism to a fully integrated network-information age—*post-everything*. Gulf War 1 was slotted into sweeps week, preprogrammed, hyped like a miniseries, the opening salvo of the dominance of reality television. Shit, Fowler remembers it even had trailers.

"Kyle West just rained down unholy hell in Siem Reap," Fowler says to Rebecca.

"How do you plan on getting to Siem Reap fast?"

Fowler's spirits sink. "I hadn't thought about that."

"Call Grant in Indonesia," Rebecca says, assuming her regular role—reminder of *reality*. "See where the closest chopper to us is. It's your best bet."

"Thank you," Fowler says. "Genuinely." He searches for Grant's number in his cell.

"And you take your fucking assassin with you to Siem Reap."

Fowler holds up his hand, a plea for Rebecca to stop. "Larry . . . It's Tom Fowler in Phnom Penh."

74.

SIEM REAP, CAMBODIA

Kyle walks into the room and sees Lara's eyes fluttering open, finding light. "What's wrong?" she says upon seeing his face, noting the last time that it looked this stressed and dour, she ended up shooting a Chinese courier.

"I cracked it," he says.

She bolts up, fully engaged. "And?"

"It's big..." He's at a loss for words, spreads his hands apart to indicate *how big* the problem is. "What do you know about a guy named Li Bao?"

Lara shrugs. "Nothing."

"See, this is the problem with our world," Kyle says. "I'm front-page news; everyone knows me. But here's this guy trying to change the world and—"

Lara puts her hand up. "My fucking head is killing me. No lectures. Please. Just tell me who the hell he is."

"There's this thing in the Chinese Communist Party called right of succession. Li Bao's dad was one of the original council of nine in China. The guys who founded the CCP. Li had been planning to exercise his hereditary right to join the ranks of the standing committee of the politburo. He worked his way up, was given the huge post of governor of a province. But while he was there, he changed...saw what the Chinese economic miracle was all about: Worker suicide, polluted lakes, infertility. Keeping the workers totally cut off communication-wise from the rest of the world. He's been a tacit supporter of the New Left, Maoists and Social Democrats since. He wants unions, social security, workers' rights on paper, health care, and, most important and problematic for the CCP, he wants workers' wages to rise. That means taking away money from the state's coffers. The sovereign wealth plan of China is built on an inhuman savings rate imposed on the people. You allow the people to make more, you pay them more, then China looks less attractive to do business with. The moneymen move to Africa. And the CCP loses its reason to exist. They've got a compact with the people: The officials keep them working and pay them a basic wage, and the people keep electing and funding them. Li Bao wants to talk about that. He wants democracy, not autocratic capitalism. He's called a spade a spade in print too many times. And more than that, he's got some huge backers in his own country that agree with him."

"Okay. When does this become our problem?"

"The Chinese can't kill this guy. He's a legacy. They've already got enough of an image problem." Kyle runs his hands up and down his face. "But apparently, Robinson can kill him."

75.

Kyle shows Lara her laptop and points to the screen.

"Behind all the codes is Li Bao's security detail for his entire trip. I'm not sure who the recipient of the flash was supposed to be, but it sure wasn't Robinson." He points at different entries. "Look...fucking car routes, Li's arrival and departure times, the number of guards on duty. It even has physical, personal, and political breakdowns of his entire security detail. Li's areas of vulnerability at several locations indicated by percentages. This is heavy calculus." Kyle shrinks that window and opens another. "Here's a list of known dissidents in the surrounding area that Li could potentially meet with. What you have here is a complete bio-power breakdown of Li Bao for the next few days." Kyle turns away from the screen. "This flash is holding millions of dollars' of intel."

Lara stares at the screen and the blood drains from her face. "I...I can't believe this."

"What part?"

"This is someone's whole life. His whole life boiled down to charts, graphs, and statistics. That's all he is to someone. That's all he means to someone in charge." She involuntarily shudders. "It feels so wrong."

Kyle points to the screen. "I think Robinson's going to use this location. Li's going to be in Siem Reap to meet with a group of supporters. Other dissidents, some local politicians." He drums his fingers on the keypad. "That's why Robinson's been in Cambodia all this time. He's prepping."

Lara's silent, stunned by the information overload.

"Lara...we have to stop Robinson. We have to."

"No way. No," she says. "I need him. How is not having Robinson helpful to me in any way?"

"Stop being so selfish."

"My life is on the line because he ran."

"So is mine."

"I'm not dying for this guy." She motions toward the computer. "I don't even know who the fuck he is. All I know is Robinson owes me a bunch of jobs, and people want to collect. If he pulls this off, he can come back and work."

"If we let Robinson do this, there's going to be a total breakdown in China. Or worse. In fact...probably much worse." Kyle tries to convince her. "If Li gets killed, the Chinese workers are going to lose all hope. They will riot and more. And the CCP will not hesitate to crush them. We're looking at something much worse than Tiananmen Square. Tiananmen was a tragedy but considered a local event. China wasn't integrated then. They were just coming out of their shell. Now the world is watching. Killing Li would be truly revolutionary, but in the worst way possible for the people Li is trying to help."

"I'm not helping you get Robinson. I'm not," Lara says. "He will come home to me when he's done."

"No, he won't," Kyle says. "This is a suicide run."

Lara focuses. "Look. Just call Li Bao's people and tell them you have reliable intelligence of an assassination attempt on their boss. They'll take precautions."

"And when they ask who I am? Or when they trace the call? Because they always do." Kyle rises, frustrated with her. "Don't you get it? I've dealt with security forces before. Chandler owns dozens. They investigate calls only if they come from a reputable source. Someone threatens to kill Chandler every week. I need to get to Li's people. I need to explain this to them. They need to understand how much danger he's in from Robinson."

Lara struggles with the raw reality of what Kyle's saying. "No...I'd be betraying him."

"If you care about Robinson, if you want to see him again, you can't let him do this. This is too hot even for him. You've got to save him from himself."

"Stop manipulating me. He can handle this—"

"You're lying to yourself. I'd stop him myself, but I can't. I know it. If you tell me you can stop him, I won't go to Li's people. But you be fucking honest with me. Are you good enough to stop him?"

Lara hesitates, then finally has to come clean. "No way. Not close."

"Then either come with me to find Li's people or let me go. 'Cause one way or the other, Robinson's not doing this."

Lara rises from the couch. "You're not backing down from this?"

"No way," Kyle says.

"Not for nothing, but why do you care about Li Bao so much?"

"I've got enough sins on my plate," he says. "I'm not adding Li Bao to the list."

"You know the minute the Chinese figure out who you are, they're gonna deport you? They're not gonna thank you for the information."

"I know that. I know they're gonna send me home."

"And you still want to do this?"

Kyle bites his lip. "I do."

"All right." She takes her Walther from the coffee table and puts it down her pants. "There's a parking garage two blocks from here. We'll pick up a new car from there."

76.

Lara cuts between the numbered parking spaces in the basement-level garage. Kyle follows behind her, examining the assortment of European luxury cars. They walk between red and white concrete pillars, past blue arrows directing them to the entrances and exits in three different languages. There's an oil leak underneath one of the cars, and in the puddle, a chemical rainbow has formed. Lara stops to stare at the cosmic image. She turns back to Kyle and says, "King me. That's what we used to say when we were kids and saw a rainbow."

She spots a chrome Aprilia Shiver motorcycle between two luxury SUVs. "This is the one." She kneels next to it, inspecting. "Cops take notice of a stolen car here because it rarely happens. Most thieves can't afford gas. We'll stick out less with this. Also, we get in a tight spot, we've got a lot more room to play than in a car."

"Good," Kyle says. He walks to the front of the motorcycle and rests his arm against the handlebars while Lara works.

He looks to the ceiling and becomes transfixed by a flurry of moths congregating around a flickering overhead fluorescent light. His mind goes blank. He forgets his body, forgets his arm resting on the bike's handlebars. He focuses on the moths, losing himself in the first moments of quiet he's had in days.

A figure emerges from behind one of the luxury SUVs. He wears no shoes, just striped silk socks. Shoes make too much noise on this surface.

Before Kyle has a chance to react, the figure's hand secures Kyle's wrist against the bar of the bike.

He tries to shout, but the figure silences him by tracing a thin stiletto blade against the brachial artery of Kyle's upper arm, then continuing on, not breaking skin or ripping clothes, clearly an expert with the weapon. He stops at Kyle's jugular vein, holds the blade there, presses gently, pricking the skin but still not drawing blood.

Then he draws Kyle close by the waist and whispers:

"There's my shadow."

Before Kyle can even process this, Robinson knees him in the kidney, throws him face-first onto the gravel floor, and starts kicking him. Then he stops suddenly and laughs.

"Know what, Kyle?" he says, breathless. "This hurts way more than you think without shoes." He curls his toes, cracks them back into place, and resumes kicking.

Kyle rolls over and screams, *"Run, Lara, run.* He found us."

Robinson mockingly echoes Kyle. "Yeah, Lara, run...Run and don't look back." He turns his head. "There you are."

Lara's standing behind Robinson. Her face is a blank screen waiting for Robinson to start the show. She's back under his control. He takes her hand and kisses her fingers, more proprietary than affectionate. "You've been magnificent. Truly."

Kyle's been conned by Lara, probably from the first moment. The anger rises in his stomach and explodes out his mouth in a scream.

"I know," Robinson says. "It always hurts. No matter how many times it happens." He kneels down, puts his hand on Kyle's chest, which is heaving with anger. "Everyone's betrayed you. It doesn't seem to stop. I know. Life's been the same to me." He rises and offers Kyle his hand. "But now you've got to get up and walk with me."

Kyle slaps it away. "I'm not helping you kill me." He gets up on his own.

Robinson takes Kyle by the neck, points to his car. "I'm right over here," he says. Then he punches Kyle in the face, knuckles first.

Lara winces.

Kyle collapses onto the floor, curls into himself.

Robinson leans against a red pillar, lights a cigarette, and watches the pain play out on Kyle's face. "All right. Up. We've gotta roll." He says, clapping his hands.

Lara goes over to Kyle, kneels next to his beaten body. "You've got to get up."

Kyle shakes his head. "You fucked me. Why? Why'd you do it?"

"It's what I do."

Kyle turns to Robinson and watches him shake the violence out of his hand, opening and closing it until the numbness fades. He can't look at Lara. He knows he never should have trusted her, and maybe he never did, but it doesn't make her betrayal hurt any less.

"I'm sorry," she whispers. "I am."

Robinson tosses the cigarette, claps his hands together again, a demonic father on a road trip. "Come on. We gotta go. Kyle, either you get up on your own or I'm coming over."

Kyle hoists himself up and holds his head in his hands, cupping his bloody nose. He can't get over how much his face hurts. This seems to be the take-home lesson of his sentimental journey through Cambodia as Robinson: There are a myriad of ways you can get hurt, and they all *hurt* more than you'd think.

Robinson tosses Kyle into the passenger seat of his SUV, then slams the door shut. Lara comes up alongside him. "Go easier on him. He's really hurting."

Robinson nods. "Noted." Then he smiles, and it looks the prelude to a viper's kiss. "It's your fault, though. You shouldn't have fucked him. The way he screamed out. That wasn't just pain. There was pride in there too."

77.

Kyle sways in his seat as Robinson steers the car into the swirling vortex of motos and tuk-tuks.

Kyle lifts his head. Blood streams out his nose in parallel rivulets. He uses the tail of his shirt to wipe it.

Robinson starts to sneeze and can't stop. Seven or eight in a row. "I've been on a lot of public transportation, so of course, I got a cold. All that recycled air. The curse of travel in a globalized world." He wipes his nose with the cuff of his sleeve. "We've never been closer together. Right? Never had more of a chance to share our thoughts...and germs. Only thing is, there's very little of the former and a whole fuck of a lot of the latter. But that does seem to be the truth behind most revolutions and breakthroughs, doesn't it? Industrial revolution. Information revolution. Unfettered freedom and access...then the viruses come."

Kyle's head is pounding; he's seeing double, and that combined with Robinson speeding spins his stomach.

Robinson hacks. "God. The pressure is right behind my eye. Pushing right on it. Do you know what that feels like?"

"Just kill me. Just get it over with."

Robinson keeps his eyes on the road. "I can't kill you in the open. We need to be near water. I can't have anyone finding you for a few days."

Kyle mops more blood from his upper lip. "Why me, man? I was some stranger to you... just some innocent fucking stranger."

"No. You're not some *stranger*. And you're not innocent. No one innocent ends up where you were. No one innocent ends up in Phnom Penh. You and I were able to meet because the universe brings people like us together. Some artists are criminals, some write code for private concerns, but all artists come together eventually. That's what we both are." Robinson slaps his hand against Kyle's arm. "You think this means anything? Skin. I *borrowed* you. That's it. Names are just sleeves for identity. Bodies are receptacles."

"So life means nothing to you?"

"No. It means a lot. The name and the body mean nothing."

Kyle rests his head back, finds a tissue in his pocket, stuffs it up his nostril.

"Don't pack that," Robinson says. "Use pressure. Packing will just jam things up."

"Why'd you pick me?"

Robinson points to his own face, then Kyle's. "You mean, outside the obvious?"

Kyle nods. "Yeah. Outside that."

"The Chinese got on me. Li's people. Then Li's people called their friends in the secret service in. I knew I couldn't prep with that kind of heat. They are a tenacious group. I needed a believable diversion to buy me time to do a few *errands* of my own." He laughs. "*Entrez vous.* I needed you to send everyone in one direction while I went in the other."

"That's it? I was a diversion 'cause I look like you?"

"I needed you for two very specific things, and Kyle... you sure didn't disappoint. I left you a trail to follow so you'd make all my personal appearances. I had to. Unfortunately, like most institutions, mine is still inherently misogynistic. Personally, I'm a gynocrat. Give the ladies a whirl, I say. But the world hasn't caught up with me yet." He flashes Lara a smile in the mirror. "People needed to see me in person. For that kind of deal, it would have been inexcusable for me not to see Protosevitch. If I'd just sent Lara, it would have been an insult. And from what I hear, you and he got along famously. And the courier. Well, Lara handled him. But I needed his people to see you there...to see me there. Clearly, I can't be in two places at once. Kyle, the Chinese are so fucking lost right now. They have no idea where I'm going to pop up next. We've stayed ahead of them the whole time. You've been magnificent."

Robinson pauses, pushes in the car lighter, waits for it to eject, then fires up a cigarette and coughs.

"And most important, I needed you because I knew if Lara could keep you alive long enough to get the intel for me, you could crack the Chinese encryption. I mean, hell, you wrote most of the encryption the Chinese ripped off from us. You gave me the final key. You signed Li's death warrant."

"Who was the courier? Why'd he have to die?"

"He was just some CCP underling with a gambling problem. Needed cash. The Chinese secret service has a whole document worked up on Li's little trip here. There's a war in the CCP, Kyle. Li has people loyal to him in there. They're watching him too. They don't want anything to happen to him, and I needed to know if Li's people changed his schedule after his security spotted me. So this little courier got industrious. Swiped the plans from the CCP and scheduled a rendezvous with me. But I'll be damned if I'm paying someone like him."

Kyle's torn between rage and despair. "Why Li? Why does he matter to you?"

"He doesn't," Robinson says. "Someone paid. That seems like enough to me."

"Who paid?"

"People who can. Why do I care?"

"Small-time...you're small-time."

"It's a small-timers' century, Kyle. And this one belongs to me. You think the past ten years have been a sad speed bump on the way to a better world? The post-Wall euphoria—*that* was the speed bump to where it was all heading; 9/11 was the starter's pistol. Game on. Whole world's up for grabs again. Last century was the devil's century. Top-down totalitarian. Hell on earth. Big management. And it failed. This one...act two...belongs to the *small-timers.* The technocrats. The damned middle managers and entrepreneurs. People like us. No more grand blueprints and narratives. Just a bunch of small-timers making a go of it." He sounds a little disappointed. "You and I could've played it together, circumstances being different, of course. It could've been great. But spiritual cousins end up enemies in this thing."

"Thanks for those two bodies you left for me in your hotel room. The CIA has me on the hook for those."

"Oh, them. Li's private security people have been merciless about tracking me. Sorry about that. You understand, right? I was in a rush."

"So the people who picked me up at the airport?"

"Li's people. Private security. Same as the ones in the hotel room. Those two were so young, I felt bad killing them. Young start-ups always want a chance at someone like me. It's their best shot at fast advancement. You take me...you write your own ticket to the sky." He smiles, like a man reminiscing about an illicit one-night stand. "I turned on the lights. We saw each other. There they were in the light. I was better; I took them both apart. But they fought me till the bitter end." He drags off the cigarette. "Knowing the Chinese, they were probably underpaid for what I put them through. And the CIA...don't worry about them either. I had that taken care of."

Kyle focuses his rage, focuses his pain, starts to think. "Wait...back in Phnom Penh, those weren't Chandler's people trying to kill me. Chandler's people would never have let me get away. They were yours. You needed me to come back to you. You needed a reason to force me to take your passport."

Robinson turns to him, cigarette clenched between his teeth, like a shark with a small fish. "Now you're getting it."

Kyle turns to Lara. Her face is remote. *What is she thinking?* he wonders. Can he make out the signs of struggle? Is she torn between her lover and her new friend? Was he ever a friend in the first place?

Did she really play him the whole time? Because it hadn't felt that way.

Kyle turns back and increases the pressure on his nose. He knows Robinson screwed him, but it was only possible because of Kyle's refusal to avoid taking responsibility for his guilt. Everything spread from there. He can admit it now. His desire to evade reality unleashed Robinson, belched him from his own unconscious like some secret sharer to liberate and punish him. And now Li Bao's going to be the next person to suffer because of him.

Suddenly, he has an urge to do something destructive, something to put an end to it all. If he's going to die, he refuses to die passively.

"Look at you," Robinson says. "You're on fire." He laughs. "It's no fun killing someone submissive. But I can't have you boiling over; believe it or not, you bleed more that way. And I don't want to have to hurt you." His smile has a tinge of sadness. "It'd be like hurting myself."

Kyle concentrates his anger in his left arm, raises his elbow to the passenger-side window, and bashes it. One crack and the glass spiderwebs. He gives the glass one more shot, and seconds later, the window shatters in his lap.

Robinson swerves the car. "Shit—"

From the backseat, Lara struggles to stop Kyle.

Kyle grabs a jagged shard, slicing his own hand in the process, and jams it into the meaty area between Robinson's shoulder blade and neck. Blood spurts, a steady fountain, the sanguinary consequence of slitting skin in a sensitive area surrounded by nerves and vessels.

Robinson takes his hands off the wheel, tries to wipe all the blood from his eyes while steering the car with his knees.

Lara tries to squeeze herself between the divide separating the two seats.

Kyle reaches over, slams down on the door panel, unlocks the passenger side, and jumps from the moving car.

He lands hard on his side, then gets up and takes off in a dead sprint.

The car screeches to a halt on the side of the road. Lara jumps out of the backseat and joins Robinson in the front. He turns to her, blood spurting, and hands her his gun. "Stop him," he says, furious.

Lara runs to the middle of the road, tries to set up a clean shot. *"Kyle, stop,"* she yells. "I'll shoot. I will."

Kyle doesn't turn around. He'd rather take a shot in the back than slow down.

He reaches the pier, takes a running dive into the river, and starts swimming past the limits of his body, muscles burning and aching.

Lara gets back into the car, gun at her side. "He jumped."

"I noticed." Robinson looks at her, his neck spurting, more annoyed than anything else, and says like the ultimate disappointed parent, "He's your problem now. Get out. Go get him, and don't miss this time."

Kyle swims through the thick dregs of the Mekong.

He wades for a few seconds, then catches his breath and floats through a patch of pollution. Planks of diseased wood, pockets of redolent food—mealy fruit, rotten meat, hundreds of bruised UN-donated potatoes—and strange sci-fi vegetation, stems and vines, rising from an unseen source. He's going to need one hell of a tetanus shot after slogging through this sun-spangled septic tank.

He swims through an assortment of corroded hubcaps and floats over to the rickety deck of a moored houseboat. Two children wearing nothing but torn cloth diapers watch him with a mix of awe and fear as he hoists himself onto the boat's deck.

Kyle beaches himself on the wooden planks, rolls onto his back, and breathes in. He's strained the limits of his lungs; his chest feels like there's a hot coal in the center. His arms and shoulders tremble.

The children don't move, just stare at him like he's some mythical object dredged from the depths of the sea.

Kyle shakes off the water, walks the length of the boat, and rips a threadbare towel off a rope acting as both a drying line and substitute sail. He wraps it around his wounded hand, holds it tight.

He walks to the edge of the houseboat and makes the jump from the boat to the shore. It's farther than he thought. He goes down on one knee upon impact and allows the rest of his body to follow. He's overcome; he still can't catch his breath.

He hobbles across the shore until he hits the main road.

Hitchhiking isn't an option. No one, no matter how many good Samaritan impulses that person is harboring, would pick up someone in his condition. His only hope is to walk until he finds a stand where he can rent a moto.

He sticks to the side of the road and walks with the traffic. He runs his hand along the sleeves and shoulders of his suit, swats away any refuse left over from his plunge.

He weighs his options. Surrender is the only viable one he can come up with. Try to find someone to turn himself in to and tell him Robinson's plan. The problem is, who is he supposed to surrender *to* at this point? Why would anyone believe him?

He looks down, and his hand is seeping through the towel, leaving a trail of crimson blots behind. He needs to get somewhere and change the dressing.

78.

The sun's a boiling naked ball. Below, the clouds churn like cumulous magma. Kyle rubs his eyes, which are stinging and swollen from his Mekong bath. Keeping the pressure tight on his wounded hand, he makes a right turn into the congested city and is besieged by sonic chaos.

Everyone seems to be at war with everyone else on these streets far removed from Angkor Wat's famed temples and tourist infrastructure. A wedding procession—about one hundred strong—strolls between gridlocked cars, further fucking things up. Car horns bleat at the bridal party, the members of which are decked out in traditional garb and holding cakes and gifts over their heads.

Kyle cuts between the cars.

More honking, more shouting; a cluster of hotel buses try to merge. This is a city composed of people who can't stop yelling "Fuck off" at each other, and the merciless sun hanging above clearly feels the same way about them. *Fuck off,* it says. *Don't touch.*

Kyle mixes in with the wedding party, dashes across traffic to the opposite side of the street, and hits a wall of vendors selling spinning street meat, fried bugs, and flamboyantly patterned fabric.

He walks on, trying to mingle gently with a crowd that doesn't share his goals, a crowd who seem to be staring and then—intentionally or unintentionally—knocking into him. And there's a simple explanation for this.

On either end of the street are police officers handing out Wanted flyers with Kyle's picture adorning them.

He thought seeing his face on television for a year alongside Chandler's would have inured him to losing control over his image; however, there's something about the tactile nature of his photo being *distributed* that unnerves him in a way pixelation never did. He could always turn off the TV, shut the computer down, so somehow—in his own mind—he still controlled the flow of his face. Not anymore.

His hand throbs; he feels his pulse hammering in the wound, cellular conversation. He's completely soaked through the towel. No more time. He has to change it.

He has to stop.

He rounds the corner, swiftly snatches a long lime-green silk scarf from a fabric vendor's table while the owner is busy scolding her kids, and ducks into an alleyway. He shares it with several children trying to set insects on fire by focusing sunlight through a shard of glass.

He removes the saturated towel and readies himself to examine the wound. He's not squeamish about other people's injuries, but he's seriously queasy when it comes to his own.

The cut is a clean slice across the length of his palm. From a psychic's standpoint, he cleaved out over a third of his future.

The bleeding is heavy, but what's making the wound throb is the crud from the Mekong in the gash. He needs to rinse it out. Some stitches would be optimal, but there's time only for the essentials.

Water.

He'd like to flush the wound with bottled water, but his wallet and the bills inside are drenched, so he can't pay a street vendor. If he uses tap water on it, he's going to get an infection. If he doesn't clean it out, he's going to get an infection. There are no good options, only possible palliatives.

He grits his teeth. He's got to clean it.

He walks down the alley and finds the back entrance to a restaurant. Next to the dumpster brimming with putrefied vegetables, chicken appendages, and bloated flies in a post-buffet state is a garden hose. He opens his palm, works the nozzle, lets the stream run through a chain of brown coughs, and then lowers it onto his hand.

It burns more than he'd imagined. Feeling faint, he leans against the wall for support while the stream runs over the gash, and a blood-spangled puddle collects around his feet.

He cuts off the water flow, drops the hose, and starts to pat the wound dry with the scarf. He averts his gaze, looks toward the mouth of the alley—and sees Lara round the corner and begin sprinting toward him.

79.

Kyle palms the silk scarf and shoulders the steel side door to the restaurant. The door gives and crushes the cheek of a chef hauling a colander of green beans to the stove. He goes down to the floor, instantly unconscious. Green beans soar and scatter. Kyle flops inside.

It must be four hundred degrees in the kitchen. In every direction, an appliance or stovetop is sizzling, spitting, boiling over, or about to be overrun with flames.

Before the staff can ask questions or chase him out with a cleaver, Kyle bursts through the cheap plastic sheet separating the kitchen from the restaurant proper, which is about the same size as the kitchen. The walls seethe with flashing neon characters and splattered sauce. The air is a pungent mix of spices, sweat, and Freon.

There's not enough room between the tables for Kyle to run. He jumps across them in a mad dash to the door, upsetting people's meals and causing a melee among the diners.

Lara smashes through the steel door and follows his path.

Kyle makes it out the front door, spills back onto the teeming street.

He knows being in the middle of a crowd isn't going to keep Lara from shooting him. He also knows he's not going to outrun her. His only hope is to get away from her.

He looks back; she's getting closer, almost at the door.

There's only one option left.

He shoulders through the crowd, making his way toward the cop at the end of the street. He doesn't turn back, but he hears Lara crash through the front door of the restaurant.

"*Kyle...stop,*" she yells.

He picks up the pace until he reaches the end of the street, where he's face to face with a local cop holding a stack of Wanted flyers featuring Kyle's close-up.

He stops, catches his breath. "I'm turning myself in to you," he says.

The cop clearly has no idea what Kyle has said. *Come on,* Kyle thinks. *Even this is going to be a struggle. Jesus Christ.* "I am turning myself in to you," Kyle repeats slowly, nodding and with accompanying hand motions to indicate handcuffs.

Once again, the cop stares back.

Behind him, Kyle hears Lara tossing over pedestrians and speeding his way.

No time.

Do I just grab this guy's gun and point it at him? No, he thinks. *No need to add to my perpetually expanding criminal record.* He grabs one of the flyers from the stack, holds it up next to his face, points at the photo, then at himself. *See? It's me. I can't make this any more obvious.*

And now the cop gets it.

Really fucking gets it.

He draws his gun, trains it on Kyle, and starts shouting instructions in Khmer.

Kyle has no clue what the instructions *actually* are, but he's more than happy to put his hands up, get down on his knees, and stay still. The cop keeps his gun level, grabs his walkie-talkie, and speaks animated Khmer into the apparatus.

Kyle waits for him to finish, keeps his hands locked above his head.

The cop commands Kyle to get down on his stomach—at least, that's what Kyle takes from the exchange—then walks in a circle around him shouting incomprehensible orders while waving his gun.

Kyle turns his head and sees Lara staring, gaping at the scene. He can only imagine what she must be thinking.

That he's cracked, finally gone suicidal.

But Kyle figures rage is her primary emotion, because as crazy as she is, she's not going to gun him down in front of a cop and risk being shot and killed herself.

They share a last skewed look and then she storms off, leaving Kyle to sort through the consequences of his Pyrrhic victory. Now he's going to have to deal with the Chinese, who are about even with Robinson in terms of complicating issues.

Because even if Kyle does manage to convince them he's Kyle West, not Robinson, they're going to be just as *thrilled* to have Kyle West in their possession.

80.

Robinson stands on a makeshift tarp of hotel-room towels and a tropical-themed shower curtain—banyan trees and a breeze. His feet are bare and streaked with dots and dashes of blood. He takes a generous gulp from a bottle of Grey Goose, then puts his cigarette on the lip of the cream-colored sink.

The bathroom mirror is a severe square bordered by naked halogen bulbs, providing him with both an excellent spot to perform DIY surgery and about the hottest fucking room one could imagine. Orbs of sweat drip from Robinson's forehead down his nose, lips, chin, earlobes.

He takes a drag off the cigarette and squints through the smoke while making a pragmatic assessment of the surgery required.

The shard of glass Kyle jammed into his neck left a ragged puncture wound between his neck and shoulder, right in the area above his trapezius muscle, a knotty mix of tendons of particular importance to comfortable sleep.

Robinson leans into the light, separates the flaps of lacerated skin, and looks inside. The halogens do a languid dance against the seeping and shifting fluids, and he sees abstract figures and shadows in the interplay; it's like watching time-lapse photography of clouds.

He snaps back to reality, picks up a threaded needle from the countertop, and holds it in his hand. He's shaking too much to make the first stitch. Nothing will go right if the first one isn't even.

He tries to muster his inner reserves, takes another belt of booze, but he's lost too much blood and can't get his body to stabilize. He studies himself in the mirror, fascinated by his own destruction.

Lara walks into the bathroom, soaked in sweat, her clothes clinging, and helps herself to Robinson's cigarette. "You need me?"

Robinson keeps staring in the mirror. "Yeah. I can't get the skin to line up to make the first stitch."

"You want me to wash up first?"

"I don't know how much longer I'll last before I pass out."

"Okay," she says.

"Fuckin' Kyle stabbed me at an angle." He laughs. "I would've done the same."

"About him..."

"Later," Robinson says. "I'm going to pinch the skin together and you put in the first three or four stitches. I can finish up the rest."

"How many you think you need?"

"Twenty, maybe. Give or take."

"Christ," Lara says. "I don't think..."

"Just line up the skin and close it. When I get back home I can have a real doctor redo it." Robinson takes another shot of vodka and arches his back so Lara can start.

She leans in, stabilizes him against the sink—in case he reflexively jumps on the first stitch—and pinches the two flaps of skin together so they line up. "I'm starting."

"No need to tell me," he says.

Lara powers her way through the first stitch, trying to keep the skin straight. "Okay?"

Robinson coughs, breathes in. "Do a few more. You need to leave me with a straight line to work with."

Lara goes back to work, starts the second one. "I need to clean it off. There's too much blood. I can't see what I'm doing."

"Fuck it," he says, visibly in agony. "Don't stop. Just keep going."

She spits on her hand, clears away a spot, and continues on.

"Christ," he says. "You sew like a fucking Russian. It's brutal."

She snorts a little to stifle a laugh and keeps going.

"Enough," he says. "How many is that?"

"Around six."

"Fine. I'll finish it later."

Lara backs away. Robinson turns around, takes a drink of vodka, and offers her the bottle. She drinks. Their eyes lock, eliminating the need for conversation.

Robinson opens his arms to invite her in. "Come here." She acquiesces, and he holds her close. "Now, tell me."

She speaks into his shoulder. "I couldn't find him. I've been looking this whole time."

Robinson pushes her away, fixes her with a glare, which she tries to match. "You're lying," he says. "You never have to lie to me. You know that by now."

"I'm not. I looked all over the city. I couldn't find him."

"Just tell me the truth."

"I couldn't..."

"I just need to know what I'm walking into tomorrow."

"He won't be there."

"You found him. You couldn't pull the trigger. It's my fault. I left you alone with him for too long."

"He just... he just disappeared, Julian."

"Hey," he says. "Hey. I'm human. It's hard to kill someone you've spent a few days with."

"It's not that."

"I'm not mad at you," he says, and brings her back inside his arms. "I just need to know if he's a factor I have to deal with."

"He isn't. You won't need to worry about him."

He runs his bloody finger over the inside of her forearm in soft strokes. "Don't be embarrassed if you liked him more than me. It's okay. Just talk to me."

"I didn't like him more."

"You can like him all you want. I just want to know about your *interaction*."

"The plan is solid. You really think you need to worry about him? He's just a computer guy."

Robinson suppresses a smile. "Just tell me."

She's cracking under Robinson's calm, can't hold back her panic. "I love you. I do."

"I know that. And I love you."

"He won't be there tomorrow," she says, starting to breathe unevenly. "He won't. I swear."

"You never need to be afraid of me," he says. "I love you." He makes it sound like a veiled threat.

She starts to cry.

"Just tell me."

"I found him," she says. "I did. I found him."

"Okay."

"I'm so sorry," she says. "I am."

"Don't be sorry. Just keep going."

"I had him cornered on the street. He saw me and turned himself in to the cops. I couldn't...I couldn't shoot him. I couldn't do it."

"Did you have the shot?"

She can't stop herself from saying it. "I couldn't have done it even if I'd had the shot."

Robinson ignores this. "What did the cops do?"

"They took him away. They have him now."

"That's fine," Robinson says. "Then he won't be a problem. By the time they figure out who he is, I'll be done."

"Yeah?"

"Yeah."

"Do you want me to keep going with your shoulder? Now that you've had a break?"

"No. I can finish it later."

She looks up. Robinson's gaze gives it all away. In one fluid motion, he sweeps her at the ankles, and before she has a chance to react, she's cradled in his arms, being lowered into the tub.

Her journey ends with her head angled against the drain.

Robinson slams the shower on. Her face fills with water, and before she has a chance to choke, he fires two shots directly into her brain with his eyes closed.

He keeps the shower running while he washes his hands and watches the chips of her skull and cheek swirl down the drain.

81.

This section of the Prey Lang forest has been marked for active de-forestation and forced population removal for several intersecting reasons.

The government needs the occupied lands to plant corn, beans, and cassavas to feed the population—which keeps growing, despite officials' best efforts—and also to lease to the Chinese and Saudis, who are prepared to pay handsomely to plant their own crops on it. Also, timber is one of Cambodia's most prized exports, and the state can't subsist solely on ill-gotten gains and aid money; it needs to exploit that resource. Finally, clearing the land of its inhabitants is part of an active plan to relocate people from the countryside to the cities. People in cities are easier to monitor. It's hard for the state to exert draconian control when a third of the nation's populace exists effectively off the grid.

A combination of chain saws and controlled fire works over the forest.

Heavily armed men in khaki clothes lead a march of the forest's former residents, who haul their meager possessions in wheelbarrows or by hand. The people started squatting here over thirty years ago when the Vietnamese kicked out the Khmer Rouge. They have no rights, no legal title for the land, no hope of combating the state.

Some weep, some explode with anger, only to be put down with a gun barrel to the belly.

But no one bothers speaking.

And Robinson moves right into the middle of it. His intelligence was right. This is the perfect point of entry. He can move freely and cloak himself in chaos.

Workers wearing gas masks transport large branches, brush, and tree stumps to a pile, then douse it with gasoline and start a fire when the pile reaches a designated height. The squatter shacks have been stripped of their usable timber, and whatever's left will be razed.

Robinson puts on a gas mask, secures his duffel bag to his chest, and crisscrosses through the smoke, people, and destruction without attracting attention.

He stops at an area blighted by drought, the soil something out of science fiction, the grass reduced to intermittent wisps of brown. He pounds his heavy-soled boots on the dirt, which is so rigid his seismic activity barely dents the surface, the impact registered by patterns of thin veins.

After stomping several hundred square feet, he's satisfied—he's found what he's looking for. He removes his gas mask, wipes away sweat, kneels down, pulls a small shovel from his duffel bag, and begins clearing away soil.

The workers let machine-gun rounds off in the air to get the migrants to pick up their pace.

Robinson stops digging when he hits steel. He clears the dirt away, and underneath, there's a grate, roughly the size and weight of a city manhole cover. He uses the lip of the shovel to pop up one side of the grate, then slides three fingers under the lid and lifts.

He pushes the grate to the side, drops the duffel bag down the exposed hole, then lowers in his legs and kicks around until he finds what's he's been searching for.

A ladder.

With one leg stabilized, he pivots, turns his body, and lowers himself in farther.

Before he's too far down, he reaches into his pocket, pulls out a penlight, turns it on, and fixes it between his teeth.

Then he places the grate back over the hole.

He reaches the bottom of the ladder, and it's a ten-foot drop to the floor. He uses the penlight to find his duffel bag in the dark and extracts a tactical hiker's flashlight from inside. He's seen this spot only on a map, but now it's real.

Thank Christ, he thinks, *that I don't have claustrophobia, 'cause it is close in here.* More tomb than tunnel. Barely high enough for him to stand or wide enough to stretch out his arms. Unlike drug tunnels, there's no breaker lights and, more important, no ventilation, no fans, no air-conditioning.

He shines the light down the shaft. According to his intelligence, it's about a mile and a half. And he's going to sweat every square inch of it.

He adjusts his legs and back to the height, drops the duffel bag in front of him. He's going to have to *carefully* push it the length of the tunnel. When not requisitioned by someone like himself, this tunnel serves a practical use. It's the second stage of a four-tiered journey for Cambodian dissidents and NGO workers to escape to Thailand.

Robinson trudges, trying to find his pace. If he goes too fast, he can't breathe. If he goes too slow, he'll run out of air.

He stops, takes some shallow breaths, shoves the duffel bag, and continues on.

Sixteen minutes later, he reaches the end, and another ladder. He rests his hands against the rungs, opens his mouth, and tries to yawn. In his current state, he can take in more air that way. He coughs up a broken cloud of dirt, then straps the duffel bag across his chest and mounts the ladder.

At the top is another steel grate.

Robinson pushes it up and over. He detaches his duffel bag and heaves it over his head and through the hole. He follows and surfaces inside a walk-in closet housing cardboard boxes crumpled by humidity and sinking into each other.

He rises to his feet, grabs his bag, and leaves the carpeted room.

The plastic nameplate on the desk reads Dun Vibol, and the office furniture reflects the man's occupation, nonprofit human rights lawyer. Everything appears to have gone through at least two or three different owners—all seemingly abusive—from the wooden desk that looks like it was involved in a knife fight to the cratered filing cabinet to the graffiti-branded computer that still needs a tower to run.

Robinson removes Zeiss night-vision goggles, a FatMax measuring tape, and a collapsible handheld telescope from his duffel bag.

He approaches a window made of four distinct panes that each open independently. He opens them individually, then takes a measurement of the entire frame.

He extends the telescope out the window, surveys the buildings across the street and the ground below. He's pleased. His abstract calculations match the physical reality of Mr. Vibol's office.

Robinson dumps all his supplies back into the duffel bag, picks it up, and returns to the closet. Before closing the door, he attaches a small wireless camera to the bottom of it, just above the gap between wood and floor. The lens feeds imagery directly to a handheld television.

Mr. Vibol is in court most of the day, but Robinson still needs to monitor the coming and going inside the room.

He settles in the closet, leaving the tunnel uncovered so he can dive down at a moment's notice. He extracts the rifle cases from the duffel bag and slides on surgical gloves. If he has to leave something behind at the scene, he doesn't want anyone to get his prints.

He sits there, building his gun and watching the outer office on his handheld screen.

82.

Kyle's handcuffed to the leg of a metal desk inside the police station at Siem Reap, a recently erected but still ramshackle stucco sandcastle surrounded by high-tension power lines. On the wall behind him are framed anticorruption commendations from Hun Sen's office.

Two members of the Chinese secret service, Agents Di and Lai, sit across from Kyle. Even though the room is sweltering, they haven't taken off their sunglasses, blazers or loosened their ties. The pair strike Kyle as taking their role as the literal embodiment of their nation seriously. They will not drop their façade for something as mundane as heat.

Kyle forgets his hand is cuffed and nearly falls over when he tries to use it to punctuate his conversation. "Look, we keep going over this. Maybe you should just let me talk to Li Bao's private security."

"We are in constant contact with Li Bao's private security. Many of them were former colleagues of ours who went to work for him out of loyalty to his message," Agent Di says. "He's very popular in certain circles. More so than the CCP."

Agent Lai lights a cigarette and offers one to Di, who accepts. They smoke in total silence, a fly caught in the window screen offering the only auditory interruption.

"What can I possibly do to convince you that I am *not* Robinson?" Kyle says.

"Look at it from our perspective," Di says. "All of our intelligence on Robinson dried up a week ago. He was seen in Phnom Penh, and then—"

"Then," Kyle interrupts, "I traded passports with him."

"A passport you seem to have lost."

"I had to jump in the Mekong. It's somewhere in there."

"Right," Lai takes over. "Then Robinson reappears all over the place, but this time he's *you?*"

"I was trying to find him."

"Look at it from our perspective," Di continues, obviously trained in dialectic. "You were at the scene of the murder of two of Li Bao's security guards. You accompanied a woman who killed one of our former employees. Then you injured several of our agents in a car chase. Even if you are not Robinson—as you contend—you still have a lot of explaining to do."

"I understand. I really do," Kyle says. "But look...please, please alert Li Bao's people that there's going to be an attempt on his life in a few hours."

"They've been aware of it for weeks," Di says. "Attempts on Li Bao's life are not as infrequent as you seem to believe."

"I'm fucking serious," Kyle says, once again forgetting his wrist is chained and stopping short of falling over. "Robinson is going to kill him."

"As far as we are concerned, you still are Robinson," Lai says.

"You took my fingerprints, right? That should tell you who I am."

"Unfortunately," Lai says, "the computer systems are down in this office. We had to fax your prints to the Chinese embassy. We'll have to wait."

"What happens in the meantime?"

"Our embassy is sending its helicopter over," Di says. "You will board it with us. Then we are taking you back to Beijing. If you are Robinson, you are quite a prize for us. And if you're Kyle West, as you claim," Di continues, "you are also quite a prize for us. Either way, it's a very estimable position for us to be in."

"I know that. I know. But your man is going to be killed. I turned myself in knowing I could end up in China. I turned myself in to warn you. You can take me wherever you want, but you have got to save him."

"If you are Robinson, you are no longer a threat to Li Bao. We have you. If you're not Robinson, you've told us Robinson's plan. Do you really think he'll go through with it knowing you've been captured and are talking to us?"

"Absolutely," Kyle says. "He will absolutely go through with it."

"Mr. Robinson is a professional," Lai says. "If his plan is blown, he will try on another occasion. And we will be ready for him."

"Robinson is not going to let this stop him," Kyle says. "I've been him. I know how he thinks. He's . . . he's not as attached to life as you or me."

"This is all very interesting," Di says. "We can continue on the plane ride. In the interim"—he rises, pushes in his chair—"we have other business to attend to."

Kyle's dying to rub his eyes, scratch his nose. "Wait . . . wait. When does the chopper from the embassy get here?"

"Another two hours or so."

"Just listen to me, okay? You have to make Li Bao change his schedule. Just do that for me. Promise me."

"We told Li Bao's people to do that when you first told us your story," Di says. "We've done all we can. Li Bao gets many threats. It's up to his people how seriously they choose to take this one."

"He's never had a threat like Robinson," Kyle says.

"Who I'm still not convinced you're not," Lai says, and he follows Di out of the room.

They lock the door behind them and leave a guard stationed outside to keep an eye on Kyle.

83.

Kyle tries to lift up the table so he can slide his cuff off the leg, but it's bolted to the floor. Frustrated, he slams his fist down on the table.

Well, he thinks, *a situation that was already fucked up has now reached new heights. Not only is Li Bao going to be dead in a few hours, because these guys won't take me seriously, but China's going to be reduced to riots, and I'm going to be there to see it all burn down.*

He stops fussing with the cuffs when he hears talking outside the room. He can't make out what the voice is saying, but it doesn't sound Chinese.

The lock turns. Kyle tries to duck, certain Lara or Robinson managed to track him here, intent on finishing the job. So he's surprised—*pleasantly* wouldn't be the right word, but it's not far from the sentiment—when the door opens and the CIA agent from the hotel steps inside.

"You sure fucked up downtown traffic," he says. "I just came from there. They're still cleaning it up."

Kyle stays quiet, not sure how to this play this.

"No balcony for you to jump off this time," the agent says. "You remember me?"

Kyle nods. No words feel quite right.

"I'm Fowler."

"You're CIA. I remember you said that..."

"Before you jumped. That's right."

"Well, if you're here to arrest me, you're a little late. I'm already booked for a flight to Beijing."

Fowler pulls out a chair, sits across from Kyle. "I know you're not Robinson."

"Great," Kyle says. "Why don't you tell them?"

"They don't care. If you're not Robinson, you're Kyle West. They've got big plans for you either way. Think of the spies they can trade you to the U.S. for. Christ, you're worth at least two or three nuclear thieves."

"So you're going to let them take me to Beijing?"

Fowler lights a cigarette, evades answering. "I want Robinson. And I need you to help me get him. You really think he's going to try and hit Li Bao? The Chinese think you're bluffing."

"I *know* Robinson's going to hit him."

"Know where he's going to try it?"

"I do."

"Does Robinson know you know?"

"He does."

"You see him recently? Can you point him out for me?"

"Yeah. I'll know him. Definitely."

"Okay. All I need to know." Fowler drums his fingers on the table. "We gotta go."

Kyle indicates his cuffed hand.

"I can take care of that. That's not the problem," Fowler says. "Thing is, I can't just waltz you out past the Chinese. In the name of interagency-fair play...they did get you first. Plus, I'm not actually on official business. And I scoped this place out. No back doors, no private exits. Nothing. We can only go out the front door." He pulls out his gun, puts it on the table, and sucks down the rest of his cigarette. "But I've got a plan."

84.

The guard posted outside the interrogation room hears two shots explode in quick succession. He bursts inside, gun drawn, and sees Kyle holding Fowler in a headlock and pressing a Glock against his temple.

"This man is my hostage," Kyle says. "Do you understand that?"

The guard looks down, sees powder burns on the floor and the remnants of Kyle's handcuffs rearranged by bullets.

"Against the wall now," Kyle says to the guard. "Turn around and face the wall."

The guard doesn't appear to understand a word Kyle says.

Fowler repeats the instructions in Khmer, then looks up to Kyle. "Go easy on the neck. Hurt it years ago."

"Sorry," Kyle says.

"Stay in character. You're doing fine."

Kyle marches Fowler into the hall, gun barrel still against the side of his head. Officers spring from behind their desks, scramble, unsure how to react.

"*Do not reach for your guns,*" Kyle shouts. "Do not move. Everyone, sit down right now." He gets louder. "Now. Sit down now."

The officers obey. They clearly have no interest in heroics.

Kyle watches Agents Di and Lai rush in, draw their guns, and block the front door.

"Drop them," Kyle says, spinning around to face them. "You are not taking me to China."

"You're making a mistake," Di says.

"No. You are," Kyle says. "Drop them."

"Look at this from our perspective," Di says.

"Shut up and drop the guns, for fuck's sake!" Fowler yells. "This guy's serious. And I'm not taking a bullet."

"You get in touch with the American embassy, and you get in touch with"—Kyle motions toward Fowler with the gun—"this guy's bosses. You tell them I've got one of their senior officers as a hostage and I want to talk. No one's taking me anywhere. I go where I want and on my terms. You get that?"

"We can't let you do that," Lai says.

"You want the death of a CIA agent on your heads? Think the CCP will like that one? You let this man die, your next job'll be rounding up Uygurs."

Fowler whispers to Kyle, "Make your way to the door. Don't hesitate. They're not gonna shoot. Trust me."

Kyle inches closer to Lai and Di. "Out of my way. Out of my way *now.*"

"Okay. Okay." They acquiesce. "How do we find you once we've met your demands?"

"You won't," Kyle says. "I'll find you."

"You're only making this worse for yourself," Di says.

"You can't be serious. Now, get out of the way."

"Move it," Fowler says. "Out of the way. I'm not taking a bullet, I told you."

Di and Lai drop their guns, step to the side.

Kyle marches Fowler out of the station, gun against his head, and doesn't speak until they're out of earshot. Then he says, "You're gonna have to tell me which one is your car."

"First you give me back my fucking gun," Fowler says. "You may not be Robinson, but I still don't know who the hell you really are."

85.

Fowler's floored the car, but even a judicious application of speed can't compensate for the fact that traffic here doesn't play by linear rules. Horns punctuate the pressure building inside the cars.

"Fuck," Fowler says, slamming on the wheel. "Fuck. Do you know how Robinson plans to do Li Bao?"

"I know where Li's going to be when Robinson takes his shot. I *don't know* where Robinson's going to try to make the shot from."

Fowler sticks his head out the window, scopes out the traffic. "This won't do."

"Li's gonna be in a conference room. Robinson's gonna have to try to take him from one of the surrounding buildings. Or a roof or something, right?"

"Hold that thought," Fowler says. He gets out of the car and walks between the gridlock, keeping out of the way of the motos that have the same idea as him.

He stops by a police car stalled in traffic and motions for the cops to roll down the window. "I'm CIA," he says, then hands them his ID and waits for their general confusion to pass.

It doesn't.

Fowler takes his ID back, examines the siren on the roof, checks that it's portable, and then rips it off. "I have to borrow this for an ongoing op," he says to the cops. "You'll get it back. Thanks for your cooperation."

* * *

Fowler activates the police alarm, slams it atop the hood of his car, then jumps inside. "We're back in business," he says to Kyle, and proceeds to take a severe right, hop the side of the street, and drive between traffic and street vendors, the siren blaring the entire time. Pedestrians scatter and scream.

"You know it doesn't help Li Bao's cause if you kill us before we get there."

"Fuck you care?" Fowler says. "Half an hour ago, you were about to get on a plane to Beijing." He smiles. "Don't worry. I've been waiting years for this."

"For what?"

"For *something*."

Fowler brings the car to a screeching halt and double-parks on the main street of the Central Business District, where the past sixty years of Cambodia's architectural history can be viewed in a chronological clusterfuck. A sleek gym and a swanky lunch spot share the block with a dragon-themed hostel and a colonial hotel.

Kyle points across the street to a high-rise that's an awkward mix of Confucian grace and prison surveillance. The central tower is curved, recessed back from the street, and constructed from thousands of individual windowpanes. "That's it," he says. "That's where Li's taking his meeting. Twelfth-floor conference room."

"We start here, then," Fowler says. "Get them to check their security footage. Then we track every building on this street that faces into the conference room's window."

Robinson sits inside the closet, steel cover close to his left hand.

In his palm, he cradles the handheld television. He hasn't stopped watching it for four hours, entranced by the miniature images punctuated by arrhythmic shocks of static. Finally, he feels like he understands the popularity of reality television. It has nothing to do with the digital aesthetic, the raw presentation, the fly-on-the-wall excitement of delving into a particular family or subculture. Reality television gives you something narrative can't. The lure of reality television is that *something real* could happen.

Now, the stroke of genius is that *nothing* ever happens, and that's purely by design. It's the same thing with advertising. The product can never actually deliver what it's supposed to. Television used to show you your dreams; now it tells you what to dream.

Robinson keeps one eye trained on the screen while he pulls his rifle close and drops two bullets smeared with accelerant into the chamber.

Fowler and Kyle luck out. The high-rise's manager—Mr. Lay—is on-site and speaks English. Fowler meets him at the security desk, shakes his hand, moves him into a corner bursting with natural light and artificial trees sprayed silver, and shows him his ID. "You may have a security crisis in your building," he says. "We believe this man"—he pulls out his BlackBerry and shows Mr. Lay the résumé photo of Robinson—"may be somewhere inside your building and about to commit a crime."

"Tell me how to help," Mr. Lay says, adjusting his cuff links, silver and sleek, like he's melded with his office building.

"Couple of things. Is this place open twenty-four hours?"

"No," Lay says. "We close at ten. Reopen at six."

"I need you to go over all your security tape since six this morning. I need a list of every single tenant in this building, and you need to find out if any of them called in sick today. If someone has, I want the name. Do you have a sign-in sheet or do you just scan ID?"

"Scan for tenants. Sign-in sheet for guests."

"Do you hold on to the guests' IDs?"

"No. They just need to sign in."

"I need a list of all guests too. How many people work security here?"

"Six. Rotating shifts."

"If they can't have it done within the next half hour, I want you to call in the second shift. Understood?"

Mr. Lay nods. "I will do anything I can to preserve the building's reputation."

"Good. And don't wait until you have everything covered. Text me constant updates."

Fowler nods at Lay and then walks over to Kyle, who has been waiting at the security desk. "We go across the street, do the same thing there. We need to be sure he hasn't accessed a building directly. With the buildings that aren't modern, we'll do a house-to-house."

Kyle motions toward Mr. Lay. "You think he can get this done?"

Fowler shrugs. "Yeah. No one wants an assassination in his building."

"Look . . . I'm already fucked. Why don't you just call the CIA and bring them in? We need the help. I don't care if they take me in."

Fowler pulls a cigarette from his front pocket and lights it. "I appreciate your selflessness," he says mockingly through the smoke, "but it's entirely unnecessary. CIA in Cambodia isn't much bigger than the two of us. Plus I got orders from Langley not to investigate Robinson. Even if we stop an assassination, they're still gonna be pissed I disobeyed orders. They're big on orders."

Robinson checks his watch. Not yet. He's dying for a cigarette but knows he can't leave any traces behind, like his saliva on the filters.

He rolls up his sleeve, rips the nicotine patch off his upper arm, dips into the duffel bag, pulls out a fresh one, and affixes it. Then he pops two pieces of Nicorette into his mouth and chews. He's dying for something to do with his mouth. A gun may substitute for a flaccid penis, he thinks, but nothing can take the place of a cigarette.

He rises from the floor, stretches out his cramped arms and legs. He's been bunched up, ready to make a quick dive down the tunnel, but he's feeling secure now. Not safe—something can always go wrong—but secure enough to move around. Who could know he's here? Cocooned in the anteroom of a third-world lawyer's refugee escape hatch. Well, someone still might. Chew your gum. Stay mobile.

He rests his rifle against the wall, shakes his limbs.

Kyle waits in the corner while Fowler finishes talking with another building manager and then gives him a shoulder slap and sends him a text with his phone number. The manager smiles; he's obviously excited to be part of Fowler's project and entrusted with such responsibility.

Kyle can tell that Fowler has led men before, and led them well. He carries an air of confidence that assures his subordinates that he's got this under control, that they just need to follow him. It's the hallmark of an older generation, Kyle thinks, one that actually believed in centralized power.

Kyle could never lead anyone, could never boil instructions down to their essence. He relied on other people intuiting through the clutter of his monologue that there was a streak of genius in him and then hopefully letting him act on it. Alone.

In fact, Kyle thinks it's a failing of his entire generation. *We can't communicate anything—power, authority, desire—face to face anymore. We communicate only through pulsating pink boxes in the corners of screens. Every encounter is so fraught that it's easier never to meet, to let the encounter occur in a tiny shell that's controlled by two, free from baggage, free from flesh.*

Men like Chandler and Fowler don't have that problem. They don't care about subtext or history. They only want others to follow orders.

Fowler rushes back to Kyle. "All right. This is the biggest building with a room facing the conference room. They're gonna lock the place down until they finish the search." He looks at his watch. "How long until Li Bao's limo gets here?"

"Fifteen minutes. Give or take."

"Yeah." Fowler nods. "Time to house-to-house."

On the block, Fowler scans the remaining buildings. "Brass tacks. Break this down. His cleanest shot is from inside the conference room, right? And Mr. Lay's guys are looking there for us. Across the street, where we came from, is good, because it has window access. And the people in there are looking too." He points. "If he's not in one of those...that's the only other building tall enough for him to get a shot. Drawback is, it's a terrible angle to shoot from. He goes farther up or down the block, he can only get a shot from a rooftop.

He could...but it's not ideal. Too many angles and too many people. Shooters are fine with distance, but they hate angles."

"You've done this before."

Fowler nods. "Yeah. I've worked cities before. Never liked them."

As they stand scoping out Robinson's potential strike points, Li Bao's armor-plated limo speeds down the street, so weighed down by heavy metal that it's practically kissing the asphalt and sending up sparks.

"Shit," Fowler says. "They're trying to confuse Robinson's clock. Have Li show up early...force Robinson's hand." He watches the limo. "I gotta flag them down."

Kyle doesn't want to see Fowler get shot. He needs him. "Li's got a ton of guards."

"Yeah. None of whom have survived encountering Robinson. If Robinson starts shooting up the street, I can help these guys."

"So what do I do?"

"Go to that building. Check out the twelfth floor. If Robinson doesn't try to potshot the car, then I'll move to the roofs, start looking there." He puts his hand on Kyle's shoulder. "Just keep in touch with me."

"I don't have a phone."

"Take this," Fowler says and flips his phone to Kyle. "I'll get one from the guards."

Fowler takes off toward the limo without an ounce of hesitation. He's built and primed for moments like this.

Kyle looks toward the building Fowler indicated, eyes the twelfth floor, and counts the windows. There's only three that could offer any reasonable shot into the conference room, and, as Fowler pointed out, they're angled shots that don't provide a shooter any favors.

Robinson slides a black flak jacket over his shoulders and unzips the pockets. A disposable cell phone goes in the right, extra ammo goes in the left. He runs a wet wipe over the telescopic lens, lines up the sights, finds equilibrium.

Time means nothing to him anymore. It's not liquid, not diaphanous, just simply *not there*. He's become a bullet, and he exists in bullet time. Pure force, buried in eternity and beyond measurement.

Kyle knocks on the first door and is greeted by a middle-aged Cambodian woman sporting the country's omnipresent striped pajamas. She doesn't speak English, doesn't want to let him in. She whips her head to the corner, calls out to a shirtless man playing with a large blade as if it were a kitten. He completely ignores the woman, keeps up his knife work.

Kyle pushes into the room, and inside there's a tableau of African illegals—mostly mothers and their postadolescent daughters—sitting at sewing machines. Their feet ride the pedals; their hands hold the fabric straight. They finish one garment, start up the next, never bothering to notice Kyle.

Kyle can't believe his eyes. What the fuck are African workers doing in Cambodia?

Then he remembers an NGO worker he talked to one night at Armand's, a young guy, under thirty, and heading back to the States the next day, which was why Kyle felt comfortable with him—he knew he'd never see him again.

The NGO worker told Kyle his organization was so successful lobbying for Cambodian workers' rights, for more humane conditions and pay raises, that the Cambodian business owners had fired all the indigenous labor and begun importing it from Senegal to save money. The guy truly had to laugh in order not to cry.

He told Kyle that he finally understood that innocence was the worst vice of all, that due to his willed denial of the facts on the ground, he'd managed to fuck two different sets of people.

"Welcome to globalization," Kyle said.

"Globalization is just the newest euphemism for how we've always been. The worse things get, the more polite the terms become. I think when they finally reintroduce forced labor, they'll actually have the balls to call it a renewed birth of genuine freedom."

Kyle starts flittering around the sweatshop, looking in closets, opening the window to the fire escape.

The shirtless guy walks over, taps Kyle on the shoulder, and presents him with several new bills wedged between his thick fingers.

"No. No," Kyle says. "I'm just looking."

The guy nods. "I know. Labor inspection."

Kyle keeps looking, ignores him. "No. No. You keep it."

The guy shrugs, confused but thrilled not to have to part with the money.

Kyle's satisfied. Nothing here. Time to move to the second potential spot.

Kyle exhausts his minimal Khmer—you don't pick up a language when you're in exile and afraid to talk to anyone—gaining access to the second room, which is a massage parlor split into two distinct sections. In the outer area, there's the more Westernized version of a massage parlor: a woman, a towel, and some scented lotion. In the inner area, there's the Khmer variety, which features heated glass and someone to walk on your back and crack joints into place.

Kyle explores the outer room, scanning men's faces and finding no Westerners. The inner area has private rooms that are closed off with beaded curtains, red silk, or flowing silver tinsel.

Kyle starts probing the rooms one by one and gets the same reaction in all of them. Shouts of rage from paying customers who don't stop yelling until the topless masseuse forces him out with a firm shoulder shove.

While he's in the last room looking around and trying not to upset altars of burning joss sticks, Kyle's cell phone goes off.

"Hello."

Fowler's breathless. "It's me. Where are you?"

"In a massage parlor. But it's not what it sounds like."

"Are you currently in a massage parlor?"

"Yes."

"Then it is what it sounds like," Fowler says. "Okay. Situation as follows: Li has been safely escorted into the conference room. His family is secured in the limo. No sign of Robinson in either building. You find anything?"

"I've just got that one office left."

"Okay. I'm gonna start a roof-to-roof, but I gotta tell you, if he were gonna take a shot, it would have been at the car. Conference room's surrounded in double-paned bulletproof glass. How the hell's he gonna get through that? He needed to take them on the street."

"You know better than me."

"I don't think he's showing. No way he can get through that glass. I think you turning yourself in spooked him. He'll try again somewhere else."

"I don't know..."

"Look. Check the office. I'll check possible roof nests. Then you call, and we'll meet up."

Robinson's popped in another piece of Nicorette and now has a wad the size of a small potato wedged in his check. He chews it like cud, hoping to feel some kind of surge, hoping to feel it in his heart.

He checks his watch again. Not yet.

The final room is the law office of Dun Vibol according to a small sign on the door. Kyle knocks. Silence. He tries the knob. Bolted. He steps back into the hall, weighing his options.

He can walk away on the assumption Fowler's right and that Robinson's a no-show. Or he can break down the door, which is not only illegal but a flagrant violation of poor Mr. Vibol's privacy.

Fuck it, Kyle thinks. *I'm already wanted in two countries, and considering I've been instrumental in violating privacy* worldwide, *I don't have to worry about protecting my reputation on that front.*

He shoulders the door hard twice, taking off one of its hinges, and he's able to slide his hand through the gap and unlock it.

Robinson watches on his handheld screen as Kyle enters the office, and he can't help but crack a smile. Thank God Kyle decided to crash. Assassination has always been Robinson's least favorite line of work, all that waiting for one or two shots.

He couldn't be happier to see Kyle right now.

But it's still too early to make his presence known. He tosses his bag down the tunnel, slides the rifle under his armpit, puts the hand-held in a jacket pocket, and descends.

Kyle searches the office, checks corners, looks behind furniture and under the desk.

He slows down; he knows he's not thinking, just going on blind instinct. *Robinson never does anything by instinct,* he thinks. *You'll never stop him unless you think like him.*

He backs up, sees the closet door in the left-hand corner. He tries the knob and it turns. Before he steps inside, he takes a moment to wish Fowler had left him a gun instead of a cell phone.

He hits the lights, sees Mr. Vibol's cardboard crypt of files and his shabby shirts and blazers. He checks the perimeter, then goes down on one knee and feels around the carpeting.

He stands up, moves to the corner. There's something strange about the way the carpet lies. There's something worth investigating here.

He pounds on the area with his shoe and hits steel.

"The hell is that?"

He finds where the carpeting begins, starts pulling it up. He rips up section after section until he exposes the steel grate.

He digs his fingers under the lid, pops it up, and is enthusiastically saluted by the slim nose of Robinson's rifle.

"Kyle," Robinson says while surfacing, gun-first. "I'd almost given up hope."

Kyle backs—actually falls—into the corner, overcome. *This is really happening,* he thinks. *Really happening.*

"So we've got some catching up to do," Robinson says as he leads Kyle into Mr. Vibol's office. "My situation's changed since we last met. Things are always so fluid in this line of work. What do you say to one last job together?"

"I think I've done enough for you."

"Kyle, you've got to stop acting as if our deal was so one-sided. It's such a profoundly negative way to reflect on your experience." Robinson steers him toward the window and crouches down on the right side. He places Kyle on the left. "So. Bring me up to speed. You got yourself arrested, I hear."

Kyle nods. "Turned myself in."

"How'd you get loose?"

"Took a hostage."

Robinson laughs. "Sometimes you have to." He pulls a disposable phone from his pocket. "I've had a few changes myself. First off, my shoulder is fine. Thanks for not asking. Second...Lara has very suddenly left my employ."

Kyle lowers his head. Anything not to give Robinson the pleasure of his reaction.

"It was a mutual decision a long time coming," Robinson says. "We've both got the same gift, you know. You and I. Everyone close to us dies, but somehow we keep going. Know what they call that?"

Kyle can't bear the thought of Robinson being right. How can you live in a world where someone like Robinson can be right?

"They call it luck. We've both got it," Robinson says. He racks the rifle, then points his gloved finger across the street to the conference room's window. Li Bao appears as a dot addressing a congregation of specks.

"Can you believe it?" Robinson says. "Millions of dollars to shoot at a dot. It truly is God's work."

Kyle counters, "You know that glass is double-paned and bullet-proof, right?"

Robinson gestures with his head. "Around the window trim. Already taken care of. While you were off the past few days being me, I was doing prep work. The window border is lined with plastique and a charge." He holds up the disposable phone. "*You* dial the number, the charge goes, the window blows, and I get my shot."

"You? As in *me?*"

"Yes. *You* make the call."

"No way. No."

Robinson crouches on one knee, moves in closer. "Kyle, I'd like to advance a radical proposition. *You* take Lara's place. You be my new public face. Think about what we could accomplish together. Even better, think about what you could accomplish if you were like me. Unencumbered by laws, nations, treaties, stockholders. I exist in a world where none of that matters. You could be pure again. You don't have to go to jail, don't have to worry about Chandler. You really want to go back home and live in *that* world again? You're not like those people. They don't understand you. Or you them. I understand you. I really do." He smiles. "I'll get you a new passport, a new identity, more money than you could ever need. I can get you anything you want. I'm the magic man." He laughs. "Think about it." He checks his watch. "Thirty—actually, twenty-eight seconds for you to decide. The job is yours if you want it. All you have to do is make this call."

There it is, Kyle thinks, *the speech. The same one Chandler gave to me. Go to sleep, lend me your gifts; pay no attention to the man making the offer. Listen to the melody, not the lyrics.*

Only this time, Kyle knows enough not to say yes.

"No," Kyle says. "I can't."

"Yeah. I figured you might say that." Robinson purses his lips in disappointment, a sour petulant pucker, and then checks his watch. "So here's your other option." He points to Li Bao's limo waiting right below their window. "Since there's been all these assassination threats, Li Bao doesn't travel anywhere without his family. He's afraid to leave them vulnerable. Someone may snatch them to get to him. They're in the limo right now. Wife and two kids. Waiting for him to come out of that conference room." He smiles. "I've got a charge buried in that car. Another one of my *errands*. And they're not gonna find it." He shakes the phone in Kyle's face. "Now, my charge may not destroy the whole thing. With all that armor...it'd take a nuclear bomb. But the charge will force everyone out of the car. And while they're all terrified and running, I'll shoot every single one of them down. One of Li Bao's daughters is only three. She'll be the first one I hit." He checks his watch again. "Think about it.

You make one call, only Li Bao dies. You don't make the call, I kill the whole family." He pops another piece of Nicorette. "Fifteen seconds to decide."

It takes Kyle *two seconds* to realize there's no way to counter Robinson's plan except to try to disarm him. It's surely suicide. But Kyle's reached some small peace with the fact he's not leaving this room alive. "Okay. Okay," he says. "I'll make the fucking call. I'll do it."

Robinson smiles, gives Kyle's cheek a patronizing pat. "It's the right thing. I'm proud of you. Li Bao's daughter sure appreciates it."

Kyle nods, sizing up how he's going to attempt to take out Robinson. He needs to find some way to briefly tilt the situation to his advantage, because he doesn't have brute strength on his side. "Yeah," he says, distracted.

Robinson points the rifle out the window, adjusts the angle on the telescope. He's not going to try to set up an exact shot, because once the charge blows, everyone's going to scramble. He's going to be shooting at moving targets, so he needs to have his scopes straight to deal with the awkward angle. He listens to his heartbeat, clockwork thumps against his chest. That's how he knows when to shoot. His heartbeat.

Robinson turns toward Kyle with the phone in his hand and, for a split second, brushes against his own boot, and in that rotational sliver, he unsheathes a triple-play military blade.

He drives the knife into the center of Kyle's stomach, rips it up and to the left, then goes up a few more inches and leaves it stuck inside.

Kyle's incapacitated and terrified. The horror outweighs the pain, because he can't move, can't gurgle out words. He's frozen. Robinson stabbed him in that exact spot to arrest movement. The one thing *not arrested* is bleeding. That's a steady stream, which is already soaking his legs and the surrounding area.

"Don't move. Another three inches and that blade's in your heart." Robinson runs his latex-covered hand through Kyle's hair. "Listen. Listen. Calm down. I had to do that. But you're not going to die. You won't. I just had to be sure you couldn't talk. Stop trying to talk."

Kyle can't *stop trying.* He's freaking out. He's trapped in his own skin, and Robinson's taken over the controls.

"You're gonna bleed out if you don't stop," Robinson says. "Everything's going to be fine. You're in shock. But it's a clean wound." He smiles. "I know how to do this." He places the phone before Kyle. "Open and close your fist. You can do it. Open and close."

Kyle can't move.

"Open and close," Robinson says. "Come on. Try it for me."

Kyle's fingers spring to life, close into his palm, and then retract. He can't believe it. Robinson is some kind of artist with a knife, able to rearrange your body so it responds only to him.

"Good." Robinson places the phone in Kyle's palm. "Okay. Now, when I tell you the number, you're going to dial it. You dial. The window goes. I get Li Bao. Then we get you fixed up. Okay?"

Kyle's face is a rictus of pain playing across his lips and forehead.

Robinson aims out the window, glares through the scope. "Four-four-five..."

Kyle shivers; he's losing feeling in his legs. He's bleeding fast and still trying to talk.

"Focus for me. Don't look down. Four-four-five..."

Kyle punches in the digits with shaking, blood-soaked fingers.

"Six-six-seven..."

Kyle's lungs start to seize; he hacks up blood and holds his side. Something's not going right. This is happening too fast.

"Six-six-seven..." Robinson repeats.

Holy shit, Kyle thinks. *I'm dying. I'm actually dying. Robinson lied to me again. He killed me.*

Kyle dials the next three numbers, getting progressively weaker with each digit.

Robinson's finger teases the trigger. "Eight-eight-four-nine." He repeats it. "Eight-eight. Four-nine."

Kyle hits the first two digits.

"Four-nine, Kyle. Four-nine. You can do it."

Kyle chokes back blood that erupts from his stomach and shoots up his throat.

"Four-nine," Robinson says, losing patience. "Four-nine."

Kyle looks at his hands. The color seems to have evaporated from his skin. The same thing is happening to the room itself; it's gone gray and spinning.

He figures he's got less than thirty seconds before he passes out.

He coughs, his chest heaves, and he punches in the last two numbers.

On the street below, Fowler stands by Li Bao's limousine talking with Li's private security and waiting for Kyle to call.

Suddenly, his phone rings. He flips it open, says "Hello," but there's nothing on the other end. "Kyle. It's me."

He looks up toward the office window for signs.

Before Robinson has a chance to question why the window didn't explode, Kyle musters up his last reservoirs of incautious fury, the death drive of someone with nothing left to lose. He crashes into Robinson and throws him to the ground. The rifle goes spinning across the floor.

Then Kyle throws himself out the open window—feetfirst.

It's a twelve-story fall, but he already ran the figures, knew the consequences if he didn't jump in this position. There's a knife jammed in his stomach, and if he lands on his back, his guts will literally fly out of his mouth.

He knows exactly where he's going to land. He's floating toward a metal embrace with the roof of Li Bao's limousine.

Feetfirst, he prays. *Feetfirst. Or at the very least, let me land on my knees. Either way, I'm breaking something on impact. It's just a question of how high up on the leg.*

And landing on his knees it is.

The alarm system in the limo goes into overdrive upon his crash. Something internal has gone haywire and it keeps repeating the same sound, like a concrete symphony, and in true city fashion, this gets all the other car alarms involved in a furious dialogue, an orgy of squawking, signifying nothing.

Even though Li's limo is bulletproof and armor-plated, a grown man who falls twelve stories and lands on it is going to leave behind some serious dents. Accordingly, upon Kyle's impact, the roof caved in and curved like a government statistic. The windows spider-webbed. The undercarriage—already hanging low—went right to the ground. Oil is streaming out, and the smell of gas is everywhere.

"The fucking thing might blow!" screams one of the guards.

Kyle can't help but smile. His plan worked.

Li's security men immediately pull the wife and kids out of the backseat, rush them to the other side of the street, throw them to the ground, and ready themselves to be shields.

Once they've settled the family, the agents look up, note what window Kyle dove from, and open fire on Robinson.

Robinson turns to the side of the window, using the angle to his advantage. Bullets rip up the surrounding area, shredding the walls, launching clots of rotted wood and decades of moldy files from Mr. Vibol's desk.

When there's a break in firing, Robinson peers outside and sees Kyle on the limousine roof, still on his knees, unable to move, holding his side and looking like a Pre-Raphaelite sculpture testifying to the nobility of suffering.

Robinson smiles, an anarchic riot across his face; even his cheeks and eyebrows get involved, because, let's be honest, this denouement is far more to his liking. Sure, the people who hired him to kill Li are going to either kill *him* for this or place him in indentured servitude for years. He knows it.

That said, they'll have to find him first, and that gives him a reason to indulge in his favorite activity: going liquid. He wasn't created for a rooted world; it stifles his creativity. His line of work has always been an excuse for him to have the life he wants. *Other people's lives.* Hundreds of them, all in different places.

Unfortunately, he doesn't have any more time to admire Kyle's reshuffling of the deck; he's got to get out. Not only has Li's security reloaded, but Fowler's run through the front door to get him.

Robinson leaves the rifle by the window, darts to the closet, dives back into the tunnel, and leaps the last few ladder rungs. Once below, he pulls plastique and charges out of the duffel bag and leaves the rest behind.

He tightens the loosened rifle strap around his neck and attaches the handheld television to the cord. He needs to watch Fowler to know when to activate the charges.

He barrels down the tunnel, forced to run a five- or six-minute mile in a space with no air. It's going to hurt; he's going to feel every foot of it.

Fowler explodes into the office, gun drawn, and lets off several warning shots. There's no return fire. The room is empty. The fucking guy is gone.

He sees Robinson's rifle still at the window. The guy left everything behind and ran. Ran where?

The window Kyle launched himself from is the only one in the office. Obviously, Robinson didn't escape that way, and Fowler banged on every other door in the hallway and Robinson hadn't run through to dive out one of their windows onto the street.

No, Fowler thinks. Somehow he's got to still be in this room.

Fowler tosses the desk on its side, does the same with the filing cabinet. Nothing. Water-stained carpet and mildew. He moves to the closet, rips all Mr. Vibol's clothes off the rod, kicks over the boxes, pounds against the walls and floor, looking for an opening.

Nothing. Where did this guy go?

He steps out of the closet and stands in the middle of the room with his hands on his hips, breathless, furious. Robinson isn't getting away from him.

When Robinson shoots, he listens to his heartbeat. When he runs, he sings under his breath to keep time. Speeding through the tunnel, his sides splitting, phlegm pushing against his throat, he decides to go with Johnny Cash.

Fowler goes back into the closet; something's bothering him about the spot. He pounds on the floorboards, drops to his knees, and sees a small slice in the corner of the rug.

He follows the cut, rips up the carpet, peels it back, and finds the steel cover.

While Robinson pastes more plastique, he checks the handheld and sees Fowler fussing with the lid.

He starts sprinting, pushing himself harder. His calves and quads shake with effort.

He spits out the running residue coating his tongue, wipes the sweat from his eyes, and increases the length of his stride.

Fowler pulls off the steel, peers inside, and sees the ladder leading to the dark hole.

"Son of a bitch," he says, then punches in the number for Li's security on his phone. "Robinson used a fucking migrant tunnel. Get anyone you can spare up to the office on the twelfth floor. I'm going down after him. We gotta move. He's got a good head start on us."

Robinson reaches the end of the tunnel, glimpses the ladder back to the surface, pastes one more plastique bomb, and lays in the charge.

He scales the ladder and pulls out another disposable cell phone that acts as the trigger.

He has to slap himself hard across the face until his cheeks flush. He's about to faint from oxygen deprivation, and this is not the time for him to pass out.

Fowler drops to the dirt floor of the tunnel and freezes when he realizes how narrow and air deprived it is. There's no way he can catch Robinson under these conditions. He's got to swallow his pride and wait for Li's security to arrive.

* * *

Robinson hits the top of the ladder, pushes up against the steel grate.

He punches the detonation number into the phone and waits to surface. He wants to hear the seismic rumble that presages the blast.

He loves to listen when he makes things explode.

Fowler hears the roar from the back of the tunnel. Heat and smoke swell toward him. Destruction follows its own immeasurable clock, but in Fowler's experience, it always arrives faster than you'd think.

"Fuck me!" he yells, and he scrambles up the ladder, two rungs at a time, back into Mr. Vibol's office.

Fowler surfaces and tries to get the steel cover back on in an attempt to contain the damage to the tunnel itself. But the fire has other plans.

Before Fowler can secure the lid, it flies off from contained force, nearly decapitating him, and lodges itself into the wall, quivering with unspent energy.

The floor begins to heat up and crumble.

He's got to get the hell out of there.

He rises, darts through the office, jumps over the desk and filing cabinet he tossed aside. Flames punch through the walls; the floor growls and hisses as sections come loose and collapse.

He makes it into the hallway, sees Li's security heading toward him, and yells:

"Turn back. Get the fuck back. He blew the tunnel. This place is gonna go."

They don't need to be told twice, take off back in the direction they came from, Fowler on their tail.

The door to Mr. Vibol's office flies off, and flames—with crackling blue tongues—froth into the hall. Inside the office, the heat mounts; the wallpaper bubbles and explodes, the wall underneath follows, and the fluorescent lights pop and dump their contents into the fire.

* * *

Robinson walks through the woods, already aflame from deforestation, already a future ruin when his inferno joins in. He couldn't be happier to contribute, couldn't be happier to overflow the heavens with the acrid afterglow of his destruction.

He throws his head back, luxuriating, savoring, breathing in his true métier.

THREE WEEKS LATER

86.

NEW YORK, NEW YORK

The problem with being your own boss, Neil O'Donnell has come to realize, is that the productivity of your day is solely in your own hands, and right now, his hands are occupied, first pouring gin and tonics, and then sliding off Katya's—his newest intern's—jean shorts.

Neil takes a drink, clenches an ice cube between his teeth, and starts running it down Katya's torso, neck to navel, with some stops in between.

Katya entered Neil's hallowed employ last week. Things with Katie, his earlier intern, didn't pan out and only reinforced a lesson Neil's college writing professor tried to impart almost twenty years ago:

"Don't starting sleeping with your students. Ever. They eventually want you to read their work. And you never want to do that."

Neil's cell phone rings. He doesn't recognize the number, but it's eleven in the morning, and people call him at that hour only with dire emergencies.

87.

PHNOM PENH INTERNATIONAL AIRPORT

Kyle stands at a pay phone, slouching against the metal shell, and winces in pain. His side is still taped up, stapled, wounded, and draining. He had to lose his spleen and some semi-crucial inches from his small intestine.

"Hey," he says, voice cracking. It's still a strain to speak.

"The fuck have you been?" Neil explodes. "It's been weeks. I thought you were dead. What number is this?" He tries to control his word flow. "You have no idea how pissed off I am at you. I was actually going to ask the government for help to find you. You know how scared I was if I was even thinking of involving the fucking government."

"Calm down. Okay? I don't have much time."

"Okay," Neil says. "Okay. Sorry."

"Remember you said if I wanted to come home, you'd have a lawyer waiting for me when I get off the plane and that you'd run an exclusive?"

"Of course I remember."

"Well," Kyle says, "you've got about twelve hours or so to make that happen. I'm at the airport."

Just when Neil had started recovering from the shock of hearing from Kyle, he gets hit with this. "What?"

"I'm coming home."

"That's . . . that's fucking fantastic. I'll get working right now. I'll start making calls."

"Look," Kyle says, swallowing hard, "before you do that, there's something you need to know. You need to read between the lines a little, because I'm not sure how...secure this call is. You get me?"

"Yeah, man."

"When I talk to the lawyer and I talk to you...you're...you're gonna find out some stuff about me you're not going to like."

"Like what?"

"Like I didn't run for exactly the reasons I told you I did."

"Oh, that," Neil says. "Yeah. Well, I kind of figured."

Now it's Kyle's turn to explode. "What?" he says and feels the sting in his side.

"I sort of suspected but suppressed it. But when you didn't come back even to avoid being held in contempt, I kinda knew. I mean, if the threat of going to jail wasn't enough..."

"You suspected me?"

"Had no choice."

"And you still kept talking to me?"

"Well...it kinda made me like you a lot less for a few months, but then I just missed you—and whatever you'd done, I wanted you back around," Neil says. "You're still my best friend, no matter what, right?"

Kyle's caught in the sensory limbo between smiling and crying. "I don't know what to say."

"'Thank you.' That's a good start."

"Thank you so much."

"Wow," Neil says. "You put a little extra on that."

Kyle laughs, sniffles. "I'll see you real soon, okay?"

"Yeah," Neil says. "I'll start making calls."

"And don't spare any expense." Kyle cradles the phone between his chin and shoulder. "I'm gonna need one hell of a good lawyer."

Neil laughs. "Done."

Kyle hangs up the phone, picks up his cane, which is resting against the booth, and drags himself back over the café area on a broken ankle still encased in plaster.

88.

Kyle joins Fowler at a plastic oval table.

"Everything good?" Fowler says, pushing a cup of coffee over to him. "You make your call?"

"Yeah," Kyle says. "We're good."

Fowler dips into his blazer pocket, pulls out a flask, dumps several shots' worth of whiskey into his coffee, then grabs Kyle's cup and does the same. "For the road," he says. "Long flight. And I don't have the budget for us to drink the whole time."

Kyle nods in thanks. "Can I mix this with painkillers?"

"I recommend it," Fowler says. "I can't afford the duty-free shop either, so I picked that up in town before we left."

Kyle tastes it, suppresses a gag. "What is *that?*"

"They call it Old Crow."

"Yeah, they do," Kyle says. "Does it get better at any point?"

"No. Not at all," Fowler says. "But it doesn't get any worse."

Kyle raises the cup to his lips.

"It works better if you don't smell it," Fowler says, and then pulls a plastic bag out of his pocket and slides it across the table.

Kyle's passport.

"You're gonna need this," he says.

Kyle unzips the bag, removes his passport, and flips through. He's Kyle West again.

"Use it more wisely in the future," Fowler says.

Kyle forces down another slug of Old Crow. "So I know what *I* get for going back: I get to go to jail and be let out periodically to testify. What do you get for being the guy who brings me back?"

"Oh...probably jack-shit," Fowler says, laughing. "They put me out to pasture a while ago. I wasn't made for the current incarnation of the Agency."

"Maybe they'll let you go back home too," Kyle says. "Maybe you can use *me* to get that for yourself."

Fowler takes another sip. "I'm not all that sure I want to go back. I never liked the States much."

"Why?"

"I don't...I don't really relate to anyone there. You send me out to dinner with people my age, I don't have anything to talk about. I fell in love with Southeast Asia when I was a teenager. It's too late for me to go anywhere else."

"After my prison term is up, I may join you. I got to like it there too. And the States isn't exactly going to be bursting with opportunities for me."

"You come back, you know where to find me."

"Any news about Robinson?"

"We're trying to trace whoever hired him through the money. He didn't leave us much of a crime scene to work with. And he's somehow managed to stay entirely off the grid. I mean *entirely*."

"Money come up with anything yet?"

"Nah. We can't investigate most of the suspects. Either they're already under investigation and we'd be intruding on another operation in progress or they've been shut down and the files destroyed."

"He's gone. And you know it."

"Everyone gets caught eventually."

Kyle raises the Styrofoam cup to his lips. "Do they?"

"I hope so." Fowler smiles. "Nothing in my experience leads me to believe it, though."

Over the PA system, Kyle and Fowler's flight is announced.

"Gate forty-six," Fowler says. "Finish up your coffee."

"I think I've had enough Old Crow."

Fowler looks at him, lowers his head a little. "Back at the hospital, I told you that you did good. You probably don't remember. You were busy dying. I'm sure you had other things on your mind. But I meant it. And I still do. You did real good back there. You saved Li, and you saved his family."

"Thanks," Kyle says. "And you're right. I don't remember."

"Maybe you won't have to go to jail. Li Bao's been singing your praises to the Americans for weeks."

"No." Kyle laughs. "I'm going to jail. Li Bao can hold a parade in my honor and they're still throwing my ass in jail."

"Maybe..."

"I embarrassed Congress. They don't need any help in that department, and I kept it up for a year. They're sending me to jail out of spite. Also, you're forgetting one thing..."

Fowler looks at him.

"I did wrong."

Fowler pushes in his chair and helps Kyle get to his feet.

"Thanks," Kyle says. "I'm still not quite operational."

Kyle and Fowler hook a right, step onto the escalator, and descend toward the boarding gate.

"You know, you're not quite the asshole I thought you were," Fowler says. "Someone does what you did, invents a more efficient spying program for Chandler, I gotta think the guy's a championship asshole."

"Don't get too sentimental. You didn't know me a year ago."

They hit bottom, and Kyle gets his passport ready, leans his weight on the cane, and walks as best he can, supported by Fowler's hand at his waist.

"You're lucky you're alive," Fowler says while they walk. "Few people survive major surgery in Cambodia. Most people drown in their own blood before they even make it to surgery. First thing you do when you get home is find someone to look at that."

Kyle approaches the attendant at the gate, hands her his ticket and passport.

"Washington, DC. One way," she says, inspecting both.

Kyle nods in affirmation. "That's right." *Home,* he thinks, *home, to be subject to the vicissitudes of fate and, even scarier, to the byzantine American legal system and Congress.*

At least I've got my name back.

89.

KENYA, AFRICA

Lamu Beach has been rendered private for the next few days. Armed guards—baking in the sun in their black uniforms—stand at several access points checking identification, making sure none of the locals sneak in and disturb the legion of visiting businessmen.

The National Oil Corporation of Kenya is hosting a conference this week to receive bids for exploratory crude drilling. The country is relatively untapped as a crude exporter, and the discovery of viable resources in Uganda has everyone from Texans to the Chinese to the Russians to the French and Germans besieging the continent and placing bids.

Yachts and sailboats navigate the calm and convivial waves. The shoreline is littered with sand dollars and hot-pink aquatic life. The sand itself is iridescent white, almost like salt, and it squeaks under bare feet.

Robinson emerges from the crest of a wave, stands, and rubs the water over his face. He wears black bathing trunks that end above the knee. The modesty of his attire sets him apart from the Russians and Europeans, who favor a more crotch-suffocating fit.

Robinson walks to the shore, steps over cracked scalloped shells, and sits down on his white beach blanket. His skin is in the awkward stage between burning and tanning. He takes a sip of bottled water and lights a cigarette. Almost absentmindedly, he rubs a still-forming scar on the side of his neck.

He turns around, notes the armed guards, and waves at a passing tourist. "Gérard," Robinson says, paying close attention to the French pronunciation, and waves him over.

Gérard strolls over to Robinson's blanket, flip-flops filling up with sand, umbrella tucked under his arm. His torso is slathered with sunblock, and dark chunky lenses shield his eyes.

Robinson rises to greet him, and the resemblance is startling.

They're the same height, have the same color eyes, the same body type—mesomorphic muscularity in the shoulders and chest, but with a tendency to hold weight in the middle—and the same dark hair, although Gérard's is shorter and thinner and parted on the side while Robinson's is slicked back.

"How are you up this early after last night?"

"Lying down wasn't getting me anywhere." Robinson smiles. "Figured I might as well get tan with a hangover."

Gérard laughs, points to Robinson's cigarettes. "May I?"

"Of course," he says. "When's your meeting with the Kenyans?"

"Tomorrow at two. Yours?"

"Today," Robinson says. "Four o'clock."

"I don't even know why I'm going." Gérard lights the cigarette. "Chinese can outbid us all. Only thing I can offer is Gallic charm."

Robinson laughs. "A contradiction in terms."

Gérard exhales smoke. "Four o'clock today."

"Right. I head out tomorrow morning."

"Back to the States?"

Robinson nods.

"Then that's it?"

"For now."

"But who will show me how to fill my nights? I'm no good on my own."

"We still have one more," Robinson says. "My room at eight. Dress to the nines. Party starts there, then we move out after sufficient social lubrication."

"Bien." Gérard slaps Robinson's knee. *"Bien.* One last hurrah. Just the two of us."

"Well, not exactly just us. I've procured us company of the supple kind."

Gérard smiles. "I had hoped."

"What's your taste?"

"You choose for me. Your taste is impeccable."

"What do you have at home?"

"Why?"

"A friend of mine in Berlin owns a nightclub. Runs a legion of the most beautiful girls you could imagine. Not a flaw in the bunch. But you know which girl makes the most money?"

Gérard shrugs.

"The goth girl covered in tattoos. Pneumatic body. Piercings. Bottle-dyed black hair. *That* girl makes more money than women so perfect they border on parody." Robinson takes the cigarette from between Gérard's fingers and inhales. "Want to know why that girl makes so much?"

"Why?"

"No one has anything like her at home. Men go out, they want something *new.* So I ask again: What have you got at home?"

"Brunette. Petite."

Robinson sends the smoke out his nose. "Then I work from there."

"I look forward to your selection."

"And don't forget your passport, just in case we decide to leave the city limits. We don't want to get caught in a random inspection."

"Thank you." Gérard nods. "I always leave it behind in the safe."

"It's what I do." Robinson smiles, practicing in his head how to say Gérard's name with the proper intonation and estimating how much of his own hair he's going to need to cut off and shave back to make this work.

Gérard returns the grin, and Robinson slowly molds his own to match his new friend's.

"It's what I do," Robinson repeats softly as he buries his toes in the soft hot sand.

Acknowledgments

Nicholas Mennuti

My mother, Virginia, the champion of taking a late-night phone call where I wonder what I'm doing with my life. Michael Bitalvo, the perpetually good-natured recipient of many a rough first-draft. John Schoenfelder, for getting this process started, and Josh Kendall, for steering it to a firm landing. Jonah Straus, for reading one of my short stories and offering to rep me. Sven Birkerts and Stephanie Dickinson, for giving me my first publications. And at the risk of invoking my superiors, Cliff Martinez, whose aural soundscapes provided the book's unofficial soundtrack, and Graham Greene, for showing any thriller writer how it's done. And lastly, David Guggenheim, collaborator and best-friend...a hefty job description for one man. And like everything else, you carry it with grace.

David Guggenheim

To my amazing parents Peter and Leni; my brothers and idols, Marc and Eric; all my unbelievable nieces; Nick Mennuti, a great writer, friend, and shrink; producers extraordinaire Scott Stuber and Alexa Faigen; my incredible reps, David Boxerbaum, Adam Kolbrenner, and Jamie Afifi; and the holy trinity of storytellers, Ian Fleming, William Goldman, and Lawrence Kasdan.

Nicholas Mennuti is a graduate of New York University's Tisch School of the Arts' dramatic writing program. His short stories have appeared in *Agni, Skidrow Penthouse,* and the *Ledge*. He lives in New York City. *Weaponized* is his first novel.

David Guggenheim wrote the 2012 Denzel Washington hit *Safe House* for Universal, and the Nicolas Cage thriller *Stolen* for Millennium. He also penned the sci-fi adventure film *364;* the action film *Narco Sub,* which was to have been the late Tony Scott's next feature film; and *Puzzle Palace,* a contained thriller, for Summit Entertainment. His most recent spec script, *Black Box,* sold to Universal with Madhouse and Bluegrass Films producing. *Weaponized* is his first novel. He lives in New York with his wife and two children.

MULHOLLAND BOOKS

You won't be able to put down these Mulholland books.

YOU *by Austin Grossman*

MYSTERY WRITERS OF AMERICA PRESENTS: VENGEANCE
edited by Lee Child

FIFTEEN DIGITS *by Nick Santora*

THE CUCKOO'S CALLING *by Robert Galbraith*

POINT AND SHOOT *by Duane Swierczynski*

MURDER AS A FINE ART *by David Morrell*

ANGEL BABY *by Richard Lange*

THE SHINING GIRLS *by Lauren Beukes*

KILLER AMBITION: A RACHEL KNIGHT NOVEL
by Marcia Clark

SKINNER *by Charlie Huston*

WEAPONIZED *by Nicholas Mennuti with David Guggenheim*

THE DEMANDS *by Mark Billingham*

SHAKE OFF *by Mischa Hiller*

Visit mulhollandbooks.com for
your daily suspense fiction fix.

Download the FREE Mulholland Books app.